JOHN FRANCOME

Storm Rider

headline

First published in 2010 by
HEADLINE PUBLISHING GROUP

First published in paperback in 2011 by
HEADLINE PUBLISHING GROUP

7

Cataloguing in Publication Data is available from the British Library

ISBN 978 0 7553 4995 1

Typeset in Veljovic by Avon DataSet Ltd,
Bidford-on-Avon, Warwickshire

Printed and bound in Great Britain by
Clays Ltd, St Ives plc

Headline's policy is to use papers that are natural, renewable and recyclable products and made from wood grown in sustainable forests. The logging and manufacturing processes are expected to conform to the environmental regulations of the country of origin.

HEADLINE PUBLISHING GROUP
An Hachette UK Company
338 Euston Road
London NW1 3BH

www.headline.co.uk
www.hachette.co.uk

Storm Rider

Prologue

There were three men in the Land Rover as it drove up the track towards the ridge of tall trees on the far side of the top gallop.

The man at the wheel – barely a man, in fact – was the youngest. A skinny slip of a lad but wiry and strong. No matter how much skill you had as a jockey you had to be strong to control the explosive power of a fully grown racehorse.

Next to him, his passenger maintained his silence. He'd barely said a word for hours. It was shock, the jockey thought.

The third man was also quiet, which was no surprise. He was dead.

It was one o'clock in the morning but the jockey drove without lights. The moon was full and the sky was clear. Anyway, he knew the track.

He was scared and excited. In a life of rebellion, this was the most terrifying – and the most thrilling – thing he had ever done. He had no feelings about the dead man behind him but they ran deep for the passenger by his side, and for the woman who had sent them on this macabre mission. He was doing it for them, the only people in the world to whom he owed anything.

He parked where the trees were tallest, huge conifers towering above, blotting out the moon. This was it. His heart was pounding.

The passenger looked at him, like a man slowly waking. He spoke. 'We're really going to do it?'

'It was your idea to put him here.'

'I wasn't serious.'

The jockey gripped his arm. 'Well, I am. Get out.'

Chapter One

Two years later

Rosemary Drummond let the dogs go on ahead as she strode up the gently sloping meadow. It was good to get out of the house after being cooped up all morning and she was as invigorated as Lodger and Porky, bounding happily fifty yards off. There was something about the aftermath of a dramatic storm and this had been more than a mere storm – the local radio was calling it a 'mini-tornado' as it chronicled a trail of damage around Lambourn. But now the winds had died down and it was as if nature had given the world a good scrubbing. The air was clean and the cloudless sky a pristine blue. She filled her lungs and lengthened her stride. She wasn't much for gyms and jogging and other modern exercise fads. Give her a stiff walk with the dogs any day and when she wasn't up to it they could ruddy well shoot her – or pack her off to that clinic in Switzerland. Life wouldn't be worth living.

They'd phoned from the yard to warn her that a couple of the trees had come down on the drive, in case she was thinking of motoring up to see Anna. She appreciated the thought, though it was only three quarters of a mile from the gatehouse to the Hall and when had she ever used the car for that? To be fair, she did when short of time or in emergencies. She supposed that Anna's current indisposition might count as that and resolved to drop in on her daughter later, after dinner when there was a chance Edward might be back. It would be more entertaining to discuss the day's racing at York than be obliged to sympathise with her daughter about being pregnant. No one ever said having children was a picnic. She wouldn't have done it more than once herself if circumstances hadn't forced her.

She was across the meadow now, taking the footbridge over the stream and heading up the bridle path. The dogs were out of sight but she could hear them heading in the direction of the all-weather gallop, which was not the route she wanted to take. She called and was rewarded twenty seconds later by the appearance of the lurcher, a rangy deerhound/greyhound cross, his brindled coat streaked with mud. His companion, a biscuit-coloured Norfolk terrier, shot into view after another peremptory shout and Rosemary shooed them up the path leading to the northern boundary of the estate.

This was her favourite walk. From the top by the trees she'd be able to look down over the entire property and see for herself what damage the storm had caused, aside from the old lime trees on the drive. Though she no longer lived in the Hall and the chief responsibility for the upkeep of the fifteen hundred acres had passed to her son-in-law, Edward, Rosemary still felt a deep-seated proprietary interest in the estate which had been in her family for over a hundred years.

She felt her breath shortening as the gradient increased but she stepped off the path and headed upwards, determined to obtain the best vantage point before she took a breather. Eventually she reached the shadow of the beech and conifer woodland that marked the boundary of their land. Pitchbury estate was spread out beneath her like a handkerchief of greens and browns, with the terracotta roofs of the yard buildings at its centre. In the near corner to her right sat the old gatehouse, a solid two-storey edifice where she lived these days with her firstborn, Freddy. The drive bordered by lime trees wound from the gatehouse to Pitchbury Hall, the Georgian mansion that her great-grandfather Neville Pym had bought in his declining years, after he'd sold his watch-chain factory in Birmingham.

Her grandfather had run through his old man's cash and her own father had only hung on by turning the building into a hotel. But the Pyms had not been cut out for the graft of serving the public. In Rosemary's opinion, after Neville, the male Pyms had shied from any graft at all, short of the self-indulgent variety. It was she who had saved the estate and preserved the family presence by marrying Jack Drummond, a genius with young horses, who had turned Pitchbury into one of the best training establishments in the country. And now Anna had performed the same trick by marrying Edward Pemberton, a trainer worthy of inheriting Jack's yard and continuing the Pitchbury tradition. There was a lot to be said – and she said it frequently – for improving the bloodline, in humans as well as horses.

Damnit, she missed Jack. Dead at seventy-five. At his funeral someone had said he'd had a good innings but she couldn't agree. These days seventy-five wasn't old, especially from the vantage point of someone in her sixties. She'd noticed that the fellow with the cricketing metaphor was on the right side of forty.

Enough with the doom and gloom, she admonished herself. Where on earth had those dratted dogs got to? The stand of trees was some thirty yards deep but behind that was the old wall that flanked the road into Lambourn. It was kept in decent order but who knows what damage the weather might have done to the ageing brickwork. The thought of Lodger and Porky escaping on to the busy public carriageway was alarming. She called their names in a voice that demanded obedience – not that it always received its due from Porky, the little terrier. But not even Lodger, the lurcher, heeded his mistress's voice on this occasion. Irritation at this disobedience was rapidly being overtaken by concern. This time she reached for her whistle.

All around were signs of the winds that had battered these trees during the morning. Branches littered the gleaming green turf. Suppose some sizeable limb had smashed on to a decayed portion of wall? Her dogs would be over like a flash, eager to explore the forbidden territory of the roadside. Rosemary wasn't one for panic but she blew hard on the whistle and strode out briskly.

Rounding the curve of the treeline, she came to a sudden halt, shocked by the sight of a wall of green directly in front of her where it had never been before. She looked up in astonishment. Here was the highest point on the ridge and the familiar bank of conifers was broken, as if some great hand had reached down and flicked the tallest tree out of line. The top of the tree, some twenty feet of trunk and foliage, now barred her path.

But at least she had found the dogs. She could hear them scrabbling, panting and frolicking in the wreckage of the wood to her left and she called to them again. She was answered by a bark but the animals did not appear. There was more barking, higher pitched this time, followed by growling from the other dog. The lurcher had found something – a rabbit, maybe – and the terrier wanted in on it. Typical.

Rosemary turned towards the commotion, along the trunk of the ravaged tree which rose above her head, the damaged top evidently still attached to the main stem and hanging over her like a giant hinge. She had to bend and weave through the barrier of its leaves and branches which snagged her clothes and jabbed into her face. The core of the tree was brown and dry, she noted. A separate climate obviously existed inside the embrace of these big conifers.

'Come out of there, you silly brutes,' she yelled, not relishing her progress. Talk about scrambling through a hedge backwards.

Then suddenly, pushing through a final barrier of leaf and branch, she found space to unbend and there were the dogs a few feet in front of her. Sure enough, the lurcher had something in his jaws and the terrier was snapping at him, trying to get his mouth around the object too.

It wasn't a rabbit. It looked black and leathery. Was it a shoe?

'Give it to me, Lodger,' she ordered and, glory be, the dog obeyed, allowing her to detach the article from his jaws. Obviously it wasn't worth eating.

'You've found an old boot,' she said, hefting it in her hand. 'Someone must have chucked it over the wall.'

But even as she said the words, she realised that they didn't make sense. There was no way anyone could have thrown an article through the barrier of trees to this point, thirty or forty yards from the road.

Anyway, it wasn't a boot. It was a rather elegant man's shoe, size nine or ten, whose brown leather had weathered to a wrinkled black – she could see traces of the original colour inside the rim. But it wasn't the colour of the shoe which was setting her heart skipping to an unfamiliar rhythm, nor even the spidery traces of sock material attached to the interior. It was the bone. The wearer's foot was still inside.

She tried to clear her head, fighting the gruesome thought. She was only sixty-four, far too young to be going doolally.

The dogs were barking fiercely, trying to attract her attention.

'Shut up, you silly sods,' she muttered. 'Let me think.'

But they persisted. She'd taken their shoe but they'd found something else – something out of their reach.

She looked up, following their agitation, and she saw it too. A hanging object, attached to the broken tree trunk and part of it dangling like an arm. It was an arm. At least, it was the arm part of a jacket and at the end of it was something whitish and familiar in structure.

She was looking at a skeletal corpse, held together by clothing, tied high above the ground to the trunk of a tree and concealed from sight. Only the tree was no longer standing.

All this was clear to her in a flash, as was her duty. Still holding the shoe clear of the dogs – it was evidence! – she took her phone from her pocket.

York racecourse was a track where Edward Pemberton still felt like a novice in the business of training horses. At other courses on the circuit he considered himself a seasoned campaigner, almost ten years in the training game with some good wins under his belt and quality horses in his yard. But he'd yet to land a significant victory at York and, in his opinion, it was only by winning the big battles that a man built a heroic reputation.

Edward was given to military analogy. He'd spent nearly ten years in the Household Cavalry, just missing the first Gulf War but including two tours of Bosnia in the nineties, before getting stuck into a career in racing. As a boy, horses had always been a distant dream but the army had made the horses possible for a plumber's son from Coventry. He owed the army everything and the principles he'd learned in the service – dedication, conformity and hard, hard work

– were those he demanded in his yard. The fact that he didn't always get it was a daily frustration.

Chief among his present dissatisfactions was not having a decent filly to run in the day's best race, the Musidora Stakes. Second to that was the prospect of driving back to Lambourn this evening, a 200-mile journey, only to return for tomorrow's racing. He knew everyone thought he was daft to subject himself to so many hours on the road but he'd sworn to himself never to leave Anna alone for the night if he could help it. As a consequence, he had the reputation of a devoted husband and he was content to leave it at that. It was true he was concerned for his wife's well-being, particularly in these delicate early months of pregnancy when she was plainly suffering. It was also true that a man couldn't police his property with any certainty from a distance of two hundred miles.

'So then, Ted,' said his short, pinstripe-suited companion as they found a vantage point in the stand, 'what's our chances?'

Edward smiled at Sir Sidney Tobin and ignored the fact that he had been asked that same question twice already. He didn't like having to repeat himself any more than he appreciated being called Ted, but Sid – as Tobin insisted on being known – though a man feared in boardrooms from New York to Shanghai, was a surprisingly nervous owner. He was also a very rich one who was considering sinking more of his personal fortune into racing. Naturally Edward was eager to see the benefits at Pitchbury. As far as the trainer was concerned, no race was unimportant, but the six-furlong sprint due off within the hour – featuring

Sid's chestnut three-year-old Paper Sun – was of particular significance.

'I told Will to ride him how he wants to. He knows him better than anyone,' Edward said.

Sid nodded thoughtfully. 'And this jockey's the business, is he?'

Will Morrison was the stable jockey at Pitchbury but he'd not ridden Sid's horse in a race so far, that honour having fallen to an outside jockey Sid had insisted on. But after Paper Sun's most recent, disappointing outing – second from last at Ascot – the owner had agreed to hand the reins to Edward's man.

'He's got a real feel for horses,' Edward said. 'They respond to him. The buzzy ones relax and the lazy ones try harder. It's freaky to see.'

'He's only a kid though, isn't he?'

'Twenty is quite old enough.'

Sid didn't look convinced and Edward could guess the reason why. It was the reason he himself was not entirely comfortable with the lad, for all his brillance.

'That thing he's got in his ear,' said the owner, 'what's that all about?'

Edward laughed. 'It's just an earring, Sid.'

'I don't see any of the other jockeys round here with earrings – or coloured stripes in their hair.'

'He's just a bit flamboyant, that's all. Likes to express himself.'

'Huh.'

Edward could see Sid bottling up his disapproval but said nothing, though he had a lot of sympathy for Sid's views. If it had been down to him, he'd never have kept his unconventional jockey on in the first place, for all his promise. But Edward's arm had been twisted. Sometimes a man had to listen to his wife.

The sound of movement in the room woke Anna from her fitful sleep. The wind had stopped rattling the window frames and bright sunlight lit up a rectangle of peppermint-green carpet. Her mother had complained that the colour was too cool for a bedroom and on cold winter nights Anna acknowledged to herself she might have made a mistake. Not now, though. The pale green was soothing.

'How are you feeling?' The voice came from beyond the shaft of sunlight and she raised her head to see Katherine standing by the door, holding a tray.

Anna didn't know how she felt, half of her was still asleep. The other half – oh Lord! – the familiar feeling gripped her body as she pushed herself into a sitting position and lunged for the bowl on the bedside table. She would have thrown up the entire contents of her stomach if there'd been anything of substance inside her to vomit.

Instead her heaves produced just a thin trickle of snotty drool that hung in strings from her lips. She lifted her hand feebly to wipe them away.

'Poor you,' said her cousin, somehow managing to deposit the tray and be by her side in an instant.

Anna felt a comforting arm slip around her shoulder and a damp cloth on her face. 'Thank you,' she murmured. 'I feel such a fool. I'm not ill – I'm just pregnant.'

Katherine chuckled. 'Same difference in my book.'

Her cousin was childless which, given that she'd just turned forty and was unmarried, Anna assumed was likely to remain the case. Elegant, quick-witted Katherine, the picture of a prosperous single woman, had not been without disasters in her personal life. She'd lost a baby at the same age as Anna was now. Which made her sympathy and good humour in these circumstances all the more admirable.

'You're coming up to three months,' Katherine said. 'There's a good chance it will ease off after that.'

'And there's a good chance it won't.' Anna had spent a lot of time recently canvassing the mothers she knew. Everyone seemed to have had a different experience.

Her cousin nodded, acknowledging the point. 'I've brought you some tea and biscuits.'

'Ugh.'

'You've got to get some nourishment. They're ginger biscuits – ginger's good for nausea. NASA astronauts used to take ginger on their missions for travel sickness.'

Typical of her cousin that she would know that kind of stuff. Her mother had a theory that Katherine's obvious intelligence had been a barrier to her finding a husband. Anna thought it was more relevant that she had wasted too many years on men who were already married. Sometimes, however, she thought her mum might have a point.

'Shouldn't you be working today?' she asked. Katherine was a freelance book-keeper. She worked for several small businesses in the area.

'I switched things round – that's the advantage of

being a one-man band. Besides, I didn't fancy driving over to Devizes in that weather.'

Anna had been distantly aware of the storm raging outside. There'd been no question of her getting out of bed, let alone venturing out into the rain and wind.

'Was it really that bad?' she asked.

As Katherine embarked on chapter and verse – she knew whose barn had lost a roof and which chimneys had come down – Anna reached for a biscuit and began to chew. She owed it to herself and the baby. And her husband, mustn't forget him. The thought prompted another.

'What's the time?' she asked, cutting into Katherine's monologue. 'I don't want to miss Paper Sun's race.'

Since her discovery of the body, Rosemary had felt exhilarated. It wasn't every day she went for a walk and found a corpse. If it weren't for the grisly nature of her find, she might have admitted that she hadn't enjoyed herself as much since she and Katherine had made a small slam in a bridge tournament back in February.

She had rung the emergency services promptly and been put through to the police. After that, there had been some confusion as she tried to explain the precise nature of her emergency. Yes, she'd found a body but there was no need to send an ambulance. In fact, she'd only found part of a body but the other bit was plainly visible up a tree. And though her discovery was a direct result of the storm that had stretched the emergency services very thin – unstated, but plain from the tone of the control officer on the other end of the line – she could say that the cause of death was unrelated. No, she wasn't a medical professional but there was no doubt in her mind that the person she'd found was categorically deceased.

After that there'd been a degree of toing and froing about her precise location and how long it would take for anyone to reach her. In the end, after insisting that her call was high priority – 'I'm reporting a dead body, for God's sake!' – and getting a promise that she would be attended to 'probably within half an hour', she had rung off in a bit of a huff. Not that that put her out of sorts; she took a degree of pleasure in the cut and thrust of dealing with officialdom.

Throughout the conversation she'd been clutching the shoe, keeping it out of the dogs' reach, but the notion of continuing to safeguard the noxious object until the police deigned to show up was not pleasant. Her situation would be improved if she could get the animals off her hands. They would only be in the way when the police arrived, especially if they brought dogs of their own. The authorities would want to bring in vehicles and set up a crime scene. She'd seen what happened in TV police dramas. There would be tents and forensic chaps in funny white suits and teams of men on their knees combing the undergrowth for clues. And good luck to them with that.

She rang the yard office and got hold of one of the lads. The yard secretary hadn't been able to make it in and Tom, the head lad, was supervising the removal of the trees that were blocking the drive. She asked to speak to Freddy. It hadn't been her intention to involve her son but, on reflection, there was no alternative.

The dogs would not be happy if she handed them over to anyone else. Besides, Freddy was so much more dependable than he used to be – if she gave him a task, and precise instructions, he could be trusted to carry it out without supervision. And he had any number of day-to-day jobs to do in the house and in the yard which he performed with complete reliability. Problems only arose when the unexpected came along. Rosemary had no doubt that finding a dead body in the grounds came under this heading. It would have to be broken to Freddy, of course, but not yet and not without care. All the same, right now she needed his help.

'Hi, Mum.' His familiar deep voice came down the line. He sounded so adult, and looked it too, standing at well over six feet and dwarfing all the other men in the yard. His face was broad and handsome and he looked you squarely in the eye with interest and sympathy. Freddy had never been short of female admirers, though Rosemary had had to police them closely as she did everything around her son. He was the guilty cross she had to bear. Her once-upon-a-time golden boy who had been robbed of his birthright by her neglect.

'Freddy, I need a favour.'

'Of course. How can I help?'

He sounded eager but this was the tricky bit. 'You know there's a bit of a flap on today, don't you?'

'There's trees down on the drive, Mum. Tom's been sorting it all out and he's left me in charge here. I've got to carry on as normal.'

'Yes, dear. That sounds excellent. But I just need you

to bring the Land Rover up to the top end and collect the dogs. Take them back home and give them a bit of a hose down, they've got absolutely filthy.'

'But Tom's left me in charge here. I don't think I should leave without asking him.'

'It's OK, darling, I've just spoken to him and he's given me permission to ask you.'

There was a pause and Rosemary wondered if Freddy was going to baulk at her instruction. But he simply said, 'OK, Mum. See you in a moment.'

He really was much better these days.

As Will settled Paper Sun in the starting stalls he could feel the animal humming with suppressed energy beneath him. He felt exactly the same himself – eager to fly off down the track ahead. He had every confidence in this horse and was desperate to show what he could do with him. He'd ridden him a lot at Pitchbury and it rankled that this was the first time he'd been given a race on him, thanks to the owner's insistence on a better-known jockey. Not that it had done Sir Call-Me-Sid much good, Paper Sun had hardly prospered under better-known riders. And now was the time to show the ignorant old fart what he'd been missing.

Edward had given him carte blanche to ride the horse as he liked and Will intended to do just that. He knew that Paper Sun preferred racing on his own – even in his work on the gallops at home, he disliked being close to other horses. Will had a plan to turn this to his advantage.

And if it didn't come off, he didn't see what anyone

would lose. Sir Sid had yet to win with the horse, whoever was riding. In any case, he already thought Will was a twat – the jockey had read it in the other man's face as they'd said hello in the parade ring.

The stalls sprang open and they were off. Paper Sun was drawn highest, which put him on the stand side of the other fifteen runners. According to the statisticians, the middle draw was favourite.

The group of horses to his left thundered straight ahead, down the centre of the course. Will ignored them and took a line towards the stand rail, twenty yards over to his right. Hardly anyone ever went down there but the ground was better – he'd run along it before the meeting and seen for himself. He'd also cantered from one side of the course to the other on the way to the start to make doubly certain. He grinned to himself as he and his mount took a separate path away from the pack, which was just the way he liked to do things.

Edward could feel his stomach beginning to knot. Will had told him how he planned to ride Paper Sun and he had gone along with it but the tactic seemed to have backfired. Sid, the millionaire owner he was trying to impress, was not a man who missed much, particularly when, on the big screen on the other side of the course, it was clear that Paper Sun was wide of all the other runners and some way behind them.

Edward deliberately avoided the other man's eye but he could not avoid his voice.

'What the bloody hell's he up to?' Sid muttered. 'Has your idiot with an earring lost his marbles?'

*

For the moment Anna had her physical discomfort in check, there being nothing like distraction to dull pain. Katherine had propped her up with a bank of pillows and tuned in the television to the racing at York. Throughout their marriage, Edward had resisted the idea of a TV in the bedroom but he had not objected when it made an appearance a few weeks ago – anything to help Anna get through the day got his vote. She was pleased to think he would certainly approve of her choice of viewing.

She was chewing on her second biscuit, perplexed by the action on screen.

'He's miles behind already,' she exclaimed. 'Edward told me he was going to win.'

'Doesn't he always say that?' Katherine was looking no less intently at the screen.

'No. Anyway, Will was really confident too.'

Katherine did not respond to this – it went without saying. Then she said, 'He's taking the stand side – maybe the ground is better over there. Not so churned up or something.'

Anna studied the screen. There were two races taking place: fifteen runners charging in a bunch down the centre of the broad course and a lone runner, Paper Sun, eating up the ground on the stand-side rail. He was going well, no longer miles adrift, though it was hard to tell exactly where he was in relation to the others.

Katherine was right, Will had spotted the better ground but would he be able to make the most of it? Anna nervously nibbled her biscuit.

*

By sticking his neck out, Will was well aware that he'd end up either a hero or a bloody fool and quite possibly both, in the eyes of someone like Sir Sid. But he'd been certain the virgin ground on the stands rail was quicker. It wasn't by much, but it didn't need to be to make a big difference. He compared it to running on a beach – by the water the sand was wet and firm but above the tideline it was dry and soft, and much harder to travel on.

He crouched low on the horse's shoulders, coaxing every ounce of effort out of Paper Sun. They were well into the sharp end of the contest now, with only a furlong to go. Though they were approaching the stands, heaving with vociferous spectators even on this blustery unsummery May day, Will could hear nothing except the white noise of his own concentration. Even the pounding of Paper Sun's hoofbeats and the rustling creak of harness and tack were lost in the intensity of the moment.

He didn't use the whip – what was the point? He could feel Paper Sun racing as if a lion was on his tail. Nor did he glance to his left to see how they were faring in comparison to the other runners. All that mattered was arrowing his own animal over the turf towards the line. The result was now out of his hands, he could do no more. He'd followed his racing instincts the best way he knew how and, whatever the result, he'd stand by that.

Edward had never seen such a transformation in a human being. Sid had progressed from doleful resignation to beaming triumphalism in the space of thirty seconds.

'Come on, Sunny! Come on, boy!' he bawled in the broad cockney of his years on his dad's barrow in Berwick Street market. 'Come on, you lovely bastard!'

Edward shared his owner's delighted incredulity as Paper Sun's route up the stand rail took him to the finishing line a clear length ahead of his nearest rival. What a rider! He was convinced nobody else in the world could have done that. Will had pulled off a spectacular victory, vindicating Edward's decision to talk the owner into giving him the ride.

He grinned broadly as he greeted his jockey in the winner's enclosure.

'You cheeky bugger,' he said, holding out his hand. 'Fantastic.'

Will accepted the praise. 'Thank you.' There was no humility in his tone, just the arrogance of a winner. But a winner was what every trainer wanted on his horses. Every owner too.

'You nearly gave me a bleeding heart attack at the start,' announced Sid, pumping Will's arm.

'I'm just trying to make your day a bit more exciting, sir.'

'You did that all right, son.'

Edward would happily have stopped the afternoon there, in the moment of victory and mutual congratulation.

Then his phone rang.

Rosemary didn't want to disturb Edward's afternoon at York – years of marriage to a successful trainer had instilled into her the sanctity of racecourse time. Though a trainer might seem to be breezing through the afternoon, glad-handing owners while his staff scurried around doing the hard graft, she knew well enough that time on the course on race day was as important as anything else in a trainer's life. And maybe more so, because he was in the public eye, the face of his yard. And today Edward was attempting to keep Sir Sidney Tobin happy, which wasn't an easy task given their history of failure. The last thing she wanted to do was distract her son-in-law when he was hard at work.

But something as momentous as the discovery of a dead body on the gallops at his yard could not be kept secret. Two uniformed policemen had turned up at the gate on the Lambourn Road where the right of way passed into the Pitchbury estate. She'd led them along the path to the yawning gap in the trees, where she had now replaced the shoe on the ground beneath the body. Earlier Freddy had driven the Land Rover up the track from the yard and the dogs had happily jumped in the back. For a moment Freddy had looked at her curiously, as if he were about to inquire what on earth she was doing out here on her own but she sent him on his way briskly and he'd simply obeyed.

The coppers were polite but distracted, as if they'd already made up their minds that whatever bee she had in her bonnet was a waste of time. She'd not promised them a bleeding casualty or a life-or-death mercy dash, after all, and on this turbulent day, their efforts could be better expended elsewhere.

Divining this, Rosemary had kept her mouth shut

until they were standing in the arch of the wrecked conifer. 'First my dogs found this,' she said, indicating the shoe. 'And then I looked up and saw that.' And she pointed up into the branches where the dead thing hung, some six feet out of reach.

That had done the trick and all signs of distraction had vanished instantly. Now more vehicles had poured through the gate and the area of woodland had been cordoned off with blue-and-white-striped police tape. She had been informed that a specialist team of investigators was due imminently and she was the first person they would need to speak to. The two coppers who were first on the scene had urged her to sit in their squad car and praised her for her calm in the face of such a horrific discovery. 'My nan would have had the screaming heeby-jeebies,' the younger confided. The other said that she'd probably get her picture in the papers.

It was this comment that had prompted Rosemary to find some space away from the invading emergency personnel and call Edward. The policeman was right, journalists would be on to her morbid discovery before long and she owed the yard a call to alert them to the drama. But Edward, though a couple of hundred miles away, had to be informed first. He was the boss.

Edward assumed his mother-in-law was phoning to congratulate him. He even said as much to Sir Sid as he glanced at his phone and looked for a quiet corner to take the call. He didn't wait for her to start the conversation.

'Bloody brilliant, wasn't it? I hope you had some money on him.'

'What are you talking about?'

'Paper Sun, of course. He won. Didn't you watch it?'

'Forget horses for a moment, Edward. I've got some serious news.'

A chill gripped him. 'Has Anna lost the baby?' It was the worst thing he could think of.

'As far as I know Anna and the baby are absolutely fine. Now be quiet and listen to me.'

What she told him came from completely out of the blue and wiped all the pleasure of Paper Sun's victory from his mind.

'How do you know it's a body?' he said when she'd finished.

'Because I saw it. It's got a hand with fingers. And a foot. The police saw it too. Some of their people are here but there are more on the way and the press won't be far behind. This is going to be all over the news, Edward. You've got to be prepared for it.'

He could understand that but other issues were coming into focus. 'Is it a man or a woman?'

'I don't know. It was a man's shoe, so I suppose it's a man.'

'What did he look like?'

'I told you, he'd rotted away. The foot had fallen off – it's just bone. You can't recognise anybody.'

'How long do you think it's been up there?'

'How should I know, Edward? They've got experts coming and they'll tell us all that. I know it's ghoulish and probably going to cause a bit of an upheaval but it's rather exciting, don't you think?'

Edward didn't think that at all and neither would Rosemary when she had a chance to consider things properly. It was time to bring her down to earth.

'In your opinion,' he said slowly, 'could this body have been up there for years? Two years, say.'

'Quite possibly. It looked like it had been there for ages, as if it was becoming part of the tree itself. There was only bone in the shoe. Why two years?'

'Because Glyn Cole disappeared two years ago.'

There was an intake of breath from the other end of the line.

'Oh my God! Why didn't I think of that? Glyn could easily have been wearing a shoe like that.'

Racecourse chatter boomed and swelled around him but Edward was in a bubble of silence, speechless for a moment, as was Rosemary on the other end of the line. Both of them taking in the implications of the discovery of Glyn Cole's body – the man who had nearly stolen Edward's wife.

'Look,' he said finally, 'when the police talk to you don't speculate about his identity. Maybe we've got it wrong. Maybe it's not him.'

'All right,' she replied. 'I won't say anything. I suppose it might not be Glyn.'

He could tell from her voice that she wasn't convinced. And neither was he.

Chapter Two

'I can't believe it,' Katherine muttered as she clattered around the kitchen in Pitchbury Hall, hunting through the cupboards. 'It can't be true.'

'I don't see why not.' Rosemary was watching her from across the well-worn pine table, her hands clasped around a cup of camomile tea. The dishwasher hummed quietly in the corner, taking care of the dinner dishes, though there had been few. Anna was in bed upstairs and Edward was still making his way back from York. For the moment, aunt and niece were on their own. 'It could easily be Glyn,' Rosemary added. 'It would account for his sudden disappearance.'

'So would lots of other things, like running off and leaving the rest of us to clear up his mess. That's what Glyn always does. I bet he's getting pissed in some Spanish bar at this very moment while some doe-eyed local girl feeds him tapas or whatever they eat.' She yanked open the last drawer with some violence.

'What are you looking for?'

'Cigarettes. Tammy keeps a spare packet in here somewhere.'

'Really?' Rosemary wasn't surprised. Tammy Turner helped out at the Hall during the week. It was a temporary arrangement that had been going since she had quit college at Christmas. Rosemary had seen Tammy with a cigarette in the kitchen garden – she knew better than to smoke in the house.

'Aha.' Katherine turned, holding up a silver packet of Lambert & Butler. She held a box of matches in her other hand. 'Sorry, Aunty, but I'm off for a smoke. I'll be back in five minutes.'

Rosemary said nothing as she watched her go, presumably to sit on the back step in the evening chill. She thought Katherine had quit years ago, certainly it had been a long while since she'd seen her with a cigarette in her hand. Personally she thought smoking was a senseless habit but provided Katherine didn't stink up the indoors, Rosemary wasn't going to object. In any case, her niece was long past the age when she welcomed the advice of her elders.

She pondered Katherine's sudden need, however. It was the mention of Glyn, of course, which she had confided as soon as they were on their own. That had not been till late in the afternoon. News of the discovery of the corpse had reached the Hall while she was still in the clutches of the police who, fortunately, had not asked her about its possible identity. She would have refused to speculate. But with Katherine, it was a different matter.

'It must be Glyn Cole,' she'd said as Katherine rustled up some dinner; Anna had refused to come down to the kitchen on the grounds that the smell of food would make her feel worse.

'But it could be anyone,' Katherine had exclaimed. 'Couldn't it?'

Rosemary had been turning it over in her mind since the conversation with Edward. The nature of the shoe, the general size of the corpse, the fact that it must been have been hidden for a long time to be reduced to that state . . .

'If I were a bookmaker,' she'd said, 'I'd have Glyn down as a very short-priced favourite.'

Katherine hadn't eaten much supper, she'd observed, though she'd downed a couple of hefty gins despite the tonic being flat and had now resorted to tobacco.

Rosemary berated herself – she should never have mentioned Glyn. She'd not said anything to Anna, after all, being only too well aware how distressing proof of his death might be. But she'd not anticipated Katherine's reaction. On reflection, she'd been thoughtless, too selfishly bound up in the drama of her own part in the discovery. Now she thought about it, why wouldn't Katherine be upset at the thought of Glyn's body coming to light? Though her niece's fling with Glyn was many years in the past – and never that serious, surely? – she had done the books of his antiques business up until his disappearance and they had remained friends.

Come to think of it, maybe Katherine had continued to carry a torch for Glyn, a handsome man with soft wavy hair and mischievous eyes. Who was to say that he and Katherine hadn't continued to romance each other when he was between girlfriends? He went through women like a dog through bones – an uncomfortable image in the light of what Rosemary had seen that afternoon. She tried to put it out of her mind.

Katherine had always shown poor judgement in men. In Rosemary's opinion, her niece had wasted her best years on a man who plainly enjoyed having his cake and eating it. Her ill-judged scheme - getting pregnant - to get him to leave his wife and children was always doomed, even before the pregnancy went wrong in such a spectacular fashion. What man who likes his creature comforts abandons a wife due to inherit upwards of ten million pounds? The whole business had been a disaster. Katherine had lost the baby, plunged into depression and taken an overdose. Not that Rosemary had been too surprised at the time.

'She's as flaky as her mother,' she'd said to Jack.

'She'll pull through,' he'd said. 'She's tougher than she looks.'

She saw now that her late husband had always been Katherine's staunchest supporter. And he'd been right about her, Rosemary conceded that too. Her niece had gone back to college, got some book-keeping qualifications and turned herself into an independent businesswoman, a rather successful one too, judging by the car she drove and the clothes she wore. Rosemary had misjudged her. Had maligned her, too, by holding a grudge against her as an adolescent - though there had been mitigating circumstances. Any mother might succumb to irrational resentment when her own child's life is in danger.

The back door flew open and Katherine returned.

She threw the cigarette packet back into the drawer. She looked suddenly more resolute. She studied Rosemary with concern.

'Are you feeling all right, Aunty? It must have been a hell of a shock for you today.'

Rosemary supposed it had been. Maybe these morbid thoughts of the past were an indication that it was all getting to her.

Katherine filled the kettle, slamming it down with a thump.

'OK,' she said, 'I suppose it could be Glyn. But, whoever it is, how the hell did he die up a tree?'

The same question was running through the mind of DCI Alan Greening as he stood on the hillside above Pitchbury Hall. He was watching floodlit Scenes of Crime personnel, ghostly in their forensic suits, as they examined the ground beneath the fringe of trees where the afternoon's bizarre find had taken place. The corpse had been removed from the scene.

Naturally, there had been some protests.

'Can't we do this tomorrow? In daylight?' inquired Sean, the senior SOCO, without much hope – he'd worked with Greening before.

'I'd like as much done now as possible.'

'But it's hardly urgent, is it? That bloke must have been up there for ages. No vital clue is going to disappear overnight.'

But Greening had not budged. Who knew what tomorrow would bring? A multiple pile-up on the M4 or a mass murder in Reading might rob him of forensic resources. Experience had taught him not to take anything for granted. These men and their expertise were here now, let them get on with it.

He knew what Sean was thinking – that it was all right for him, he didn't have a wife waiting for him to come home and uncork the Beaujolais or two kids eager for storytime and a laugh before lights out. Well, that was true these days, but he had been in those shoes and nights like this, poking around crime scenes when his shift had run overtime, were probably the main reason no one was waiting on his company any more. It certainly simplified things. You marry the bloody job, he'd been told on week one in plain clothes.

'Got anything yet?' he asked Sean.

'Two crisp packets, an empty Coke can and a pile of fresh dog crap. Plus, of course, a few hundredweight of branches, twigs and assorted flora.'

'A Coke can? New or old?

The other man shrugged and his suit rustled. 'Hard to tell. They're not exactly biodegradable, are they? You're meant to recycle them. However, I can reveal it was a Coke Zero.'

Greening pulled a face. He was an expert on soft drinks since he'd cut down on the booze but he was still to find one he liked. 'Zero's been out for a few years now, hasn't it? It might be relevant.'

'How?'

'Our friend up the tree might have drunk it.'

'What? He tied himself into a tree to have a picnic and couldn't undo himself?'

Greening couldn't decide if the other man was being funny. He wasn't known for a sense of humour.

'Not so far off. If you can't find me something better, like a knife or a razor or a gun, a Coke can might fit the bill.'

Sean's face was in shadow and couldn't be read, but it was plain he didn't follow Greening's line of thought.

'What are you getting at, Alan?'

'I'm thinking he might have climbed up there, way out of sight, lashed himself firmly to the tree and done himself in.'

'With a Coke can?'

'He could have taken pills and washed them down with the Coke.'

Sean thought about it. 'I suppose doing it up a tree is one way to make sure some busybody doesn't rush you off to hospital and pump your stomach.'

'Indeed.' Greening thought the idea had its appeal – drifting out of life way up above the ground, caressed by the breeze, lulled by the creak of branches and the music of birdsong. But were he to choose such an exit, he'd make sure he had something more ballsy to accompany his poison than an anemic, calorie-free can of brown water.

'Of course,' he added, 'there's plenty of other ways he could have killed himself. Even if you don't find a weapon on the ground, there might be one in his clothing.'

'So you think this is a suicide?'

'Not necessarily. Someone could have put him up there. It's a good place to hide a body when you think about it.' He considered the small group of men ahead of him inching through the undergrowth on their knees as if proving his point. 'You know, Zoroastrians believe in sky burial. They place their dead in towers and expose them to the elements so that vultures can pick the flesh from the bones. Not that we have vultures in Berkshire, but there's a kind of similarity in this, wouldn't you say?'

This time he could read the incomprehension in Sean's face. It was mixed with something else – pity. 'Jesus, Alan,' he murmured. 'I'd say retirement can't come quick enough for you.'

Will was sitting in the hotel bar when his phone rang. He'd been ducking calls all evening because he owed it to Tammy, who'd come up specially to see him ride. But this was one he had to take.

'Sorry,' he said, getting to his feet. 'I'll be as quick as I can.'

She gave him permission with a wave of her hand and a tight little grin that did not disguise her disappointment. He put that look out of his mind as he headed for the quiet of the corridor.

'Will.' Anna's voice was low and tremulous. 'Have you heard?'

It was unusual for Anna to phone him – that's why he had taken her call.

'Heard what?' he said.

'Didn't Edward say anything to you?'

'Only about my ride. What's up?'

'The storm brought down some trees in the grounds, on the drive and up on the north side. They've found a man's body.'

Will said nothing but his heart was hammering.

'Can you hear me?'

'Yes, of course. Carry on.'

'The police are up there now and they've been interviewing my mother.'

'Why?'

'She found him. She was out walking the dogs and they found his shoe.' Anna began to cry. 'She said the bone was still in it.'

'Jesus.' Will felt like weeping himself. He walked down the corridor and out into the forecourt of the hotel. Rain was falling in thick sheets. He took no notice.

'It's him, isn't it? Mum and Kathy are downstairs and I know they're talking about it but they haven't said anything to me. It has to be Glyn, doesn't it?'

He took a deep rainy breath. 'The trees by the top gallop along the Lambourn Road?'

'Yes.'

'Then he's been found, Anna. I'm sorry.'

'What are we going to do?'

He wanted to say he didn't have a clue but that was hardly helpful. Anna was older than him, the respected wife of a pillar of the community and about to be a mother; she was more mature than him in every way. But he was the one who fixed things – like he'd done for her before.

'Listen, we do what we've always done, carry on as normal. Be as curious and as ignorant as everyone else.'

'And what about Freddy?'

Will hadn't yet considered Freddy. But he was the most important of them all.

He took a deep breath. 'You'll have to talk to him.'

'I suppose so.' She sounded uncertain.

He wished he could do it for her but he was two hundred miles away. He simply couldn't fix everything.

Anna put her phone down and, suppressing the familiar queasiness in her stomach, began to dress. She found jeans but rejected her first choice of a shirt in favour of a vest - why fiddle with buttons? - and pulled a thick sweater over the top. She brushed her teeth in the little bathroom next door to the bedroom and splashed her face without scrutiny - she knew she looked a mess. All the same, she dragged a brush through the thick golden mane of her hair.

Before she went downstairs she forced herself to stand upright and breathe slowly. She'd been too feeble lately, giving in to the surprise and unpleasantness of her condition. But she wasn't ill, she was going to have a baby. It sounded romantic but the reality wasn't pleasant. Too bad. She'd never met a mother yet who claimed that it was. Or who said it wasn't worth it in the end.

But her condition wasn't the issue at the moment and she couldn't afford to hang around in bed feeling sorry for herself. The discovery of the body - Glyn's body - was a crisis and until Will returned from York, she had to deal with it on her own.

She went downstairs softly, following the sound of voices to the kitchen. It was beneath her to listen at the door but she had no doubt they would be talking about the body. Had they made the connection yet with Glyn? From their faces and the silence that fell as she appeared in the doorway, she would bet that they had.

'I need some fresh air,' she announced, 'so I'm just popping out for a moment. I can't stay in bed all the time.'

They started to raise objections but she overrode them. 'Honestly, I'm feeling a bit better. I won't be long.'

That was a fib. She didn't see that walking to the gatehouse and breaking the news to Freddy could be done in under an hour. But right now all she wanted to do was get out of the door without a fuss – and without company.

Tammy hid the disappointment that was growing like a lump in her chest. The evening wasn't going as she had hoped. The day had been brilliant, though, from the moment Will had picked her up on the corner of her road first thing. The problems of her life were a dead weight dragging her down and driving up to York had been like making a break for freedom.

There was no special reason for them to keep their friendship secret, apart from not wanting to be the subject of general gossip. She knew what they were like in the yard, what they would say. 'Heard the latest? Will is shagging that bird up at the Hall – Tammy with the tits.' Only it would probably be even more offensive than that, the crude sods.

As it happened, he wasn't shagging her – not yet. That was one of the – unspoken – reasons he had invited her to accompany him to York and she'd thought hard before she'd said yes. She'd only had one serious boyfriend before – one and a half, to be truthful – and the thought of throwing in her lot with Will was daunting. Her father disapproved of him already which, as she was still living with her parents, could not be lightly disregarded. And Will wasn't popular in the yard, he had a knack of rubbing the other lads up the wrong way – not that that should have mattered but somehow it did. It had all added to the allure of escaping north with her sexy jockey to find some space of their own.

The day's racing had been great, of course. She might not be much of an expert when it came to horses but she could appreciate the spectacular nature of Will's win on Paper Sun. It had been the talk of the course and even Will, a man who specialised in shrugging off compliments and playing it cool, had not been able to wipe the flush of triumph from his face.

Their romantic interlude had been proceeding well until he had taken that phone call. It irked her that he had taken it in the first place. Then, he had been gone for a long time. At least, ten minutes feels like a long time when you're a girl alone in a bar crowded with noisy male drinkers. She'd had to fend off a couple of unsubtle approaches. And when Will returned he seemed unaware that he was soaked through.

Now they sat across the table in the hotel restaurant, both of them pushing food around their plates. She'd lost her appetite but she supposed he had the excuse of keeping an eye on his weight.

Upstairs the bedroom awaited and it no longer

seemed to beckon with seductive possibility. She wondered if she should ask him to book her a separate room, but it would be a humiliation she was reluctant to inflict. In any case, the hotel was obviously full.

'Have you dried off yet?' she said, to break the growing silence.

'Oh sure. Nearly, anyway.'

'I can't believe you didn't notice you were standing in a monsoon.'

He shrugged and grinned suddenly, which disarmed her. He wasn't a smiley sort of person. His face was all angles and planes – high, sharp cheekbones and narrow jaw with a naturally serious expression. So his sudden smile was always a surprise and his black eyes turned on her full beam were a delight.

'Let's go upstairs,' he said.

Anna was right – the walk from the Hall had done her good. The sky was clear and full of light from the moon. She met no one as she took the footpath past the stables and joined the lime-tree drive to the gatehouse. On the way she noticed the fallen trees, which had been dragged clear of the carriageway and were awaiting the attentions of the chainsaw. The gaps in the avenue, even in the dim light, were obvious and ugly, and a reminder of the discovery up the hill. Not that she needed reminding. Her eyes kept turning in that direction and, though the view was obscured by the roll of the land and its fringes of woodland, she was sure she could make out the glow of lights against the charcoal of the sky. The police would be working through the night up there, applying their expertise to the mystery of Glyn's death. The thought was terrifying and made her walk faster.

She knew Freddy would be at the gatehouse. His habits were set in stone. At the end of a day's work at the yard he would go home for tea and toast (Marmite and peanut butter on one round, strawberry jam on the other). Then he would set about the chores that Rosemary had left him, chopping logs, cleaning shoes and other masculine tasks, though he was also a slow and skilful wielder of an iron. He would walk and feed the dogs and, if his mother was busy, prepare supper – he had a small but tasty repertoire which Rosemary was always trying to persuade him to expand. After that, he would watch television or, if none of his favourite programmes were on, play games on the computer. At ten o'clock he would go to bed and be up at 5.30 the next morning in time to start his day at the yard.

This routine varied only on Friday nights when he walked half a mile down the road to the White Hart, where he would spend the evening slowly drinking quantities of ale. In his younger days there had been many scares when he'd not returned home after closing time. Rosemary had regularly got into the car after midnight and driven round the locality searching for him. Several times he'd been discovered unconscious by the side of the road and more than once she'd had to retrieve him from a police cell. But these escapades were firmly in the past. All the Pitchbury lads who drank in the Hart were under instructions to watch out for him and Freddy himself had restricted his drinking, out of consideration to his mother. 'I'll text you when I'm on my way,' he'd say to Rosemary as he headed for the pub on Fridays and he invariably did so, sending a prepared message when he left so she could measure his progress.

But today was not a Friday and Anna was confident her brother would be engaged in his usual pursuits.

It was a long two minutes after she rang the bell before he opened the door but she knew better than to summon him again. It would have taken him time to adjust, to pause his activities on screen and make his way down the stairs from his bedroom.

Naturally he was surprised to see her, but pleased. His little sister could upset his routines any time she liked and he would be happy. 'Anna.' His face split open in a grin which stalled a second later as he sought a reason for her sudden appearance. 'Are you all right?'

'Yes, I'm fine.'

'But what about the, er . . .?'

He meant the morning sickness – the every-bloody-hour-of-the-day sickness. During her indisposition he had been solicitous, bringing bunches of bluebells and cowslips up to her sickroom and, once, a tin of Quality Street, which at least her other visitors had appreciated.

'It's not too bad. I'm learning to cope a bit better, that's why I've come out for a walk.'

'On your own?' He looked behind her, as if expecting to see his mother or other attendants. 'Is that safe?'

'Don't be daft, Freddy. I'm fine. Aren't you going to invite me in?'

She sat in the kitchen while he made tea, which she

sipped cautiously. He put a packet of digestives on the table and she found herself eating one – she was going to turn into a biscuit at this rate.

She wondered how to break the news. She had never discussed with Freddy the events of that dreadful Sunday just over two years ago. She didn't know how much of an impression they had left on her brother's wounded brain. He had a surprising ability to recover from life's setbacks and had carried on, seemingly unaffected. It seemed to her that he had survived better than she had and the last thing she wanted to do was to speak about what had happened. If she could have left it to Will she would have done. But Will would not be back for two days, at the end of the York meeting, and there would be no keeping a lid on matters till then. Especially with the police at work on the top gallop.

Her mother had said she had not told Freddy about her discovery when she'd summoned him to take the dogs home. It was plain she was intending to shield him as much possible. But Anna knew it was too late for that.

When he'd stopped fussing round her, trying to fetch her more tea, offering her cushions and food, he sat across the kitchen table. She waited till he'd finished dunking his biscuit before she spoke.

'Do you remember Glyn?' she said.

He looked her square in the eye. 'Of course.'

'Do you think about him sometimes?'

He shook his head. 'He's not worth it. I used to think he was a friend but then he was mean to you.'

'Well, not really . . .' It was too complicated to go

into. Keep it simple. 'You see, Freddy, I think they've found him.'

He stared at her, his face expressionless, and said nothing. He raised his mug and drank.

'Do you understand me? I think they've found Glyn's body.'

He put the mug down. 'How?'

She told him about Rosemary walking the dogs, finding the storm damage, her discovery, even his own small part in the drama in taking the Land Rover to collect the dogs.

All he said was, 'Poor Mum.'

'She's fine. You know Mum, she's rather enjoying the drama.'

He nodded. 'And she wanted to spare me the bad news.' His face cracked into a smile. 'That's funny.'

'I suppose so.' Anna forced herself to smile in turn. 'But listen, Freddy. The police are investigating. They are up by the top gallop right now trying to find out what happened. I don't think they know it's Glyn yet. All you've got to do is pretend it's nothing to do with you. Just be prepared in case it comes up in conversation or if the police start asking questions in the yard.'

'Let me guess – I know nothing. Like Manuel.' He chuckled at her puzzled face. 'Manuel from *Fawlty Towers*.'

Sometimes she wondered which of them was meant to have the impaired intellect.

She reached across the table and took his hand. 'I just wanted to warn you. I didn't want you taken by surprise.'

'What about Will?'

'He knows. I called him in York and he says we'll all be fine if we stick together.'

'And say nothing. I understand. I might be bananas, little sister, but you can rely on me.'

'You're not bananas,' she said.

'Soft in the head.' He pulled a funny face. 'Mashed-up bananas.'

It was an old childhood joke and she couldn't help laughing. She loved her brother very much. And he loved her. Why else would he have killed Glyn?

Edward was surprised to find just his mother-in-law waiting for him when he finally reached home at half past ten. It had been a long and arduous drive.

He kissed Rosemary and poured himself a large Scotch. She offered to make him an omelette and, while she cracked eggs, told him that Anna had walked down to the gatehouse. Freddy would be driving her back any moment. Katherine had been here all evening but had just gone home.

Edward listened to this bulletin without comment. Anna must be feeling a bit better if she was able to take herself off like that, though he would have preferred someone else to have gone with her. But at least there was no harm done.

He gulped down the whisky and voiced the question that had been bugging him all the way from York.

'What on earth happened to Glyn Cole?' He poured himself another. 'I mean, people get run over by buses, have heart attacks in the street, get their heads bashed in – and sometimes they bloody well deserve it. But they don't just vanish into the treetops, do they?'

Rosemary turned from the stove and faced him. 'I wonder if he killed himself.'

'Seriously?'

'He could have climbed the tree and done away with himself somehow. Anna said he was very emotional when she broke it off with him.'

Edward snorted. 'She's not Helen of bloody Troy, you know.' He fielded the flash of disapproval in Rosemary's glance. 'Sorry – you must allow the deceived husband his cynicism. I know women like to imagine men destroying themselves for their love but I don't buy it. A professional philanderer like Glyn would never have the guts.'

'Well then, do you have a theory?'

'Someone must have killed him and hidden the body. I bet he pulled some dodgy business stroke – fake antiques or something. Probably double-crossed his partners too. Clever of them to think of sticking him up a tree. Makes a change from burying a body in concrete.'

'What on earth do you mean?'

'It's what gangsters do, isn't it? I thought the foundations of buildings and motorways were riddled with corpses. Could be that half the forests in England hide bodies. I grant you it's a flaming great coincidence they chose to stick him up our trees but they are the tallest round here.'

Rosemary sighed in ill-concealed irritation and put a plate in front of him. 'I think that Scotch has gone to your head.'

She could be right. He chuckled at the absurdity of the whole business.

'Well, whatever happened, I didn't put him up there.'

She stared at him. 'Do you think I would blame you if you had?'

He reached for her hand and squeezed it. He could always count on his mother-in-law. He just wished he could be as sure of his wife.

Tammy dried herself in the shiny hotel bathroom. Though she had managed to fug up the many mirrors with the steam from her shower, there was enough glass and chrome and white tiling to sparkle impressively. As hotel bathrooms went, she didn't suppose it was that special, but she wasn't used to showers that spat an instant torrent of hot water or several large clean bath towels to choose from, let alone the endless reflective surfaces in which she could, if she chose, preen and pose.

She wrapped herself in the fluffy white towelling robe that hung on the back of the door and returned to the bedroom. Will was out for a run before breakfast. She understood it was part of his fitness regime. He'd urged her to come with him but she'd chosen hotel luxury instead. Maybe she would go running with him in future, though, if he'd put up with her tagging along. A fitness regime appealed. She could give up cigarettes, too.

The evening before had not ended as anticipated. She'd expected to be seduced, either slickly or clumsily – she'd only slept with two men and their contrasting approaches were the limit of her experience. Naturally, a part of her had been longing to find out how Will would go about it.

Instead, as they'd settled on the bed, leaning up against the headboard, he'd said, 'Tell me about your mother.'

She must have looked shocked. The sorry story of her mother's illness, which was killing her family as surely as it was killing her parent, was another reason she'd been so keen to get away for a couple of days. Except, of course, there are some things you can never escape from.

Although she'd tried to turn his request aside she'd ended up telling him just the same. About her mother's late diagnosis and then the operation that wasn't entirely successful and the succeeding courses of chemotherapy. And the way it had upset the balance of the household, with her father – a decisive type, a man of action – rendered ineffective and increasingly useless, cancer not being a problem he could solve with a snap of the fingers. In the face of the remorseless grind of the disease, it seemed to her the men of the family had crumbled. Her eldest brother, married with a young family, used his bread-winning responsibilities as a buffer and these days made the two-and-a-half hour drive from Exeter only infrequently. Her other brother, the middle sibling, was training to be a vet in Glasgow and was rarely seen. As for her, she had dropped out of college at Christmas after only one term to help at home. She'd fondly imagined that the disease would bring them all together, binding them in adversity. But, if anything, the cancer had done just the opposite, driving them apart to conquer them separately in its unique and horrible way.

She told Will more than she should, certainly more

than she'd intended. And when she'd finished, she'd felt drained of all energy and emotion. He'd not said much, just held her while she talked and wept. Then he'd pulled the counterpane over her, snapped off the light and the pair of them had fallen into a welcome sleep. At least, she assumed he slept too. In the middle of the night she'd woken and extricated herself to wash and change. When she slipped back beneath the covers in her underwear and a T-shirt, Will was awake. He slid his arms around her and pulled her body against his. She gasped in shock.

'What are you wearing?' she squealed.

'Nothing much,' he said. 'Do you mind?'

As it happened, she didn't mind at all.

So their secret love tryst hadn't turned out to be a disaster after all and here she was, happily lolling around in luxury the morning after, just as she had hoped she would be.

Will had suggested she call room service for breakfast and not to wait for him. But that didn't seem fair. She pictured him pounding through the grey wet of the unseasonal May morning. Would he be thinking about her? Or would his mind be on the horses he was to ride that afternoon? She hoped the former but she had no way of telling. She still knew so little about him.

What, for example, had happened last night when he had abandoned her in the bar to stand in the rain and talk on the phone? He'd told her it was an owner, chatting him up about a possible ride. She supposed that made sense. But he'd not told her which owner or what ride when she'd asked and she'd felt like she'd stepped out of line in putting the question, as if she were not entitled to know. But this morning things were different. Surely now she was justified in being curious.

He'd left his phone on the table on his side of the bed. Maybe she could satisfy that curiosity.

Before she could talk herself out of it, she picked up the phone and accessed the call history. She found the call in question at once, at 19:55 last night. The display showed no name, only a mobile phone number. But that didn't matter because she was sure she recognised it. She opened the address book in her own phone to make certain.

She could imagine one or two reasons why Will should be talking to Anna Pemberton last night. He rode for her husband and, naturally, she would have been thrilled at his victory yesterday. Tammy knew that Anna took a special interest in Paper Sun because the pair of them had discussed the horse the week before, when she was tidying Anna's bedroom.

But Will hadn't told her he'd been talking to Anna. He'd deliberately lied. Why?

Unfortunately, Tammy could only think of one reason and, in her particular circumstances, it was a blow to all her hopes.

She'd not be staying another night here in York.

Chapter Three

Greening had attended many post-mortems in his time and the sights, sounds and smells of the dissecting room had, regrettably, become familiar to him. The lingering odour of decaying intestine and burnt bone, the pad of rubber boots and the snapping of ribs, the moist and messy leak of bloody flesh. Nevertheless, he had worked hard not to let familiarity breed contempt. However much the object on the table might come to resemble a carcass in a butcher's shop, as an investigator among the living he could not allow himself to lose sight of the humanity they both shared. Not if he wanted to understand the circumstances that had put them together in the mortuary at the same time.

This particular procedure was different, however. It was not of the butcher's shop variety; the corpse laid out on the table before them no longer had any flesh or blood to disturb. The body was still clothed and, to Greening, it was as if the weather-beaten garments took the place of sinew and skin, for inside them was nothing but bone.

The post-mortem team was seven strong: Arnold

the pathologist and his two technicians, Sean the SOCO supervisor, DS Les Davis the Crime Scene Manager and Dougie Hannah, a forensic biologist with an impenetrable (to Greening) Glasgow accent, plus a photographer. They all had a job to do and Greening concentrated on keeping out of their way. He'd done his bit in the briefing room next door before they'd started, recapping the facts of the body's discovery before handing over to Davis who, true to form, was full of more precise information. He had calculated that, before the storm, the deceased had been concealed ten metres above the ground, attached to a Leyland cypress which formed part of a mixed growth of woodland on the Pitchbury estate. The Leyland cypress, he informed the meeting, could achieve a metre of growth a year.

'Leyland cypress?' Arnold the pathologist had said irritably. 'You mean Leylandii, don't you? My neighbour planted a hedge of them and it's shutting out my sunlight. I'm not surprised you can use them to hide corpses – bloody awful things.'

There'd been a general chuckling until Greening felt compelled to point out that until they knew more than they did, it would be dangerous to assume that a third party had concealed the deceased.

Arnold had nodded. 'Fair enough. You think he might have climbed up there himself?'

'Alan has a theory,' said Sean. 'The dead bloke was a Zoroastrian who did himself away with a Coke Zero so vultures could eat his flesh.'

One of the technicians, an attractive young woman, snorted in merriment and Davis's jaw had gaped.

'Seriously, boss?' he'd inquired. Arnold had rolled his eyes as if nothing he heard from Greening would surprise him – they'd seen plenty of each other over the years.

Exasperated, Greening had drawn the briefing to a swift conclusion with a reminder that the purpose of the post-mortem was to establish the how and when of death. If it cast light on who the deceased was, that of course would be helpful too. It all went without saying, though he said it anyway.

Now Sean and Dougie were fussing over the dead man's clothes which, fabricated to a considerable extent from artificial fibre, had retained their original character, unlike their owner. They were removing the articles to the exhibits area next door where, through a glass window, Greening could see the beginning of a bagging-up, labelling and logging-in process, overseen by Davis. Photographs were taken at every stage of the corpse's divestment as if – the thought flew into Greening's head from left field – this were a porno shoot for skeletons. But could a skeleton be said to be naked? It was not a question he would be speaking out loud, however; those present thought him odd enough as it was.

Gradually the bones were laid bare until the entire frame was stretched out on the table.

Arnold was peering closely at the pelvic area.

'V-shaped sub-pubic arch, large sacroiliac joint, long narrow sacrum – definitely a man,' he pronounced.

Greening had never had any doubt about that, nor any of them, he imagined. The size-ten shoes were a giveaway, for a start, and the Hacketts label inside the collar of the jacket. But he supposed it was just possible some six-foot Amazon could have been dressed in such a fashion. It was as well to make things clear for the record.

That having been accomplished, Greening was keen to get on with things. 'How long's he been up there, Arnold?'

The pathologist, a big square man who looked faintly ridiculous in his white plastic pinafore, turned slowly to face Greening. He spoke through his face mask. 'A minimum of three or four months. The body decomposes pretty quickly, especially exposed to the elements. The insects and birds do their job.' Arnold's mouth was obscured by the mask but, from the crinkling of his eyes, Greening imagined the pathologist was grinning. 'We might not have vultures but we have our own carrion eaters. As you can see, there's only bone and a bit of hair left.'

There was hair on the skull, pale brown and fine, longer than the average male cut. It looked incongruous, like a wig that had been popped on the dead cranium for a joke.

'What about a maximum timescale?'

'I couldn't say at present – and don't ask me to guess from the state of the corpse. You'll probably have better luck with the clothes.'

That was true. It would be painstaking but there was a good chance they could track down manufacturers and unearth dates for the release of at least one of the garments the man had been wearing. That would give them some kind of time-frame.

'OK. So what about a cause of death?'

Though masked, Arnold pantomimed exasperation. 'Give me a few minutes to breathe, dear boy. As you can see, I don't have much to work on.'

'I know, Arnold. In which case, it shouldn't take you long, should it? Check his bones and tell me if there's a bullet hole or a neck fracture or anything obvious like that.'

But Arnold took his time, as was right and proper. Greening didn't really mind. For all his stated impatience, he knew there were some things not to be hurried. This poor fellow had spent months, maybe years, decaying above the earth; he was not to be rushed now.

Arnold was peering closely at the skeleton's hands. 'There's signs of damage here, to both hands. Look.'

Greening bent closer and Arnold pointed to plainly visible cracks and dislocations in the bone.

'He's taken blows on the phalanges - the finger bones. And the capitate on this hand - the largest bone in the wrist - has been badly chipped. I'd say both hands have been hit repeatedly by a heavy object.'

'Hit from above or below?'

'From above, definitely. He might have been holding on to something and, whack, he's taken a hit on the back of the hand. Both hands.'

Greening could picture that. It also tied in with something else. While disrobing the corpse, they had removed a wristwatch whose glass face had been missing. It was likely that one of the blows to the hand had dislodged it - which was interesting, but only up to a point.

'These injuries wouldn't have killed him, would they?'

'No.'

'So what did?'

Arnold stepped back from the table and shook his head. 'Sorry, my friend, but I don't know. There are no fractures, no indentations of the skull, no scarring of the bone from a knife.'

'No bullet holes?'

'Absolutely no bullet holes. I suppose I might have missed something but, on a first examination, I can see no anatomical reason why this man died.'

That was a pity but not a surprise. Somehow a skeletal wound would have been too easy. In his present state, there was no way of telling if the man on the table had bled to death, or choked, or ingested poison – there were so many ways to take leave of life.

But, up a tree? Greening had never come across a body up a tree before. Of course solving his death would not be easy.

'Thanks anyway, Arnold. Maybe we'll get lucky some other way.'

A sound that was hard to interpret came from across the room. It was repeated and Greening finally recognised his own name, spoken by Dougie.

'You're looking for a slice of luck?' he said. It was a pity the young man's mouth was obscured by his mask – lip-reading might have helped.

'You bet.'

'I think we've got it.' The criminal biologist was holding something in his gloved hand. 'I've just found his wallet.'

Greening understood that all right.

'You Scotch genius,' he said. 'The whisky's on me if there's anything in it.'

The body, so they had established, had been in a sitting position, its back to the trunk of the tree, with a leg on either side of a lateral branch. A rope wrapped around the torso had secured it in place and was knotted over the chest. Greening thought it quite possible that the dead man could have tied himself to the tree but he was no expert. Dougie would be examining the rope in detail in due course but Greening wouldn't mind betting it was a multi-purpose article, probably synthetic and doubtless widely available.

For the moment, though, he and Dougie were focused on the wallet which they were examining in the exhibits area. All things considered, it was in good condition. The article was uncomplicated, made of black leather, some four by five inches in size, which opened like a little book to reveal a selection of compartments for banknotes and cards. Greening had owned one very like it for some years.

Greening concentrated on the Scots lad's words, determined not to miss anything of importance.

'We found it buttoned into the back pocket of his trousers. It was sitting over his left buttock. You can see where fluids released by the body as it putrified have stained one side but the other is hardly damaged. It looks like it got soaked once or twice but it was protected by the material of the pocket and by his jacket, which would have helped keep the rain off. Not that much rain would have penetrated those trees.'

'You've been up to Pitchbury?'

Dougie nodded. 'I had a quick look on my way over.'

Greening was pleased. The scientist had not been given much time to answer the summons. The eagerness of youth was a quality to be admired – and nurtured.

'I'm impressed,' he said. 'Come on then, lad, let's have a look at what we've got.'

Greening was itching to grab the thing himself and empty its contents on to the counter but he knew that would not do – not these days, anyway. He must behave as if he were in a laboratory, his very presence a potential contamination of evidence. He stifled the gremlins of impatience as Dougie's gloved hands slowly tweezered out the dead man's valuables and laid them out for inspection: three credit cards, a debit card, an organ donor card – too late for that – a clutch of store cards and five remarkably pristine twenty-pound notes.

Greening peered at the name on the cards: Glyn L Cole. The latest 'valid from' date was 12/07.

Gotcha. His deceased now had a name and he had met his end at some point between December 2007 and, on the basis of Arnold's minimum timing of three months from the present, February 2010.

He felt a rush of elation that was matched by the gleam in Dougie's eyes.

'Glyn Cole,' said the Scot. 'That's a quick result, eh?'

'Looks like it.' Greening tempered his enthusiasm. 'But we need to corroborate to be certain.'

'You mean in case our skeleton was carrying another man's wallet?'

'Exactly. Tracking down this Mr Cole's dental records should do it.'

Dougie chuckled. 'You're hardly going to get a visual ID, are you?'

Greening did not join in the merriment. The notion of asking some poor nearest-and-dearest to look over the collection of pale bones next door was grotesque. Though should he himself be in Cole's position, he would have two ex-wives ready to scrap over the honour of identifying his remains. He suspected they would both love it. And, after two ruinous divorce settlements, he had much in common with the skeleton on the table. There was more than one way to have your bones picked clean.

'Sir.' Dougie didn't have to call him Sir, he wasn't in the police service, after all, and the deference to his years grated. But Greening said nothing, just responded to the urgency in the young man's tone. What else had he discovered?

Dougie laid out Cole's business card. In a florid script on a simple white background was printed 'Glyn Cole, Antiques', followed by an address in Hungerford and a short list of contact numbers. A line along the bottom of the card read 'Member of the British Antique Dealers' Association'.

Greening conjured up a vision of a well-heeled gentleman, an upstanding member of a respected trade body, probably an expert in Spode and Chippendale.

'There's something else.' Dougie was probing the

final compartment in the wallet which seemed reluctant to release its last treasure. Eventually he extracted it, a small square purple envelope, its contents bulging in the familiar shape of an O.

Dougie couldn't help himself. 'Looks like he was prepared for everything up that tree.'

Greening quickly revised his opinion of the august Mr Cole. Not that there was any reason why an antique dealer should not be carrying a condom.

Will sat in a corner of the changing room at York. Apart from the valets and the odd early-bird rider like himself, the place was quiet, which was exactly what he required. He wasn't much of a socialiser.

When Will had first begun attracting attention for his riding he'd been surprised to read his racing style described as 'ruthless'. It was true he wanted to win every race he took part in and that he was no respecter of reputations, but that was true of every other jockey, wasn't it? That was the point of a race – a competition pure and simple to find the best horse and rider on the day.

At first he'd brooded on the matter. Were they implying somehow that he had no skill? What rubbish. He could coax a horse into doing something it didn't want to as well as anyone. He had a feel for what the animal was thinking. When he was in the saddle, it was like being tuned in to a radio channel – he picked up every signal from his mount and reacted instinctively. And, unlike some of his companions in the weighing room, he didn't make a big show of it. He liked to get on with his business without fuss.

He envied the lads who were able to laugh and joke on the course but he didn't trust himself to relax like that. For him, riding races was a serious business, the one thing in life he wanted to do, and he concentrated on his job for every second he was on the course. Nothing else mattered but the race ahead and he shut every other consideration out of his thoughts. If that came over as ruthless, it was too bad. He preferred to call it being single-minded.

But today he was having trouble shutting things out and getting in the zone for the afternoon of racing ahead. Other thoughts kept invading his mind: Anna and the discovery of the body, Glyn Cole and Freddy. But, troubling though they were, he knew he would be able to dismiss them for the time it took to get his job done. What he was finding difficult to shake was the picture of Tammy sitting silent and remote in the passenger seat of his car as he drove her to the station.

He didn't know what he'd done wrong. Thanks to Anna's phone call, the evening before had not been a brilliant success but he thought they'd got over that. The night they'd spent together had more than made up for the awkwardness in the restaurant. And when he'd left her first thing that morning to go for a run, she'd seemed happy with him, with the prospect of the day ahead at the races and of their next night together. But by the time he'd returned she'd changed. She picked at breakfast and demanded to be taken to the station. And she'd refused to explain why.

He couldn't understand it. How could the

connection between them burn so bright and then vanish as if it had never existed?

It wasn't just a physical thing with Tammy, that's what hurt. They'd shared confidences – things he'd never told anyone before.

He'd told her about Mr and Mrs Pilling, his foster-parents, and their farm in Shropshire. And how poor, thin Mrs Pilling was the only mother he'd ever had and how he reckoned old man Pilling and his two burly sons had so worn her out between them that she died of exhaustion. The father had tried the same trick on him, putting him to hard labour on the farm from an early age. And when the two Pilling boys had upped sticks and headed for proper paid work in Wolverhampton, there'd been just the two of them to run the ramshackle old place where nothing was new and everything was botched together and there was no time for schoolwork after hours and his teachers soon dismissed him as another bone-headed son of the soil.

But there had been compensations, he'd told Tammy. He'd learned how to fix things – tractors, boilers, almost any kind of engine. He'd learned how to ride, poach game and treat the agents of the state, from social workers, to schoolteachers and policemen, with the contempt with which old man Pilling believed they deserved. And he'd developed a self-sufficiency that had stood him in good stead since Pilling dropped him off at the jockey training school at the age of sixteen with two suitcases and fifty quid. 'I reckon that makes us quits,' he'd said and driven out of Will's life for good.

He'd not meant to tell Tammy so much but it seemed only fair to share something of himself after she'd told him about her mother and wept in his arms. Lying there in the dark with her, it had been easy to talk. It had felt right but it must have been wrong – why else had she flown so abruptly?

Will didn't know a lot about girls, not in any depth; he'd never commanded affection or offered his heart before. He was swimming in deep and strange waters. What was it he'd said or done? He'd probably been clumsy and strange and off-putting but he'd been sincere. He'd given himself to her as honestly as he knew how.

But that gift had not been what she wanted after all. They'd spent one night together and she'd turned and run. Obviously he'd misread all her signals. He had repulsed her and now she hated him. To think that, as he'd splashed round the damp streets in his early morning euphoria, he had thought he was in love.

After a quick conflab with Davis, to make sure they were on the same page, Greening quit the mortuary without regret and returned to his car in the hospital car park. He called DS Yvonne Harris, who was in charge of the incident room back at Farley Road nick.

'We've had a good result,' he told her before he recounted the discovery of the wallet and its contents. 'So check Missing Persons pronto and ring me back.'

'Yes, boss,' she said in her vaguely insulting style, as if the notion of anyone being her boss was ridiculous. Twice now, during tipsy nights in the pub, he had told her to cut out the boss and guv stuff when it wasn't necessary. 'It's a habit,' she'd said. 'Besides, if I have to work in a male-dominated hierarchy, I think it's important to maintain propriety.'

He wasn't quite sure what she meant by that. Though she was a good officer, sharp and intuitive, in personal matters she could be irritatingly ambiguous. Like using the word propriety while swinging her long white shiny legs casually backwards and forwards as she toyed with her wine glass. Propriety, in Greening's view, was not going for an off-duty drink with a middle-aged and lonely divorced man while wearing a skirt that barely covered her bottom. Yvonne liked to tease and was not averse to manipulating males in her own fashion. Greening had no doubt she'd go far.

'Have you found out how he died?' she asked.

'The post-mortem did not reveal any anatomical injury.'

'That's a pity.' She made it sound as if it was his fault. That was another thing about Yvonne, too often she reminded him of both his wives. 'And you still have no idea what he was doing up a tree.'

'We –' he laid stress on the word – 'are still in the dark about that.'

'Les Davis says you think he was a member of a religious cult. That he climbed up a tree to be pecked to death by birds.'

'Les is talking out of his arse,' he snapped, 'and you are making mischief. Just check out Missing Persons, like I asked you to do five minutes ago.'

'Yes, boss,' she said in her irritating fashion. 'You

haven't forgotten the press conference, have you? They're already turning up downstairs.'

That was another thing she had in common with his wives. Yvonne always had to have the last word.

Edward was in a foul humour as he forced himself to be charming to the race-goers in Sir Sidney Tobin's box at York. He reckoned he'd got away with it pretty well but Sid was too shrewd to be fooled.

The owner cornered him. 'What's up, old cock?'

'Couple of things on my mind. Nothing to do with Liquid Assets though – he looks tip-top.'

Liquid Assets was Sid's runner in a Maiden Stakes that afternoon, a horse bred by Rosemary who had been reluctant to sell. Finally a deal had been arranged with the proviso that, should Sid ever decide to have the horse trained elsewhere, Rosemary would have the option to buy him back. Liquid Assets was Freddy's favourite horse, he'd been present at the birth and had lavished attention on him ever since. If only for Freddy's sake, it was important the horse remained in the yard.

Sid wouldn't be fobbed off. 'Anna's OK, isn't she?' Sid had visited Pitchbury within the last month and witnessed Anna clutching a sick bucket. It had left an impression.

'Still feeling rough but she's coping. But something else has come up and the yard might be splashed all over the media. It could be a real hassle.'

Exasperation flitted over Sid's doughy face. 'Are you going to spill the beans or not?'

Edward considered. He knew he could trust Sid to

keep his mouth shut. More to the point, the owner was important to the yard and he'd find out soon enough. It made sense to take him into his confidence.

They stepped out on to the balcony overlooking the course. The first race was still an hour off and the early arrivals were enjoying a good lunch. They would not be overheard out here.

'They've found a dead body on the estate. It was up a tree which was blown down in a storm. A mini bloody tornado.'

Sid's eyes widened in surprise and Edward could see him working to conceal his amusement as he said, 'Up a tree?'

'God knows how it got there. My mother-in-law found it when she was out walking her dogs. Anyway, the police are there in force, as you can imagine, and we started to get phone calls from the local media last night. This morning I had some police PR character trying to persuade me to allow a press conference on the estate. He said it would maximise publicity and get people to come forward with information if they could show the location of the body. It's actually just a few yards from a public footpath but I said it was private land and they could bog off.'

Sid laughed. 'I don't blame you.'

'All the same, the press and police are going to be prying, the locals will be gossiping and I've got eighty thoroughbreds and a pregnant wife to worry about.'

'But it'll soon blow over surely. Who is the dead person anyway? A down-and-out?'

Edward decided he'd said enough. 'No one knows yet.' That was true.

'Be a nine-day wonder, I expect,' Sid said. 'Let me know if there's anything I can do.'

Edward appreciated the sentiment, though he doubted the businessman could be of much practical help from the fastness of Canary Wharf.

Sid picked up on Edward's scepticism. 'If you need help with lawyers or press handlers, I know some good people.'

That would be true. 'Thank you. But I hope it's not going to come to that.'

'Don't let it get to you, son. That's my advice. I mean, it's nothing to do with you, is it?'

If only that was true.

Sid clapped an avuncular hand on his back. 'So how's your mum-in-law surviving? I was hoping to see her this afternoon.'

Rosemary and Freddy had been scheduled to travel up to watch Liquid Assets race.

'She's had to cancel, I'm afraid. In the circumstances.'

'You say she found this body?'

'Her dogs found a shoe with a foot still in it. Frankly, I think she's loving every minute of it.'

Greening had heard back from Yvonne as he returned to Farley Road. She told him that Hungerford antiques dealer Glyn Cole, an unmarried man of thirty-three, had gone missing in April 2008, just over two years previously. His car had been found in Swindon, close to the railway station, and there had been no sign of him since – at least, none that had been reported. A member of the local neighbourhood policing team,

PCSO Carmel Gibbs, had been most closely involved with the disappearance and she had promised to come in to Farley Road, even though she wasn't on shift, to brief him. In the meantime, he had the press conference to attend and Yvonne trusted he was not going to be late.

Greening was an old hand at press conferences, which didn't mean he enjoyed them. For one thing, the circumstances were usually grim and, for another, it was easy to get trapped in an interchange which would leave him with egg on his face and the Chief Superintendent on his back.

Today, however, was unlikely to be too bad as there were no grieving relatives to handle with care and because of the curious fashion in which the body had come to light. From the start, the meeting was infected with misplaced levity.

He dispensed the bald facts – the time and place of the discovery of human remains by Mrs Rosemary Drummond who was out walking her dogs on the Pitchbury estate after yesterday's storm. Mrs Drummond, he promised them, had agreed to answer questions following his statement.

Jimmy, the press officer, had been miffed not to have the conference 'in situ', as he put it, but the presence of the woman who had discovered the body made up for it in some measure.

'Have you got any idea who this person is?'

'All I can tell you, following this morning's post-mortem, is that the remains are of a man.' Greening wasn't prepared to broadcast Cole's identity until it had been corroborated and his family alerted.

'However,' he added, 'we have a strong lead which I shall be following up once our business here is over.'

Other questions succeeded along predictable lines and Greening responded accordingly. As yet, he said, there was no clear indication of how the man had died nor how long he had been hidden, though it was certainly months, if not years. The police were consulting a range of forensic experts in order to shed light on this and other aspects of the mystery. And no, he was not going to speculate on the circumstances which had led to the concealment of the body in a tree.

'Was he murdered?'

That, of course, was the big question and Greening ducked that too – not that he was in a position to answer it with any certainty.

'I'm sorry, it's too early to tell. At the moment we are treating the death as suspicious and the investigation team are actively pursuing a number of avenues of inquiry. However, in a case like this there are obviously many elements to be considered and I would welcome any additional information that the public can supply. I understand that the walk along the top gallop where the body was found is regularly used by locals out for a stroll or, like Mrs Drummond, exercising their dogs. If anybody saw something they think is relevant, I would be grateful if they would share that information with us.'

That seemed the right moment to introduce Rosemary Drummond who stood up for herself robustly.

'Mrs Drummond, is it true the body was in pieces

and the first thing you discovered was a skull?'

'Good Lord, no, where on earth did you get that idea?'

'But you did, I believe, first find just a bit of the skeleton, didn't you?'

'This is true. My dogs found a shoe. I thought it was just an old boot but when I looked closely I saw that it was in essence a rather elegant man's brogue that had been blackened by exposure.'

'Elegant man's brogue' was not how Greening would have described the article in question but he couldn't help admiring the lady's evident desire to make the most of her moment in the sun.

'But when I looked inside the shoe –' Mrs Drummond paused for effect – 'I was astonished to see the bones of a foot. And then I looked up . . .'

Greening had to admit she handled the whole thing rather well, ensuring that the inquiry, and she herself, would receive maximum exposure, which was the point of the entire exercise.

Will's mood had lifted as the afternoon wore on. Not that the wound that Tammy had inflicted had healed but the moment he sat astride his first ride he'd been able to put it aside. The adrenaline of his job was enough to defer the pain. Now, as he took his mount down to the start for his last ride of the afternoon, he had no thought for anything but the race ahead.

It wasn't only Freddy who had a soft spot for Liquid Assets. The chestnut two year old was a favourite at Pitchbury, possibly because he was home bred and had been something of a yard pet as a foal. Whether or not he had the makings of a winner on the racecourse was yet to be revealed. This was his first race. He had shown a fair turn of speed on the gallops, however, enough to impress Sidney Tobin who had watched him work and offered a generous price as a consequence. But a home gallop was one thing, the hurly-burly of a contest against a dozen other eager colts in front of a packed racecourse was another matter altogether.

Will was aware his mount was nervous from the moment Edward legged him up. Liquid Assets might be quick but he was sensitive, alert to every shout from the crowd and each movement in the periphery of his vision, and there were plenty of both. The real problem, however, was the starting gate. Though Will knew the horse had spent time in the starting stalls at home, here he shied away from them and was the last to be loaded. For an uncomfortable moment Will thought he wouldn't go in and the race would start without them. That would have been a disaster. But, with a bang against the open door, Liquid Assets was finally loaded.

Before they had travelled a furlong, Will knew that something wasn't right with the horse. Though well placed in the leading group, he wasn't moving with his usual fluency. All the same, he seemed eager to race and held his own through the charge along the straight. Will wondered whether he'd misjudged the animal beneath him.

Within sight of the stand, they were lying second and the leader, just two lengths ahead, was visibly flagging – plainly he'd shot his bolt. This was their moment.

Will gave the horse a tap with his stick, the signal for him to kick up a gear as he did on the Pitchbury gallops. But there was no response from Liquid Assets. He sensed that the animal wanted to obey but just couldn't.

They overtook the flagging leader but at the same time two other horses came flying past on the outside and Liquid Assets finished in third place.

'Only his first run and he's in the frame,' said Sir Sid as he and Edward welcomed horse and rider. 'I can't complain about that.'

Will said nothing, just accepted Sid's handshake and congratulations. But a moment later he whispered to the trainer, 'There's something wrong with him. He didn't feel right at all.'

'Are you sure?'

By the time they unsaddled the horse, he was hobbling. It didn't improve Will's mood to discover he'd been right.

Greening was accustomed to some of his colleagues being the same age as his daughter but Police Community Support Officer Carmel Gibbs looked young enough to be swotting for her GCSEs. She cut a tiny figure in her uniform, her vest pockets bulging with radio and other equipment, the collar of her crisp white shirt loose around her slender throat despite the tightly knotted tie. Greening was no giant but he found himself looking down on her little bowler hat with its gleaming silver badge.

Carmel had a round, cheerful face, though now her pink lips were pursed in a tight line and he could read the nerves in her forget-me-not blue eyes. She must find him intimidating – how gratifying, though not if it was going to inhibit her performance.

His impulse was to order her to stand at ease. Instead he said, 'I'm desperate for a cup of tea. The canteen or Starbucks?'

She opted for the canteen which Greening had guessed she would. Being seen with a DCI would do her station cred no end of good.

'Thanks for coming in specially,' he said as they found a table. 'You didn't have to dress up, you know.'

'No problem, sir,' she said firmly – she might be small but she sounded confident enough. 'I enjoy wearing the uniform.'

He'd bet she did. She was plainly a keen type. That boded well.

'I'm interested in a missing person inquiry that you handled in April two thousand and eight.'

'Yes, sir.' She had been clutching a blue ring binder which she now opened. It was leaved with plastic envelopes containing not so long ago, Greening imagined, her school revision work. Now she pulled out a sheaf of A4, on which, above some lines of type, had been scanned a colour photograph of a man. 'Glyn Llewellyn Cole, the proprietor of Cole Antiques in Hungerford. Reported missing on Wednesday the sixteenth.'

Greening studied the photo. A long, boyish face, clean shaven, with light brown hair growing over the ears and falling in a lock over his forehead. A good-looking man though not devastatingly so, apart from the look in his eyes as he gazed frankly into the camera. Amused, self-confident, knowing. If the photographer were a woman – and Greening had no doubt she was – her subject was propositioning her with no need of words.

'Handsome fellow,' he said.

Carmel grinned. 'He is a bit.'

'He doesn't look like that now.'

The grin vanished. 'Is this definitely him then? The skeleton in the tree.'

'We're not saying so officially yet. But we've found Cole's wallet in his trousers so it looks pretty certain. Why don't you tell me what you know about his disappearance?'

Carmel took a sip of her coffee then pushed the cup aside, composing herself before she launched into her account.

Cole had been reported missing on Wednesday, 16 April, by a next-door neighbour and by his book-keeper, Katherine Pym, who had gone to the shop that morning and found it closed. Cole lived in a small flat above the premises but he had not answered the doorbell. As Miss Pym had stood outside, wondering what to do, the neighbour approached her and said the shop had been shut since the weekend.

Greening interrupted. 'So the book-keeper hadn't been there the day before?'

'No. She only went in a couple of days a month and this was her regular day. Mr Cole hadn't said anything to her about being away, so she was a bit put out. That's when I came along. It was only by chance because I'd been dealing with an abandoned vehicle in the next road. It's possible Mrs Shaw might not have reported him missing if I hadn't turned up.'

'Mrs Shaw?'

'The neighbour. She saw me and said she was worried about Mr Cole not opening up as expected. She said she had a spare key so why didn't we go in and see if everything was all right. So that's what we did.' She looked at him as if seeking approval.

'What did you find?'

'Nothing. Well, he wasn't there. The flat upstairs was in a bit of a mess – dishes in the sink, unmade bed, clothes on the floor. But the place was in reasonable order – it didn't smell or anything. Typical bachelor chaos really.'

It struck Greening that she could have been describing his own fair abode between weekend bouts of cleaning.

'Was there any indication of when Cole was last there?'

'Sunday newspapers were on the kitchen table. The *Sunday Times* and *News of the World* from the previous weekend. They didn't look like they'd been read.'

'Were there any notes?'

She looked puzzled. 'Notes?'

'Left on the mantelpiece or somewhere obvious. Written in a wobbly tear-stained hand. You know.'

'No, sir. I didn't see anything like that. It was as if he'd just popped out and he'd be back any moment.'

'What about the shop?'

'That was much neater.'

'I mean,' Greening said, 'was there any indication that he'd been there since the Sunday?'

'Actually, it was quite the opposite. There was two or three days' post piled up on the floor and some messages on the answerphone. Miss Pym and I listened to them. There was one asking why he hadn't come to value a chest of drawers on the Monday as promised. And a couple of others – he'd missed quiz night at the pub.'

'What happened then?'

'I established that his car was gone and, later, talking to Miss Pym and the neighbour, I got the impression that Mr Cole wasn't entirely reliable. He had been known to disappear to some auction miles away at the drop of a hat. Considering that he was a grown man who could take care of himself, I was pretty sure he'd turn up when he felt like it. After all, he'd only been gone a couple of days. Mrs Shaw said to me it was possible he'd gone off with one of his girlfriends. She was a real nosy-parker.'

'They're the best witnesses,' Greening said with relish.

'Yes, sir,' she said solemnly, as if making a note. 'Anyway, even after his car turned up near Swindon station, I didn't think much of it. I put him on the misper database though. Then, after a few weeks, I got a call from his sister.'

'A local?'

'No. She lives in North Wales – that's where his family come from. It's not a surprise, is it, him being called Glyn Llewellyn? I got the impression he wasn't close to his family though. Dee, the sister, seemed to think his disappearing act probably was the latest in a line of misadventures. In the end, though, she came down to Hungerford and oversaw the closing of the shop. Then she went back to Wales. I was so busy doing other things I forgot about him till this morning, when DS Harris called me.'

She looked at him unhappily, as if the tribulations of Glyn Cole were all her fault. 'We put out a press release when he disappeared but no one came forward. There didn't seem much else we could do, him not being elderly or vulnerable or anything. So many people go missing.'

Greening subjected her to his most penetrating stare. 'You didn't murder him and stick him up a tree, did you?'

For a second, colour flared into her cheeks as she seriously considered the question. Then she relaxed. 'They told me you were a bit of a joker, sir.'

He nodded. Titchy or not, he liked her.

Chapter Four

So far, Edward had to admit, the police invasion of Pitchbury had not been as bad as he had feared. He had his head lad to thank for that. While Edward had been away at York, Tom had ensured the police had enjoyed unimpeded access to the top gallop while steering them clear of the other training facilities and the yard itself. He'd sent regular relays of lads up there, offering assistance but with instructions to keep an eye open and report back.

The day after the York meeting, a detective had appeared in the yard asking for the boss and Edward had steeled himself for intrusive requests. But the copper, a DS Davis, had only stayed long enough to assure Edward that they would stick around just as long as their job demanded and to thank him for the cooperation they had enjoyed so far. A courtesy call, in other words. Edward was cynical enough to believe the purpose of the visit was probably just to tick a box – the police being dead keen on neighbourhood relations these days – but that wasn't to say he didn't appreciate it.

Davis asked him if he had any recollection of unusual activity up on the top gallop.

'When?' he'd asked.

'Going back two or three years, say.'

'Is that how long the body was up there? No, officer, I can't say anything springs to mind.'

And that was as probing a question as the policeman asked.

Of course, it wouldn't stay that way once the dead man was identified as Glyn Cole. But three days had gone by and there had been no mention of the missing Hungerford antique dealer. Maybe the police wouldn't find any connection between Cole and the corpse. He fervently prayed that would be the case.

Two years had passed since the slimy Welsh homewrecker had almost stolen his wife and things had changed. He had forgiven Anna, as he believed she had forgiven him for all the bitterness and recrimination. And now, finally, she was pregnant, the yard was doing well, they were established in the Hall; the last thing they needed was the ghost of Glyn Cole to come calling.

But so far that hadn't happened. Perhaps he'd been worrying over nothing.

His mobile rang – his mother-in-law. 'You haven't forgotten about tomorrow, I hope. What with all this disruption.'

'I'm not the one who's been disrupted,' he said. 'You're the one who's been in the limelight.'

It seemed to Edward that Rosemary had revelled in her fifteen minutes of fame; she'd even been on local radio to describe her gruesome discovery. 'And how did you *feel* when you saw you were holding an actual human foot?' the interviewer had asked her. 'It must have been something out of your worst nightmare.'

'Well, I was a little surprised,' Rosemary had replied. Edward had enjoyed his first good laugh for days when he'd heard that. His mother-in-law had always stood high in his estimation.

'No need to worry,' he continued. 'Miletus is in fine shape. As far as I'm concerned, it's all systems go.'

Miletus was another of Rosemary's home-bred horses, a plain-looking three year old whose appearance had mitigated against a decent sale as a yearling so Rosemary had kept him, putting her faith in his breeding. 'His mother was a Group Two winner and his father had bucketloads of stamina so I don't see why he shouldn't perform,' she'd said at the time. 'He can stay at home and win races for me.'

Regrettably, he'd not managed it as a two year old but they'd only raced him in distances up to a mile. This season he'd come second over a mile and six furlongs at Haydock where he'd finished bravely, only just failing to reel in the winner. Tomorrow, at Salisbury, he was to try again over the same distance.

'Have you spoken to young Will?'

'Yes, he can hardly wait.'

Rosemary sounded a mite anxious, which wasn't unreasonable considering that a sizeable amount of cash was at stake.

The thrill of a good wager was something they enjoyed in common. In his army days, Edward would spend his money on racecourse fancies rather than beer – he still had mates from back then who called him Punter Pemberton. And when he'd got to know his future mother-in-law he'd discovered a kindred spirit. She'd delight in telling him tales of past betting exploits organised with Anna's father. In the early days, so she said, the Pitchbury yard had survived only with the help of one or two daring betting coups. Together, they had carried on the tradition, for the fun of it as much as anything else.

Miletus's contest at Salisbury had been earmarked for their next assault on the bookmakers and Will's input was essential. Apart from the compelling reason that the lad was the yard's best rider by a country mile, the plan required some skill in the execution that only Will could be relied on to supply.

'Don't you worry about the jockey, Rosemary,' Edward said. 'Leave the racing to me and you sort out the other stuff.'

The other stuff was dealing with the cash and getting it on with the rails' bookies at the right moment. It might have been thought that entrusting that task to a respectable lady of pensionable age would be a mistake. But Edward knew better than that.

Greening put the phone down after talking to Glyn Cole's sister, Dee James, and considered the doodle he had created on his pad. He wasn't much of an artist, though he'd perfected a line in soppy pussycats when his daughter was a toddler. This wasn't a pussycat but an abstract of triangular shapes driven hard into the paper with the point of his pen. He supposed it could be an iceberg floating on a jagged sea – which would be appropriate, given the conversation that had just taken place.

With laudable efficiency his team had tracked down

Glyn Cole's dentist – the book-keeper, Katherine Pym, had come up with the name – and the corpse had been duly identified as the missing antique dealer.

Greening's next task had been to inform Cole's sister and she had been harder to pin down than the dentist. When he'd finally obtained the right phone number, she never seemed to be in or willing to return his messages. 'I'm running a business here, you know,' she'd said by way of explanation when he'd finally got hold of her. 'We're making deliveries round the clock.'

'Deliveries of what?' he'd asked, trying to get a handle on a woman to whom he was about to break some bad news.

'Lamb. We raise and sell the finest organic lamb in North Wales and supply half the restaurant trade within two hundred miles. I'm sure you can appreciate I don't have a lot of time to chat.' In the background he could hear the rattle of fingers on a keyboard. She was probably checking her email as they talked.

'I'm afraid this is not a social call, Mrs James. It concerns your brother Glyn.'

'Well, I'd worked *that* out. Why else would the Swindon police be bothering me? I suppose he's turned up again.'

Greening hoped that what he had to say next would puncture her apparent lack of concern.

'Human remains of a man have been discovered in woodland near Lambourn, Mrs James, and your brother's wallet was in his trouser pocket. We've checked Mr Cole's dental records and I'm sorry to say that they match.'

'So he's dead?'

'Yes. I'm very sorry.'

'You just said that.' Her voice remained cool – no chance of this grieving relative cracking, not in public anyway. But at least he had her full attention. There was no keyboard noise now. 'You say you found "remains". What does that mean exactly?'

Greening recounted the circumstances briefly. 'Maybe you heard – it was on the news.'

'I heard about the skeleton up a tree. Good God, you mean to say that's Glyn? You're not asking me to come and look at his bones, are you?'

'That won't be necessary, Mrs James.'

'Thank the Lord for that.'

There was silence and Greening wondered if he'd got this woman all wrong. He shouldn't have sprung such sensitive information on her over the phone but Wrexham was a fair old drive, especially to see someone hard to pin down. He supposed he should have asked the local lads to go round but the circumstances made it hard to delegate.

'Are you all right, Mrs James? Is there anybody with you? I can arrange for a family liaison officer to call.'

'Don't be ridiculous. There are plenty of people here and we've all got jobs to get on with. You may or may not know, Inspector, but my brother walked out on his family the first moment he could and only ever got in touch when he needed something. This isn't so very different.' She sighed heavily. 'I suppose I'll have to organise a funeral.'

'Only after the coroner releases the body. It may be a while. We have to conduct an inquiry into his death.'

'Of course. Silly of me. I'm not thinking straight.'

At last a human reaction. 'That's perfectly understandable, Mrs James. This must be a shock.'

'Not entirely. I suppose he killed himself.'

'What makes you say that?'

'My brother would do anything to draw attention to himself. Especially if it embarrassed his family.'

Greening screwed up his doodle and lobbed it into the wastepaper basket. An iceberg, definitely.

Will found Freddy by the equine swimming pool, a domain he regarded as his own. The open-air pool was in frequent use as it enabled animals who couldn't work on the gallops to exercise without putting pressure on their joints; it was also excellent for building muscle tone and stamina. It was a rare horse who didn't appear to enjoy his regular dip. As a consequence, there was plenty for an industrious hand like Freddy to do, not only in handling and leading the horses round as they swam, but in maintaining the pool and its surroundings.

It was a mystery to Will why Freddy should be drawn to this spot, considering what had happened to him. If he were Freddy, the pool would be the last place in the yard you'd ever find him.

The older man was bending over, washing out the drain in the hosing-down area where animals were cleaned up before entering the water.

'Fancy a run up to the Rack?'

Freddy said, 'Why?'

It was a good question. Will knew he had to talk to Freddy just to see that he was OK – he'd promised

Anna. The Rack and Manger was a good ten miles off, out of the regular Pitchbury orbit, and they'd be less likely to be interrupted.

'It's lunchtime. Let me buy you a pint.'

Freddy slowly straightened up and rinsed his hands under the tap over the sink built into the pool wall. He shook his head. 'Anna will be expecting me up at the Hall.'

He'd been going up there regularly for the past few weeks, since his sister had stopped coming into the yard every day. Nothing had been said officially but they all knew it was to do with her being pregnant.

Freddy smiled at him. 'Why don't you come too?'

Will could think of a reason – Tammy might be there. He'd rung her just once since she'd fled from York and she'd not answered. Then he'd texted her, keeping it light. 'Hope you got home OK – give me a call.' But she hadn't responded at all. He'd left it for a day, unsure what to do. Then he'd texted again, asking to meet and talk. He'd got a reply to that: 'No – sorry.'

Well, sod it, surely he was owed a brush-off in person?

'OK, Freddy,' he said. 'I'll walk up there with you.'

At least it would give them a chance to talk as they took the footpath out of the yard and cut across the bottom paddock towards the Hall gardens.

As Will was considering how to open the tricky subject, Freddy said, 'That body they found, I reckon it might not be Glyn Cole after all.'

It was quite funny – not that Will felt like laughing. How many other dead men could be hidden in trees on the estate?

'Why do you say that?'

'Because it's been days now since they found him and they haven't said. If it was him they'd have said, wouldn't they?'

'I don't know.' Will had been puzzled by this too. There must be lots of ways of identifying a body, even if it had rotted away. After all, they hadn't tried to obscure Glyn's identity, hadn't been through his pockets or looked for his phone or anything. At the time the only issue on Will's panic-stricken mind had been hiding the body where no one would see it.

He supposed it was possible the police might not know who the dead man was. That would be a relief, especially if it stayed that way.

Freddy said, 'You and Anna worry too much. I told her I wouldn't say anything. So chill out, it's going to be all right.'

Will did not respond to this. Unlike Freddy, he did not believe in miracles.

They went into the Hall the back way, through the kitchen. Will steeled himself for the sight of Tammy. He'd decided he would ask her outright for a couple of minutes of her time – she couldn't deny him that, could she? Then he'd – well, he didn't know exactly what he'd say, the words kept rearranging themselves in his mind.

But there was no Tammy in the kitchen, only Anna setting some bread and cheese on a tray.

'Oh,' she said at the sight of them.

'I brought Will,' said Freddy, giving her a hug. 'Don't mind, do you?'

She shook her head, offered Will a grave smile of

welcome. 'We're going to eat in the garden if that's all right.'

Will considered making a retreat but why? The three of them hardly looked like a bunch of murderous conspirators. Besides, he was hungry.

He carried the tray out to the picnic table on the lawn.

Tammy saw the three of them from Anna's bedroom on the first floor.

She'd nearly thrown in the job at the Hall – the thought of being there now she knew about Anna and Will was abominable. But she needed the money and jobs weren't easy to get at the moment, at least not part-time jobs where she could pick and choose her times. And where there would be no questions asked should there be an emergency with her mother. Anna was a good employer, Tammy had no criticisms on that score. Furthermore, her college had promised to let her return at the beginning of the next academic year and so she was determined to keep up her studies. The flexible arrangement at the Hall suited her very well.

Now, as she watched Anna and the two men at the table, she wished she'd had the courage to pack it in after all.

She'd wanted to answer Will's call and at least make it clear why she'd left York so abruptly. But she didn't trust herself. He'd talk her round and they'd be back in some kind of relationship with her having given in. It was painful now but how much worse would it be in a few months' time if it all went wrong? At this point it was possible for her to walk away from him. They'd spent just one night together, surely that wasn't time to forge a bond that counted. What she felt was intense but shallow, like homesickness or a blow on the head. The agony would soon pass.

Bearing all this in mind, what she ought to do now was walk away from the window and run a vacuum cleaner round the rooms on the other side of the house. But she stayed exactly where she was, rooted to the spot.

The sight of Will at her table filled Anna with relief. Keeping her feelings about Glyn's discovery bottled up was killing her. There would be a moment, even if she had to stage-manage it, when she could speak to Will about how he felt, find out how he was coping. Keeping their secret was hard. The need to acknowledge it to another person was building to a necessity.

Her moment came after they'd eaten, when Freddy volunteered to make tea. He put dirty plates on the tray and walked off towards the house, whistling as he went.

As soon as her brother was out of sight she said, 'He's doing better than I am.'

'He thinks you worry too much. He said so on the way over here.'

'It's because I know what will happen to him if the police find out.'

Both of them had always been aware of the consequences; it was why they had done what they had. Only, of course, she had had much more reason.

She reached across the table and took his hand.

'I can never thank you enough for keeping him out of jail.'

Will nodded. 'Right now, I'm just as concerned we all stay out of jail. Do you know what's going on?' He inclined his head to his left, up the hill, a small gesture but one which was clear to Anna.

'They've still got the area closed off. Edward's itching to use the top gallop so he's asked them how much longer they're going to be. He hasn't got a proper answer, though. They're still busy.'

'I wonder what they're doing.'

She shrugged. 'Whatever they do. Look for clues, I suppose.'

'They won't find much after two years. Apart from the body, of course.'

'Poor Glyn.'

They sat in silence for a moment. She thought how awful it was that the man who had once shone a spotlight into every corner of her life and made it bearable was now just a thing. An object of nuisance and a threat to her liberty. She had wronged him terribly – all three of them had.

'Do you think,' she said, 'there's a chance they won't identify him?'

'I think there's every chance that they will. I'm surprised they haven't already.'

That's just what she thought too.

'Are we going to be all right, Will?'

He smiled at her, a brave keep-your-spirits-up smile that she saw right through. She appreciated it all the same.

'Of course we will. No one knows what happened

except us. If we stay strong and keep our mouths shut then we'll be fine.'

The sound of whistling from across the lawn advertised Freddy's arrival with the tea.

She withdrew her hand from Will and placed it over her slowly swelling belly. She almost wished they had faced the music at the proper time. Now, if they were discovered, the price to be paid for Glyn's death would be even greater.

Watching from her window, Tammy did not miss a thing. Anna sat with her back to the house but Tammy saw her reach for Will's hand the moment they were alone, saw Will's pale concerned face react to her words, saw him speak urgently. She was glad she could not hear what he said, just watching them together was wounding enough.

She wasn't surprised Will was in thrall to Anna. What boy his age would not be seduced by a slender beauty in a clinging summer dress whose hair flowed down her back like golden rain? Anna's skin was porcelain perfect. Tammy had seen her at her worst and wondered how, even when Anna was throwing up into a bowl or wiping sick from her lips, she still managed to look so lovely.

If that was what Will wanted in a woman, she knew she could not compete. She herself was tall and gawky with barely controllable toffee-brown hair and a tendency to knock over glasses and burn toast. If she was sick, her face turned scarlet and puffy. And she still couldn't ditch her filthy smoking habit. Why Will had ever invited her to York in the first place was a mystery.

The pair of them in the garden were still talking with intensity, his fingers wrapped around hers. The same fingers which had combed Tammy's wild hair out of their faces in the middle of the night in the hotel. And then had explored her features in the dark, softly, as if committing them to the memory of his touch.

Despite herself, though Tammy knew it was stupid to wallow in self-inflicted misery, she replayed the moments in her mind.

Down below, her once-only lover smiled at the blond beauty facing him.

Tammy lost the battle to control her tears.

Greening bent low to scramble beneath the branches of the broken tree. Around him in the thicket and on the ground, numbered markers denoted sites of possible evidence. This was the first time he'd returned to the place where the corpse had been discovered. He'd been content to leave the scene to the forensic experts. Now they were keen to show him what they had uncovered.

Sunlight filtered through the canopy of leaves and played along the reds and browns of the fallen branches. Above, through the tangle of foliage, the May sky was the milky blue of early summer. Though he was standing on almost exactly the same spot as on the evening of the body's discovery, he could have been in a different land.

Dougie Hannah, the forensic biologist, was briefing him, which was fine by Greening. It was funny how swiftly he'd overcome his prejudice against the

Scotsman's accent. He'd found it was quite possible to disentangle its thickets now that he was keen to hear every word the young man had to say.

'This is the tree where the body was concealed,' Dougie said, laying a gloved hand on a broad trunk which thrust up above their heads. 'The tornado smashed through this section of woodland and fractured this tree about nine metres above the ground.' Looking up, Greening could see where the tree was bent over like a broken straw, its innards exposed in the angle of the split.

'And our man was hidden above the break?' Greening asked.

'Correct.' Dougie pointed to the right along the remainder of the trunk which thrust over their heads down to the ground. 'He was sitting on that lateral there, hidden in the leaves and branches. He would have been completely invisible from the ground.'

'Until the Good Lord sent along a tornado.'

Dougie shot him an inquisitive look and Greening reminded himself he should keep his more whimsical thoughts to himself. His previous remarks about Zoroastrians and vultures were still causing merriment among the team.

'We've made a couple of interesting discoveries.' The scientist pointed further along the broken trunk. 'Do you see that big offshoot there?'

It wasn't hard to see the branch he was indicating since it was clearly tagged. Then Greening noticed the rope, weathered a greeny brown like the rope which had bound the body. It was tied in two places around the branch just six inches apart. An idea formed in

Greening's mind of the nature of Dougie's discovery but he waited for the scientist to spell it out.

'You see how the rope between the knots forms a loop?'

Greening agreed. He was sure now what was coming.

'When the tree was standing,' Dougie continued, 'that loop would have been a couple of metres above where the body was positioned.'

Greening couldn't contain himself any longer. 'Block and tackle,' he said. 'That's what you're going to tell me, isn't it? The body was hauled up into the tree on a pulley suspended from the branch above.'

'Exactly. Well done, sir. A pulley was hooked or tied on to that loop to provide the leverage to lift the corpse. And after the body had been secured to the tree, the lifting gear was removed. But whoever concealed the body didn't bother to climb up and untie the section of rope above.'

'Well, there wouldn't be much point, would there?'

Dougie nodded. Why bother to conceal the means by which you had hidden a corpse when the corpse itself was just below it?

'There's more,' Dougie said.

'More rope?'

'More evidence of how the body was hoisted up.' He led Greening back to the standing section of the tree. 'If you look up on this side of the trunk you can see where the smaller side branches have been broken off. There's even a couple of bigger ones that have been cut – they're tagged, as you can see.'

Greening looked up. Branches of all sizes radiated

from the main trunk but there was a clear pathway through the obstacles on one side of the tree.

'There's been recent growth, of course,' Dougie added. 'I got a tree expert in for a look and he estimated that the damage could have been done about a couple of years ago.'

That wasn't a great surprise but it was welcome information all the same.

'This is good stuff, Dougie. Crucial information. I can see I'm going to have to buy you even more whisky.'

'Actually, sir, I don't drink alcohol.'

'Please, Dougie, don't shatter my illusions about Glaswegians.'

The Scot looked both amused and embarrassed. 'I did postgraduate studies at Glasgow but as a matter of fact I come from Edinburgh.'

Greening raised his eyes to the greeny blue canopy above his head. Sometimes solving crime seemed easier than forging relationships with his juniors.

'I'll try and remember that,' he said. 'And stop sirring me, would you? My name's Alan.' Time to get back to the script. 'So, how many people do you think were involved in hiding the body? Any indications?'

Dougie shook his head. 'There's no foot marks or anything like that – it's too long ago. There's signs that vehicles come along this path and you'd probably need to transport the body up here. But, again, it's too long ago to make any specific connection.'

'They work the horses along here, don't they? I imagine the trainer, or whoever, comes along in his four-wheel drive to watch them do their stuff.'

They stood in silence for a moment, Greening hoping the scientist might volunteer something further but he didn't.

'Could one person manage it on his own?' he prompted. 'Driving the corpse up here wouldn't be a problem, the gate's not locked so you could get your vehicle in and bring it this far along the track. But how about hoisting the body up?'

Dougie pondered the question. 'You've got to climb the tree and rig the rope to support the pulley system. You attach the pulley and thread the rope you're going to use to hoist the body. Then you come back down to the ground, tie on the corpse and pull him up.'

'You've got to be pretty strong then?'

'Well, yes. The block and tackle will make the lifting easier but the skeleton was of a fully grown man, nearly six foot tall. Likely to be twelve stone at least – could have been a stone or two more.'

'So,' continued Greening, 'when you've got the body up to the height you want, you've got to secure the rope you're holding – attach it to your vehicle maybe – then shin back up the tree, manoeuvre the body into position and tie it on. And then you've got to dismantle your block and tackle, clear up the other gear you've got – ropes and whatever you've used to prune the branches – and finally scarper.'

'That sounds like a lot of work for one man, sir. But possible, I suppose.'

'Much easier for two. One to work on the ground, the other in the tree guiding the body past obstacles on the way up and doing the tying off.' Greening looked around. 'I bet it was hard work even for two.

They'd have been scared, tempted to rush but knowing they had only one chance to do it right. How long do you think it would have taken?'

Dougie considered. 'An hour maybe, if there were two of them. Bearing in mind the body was probably stiff with rigor mortis and difficult to manoeuvre. One man on his own would be here for ages.'

'And this is a public right of way – you get people out here at all hours. You'd have to do it in the night, with torches. Maybe moonlight if you were lucky. Spooky work, eh?'

'Clever though. If it hadn't been for the freak weather, the body would never have been discovered.'

'Never is a big word. There is a precedent for this, you know.'

They had scrambled out of the undergrowth, back on to the path above the long sloping paddock. Down below, the Pitchbury estate was spread out in a rolling patchwork of trees and fields. The yellow brick of the Hall glowed in the sunshine and a pair of chestnut horses mooched in the shade of an oak in the adjacent meadow. Some lucky bastards certainly knew how to live. Greening wondered how they were feeling about the discovery of a dead body on their land.

Dougie was looking at him expectantly. 'Precedent?' he said.

'Yes, something I unearthed on the internet.' He'd sourced the information in the small hours of the morning before the post-mortem. It had lingered with him ever since. 'A German gentleman suffering from terminal cancer left a note for his family, saying they would never find him. He went into the forest, climbed a tree, tied himself on and shot himself with a rifle which he'd attached to his body. He was only discovered when his corpse starting falling apart. A courting couple found his hip bone, I believe. That would put you off, wouldn't it?'

Dougie pulled a face. 'How long was he up there?'

'Twenty-nine years. He walked out in nineteen eighty and was discovered a year ago. Whoever did our man can count themselves unlucky.' He chuckled. 'Maybe the trees are full of corpses but we don't see them because we never lift our eyes above ground level.'

'Er, yes.' Dougie had divested himself of his paper suit and other protective gear. He looked like he'd had enough. 'If you don't mind, Alan, I'm running a bit late.'

Alan? Maybe Greening had made a breakthrough. 'You sure you don't want me to buy you a quick drink? A Coke Zero or something?'

'Thanks but the wife's waiting. I promised I'd take her out to lunch to make up for the past few days.'

Greening got the picture. Dougie must have been working all hours on the tree skeleton.

'Well, I'm very grateful for your efforts. Enjoy your lunch. And don't go taking your missus for any romantic strolls in the woods afterwards.'

Dougie raised a tight smile and headed for his car.

Greening regretted his parting shot but dismissed it from his mind as he considered the progress he had made. Suddenly, the picture was much clearer.

The skeleton Mrs Drummond had discovered was definitely that of missing antique dealer Glyn Cole.

Chapter Five

Though he was strictly a homebody, Freddy enjoyed chauffeuring his mother to the races. He wasn't one for getting away from it all, even a day or two out of his familiar surroundings made him uneasy. There had been holidays abroad when he was younger, in the years after his accident. But hotels full of strangers, big cities, foreign languages, these things intimidated him. Even sleepy seaside towns and cottages in the country were not to his liking. He knew he was a lucky boy. He lived in the most beautiful place in England and, for him, England was the most beautiful country in the world. At home he had everything he could ever want: a big friendly old house with a warren of rooms that was his exclusive playground, fields and woods teeming with wildlife outside his door and a training yard for racehorses just down the drive. And the people he loved lived there. Why would he ever want to go anywhere else?

But though at heart his attitude hadn't changed, as an adult he took pleasure in the occasional break in his routine, especially an outing like today's to Salisbury. On his first visit as a boy, he had been told

Queen Elizabeth had gone racing there on her way to see Sir Francis Drake, the great hero who sailed from Plymouth to defeat the Spanish Armada. It had taken some years of confusion for him to realise that the Queen Elizabeth in question was not the one who was on television on Christmas Day.

The drive to the racecourse only took ninety minutes but he allowed a good two hours in case of traffic problems. He stuck to the speed limit all the way because those were the rules. He could tell his mother became irritated when he wouldn't put his foot down, but he knew she would be even more upset if he got a speeding ticket.

All the same, as he steered the old Rover into the racecourse and carefully parked up, he could feel excitement building in his veins. Miletus, one of his mother's horses, was running and she'd told him she had a plan, which marked the afternoon as special. It meant that she expected to win some money and that he would be needed to help her place her bets.

Freddy was good with money. He knew how to keep it safe and how to do calculations in his head. And betting was fun. Whenever he went racing he spent time in the ring, watching rails bookies at work, putting a few pounds on horses he fancied – the Pitchbury ones, mostly. He never won much because he never wagered much, the excitement of the game was enough. But on one occasion last year his mother had given him £300 with strict instructions to spread it across as many bookmakers as he could, at the best prices he could find. He'd collected over £1,200 which he'd handed over proudly.

One of the pleasures in his life was earning his mother's praise.

Today she'd asked him if he would mind betting for her again. Mind? He was thrilled at the prospect. But first he was looking forward to a good lunch. She'd promised him steak and chips, or whatever else he might fancy. He wondered if today he might choose something different. But what was the point of changing for the sake of it? He knew what he liked.

Will hacked Miletus down for the race with the other runners. The start of a mile-and-six-furlongs contest at Salisbury is close to the stands. It requires the horses to run away from the winning post before they head downhill and take a fork to the left which swings them round in a loop to join the bottom of the long straight. From there it's a gruelling six furlongs back up the hill to meet the winning post from the correct side.

The course had been carefully selected for the tactics Will was about to employ. In essence, the idea was Edward's but Will was aware Rosemary Drummond had had some significant input too, even to the extent of volunteering her own horse for what they had in mind.

Edward had explained it to him in detail one morning the previous week.

'When I was in the army I had a long time to think about what I was going to do when I got out. I knew it had to involve horses. I was too big to be a rider – I'd be too old anyway by the time I left – but I wanted to work in a racing yard. The whole business fascinated me. I used to fantasise about being in charge of racehorses, how I'd train them, what ways there were to make them fitter and run faster. I have a lot of respect for tradition but I thought there had to be other methods of getting the best out of a horse. There's always something new, isn't there?

'I had a pal in the regiment who was an athlete, used to run for the army, and I'd pick his brains. I reckoned that what worked for humans must have some bearing on horses. One thing he told me was that he aimed to raise his core temperature by one per cent before a race so he could run at his best.'

Will had been puzzled. 'How did he do that?'

'By warming up hard. He told me the amount of work he used to put in before a race and I was amazed. It stuck in my mind but I never did anything about it – I mean, nobody warms their horses up before a race, do they? But when Mrs Drummond went off to the Olympics in Beijing with her bridge club friends, I spoke to her about it. She came back with some very interesting observations. She told me that in the half hour before the fifteen hundred metres final, she saw a runner do eight hundred metres twice, then four hundred metres twice, all these at about three-quarters pace, then he finished off with two hundred metres at full blast, ten minutes before the biggest race of his life. Remarkable, don't you think?'

Will had indeed. He was interested in running and was vaguely aware how the top guys went about it, but horses were different, surely?

'I don't see why,' Edward said. 'Have you ever noticed how a horse that runs off at the start often does well in the race itself? Most of the time, of course, he gets scratched because the trainer thinks he'll be more tired than his rivals. But I don't agree. I think that if he gets the right amount of work before the race and raises his core temperature to the correct level, he'll have an advantage.'

And that was the theory they were about to test.

Miletus had shown an appetite for a longer race during his last outing at Haydock and Will thought the course was perfect for what they had in mind. He could pretend to be 'run away with' before the race by giving Miletus a whack out of the view of the grandstand. Let him go a couple of furlongs. Pull up. Do another couple and have him properly warm before he got back to the start. Since the start was close to the paddock, the other horses would barely have warmed up at all and Miletus would have a distinct advantage – if Edward was right.

His whip hand obscured from view, Will cracked the horse hard across his shoulder.

For a second, he thought Miletus wasn't going to obey, that he had been taken by surprise at the command to run delivered at such a time. Then the horse's instincts kicked in and he took off, charging away from the stands.

Will pantomimed attempts to stop him. It was by no means an unusual occurrence for a horse to bolt before the start of a race and ignore his jockey's valiant attempts to bring him to a halt. As far as the spectators were concerned, it was an authentic mishap.

The plan was to 'give him a good blow' and Will reckoned he had accomplished that all right. Now he had to get the horse back to the start and apologise to the others for the delay.

Freddy was dismayed when Miletus bolted at the start.

'That's torn it,' he said to his mother.

They were standing in front of the grandstand, surveying the betting activity around the bookies' pitches lined along the rails.

'Don't worry about it,' she said. 'Just keep your eyes on the boards for the best prices.'

'We're not still going to bet, are we?'

'Yes, we are going to bet,' she said firmly.

'But he's never going to win now. He's run round half the course.'

Up on the big screen Miletus could be seen cantering back up the straight. He was almost level with the stands.

'Look.' His mother's hand closed on Freddy's arm. 'He's gone out to fives at the far end. Go and start putting money on. OK?'

Her sharp eyes bored into his. She was serious and she wanted his help. That was all he needed to know.

'Yes, Mum,' he said and began to push through the crowd to the bookmaker who was now offering 5/1 on Miletus. The price before the horse had run off with his jockey had been 7/2 and he'd been second favourite. Now the position was changing fast. As he reached the rail, the bookie rubbed out the 5 and replaced it with a 6.

Freddy grinned and handed over £200 to win. Carefully pocketing his ticket, he moved two pitches along and made the same investment. Naturally he hoped Miletus would succeed but, whatever happened, this was fun.

Edward made sure he was down at the start when Miletus finally appeared to take his place in the line. He was anticipating trouble with the starter.

That gentleman, bundled up in a tweedy winter topcoat and scarf despite the early summer sunshine, shouted at Will, 'Are you pulling him out?'

'No, sir.'

The starter's pink face registered surprise. 'Are you sure?'

Edward stepped in. 'No, let the silly sod race. It'll serve him right for running off.'

The starter looked at him, plainly about to argue the point. Then he recognised the trainer and bit back his words. 'Well, let's bloody well get on with it then. We've wasted enough time already.'

The start of the long race at Salisbury is an old-fashioned affair, with the runners lined up behind a tape like the beginning of a jump race. Will eased Miletus into the line, the tape rose and they were off, heading away from the stands for the first time – officially, that is. He and his mount had travelled that way already.

Will could feel how easily Miletus was breathing. The warm-up beforehand had properly opened his lungs and got his heart pumping. He dropped at once into a steady racing rhythm. Will tucked the pair of them into the group behind the leader who was setting off at a fair gallop.

For the moment, Will had no worries about his horse. The real test would come when they rounded the loop and began the charge back along the straight. This was the most testing part of the course at any time, since the ground rose steadily. Today's going in particular – early summer soft and clinging – would test the horses' stamina to the utmost. And Miletus had literally run an extra mile.

Freddy was basking in the glow of a job well done. He'd laid the best part of £1,000 on Miletus, most of it at 6/1. The bookies had taken an unfavourable view of the horse's behaviour and happily pocketed his cash. It was plain to him that they thought it unlikely they would be returning it. His mother, however, was pleased.

'That's excellent,' she'd said. 'Maybe you should have gone into the army – you carry out orders to the letter.'

'Go into the army like Edward, you mean?'

She'd tucked her arm into his. 'It was a joke, Freddy. I would never have put you into the services.'

Now they stood in the stand watching the race on the course screen. The horses themselves were out of sight away to the right. The course commentary battered their ears and Freddy tried to block it out as he found it confusing and he concentrated on the camera images.

As the runners emerged from the loop and re-entered the main straight, Renegade, the horse who had led from the start, was overtaken by the following pack.

'Renegade has gone,' Freddy exclaimed.

'He was never going to win. He was only in it to make the running for Cathedral City.'

Sure enough, Cathedral City was driving up the hill, ahead of the field and pulling away.

Will had kept Miletus up with the leaders all the way round the loop and he was lying second as they began the charge for home. Would the pre-race warm-up give him an edge? He was about to find out.

There were just two of them in contention now as they galloped uphill towards the finish, Cathedral City two lengths ahead. Will thought he had the edge over the horse in front. Then Cathedral City began to pull clear and in turn Miletus found a bit more. It all came down to the will to win – the desire not to be beaten. Looks counted for nothing at this time.

They were creeping closer, just a length in it now, and when Will slapped Miletus once with his whip, there was a perceptible quickening in the horse's stride. It was remarkable.

Cathedral City's jockey was working hard in the saddle and wielding his whip with urgency but Will could see the big horse had nothing more to give. He was travelling on guts and instinct alone.

That was when he knew Miletus was going to win. And, marvellous though that was, he couldn't flaming well believe it. Which was precisely how he expressed himself to the *Racing Beacon* reporter who pounced on him thirty seconds after he'd crossed the line half a length ahead of the flagging Cathedral City.

*

Greening's plan had been to start with Glyn Cole's neighbour, Mrs Shaw, to build up a picture of the antique dealer's circumstances before his disappearance. Mrs Shaw was the one who had reported him missing and she'd kept a key to his flat. What's more, young Carmel Gibbs had described her as 'nosy'. She sounded the ideal person to provide some background. Accordingly he had despatched Yvonne Harris, the only woman on his team, to see what she could get out of her.

The result was disappointing. Yvonne reported that the old biddy was useless as a witness. 'She's over eighty and hobbles around with a stick. And she's either deaf or daft – she didn't answer half my questions. Kept saying that Glyn Cole was nothing to do with her and that I should talk to his sister.'

'But did she remember reporting him missing and looking round his flat with PCSO Gibbs?'

'Only when I pushed her. She told me nothing that wasn't in Gibbs's account. She said it was before she went into hospital. It wouldn't surprise me if she'd had a stroke or something and her brain's gone.'

That was a setback but Greening had decided not to give up on Mrs Shaw just yet. Instead he'd called Carmel and asked if she knew how the old lady was doing and whether she'd had a stroke.

'I don't think so, sir. She had a hip replaced last summer and I know she wants to have the other one done. I'm sure I'd have heard if there was anything else.'

It had occurred to Greening that possibly the old lady had been told to mind her own business by Cole's sister when Dee James was sorting out her brother's things. Or else she had simply not been won over by Yvonne, who could be as brusque as any man when the mood took her.

Consequently he was now sitting in his car outside Glyn Cole's former antique shop, which had been turned into a boutique for little girls. Beside him sat Carmel Gibbs. They were waiting for Mrs Shaw to be delivered home from her twice-weekly visit to the day-care centre.

Greening surveyed the window of Cole's old shop, filled with small pink stars strung from above against a background of gauzy white drapery. Below, articles of pre-pubescent clothing were arranged on dummies around baby furniture, a doll's house and an old rocking horse – possibly the only item that might have featured on the premises from former days. Beyond the gauze, the interior of the shop appeared empty. They had been sitting there for a quarter of an hour and no customers had gone in or come out.

'Beats me how they make any money,' Greening said.

Carmel nodded vigorously. 'At least there were things going on when Mr Cole was here. He used to have music playing and his friends would come by.'

'Really?'

'He was very popular in the pub down the road. They all knew him in there.'

He looked at her with interest. 'Did you know him?'

'Only to say hello to because the shop was on my patch. After he went missing I tried to find out a bit about him. To see if I could discover where he'd gone.'

'I thought you concluded that he'd just taken off for some reason or other.'

'Well, yes, but I did wonder why he hadn't taken his phone. It was left in his car. I thought it was odd for him to leave it.'

He was tempted to say that if a man seriously wanted to cut his ties with the past, the first thing he'd walk away from was his mobile phone. But it was an academic point. The car, on the other hand, was not.

'Did anyone examine the car?'

'Actually, I did, sir. When I found out it had turned up in Swindon I went over to have a look at it in the council compound.'

'Did you? Well done.'

'It wasn't till a week after he'd gone, I'm afraid. Mrs Shaw phoned me and asked what was happening. She was concerned because she was feeding Mr Cole's cat. Nobody else seemed bothered – I mean, there wasn't any family to worry about him.'

Greening wondered who'd be hassling the police if he himself went missing in the all too foreseeable future after he'd retired. Even Amy didn't ring more than once a week now she'd moved in with her London boyfriend.

'What can you tell me about the car then?' All he knew from the information Yvonne had unearthed was its make, an old Volvo. 'Can you remember?'

'It had some bits of furniture in the back – I remember a little folding table and some lamp-shades. It was a mess, like his flat – plastic bags, old newspapers, crisp packets, empty water bottles, a dirty old sweater, stuff like that. The phone was in the side pocket of the driver's door.'

'And what was on it?'

'I don't remember the details. Just what you'd expect from a small businessman – he had loads of contacts. A mixture of friends and customers, I suppose. At least, I assume that's what they were. You can't tell who's who on anyone's phone list, can you? I just know there wasn't anything that seemed helpful. No texts that indicated what he'd been doing just before he vanished.'

Greening nodded. 'The Volvo was returned to his sister. It's a pity the forensics boys never got their hands on it. Very likely whoever killed him drove it to Swindon and dumped it.'

'They told me the keys were in the ignition.'

'They probably hoped someone would nick it.'

'What happened to the phone, sir?'

Greening considered the question. 'Good point. It was probably returned to the sister too.'

At that moment a white minibus turned into the street and parked outside the shop.

'Here's Mrs Shaw now,' said Carmel and jumped out of the car.

'At last,' muttered Greening and followed at a more sedate pace.

Freddy and Rosemary made the rounds of the bookies together to collect their winnings. Since the winner's presentation had just been shown on the big screen, the owner was widely recognised. 'I wondered why you were plunging in like that,' said one burly fellow with a grin. 'If you aren't going to go large on your own horse, when are you? Bit lucky, though.'

'Fortune favours the brave, young man,' Rosemary replied, accepting her winnings.

To Freddy's surprise they received a warm welcome in most quarters, even as hard-faced men handed over substantial sums in banknotes.

'Why are they so cheerful?' he asked.

'Because we did them a favour in beating the favourite. Once Miletus ran off, all the late money went on Cathedral City. They'd be paying out a lot more if he'd won.'

'Oh.' He hadn't thought of that but it made sense. What didn't make sense was how Miletus had managed to beat all comers when he'd bolted at the start and run a much longer distance than any of the others. He said so to his mother.

Rosemary leaned close to him. 'Remember I told you about that runner warming up so hard in Beijing?'

He nodded. His mother had told him all about her visit to the Olympics – she'd wanted him to go with her but he'd refused.

'Humans run better when they've warmed up properly before a race,' she said. 'And it's the same for horses. Only, not many people know about it.'

The penny suddenly dropped and Freddy could hardly contain the rush of excitement. 'You planned it,' he cried. 'You made him run away at the start.'

'Shhh.' Rosemary grabbed his arm. 'It's best to keep the secret to ourselves. Though I think we deserve a proper celebration later on, don't you? I've asked

Edward to host a little dinner at the Hall tonight. How do you like the idea of that?'

He liked it just fine. The euphoria of winning, the thrill of playing his part and the excitement of knowing the secret behind their coup made this a special day in Freddy's book. He didn't even mind leaving the racecourse before the end of the meeting so they could pick up some supplies for a celebration dinner.

'I can't be too lavish,' said Rosemary as they entered the wine merchants in Salisbury town centre. 'But we absolutely must have champagne.'

Freddy left the choosing of the wine to his mother. He'd be sticking to beer. Lots of it.

The minibus did not hang around. By the time Greening had crossed the road, it was already on the move, leaving a stout grey-haired woman with a walking stick and an over-sized brown handbag on the pavement.

'Hello, Mrs Shaw.' Carmel was already at her side.

'Oh, hello, dear.' The old lady was evidently pleased to see her. 'They're meant to see me to the door, you know. But they never do.'

'Never mind. Let me give you a hand.' And Carmel took charge of the bag while Mrs Shaw scrabbled at the front door with her keys.

Greening cleared his throat loudly and Mrs Shaw swivelled her head. Her face was wrinkled and weary but the eyes she fixed on him were pin sharp.

'Who are you?' she demanded.

'He's with me,' Carmel said quickly.

'Your father, dear?'

'No. This is Detective Chief Inspector Greening. We were hoping we might have a word with you about Mr Cole who used to keep the shop next door.'

'Oh.' She stood suspended in the act of stepping into the house.

'We would be very grateful, Mrs Shaw,' Greening said in his warmest tones.

'But I already spoke to one of your lot. A real pushy woman.'

'Yes, DS Harris.' Greening smiled at the old lady. 'She told me how much she enjoyed meeting you.'

'She did? Well, it wasn't mutual.' There was an awkward pause as the three of them hovered there. Mrs Shaw turned to Carmel. 'I don't know, dear. I told her everything already and I've got to have my tea so I can take my pills.'

'I'll see to the tea, Mrs Shaw,' said Carmel. 'So let's go inside. The inspector's come over from Swindon specially to see you. You must be important.'

And she coaxed the old lady over the doorstep and marshalled her down a narrow hallway. Greening followed, closing the door behind him in response to a command from Mrs Shaw not to let Buster out – a pet of some description, he assumed.

Following their hostess's orders, Carmel deposited Mrs Shaw in her sitting room at the front of the house, a room full of too much dark furniture and cluttered with framed photographs, small ornaments and a loudly ticking carriage clock. Greening guessed it didn't see much traffic in the usual way of things.

Mrs Shaw took the upholstered easy chair, leaving him to share the pink chintz sofa with an excessively furry black-and-white cat who looked at him with disdain, as most cats did.

'Is this Buster?' he said, aiming to break the ice.

Mrs Shaw nodded. 'It's a pity he can't talk or you could interview him. I tell you, he's the one with the real story to tell.'

'Oh yes, why's that?' It struck him that Yvonne might have been right about Mrs Shaw after all. Maybe she wasn't quite with it.

'Because he's Mr Cole's cat. He's been waiting patiently for poor Mr Cole to come back and now your Harris lady tells me he won't be.'

'That's correct. I'm afraid his body has recently been discovered, though it would appear that he has been dead since the time you reported him missing.'

Mrs Shaw was shaking her head and tutting in a fashion that reminded Greening of his grandmother. Did people deliberately set out to become caricatures of their elders or were they fated to turn out that way?

'A skeleton up a tree,' she was saying. 'Well, I never. I can't think of Mr Cole like that at all. He was so . . .'

'Yes?' He was keen to get a proper picture of Cole as he used to be.

'So full of sap. A man of appetites. He cleared his plate at dinner and asked for more, if you know what I mean.' The weary face looked weary no more as she spoke.

'You liked him, Mrs Shaw?'

Buster had raised his big furry head and appeared to be listening intently.

'Of course I liked him. There weren't many women

as didn't. Just because I'm a clapped-out old biddy doesn't mean I don't recognise a fine fellow when I see one. It's a hard thing to imagine a young man as full of life as Glyn Cole turned into a bag of bones. I tell you what . . .'

'Yes?' Greening leant forward, eager to encourage her. Buster climbed on to his lap.

'Whoever shoved him up some tree wasn't no woman. But I bet he got put there because of a woman.'

'Are you saying he had a lot of girlfriends?'

'Plenty. He was never short of female company next door. I could hear 'em through the wall. He was one of those men who had a chat-up line for every woman he saw. Especially if they were a blonde.'

A rattle of teacups announced the arrival of Carmel with a tray.

Mrs Shaw watched her with approval and turned to Greening. 'He'd have snapped her up for teatime, no question.'

Buster began to purr softly.

Greening brushed himself down vigorously as they stepped out of Mrs Shaw's house. He had the feeling he'd be living with cat hairs for weeks. He led Carmel at a brisk pace down the road to the pub which she had indicated earlier. 'I've no complaints about the tea,' he said to her, 'but I've still got a thirst.'

They were the only customers. 'Your Mrs Shaw, Carmel, is not so much nosy as scurrilous,' he said as he pushed her orange juice towards her across the counter of the bar. 'She appears to think Cole was sleeping with every woman who walked into his shop.'

They had listened to an hour's worth of Mrs Shaw on Glyn Cole who, according to her, though human in his 'appetites', was a kind and cultured man trying his best to carve out a successful business career, despite being dogged by bad luck and importuning females. The information, however, had been irritatingly vague. The bad luck was associated with a series of deals that had gone wrong or never come off. 'He was promised this estate up in Yorkshire – or was it Lancashire? Up north anyway. Some old boy who collected stamps. Mr Cole said he had a buyer lined up at a whacking price but the old boy's daughter went and sold the lot elsewhere at the last minute. Double-crossed him but, as he said, that's business, isn't it?'

And facts about Cole's romantic connections had been similarly hard to pin down.

'There was one blonde – bottle blonde, mind you – who used to visit him regular on Thursday lunchtimes. Forty-five if she was a day but well turned out, though she always had a button missing off her blouse, if you know what I mean. But she wasn't the only one, there were plenty of others. There was a very pretty one at the end, a proper blonde. He put the Closed sign up quick when she appeared.'

'All these females she went on about could simply be regular customers,' Greening said as he contemplated the bubbles in his mineral water.

Carmel nodded. 'She never noticed any men going in the shop, did she?'

'I imagine we'll get more sense out of the book-keeper and the assistant.'

The shop assistant, Amanda, had been employed to

lend Cole a hand on certain weekday afternoons and on the weekend. Naturally, Mrs Shaw had not left her off the list of Cole's conquests. Carmel had discovered that she had since got married and moved to one of the villages outside the town.

Greening polished off his drink. 'We could go and look up this Amanda right now.'

'Er, yes, sir.' Carmel, in her smart PCSO gear, looked a little out of place in the brown-stained interior of the public house.

'You don't mind, do you? Make a change from dealing with truants or whatever your lot do. Don't worry, I've talked to your commander. You're mine for the afternoon. You can see what real police work is all about.'

She gave him a look that was unfathomable and said dutifully, 'Yes, sir.'

They had been served by a lad who Greening had taken for an overseas student, judging by his failure to respond to Greening's banter. Now a thickset middle-aged man appeared behind the bar carrying a box and caught sight of them. 'How do, Carmel,' he said. 'Still supporting the local community?'

'Always, Len.' She shot him a grin which took Greening by surprise. It warmed up that serious little face no end.

Len put the box on the counter, cheese-and-onion crisps, Greening observed, and said, 'Is this your dad, then?'

Carmel coloured raspberry pink and introduced him. Len hastily wiped his hand on his apron and offered it.

'Pleased to meet you, Inspector. Is this just a social visit?'

'Len comes to our Pubwatch meetings,' Carmel said. 'We discuss problems with licensees. Trouble after hours. Noise nuisance. Len's been very helpful.'

'Excellent,' said Greening heartily. It was not a subject which often exercised his thoughts. There were other matters, however. 'Have you been running this place long?'

'Eighteen years. And it's a darn sight harder to make a living out of it these days.'

Greening ignored the invitation to head down a conversational back alley.

'We're making inquiries about a gentleman who used to run an antiques shop over the road.'

'You mean Glyn?' Len square face resolved itself into a sombre expression. 'We used to call him Old King Cole. Not so merry now, is he? I heard it on the radio.'

'Were you friendly with him?'

'Course. Glyn was a good customer, one of the regulars. Right from the start when he opened the shop. That was in the year two thousand. Remember all that? The Dome, the Millennium Bug that never was – and nobody had ever heard of Simon Cowell. Seems light years ago, doesn't it?'

Greening could see another blind alley opening up and moved to shut it off. 'Perhaps if we came back this evening you could introduce us to some of the other regulars.'

Len said it would be his pleasure and Greening quickly steered Carmel outside towards his car.

'You don't mind coming back this evening, do you?'

Carmel looked puzzled. 'We could have talked to Len straightaway, sir. We could go back now.'

Greening shook his head. 'I'll need something stronger than water if I'm going to listen to him. Besides, if you put on some glad rags you can charm the lads for me. We'll find out a darn sight more.'

Carmel's face was a picture. He half expected her to refuse. Instead she swallowed hard and said, 'Yes, sir. Whatever you say.'

Greening gave her his number one charming grin. 'Excellent. We'll make a detective of you yet.'

She didn't look mollified. He must be losing his touch.

Chapter Six

'Got the timing right for once,' Greening muttered as they followed the access road into the housing estate. 'I reckon that's our girl.'

A solidly built young woman in a business suit, holding a laptop bag, was opening the door of a neat redbrick two-storey house. Though detached, it stood all of ten feet from a neighbouring and identical property. A small scarlet Fiat was parked immediately outside.

'How do you know it's her?' said Carmel as they pulled into the space next to it.

'Just a hunch. Look at the hair.'

It was coiled on the top of her head and fastened with an impressive armoury of pins. But though the mass was suppressed there was no disguising the colour of glistening gold – Glyn Cole's former assistant was spectacularly blond, his favourite kind of girl, according to Mrs Shaw.

She greeted them with surprise which, to Greening's eye, looked a little manufactured. 'I don't know what I can tell you about Glyn after all this time. But you'd better come in, I suppose.'

She disappeared down a claustrophobic hallway and they followed her into a small dining room where she dumped her bag on the table. 'I heard this morning that he'd been found at last,' she said. 'I haven't been able to think about anything else all day. I've got to have a drink – do you mind?'

She stepped through a door into what Greening could see was a kitchen and he heard the sound of cupboards being opened and liquid being poured. No offer was extended to them, although it would have been refused – regretfully in his case.

He saw Carmel taking note of their surroundings, such as they were. A table, chairs and two bulging bookcases took up most of the available space. A Jack Vettriano print of a woman in her underwear covered the opposite wall. It didn't look like the home of a woman who'd once worked in an antique shop, but who was he to say? His own living circumstances were nothing to boast about.

Amanda returned with a tumbler of fizzing liquid – gin and tonic, Greening guessed. Plenty of ice, no lemon – much as he liked it, in fact.

'Will here do?' she said, indicating the table, and the three of them sat round it. Carmel laid her notebook on the polished wooden surface.

Amanda – now Mrs Yates, so Carmel had informed him – launched into a speech which Greening imagined she had been preparing in her mind. 'I worked for Glyn from September two thousand and seven until he vanished the following April. It was only part-time, while I was doing an Open University course. Business studies.' She stopped and drank, a big gulp that left a red smear of lipstick on the glass. She had full, fleshy lips and milky blue eyes. 'The hours were pretty flexible, which suited me. Glyn was a laidback employer, except when there was a big deal or a flap on. He was good to me and I'm very sorry he's dead.' She drained her glass and put it down with a clunk that echoed in the small space. 'I don't know what else I can tell you.'

Greening could think of a few things. If she thought this would be the end of the matter, she was in for disappointment.

'Mrs Yates, how well did you know Mr Cole?'

She shrugged and he noticed the brooch on her lapel, of black enamel with scalloped edging, set with pearls. So the house was not devoid of antique artefacts. How ignorant of him to make such an assumption.

'Well enough to enjoy working with him,' she replied. 'He didn't go in for any of that master-and-slave stuff like some bosses. In fact, half the time he used to send up the fact that he really was the boss.'

'Did you socialise with him after hours?'

'You mean, did I go boozing with him at the Crown after we shut up? Sure, sometimes. But I couldn't afford to sit around getting plastered all evening, I had my OU stuff to do.'

'Did he spend all his evenings in the pub then?'

'I can't say what he got up to when I wasn't around.' She thought about it further. 'It might have seemed like he spent a lot of time there but he was often very busy. He went to auctions and fairs all over the country, so there were lots of early starts and nights away. And if he was researching a collection or a particular piece, then he'd be up all hours at his books or on the computer. He really loved his business, Inspector. As far as I could tell he was good at it too.'

'Did everybody like him as much as you evidently did, Mrs Yates?'

The milky blue of her eyes darkened. 'Are you insinuating something?'

'No, no.' Greening lifted a placatory hand. The lady evidently had a temper – which was interesting. 'It's just that you paint a picture of a very likeable man . . .' He left a gap for her to fill, and she obliged.

'He *was* likeable. Everybody liked him.'

'Yet some people disliked him enough to murder him, Mrs Yates. Do you have any idea who they may be?'

Her mouth gaped, showing remarkably white and even teeth. Pretty but how sharp?

'You've got a nerve,' she said. 'I just helped him in the shop – how on earth would I know?'

Greening smiled, not at full beam however. 'I'm sorry, I was hoping you might be able to shed some light on Mr Cole's affairs. I mean, we don't have a lot to go on at present and Mr Cole disappeared more than two years ago. You were there. I'm asking for your help, Mrs Yates, because we really need it. You do want to see whoever is responsible for Mr Cole's death brought to justice, don't you?'

'Of course.' She glanced at her watch. 'But my husband will be home soon and I've got to make supper. Perhaps we could talk some other time?'

'Certainly.' Greening pushed his chair back from the table. 'We can arrange an appointment for you to come down to the station and make an official statement. You might want to bring a solicitor with you but it wouldn't be essential.'

'What?' The colour drained from her face. 'Why would I need a solicitor?'

It was his turn to shrug.

'Can't we just carry on as we are?' she said. 'Supper can wait.'

'That's very obliging of you, Mrs Yates. We'll be as quick as we can. We'd really like to build up a picture of Mr Cole's circumstances before he disappeared.'

'OK but, er . . .' she was flustered now, 'what can I say? He was a lovely man, full of energy and ideas. He had lots of friends – well, he knew lots of people, some of them customers, others just guys he had a drink with.'

'Who were his oldest friends, Mrs Yates? The people he confided in.'

'I don't know. I mean, he seemed to be very sociable but he didn't let people get too close. He didn't get on with his family and there weren't any old friends I was aware of. I used to think that, at heart, he was a bit lonely.'

'How about girlfriends?'

'I wouldn't know anything about that.' She picked up her glass and put it down smartly again when she realised it was empty.

'I gather he was popular with women.'

'Who told you that?'

'We've just been speaking to Mrs Shaw, the lady who lives next door to the shop.'

The full mouth turned down in a *moue* of disgust.

'Mrs Shaw's an old scandalmonger. And she'd have been the first in the queue if she wasn't fifty years over the hill.'

'So he wasn't in a relationship, so far as you were aware?'

'Glyn had girlfriends but no one special, not when I knew him. You should talk to Kathy Pym. I think they used to go out years ago. If he needed a female companion for an occasion, he'd ask her.'

Katherine Pym the book-keeper. Greening had been trying to pin her down but had failed to catch her at home. He had an appointment to see her the next morning.

He changed tack. 'When Mr Cole first disappeared, what did you think had happened to him?'

'At first I thought he had just taken himself off on a whim and forgotten to tell us. I mean, he could have gone on a sudden buying trip or got a call from someone with a collection that needed valuing. If it was exciting enough, I could imagine him losing track of time. When his car turned up I wondered if he'd got on a train to somewhere far off, like Scotland or Ireland. He could have hired a car at the other end.'

'And as time went on?'

'I knew something had gone wrong. I thought he'd been in an accident or had a stroke or lost his memory. It really upset me. I kept the shop going for a bit and Kathy helped me. But I only had so much time to do it and then Glyn's sister gave me notice, said she was going to close it down if he didn't come back soon. And that was it. Him going was just a mystery – like Lord Lucan, or something. Then it turns out he was stuck up a tree in Lambourn all the time. I mean, how the hell did that happen?'

How indeed. 'That's the big question, Mrs Yates.' He wasn't sure that prolonging this particular conversation would help him to an answer. He had one more try, however. 'Are you sure you can't think of anyone who would have wished Mr Cole ill?'

She shook her head. 'No.'

'Nobody he fell out with in the course of his business? Or quarrelled with in the pub?'

'I can't understand why anyone would want to harm him, Inspector. Honestly. Though I hope you find out.'

Greening got to his feet and Carmel followed suit. As she did so she said, 'That's a remarkably pretty brooch you're wearing, Mrs Yates. It's rather unusual.'

'Oh.' Amanda looked at her in surprise. It was the first thing Carmel had said throughout the interview. 'Thank you.'

'Is it a memorial brooch? It looks Georgian.'

Now it was Greening's turn to look surprised. He hadn't expected his youthful companion to come up with such an esoteric piece of knowledge.

Amanda stared at the pair of them. 'Actually, Glyn gave it to me. When I heard about him on the news this morning I put it on. It seemed . . .' she hesitated and Greening suddenly realised she was on the verge of tears, 'the right thing to do.'

Greening was caught out. He didn't know what to say. Fortunately the moment was broken by the sound of the front door being thrown open and heavy footsteps, accompanied by an angry male voice. 'You'll never guess, some bastard's nicked my space again.'

A youthful beanpole of a man in a well-worn suit burst into the dining room and froze at the sight of them. 'Blimey, what's this?' he demanded.

Greening introduced himself. 'I'm sorry I've taken your parking place, Mr Yates.' It seemed a fair assumption.

Yates swallowed, his prominent Adam's apple bobbing. He didn't look mollified. A nasty spot on his cheek glowed red.

'The police are here to ask me about Glyn,' Amanda said.

'Oh yeah?' The young man's face broke into a smile which didn't improve his appearance much. 'I heard he's the skeleton up a tree. Couldn't go out quietly, could he? Guaranteed to make an arse of himself right to the end.'

Greening observed Amanda. Her distress and embarrassment were apparent in equal measure.

'Ian, don't.'

'Oh, sorry.' Her husband corrected himself without obvious sincerity. 'Respect and that.' He turned to Greening. 'So who killed him then? Got any ideas?'

Greening played it straight. 'It's early days yet, Mr Yates. Your wife was kindly giving us some background on the deceased.'

'She'll be good at that,' Yates said, loosening his tie. 'Won't you, sweetheart?' and he pushed past her into the kitchen.

Outside, Carmel caught Greening's eye as they walked the few steps to the car but he kept a straight face, with a little difficulty.

*

Anna did not entirely resent the celebration dinner she had been required to lay on for the triumphant party returning from Salisbury races. The phone call had come through in mid-afternoon as she was napping in the bedroom. And though she was delighted to hear of Miletus's victory, the last thing she fancied doing was preparing a festive meal for eight or nine – or maybe more: for once her mother was vague.

'Freddy and I will go shopping on the way back so we can pick up provisions. Better make it simple, I suppose. We'll get smoked salmon and a few chickens. Perhaps you could knock up some kind of pudding – a blackberry crumble or something. There's fruit in the deep freeze, isn't there? We'll get ice cream. Anything else you might need?'

Just a hole to be sick in, Anna thought, but said, 'No, Mum, that's OK. Just don't expect anything special.'

'Don't worry. First stop is the off-licence. If the food's a wash-out we can all get sloshed.'

'OK.' Anna tried to inject enthusiasm into her voice but evidently failed.

'Oh, darling, I'm sorry, you're probably not up to throwing a party, are you?'

'It's all right, Mum, I'd love to see everyone.' That was true enough.

'Get Tammy to help. Tell her I'll make it worth her while.'

So Anna had asked Tammy if she'd mind staying late, to which Tammy had said neither yes nor no. She'd looked at Anna inscrutably, as if weighing the matter in her mind.

Anna assumed Tammy had plans, otherwise she'd have agreed enthusiastically. She was ever helpful and amenable, but it was important not to take her for granted and Anna chided herself for doing just that. Tammy had been a good friend to her during these early weeks of her pregnancy. You ended up feeling pretty close to the person who put her arm around your shoulders while you vomited into a bowl.

'Don't feel you have to,' she said. 'If you're busy tonight, you go ahead.'

'I'm not busy. I'll stay.'

'Thanks, Tammy.' Anna squeezed the girl's arm. The gesture was not acknowledged. 'Are you all right? If you're not well, you've got to go home.'

'I'm fine.' And she'd gone straight off to the kitchen without a smile. What was the matter? Anna wondered. Now she thought about it, Tammy had been out of sorts for days. But there could be any number of reasons for that – her mother's illness being the most obvious. But Mrs Turner's condition had not changed, as far as she was aware. Perhaps it was boyfriend trouble. Tammy had been dropping hints recently about a boy but those hints had suddenly dried up. That must be what it was – poor thing.

Anna wondered if there was any way she could help. Perhaps Tammy needed a distraction in the form of another boy. In which case, she could think of one who exactly fitted the bill.

Greening barely recognised the woman who came to the door. Out of her uniform Carmel looked less like a schoolgirl – much less. She wore tight jeans and a plain white top beneath a jacket of finely patterned navy and white thread. Her rich brown hair, freed from the prison of her hat, framed her face, which seemed prettier and more animated, no longer pinched by concern.

'You scrub up well, young lady,' he managed by way of a compliment. It wasn't much of one but he was conscious of the disparity in their ages, afraid of saying what he really felt – that she looked smashing – in case it was misconstrued. 'You make your old dad proud,' he added, which seemed to be about the right note, for she laughed.

His eyes were on the string of pearls around her slender white throat. 'Are those real?'

'I wish. They're no more real than these,' she indicated her silver teardrop earrings, 'or this,' she pointed to the glistening pin on her lapel. Not real diamonds evidently. 'I'm a sucker for costume jewellery.'

'So that's how you knew about Amanda Yates's brooch.'

'Yes, but that was the real thing. It must have cost at least a couple of hundred pounds. I couldn't afford to spend that much.'

They were walking down her street now towards the Crown, which was no more than a ten-minute stroll. Greening had decided to leave his car behind. He'd be making his way home later by cab.

'Two hundred smackers,' he mused. 'So Cole's gift was quite generous.'

'Yes, sir.'

'And that husband of hers plainly couldn't stand

Cole. You don't have to be a student of psychology to guess why.'

'No, sir.'

He looked at her in exasperation. 'So it looks distinctly possible that Mrs Shaw was right and the pair were having an affair.'

'Yes, sir.'

'For God's sake, Carmel, you're not a nodding dog. I want to know what you think. And you've got to cut out the sir business this evening. We're off duty, it's informal and I'm called Alan, got it?'

'Yes—' she stopped herself hastily. 'I don't think we can be certain about Amanda and Mr Cole having an affair. But I do think she was fond of him and that she knows things she wasn't telling us. Maybe because her husband was coming back and Mr Cole is a bit of a sore point.'

'Thank you, Carmel. That was certainly my impression. I'm inclined to haul her down to the station after all. Put her under a bit of pressure in one of those glamorous interview rooms in Farley Road nick.'

'Do you really think that's a good idea?'

'You don't, obviously.'

'I think she may be inclined to talk freely in a more informal setting. We spooked her, turning up on her doorstep like that.'

'And you've got something better in mind?'

'Would it be all right if I had a word with her? On my own. Somewhere away from her husband.'

They had reached the door of the pub. Greening stopped.

'How are you going to do that?' he asked.

'I don't know yet,' she said. She looked remarkably unconcerned. 'But I'll think of something.'

He would have pursued the topic, probably have said something sarcastic, if the pub door hadn't swung open at that moment and two underdressed teenagers lurched giggling into the street.

There was an inviting buzz of boozy chatter from within and Greening relegated Amanda Yates to the back of his mind.

'Come on then, girl,' he said, 'let's get on with it.'

'Yes, Alan,' she said as she walked ahead of him into the crowded room.

It was a long time since Greening had been in a pub of an evening with an attractive woman for company. He reminded himself it was work. Sometimes the job had its compensations.

Rosemary was revelling in the enjoyment of landing a carefully thought-out gamble, one which had brought in some proper money. She'd caught the bug from her grandfather when a little girl, though Grandad Pym's wagers were not necessarily a guarantee of increasing her pocket money. She remembered losing the lot on more than one occasion. It wasn't until she married Jack that she'd found a kindred spirit who also had the skill to have a real touch with the bookies. Of course, it had helped that Jack was a shrewd and skilful horseman, a trainer going places in the racing world. They'd pulled off some good punts years ago and ploughed the money straight back into the yard, improving its facilities so Pitchbury could compete with the best.

These days Rosemary had no need to put money into the family business, it already was one of the best and Edward had it ticking along nicely. Now, Rosemary could put her energies into raising funds for other projects. She belonged to a variety of clubs, taking part in activities from bridge to ballroom dancing, and she made it her business to recruit volunteers wherever she went. She supposed some might dismiss her as a privileged Lady Bountiful, out to chivvy and bully others into doing good. If that was the case, she wasn't bothered. In her opinion most people needed a good kick to get off their backsides and she was happy to do the kicking, if she thought it would make a difference.

In the case of her Salisbury success, the cash was earmarked for a particularly deserving cause – the local air ambulance service. They'd once rescued her old schoolfriend Helen when she'd been in a head-on collision with a furniture van. Helen had been airlifted to the John Radcliffe Hospital in Oxford in less than twenty minutes from the time of the accident which, so the doctors said, had been responsible for her making a full recovery.

That fact had made a big impression on Rosemary. Would her six-year-old son have made a full recovery if he had been flown to hospital within minutes of being found face down in the yard swimming pool? But there had been no air ambulance service in 1982.

However, the service existed now, carrying out mercy missions every day of the year, and doing it, what's more, without any funding from the government. If ever there was a worthy cause, this was it and it was top of Rosemary's list for fund-raising initiatives. In the past six months she'd organised a Halloween quiz at the tennis club, a bonfire night with fireworks for Guy Fawkes and a team to sell Christmas greenery grown on the estate. Things had been a bit quieter so far this year but the money she'd won at Salisbury – £7,000 – changed the picture. If she added that cash to the £8,500 she'd already raised, it would make a handsome donation.

But, and this nagged at her, it would be so much more handsome if it were even more. The record cheque she'd ever handed over was £17,546. She'd been hoping to beat that. There had to be a way.

Greening was quite happy playing the off-duty policeman in the pub, not that there would have been any point in pretending to be anything else after his visit earlier in the day. Len had greeted him like a long-lost friend but, having a string of pints to pull, refrained from the social commentary and introduced him to a group of middle-aged men who had colonised the far end of the bar.

An hour and two pints later, Greening had been reasonably entertained by tales of old Glyn: the time he'd organised a nude calendar in aid of local traders; the day he'd been drunk at an auction and bought a lot full of junk, which turned out to contain a stamp collection worth hundreds; the occasion he'd played in goal for the pub football team, sustained a broken finger and soldiered on to save a penalty. And then there were the girlfriend stories – Glyn was a real dog with women. These cheerful reminiscences were punctured by the occasional sombre silence and regular toasts: 'To Glyn. Who'd have thought it, eh?'

Naturally, when Greening let it slip he had seen the body in situ and attended the post-mortem, he had a host of questions to field, most of which he couldn't answer. How had Glyn actually died? Who on earth would want to stick the poor fellow up a tree? Why would anyone want to kill him?

He looked around the group. That was precisely the question he'd like them to answer but so far none of them had let anything slip that appeared of significance. Their vanished friend had already achieved iconic status, it seemed, before his body had come to light. The circumstances of the discovery had only served to reinforce his legend. He was now remote from them, a mythic figure.

As he ordered another round, just a half for himself this time, he reflected that none of his companions appeared to have been that close to the antique dealer. Glyn Cole had been a convivial drinking companion, a good man to watch F1 with on the box, guaranteed to crack a joke or put his hand in his pocket for a good cause. But his intimate life, despite the rumours of his philandering, remained a mystery.

Carmel had disengaged herself from his company and disappeared into the garden where he'd glimpsed her amongst a group of smokers. He wondered if she was having any better luck. He bloody well hoped so.

Rosemary had solved it. The solution came to her halfway through dinner when the conversation turned – unavoidably – to Glyn Cole. Frankly, Rosemary would have preferred never to have heard his name uttered ever again and she wouldn't mind betting she was not alone in the company at the table to feel that way. However, Pete the travelling head lad and Marika, Miletus's groom, were among the party and they were enthralled by the story of the body in the tree. The fact that Rosemary, who had discovered the corpse, had actually known the real man was particularly fascinating.

'If you knew him, why didn't you recognise him?' Marika asked, wide eyed.

Across the table Katherine rolled her eyes but Marika, tipsy from the champagne, didn't notice.

'I wouldn't recognise you, my dear, if there was nothing left of you but bones and your beautiful red hair.'

'Oh.' The girl wasn't quite sure how to take that – she was very proud of her rich auburn ringlets. 'I suppose not. But what was he like in real life?'

Rosemary turned that query over to Katherine, who was much better qualified to speak on the subject. She herself wasn't sure she could get through the kind of platitudes her niece was uttering without sounding a note of bitterness.

But as she listened to Katherine explain that Glyn Cole had been a charming and sophisticated man, Rosemary hit upon her solution to her funding shortfall.

She too had fallen under Glyn's spell when he'd been invited to the Hall just before she and Freddy moved to the gatehouse. At the time, Anna and Edward had not been long married and Rosemary had decided it was the moment to give them some space so they could make their own life. It had been a big decision to give up the house but she'd not regretted it.

Naturally, she'd not been able to take all of her belongings with her to the smaller establishment. In any case, the furniture and fittings and the many family mementos belonged in the Hall. So she confined herself to the things that she considered her own, one or two chairs and tables, paintings she had bought herself and, of course, her personal souvenirs. That still left many things that were, technically, hers, which she had no room for. They were moved out of the way into a couple of upstairs rooms to give Anna and Edward more space.

To keep track of everything, Rosemary decided that, for insurance purposes and her own curiosity, the household inventory should be revised and items revalued. It had seemed logical to ask Katherine's friend, the antique dealer in Hungerford, to do the job. And so, in the New Year of 2008, Glyn Cole had paid a visit.

He was a handsome man, Rosemary was not blind to that, but she was more impressed by his knowledge and enthusiasm. He also, though naturally she took it with a pinch of salt, appeared to be honest. He surveyed the cabinet of porcelain and confessed that he was no expert in this field – he recommended a couple of more knowledgeable dealers. What really took his fancy, which endeared him to Rosemary, was his passion for the collection of ancient timepieces that her great-grandfather had amassed.

She explained to him that Neville Pym had made

his fortune manufacturing chains and keys for pocket watches in the nineteenth century. After he had sold his business, he indulged himself in collecting rare and curious examples of the watches themselves.

'These are wonderful,' he exclaimed. 'Some are quite valuable.'

'I've no doubt they are,' she said. 'We're lucky they've survived in the family for so long. I'm sure my grandfather would have flogged them if he thought they could have raised any significant loot back in his day.'

Glyn had spent a long time examining one or two particular timepieces, enumerating their finer points, pointing out details she had never noticed and filling in significant background. He'd been very taken by an eighteenth-century pocket watch with a gold case whose face showed a hunting scene. And Rosemary remembered that he'd talked with remarkable lucidity about a watch from the Napoleonic era, which depicted one of Boney's victories. He'd also singled out a watch which had never struck her as particularly interesting. But Glyn picked it up and pressed a catch she had not noticed before. The watch opened to reveal a rather comic scene of a young man rogering his sweetheart by a riverbank. Glyn had given that, too, the *Antiques Roadshow* treatment and assured her it would be particularly desirable to collectors of erotic curios.

In retrospect it had come as no surprise to her that Glyn had made much of this piece, given the way he subsequently behaved with Anna. The man obviously had sex on the brain. But at the time, as the handsome antique dealer directed his well-informed and insinuating comments to her – Anna was not in the room – Rosemary had been captivated by him. But it turned out the mother had not been his target, he'd had his eyes on the daughter. And she'd not realised it! How that rankled. If she'd retracted his commission right then, how much happier life would have been for her family.

Instead, she'd encouraged Glyn to return to the Hall. It turned out that his job required more than one visit and Rosemary, being a busy woman, had not been on hand to police him. Instead, it was Anna who had welcomed him into the house and sat by his side while he pored over the family valuables, no doubt lapping up the pearls of wisdom that he laid before her. And at some point, either on that second visit or on subsequent rendezvous, the pair of them had ceased discussing the treasures of the past and turned their attention to the pleasures of the present.

Rosemary hadn't found out about the affair until it was over, when the silly girl confessed to Edward. Talk about getting the worst of both worlds. The marriage had teetered on the brink for a while and even now Rosemary couldn't contemplate her daughter's infidelity with any kind of equanimity. The girl's stupidity made her blood boil. Rosemary had never been unfaithful to Jack and yet somehow she understood how it had come about. Being in that room with Glyn as he made them look at their musty old family things in a new way, she herself had fallen under his spell. And she was stronger by far than her weak-willed daughter.

Fortunately disaster had finally been averted. But it had been touch and go for a while.

Of course, as it turned out, disaster hadn't been averted for Glyn Cole himself. After Anna had broken off with him, naturally he disappeared from their lives. And when Katherine had told her that the antique dealer had also disappeared from Hungerford, Rosemary had wondered if his absence was pure coincidence. Maybe the affair with Anna had run deeper on his side than she supposed. Certainly there were many things to love in Anna and it was plain she'd felt for Glyn in a way she did not for her husband. Maybe it had been mutual and he'd fled with a broken heart.

Well, she'd not spent much time on that romantic notion. Life wasn't a Puccini opera. She'd assumed he'd upped sticks and waltzed off, leaving everyone in the lurch - among them part-time employees like Katherine. She had no doubt he had left plenty of disgruntled customers too and was pleased her own business connection with him had not been more extensive.

But now Glyn had turned up - dead. It was ironic that she, a woman who had seen the light of his charm and watched her own daughter bathe in it, had stumbled across his skeletal corpse. Not much charm in a pile of bones.

She'd been observing Anna closely across the dinner table as the conversation turned to Glyn. Her daughter remained pale and inscrutable, though Rosemary could only guess what turmoil churned within her. She wished with all her might that she had never invited that damned man into the house.

But, even as she cursed the antique dealer in her

Chapter Seven

'What a lovely jacket.' The voice came from Carmel's left. A short woman of indeterminate years had her hand on her sleeve, reverently fondling the material between finger and thumb. 'Chanel, isn't it?'

Carmel turned to her questioner. The woman wore a pink gingham shirt and a baggy grey cardigan. She didn't look like a connoisseur of vintage fashion but Carmel knew better than to judge on appearances.

She'd moved into the garden to try and strike up some independent conversation. DCI Greening – Alan – appeared to be doing all right with the bunch Len had introduced him to.

Carmel had the advantage of knowing the area through her regular foot patrols and she'd talked first to the postmaster and then his sister-in-law who sometimes helped out behind the counter. The post office being a hub of local gossip, she'd thought that they might be a good starting point for intelligence about Glyn Cole. But they'd had nothing but far-fetched innuendo to contribute and were as keen to get information out of her. Was it true that his head had been found separately from his body?

There was a downside to being a local PCSO and when she'd caught sight of the father of a local yob who'd ended up with an ASBO, thanks to her, she'd moved to the end of the long pub garden to avoid being spotted. Which was where her new friend – Pam – accosted her.

'Where did you get it?' Pam asked, still admiring the jacket.

'On eBay last Christmas. It was a present to myself.'

Pam let go of the sleeve. 'I wondered if you'd got it from me. I had one like it in stock once.'

It turned out that Pam's husband ran a house-clearance business and she sold vintage clothes on the internet. And of course she had known Glyn Cole.

'We used to see him at all the auctions. He was very helpful in valuations on some specialist stuff.'

'What kind of stuff?'

'Medals and military insignia. Collections of odd things like matchboxes or Edwardian postcards. And watches – he was quite an expert.'

'What did you think when he suddenly disappeared?'

'Nothing really. People come and go all the time, don't they? No sooner do you think someone's a fixture than they're off into the blue and you never see them again. At least,' she rummaged in her handbag and produced a packet of cigarettes, 'that's my experience. When one husband's walked out on you, you don't take anyone's presence for granted.'

Carmel's desire for intelligence stopped well short of Pam's marital experience – unless it was Glyn Cole's, of course.

Pam mistook the flicker of alarm on her face. 'Don't worry, my dear, I shall stand downwind of you when I smoke. I must say, it's daring of you to wear your lovely jacket to a pub. You can't be sure some idiot won't spill beer down it.'

'Do you know if Glyn was ever married?' Carmel asked.

'No idea. He was brought up on a Welsh sheep farm and hated it, that's all I know. Got away as soon as he could. What he did and where he went between Wales and here is a mystery.'

She dragged deeply on her cigarette. For someone who claimed to know little and care less about the dead man, she was taking Carmel's questions seriously.

'He spent some time in Holland,' she said suddenly. 'I've just remembered. He turned up at an auction one day with a fellow called Jan. He said he used to share a flat with him in Amsterdam. It was a bit of a surprise.'

'When did he live in Holland?'

'I don't remember. Jan was a tall chap, pencil thin. He was in the trade too. Old paintings, I think – not my line anyway.'

It was dark where they were standing, at the foot of the garden, away from the lights. So Carmel saw Greening blundering down the path before he caught sight of her.

'Alan,' she called. 'I'd better go,' she added.

Pam was eyeing up the bulky figure heading in their direction. 'Is that your father?' she said.

Carmel didn't bother to correct her.

*

Anna had not had much success with her scheme for brightening Tammy's love life. The idea of nudging her into Will's company had seemed a good one when she'd thought of it that afternoon. Will was an interesting boy, admittedly not conventionally handsome, but she wouldn't mind betting a bright girl like Tammy would not set great store by convention. Will had intelligence and a sense of purpose – and the kind of self-confidence that set him apart. Edward had told her the other lads in the yard thought he was arrogant but, in his opinion, they were really in awe of his ability.

In any case, there was an air of glamour and danger about Will that any girl might find irresistible – at least Anna thought so. But she had a special reason to value Will's qualities.

So far, however, she had failed to get the two of them together. She had planned to seat Tammy by Will's side at the dinner table when she had finished her serving chores. But Tammy had claimed not to be hungry and to have other jobs which kept her from sitting down at all. By the time Anna had prevailed on her to take her place, Marika had shuffled up to Will's side and the pair of them had become engrossed in a conversation about the afternoon's racing – which wasn't in Anna's script.

After the pudding had been eaten – Anna made a point of giving Tammy credit – she asked Will to help her and Tammy clear the table, aiming to manoeuvre the pair of them into the kitchen. But everyone, even Edward, pitched in to help so that ploy came to nothing either.

Finally the party began to break up. Though there were some who would happily have sat around till the small hours tucking into the brandy – and before her pregnancy Anna would have kept them company – the prospect of getting the yard going early next morning prevailed.

She had one final bright idea.

'You've got your car, haven't you?' she asked Will. 'Do you mind giving Tammy a lift into Lambourn?'

He looked surprised but he could hardly refuse. She sought out Tammy, who was up to her elbows in soapsuds, washing glasses.

'Stop that,' she commanded. 'You've done enough for tonight and I've just got you a lift home.'

Tammy looked puzzled. 'I came on my bike.'

'I'm not having you cycling back this late. The bike can stay here and I'll come and fetch you tomorrow in the car. Leave the washing up, Will's waiting.'

Tammy froze in the act of placing a wine glass on the draining board.

'Will?'

'He's got digs in Lambourn, not far from you.'

'No thanks,' she said.

'Why on earth not? Is there a problem?'

Tammy hesitated. 'I don't know him. I could ask Miss Pym if she'll give me a lift instead.'

'But I've just fixed it with Will. Don't be put off by his manner, he's a lovely boy. You should get to know him.' Anna wondered if she was presuming too much.

'What did he say when you asked him?'

'He said he'd be delighted.'

Tammy stared at her suspiciously, as if she knew Anna was lying.

'OK,' she said and removed her apron. She did not look enthusiastic.

You can take a horse to water, Anna thought to herself. All the same, she was pleased with herself as she saw them off at the door.

Carmel placed the mug on the table in front of Greening – she'd made the tea with two bags, according to his instructions.

'I've called a cab,' he said. 'He'll be about a quarter of an hour and I'll be out of your hair.'

'It's OK, sir. You can stay as long as you like.'

He looked out of place in her cramped sitting room. She'd not thought of him as large but his broad shoulders had appeared to graze the door frame as she'd ushered him inside and now he took up most of her two-person sofa, his feet almost in the fireplace. It was true that this was a particularly small flat.

'Well,' he took a sip of his murky black tea and smiled in approval, 'I wouldn't want you having to make embarrassing explanations to your boyfriend.'

She was aware that her jaw had dropped. She snapped it shut hastily.

He pointed through the doorway to a jumble of footwear lying beneath the hall table. Amongst her diminutive pumps and shoes were a pair of man's trainers and some outsize male slippers. Greening was not the only male to invade her dainty premises and he had made the obvious deduction.

'Robbie's at a cricket booze-up,' she said, aware she was blushing.

'Weren't you invited?'

'It's a bit of a male bonding thing. Anyway, I had a better offer, didn't I? I felt like a proper detective for once.'

He took a hearty slurp of his tea and set it down. 'In that case, I hope you did better than I did. I've come to the conclusion that Glyn Cole's drinking pals didn't know much about him. They all agree he bought his round, coughed up for good causes and helped out folks in need. But they don't know much about his past or the names of these women he was supposed to be shagging. Most of them thought he'd fallen for some new woman shortly before he disappeared, and one guy said he'd seen Cole with a blonde in his car at the beginning of April, in Hungerford High Street and on the Lambourn Road. That would be shortly before he vanished.'

'That backs up what Mrs Shaw said.'

'So what? Randy bachelor likes blondes – nothing new in that. I imagine it was our friend Mrs Yates. Anyway, I'm not sure tittle-tattle about the poor fellow's love life is the point. I'd rather hear some hard facts about his business.'

'What about Katherine Pym? She should know, shouldn't she?'

'Indeed. I'm seeing her tomorrow morning. At least she should be able to tell me if Cole ever made any money.' He drank more tea. 'So, how did you get on?'

Carmel had been thinking hard what contribution she could make. Like Greening, she'd not gathered much of consequence from the late antique dealer's drinking friends. There was only one thing. 'Before he came to Hungerford, apparently he lived in Holland.'

'Really? Doing what?'

'I don't know. But I was talking to a lady who sells clothes on the internet. Pam Bellamy, married to a man who has a house-clearance business. They knew Cole professionally. She says he turned up at auctions with a Dutch friend who dealt in paintings. They used to share a flat in Amsterdam.'

Greening beamed at her. 'Really? Well done, girl.'

Carmel was puzzled, she couldn't see how this information was of significance and said so.

Greening pulled a rueful grin. 'You're right. It's probably completely irrelevant but it fills in a little piece of his background. Get enough pieces and it adds up to a picture.'

The doorbell rang loudly.

'My carriage,' said Greening, putting down his mug. 'No need to see me out.'

Tammy wondered if she could get out of the car as Will drove slowly away from the house. But then she'd have to walk home in the dark and that would be stupid. She resolved to treat Will like a stranger. She stared stiffly ahead, determined not to speak.

'I've been thinking about you,' he said. 'I think about you all the time.'

Oh God, this wasn't what she wanted to hear.

'What did I do wrong, Tammy?'

Silence. If he didn't know, she wasn't going to tell him.

He pulled the car over at the end of the drive. Maybe she would have to get out after all.

'Look,' he said. 'I don't mind if you tell me that coming to York was a mistake and that us being together was horrible for you. That I disgust you or something. But you haven't given me any reason for running away like you did. I'd rather know the truth.'

'OK.' Despite her resolve, she would have to say something. 'It was all wrong, you and me. We're not right for each other.'

He digested this.

'Fair enough. But I've got to say that I felt – I feel – just the opposite. I thought our night together was wonderful.'

Did he have to say that? He was lying surely.

'If that's how you feel about it,' he went on, 'then there's nothing I can do. But I don't want to not know you any more. I haven't got so many friends I can afford to let them go without a fight. Can't we still talk on the phone and maybe do things together sometimes?'

This time she looked at him. His face was as pale as a ghost in the moonlight shining through the car windscreen.

'I promise I'll never touch you again,' he said.

She shivered. She still wanted him.

He was staring at her, waiting for her reaction.

'Is this a plot?' she said. 'Why was Anna so keen you drove me home?'

He opened his mouth to reply but said nothing. She'd caught him off guard.

'Have you been talking to her about us?' she demanded.

'I've never mentioned you to anyone,' he said.

She ignored that. A grim possibility had occurred to her. 'Did she put you up to it all along? Is that why you started asking me out?'

He laughed but it struck a false note.

She carried on. She hadn't intended to talk but she couldn't stop herself now. 'If you're seen around with some little girlfriend, that makes good cover for you and her. Doesn't it?'

'Cover?'

'For your affair with Anna. You're screwing her, aren't you? That's why she thinks you're such a lovely boy.'

The silence in the small space was suffocating.

'Is that what you think?' he said softly.

'You were holding hands in the garden the other day. I saw you, so don't you dare lie about *that*.'

'That doesn't mean we're having an affair, Tammy. Anna has always been kind to me but it doesn't mean anything more – she's married to my boss, for God's sake.' He stared at her, as if re-evaluating her. 'Is that why you rushed home from York? Because it suddenly occurred to you I was involved with Anna?'

He made it sound as if she was deranged.

She nodded, far less sure of everything.

'But why?'

She couldn't confess that she had been through the call history on his phone and that she knew he'd been talking to Anna for ages on that night in York. He'd already cut most of the ground beneath her.

'That's just what I thought,' she said.

It sounded feeble but suddenly he didn't seem concerned.

'So it's not that I disgust you?'

'Oh no.' The words burst from her lips, she couldn't help herself.

He was smiling at her now, as if she'd given him an unexpected present. It occurred to her that no one, even confident, self-sufficient boys like him, wanted to be thought a turn-off in bed. It had been cruel of her to run out on him the way she had.

He took hold of her hand. 'So, are we friends again?'

Just his touch was intoxicating, familiar and strange at the same time. But she couldn't just let him walk over her.

'Do you swear you're not having an affair with Anna?'

He looked at her intently. 'When I first came to Pitchbury, I didn't fit in. You know Edward – he's an army man. There was one set of rules and one way of doing things and I couldn't see the sense in that. I was the yard screw-up, about to get kicked out, when Anna stood up for me. She persuaded Edward to give me a ride on a horse of her mother's and I won. That changed everything.'

'Why did she do that?'

'You'd have to ask her.'

'I might.' Maybe she had jumped to the wrong conclusions about Will and Anna but there was something between them, that was plain. If she was getting back together with Will then she'd have a right to know what it was.

But was she getting back together with him?

'In answer to your question,' he said, 'I am not having an affair with Anna or Marika or Katherine – or anyone.' He placed her hand on his chest over his heart. She could feel it beating through his shirt. 'I swear.'

He was very convincing.

Rosemary was ready to leave, though her customary irritation at being kept waiting was tempered by the fact that she was feeling a bit squiffy. She rarely drank much but it wasn't every day that she pulled off a coup at the races. Besides, she was partial to champagne.

She'd already collected her coat in preparation for the walk home but Freddy was helping Anna and Katherine in the kitchen – Anna had put him to work washing glasses. It occurred to Rosemary that now might be a good moment to refresh her memory of the watch collection assembled by her great-grandfather.

She found Edward rearranging the chairs in the dining room and, with some excitement, began to explain her scheme to expand the donation to the air ambulance fund.

'Hang on a moment,' he said, interrupting her flow. 'Let me just get the details straight. You want to sell your grandfather's watch collection and give the proceeds to the air ambulance?'

'No!' It came out as a shout and Rosemary put a placating hand on his arm – she hadn't meant to sound irritable. 'There's only one of them I want to get rid of. It's worth nearly five thousand, apparently, so we could give them a cheque for twenty. They would be very pleased with that.'

'I'll say. Are you sure about this, Rosemary?'

'Oh, absolutely.'

'But you've never suggested selling off family heirlooms before. And don't you think your grandfather's watch collection should be kept intact? Selling items piecemeal doesn't sound sensible.'

'Nonsense, you haven't been listening. For one thing, the watches were bought by my *great*-grandfather, Neville. Cecil, my grandfather, though apparently a charming man, only flogged things off. We're lucky he never got round to these watches. I'm sorry, Edward. I don't mean to give you a lecture.'

'That's quite all right.' He smiled at her.

One of the things she liked most about Edward was that he continued to indulge her now that he was her son-in-law as much as he had in the days when he was trying to win his place in the family.

'And,' she continued, 'I'm only thinking of selling one particular watch. To be frank, it's an oddity and doesn't belong with the rest. I don't know why it didn't occur to me to get rid of it before.'

'What's so odd about it?'

'Come with me and I'll show you.'

'Now?' Edward wore the look of a man who was thinking of ridding the house of guests and heading for bed. Only, Rosemary was no guest and it was thanks to her that he could consider the Hall his house.

'Yes, come on. Freddy's still busy in the kitchen. It won't take a moment.'

Katherine was coming down the hall as they headed for the staircase.

'Thanks for a lovely evening,' she said. 'I'm off. Why don't I give you and Freddy a lift down the drive?' she added to Rosemary.

'If you don't mind waiting ten minutes. We're going upstairs to look at the old pocket watches. You remember them, don't you?'

'Of course. What on earth do you want to look at them for?'

But Rosemary was already halfway up the stairs, eager to get on with it. Edward and Katherine followed and Rosemary heard him explaining what was afoot. She noted with satisfaction that he repeated the details correctly.

On the first-floor landing she turned left, only for Edward to call out, 'Keep going. They're up on the top floor.'

That brought her up short. When she had vacated the house, the family valuables had been stored in two rooms on the first floor – referred to by Anna and Edward as 'the museum'. Apparently, one of the rooms had now been emptied and its contents shifted on to the floor above. Rosemary felt miffed but recalled a long discussion about creating space for a proper nursery and moving things around. She dismissed the matter from her mind as she made for the steep narrow stairway that led up.

The key was in the lock of the first room on the top corridor, which also annoyed her. What was the point of locking valuable things away if the key was left in the door? However, now was not the moment to air her complaints.

The three of them crammed into the small room,

the first of three at the top of the house, built originally for servants but now mostly used for storage. In the main museum room on the floor below, glass and china was displayed in cabinets and ambitious, though dull, history paintings hung on the walls. Up here, no attempt had been made to show things off to advantage. Half a dozen straight-back chairs with wicker seats were stacked next to a card table laden with silver cups, old racing trophies and a pair of rearing bronze horses.

Rosemary's eyes were on the boxes and chests piled on the floor.

'That's the one,' she said, indicating a dark wooden trunk with brass handles at the bottom of the pile.

After some huffing and puffing, they cleared it of other encumbrances and pulled it into the centre of the floor.

Looking at the big lock plate, Rosemary had the sudden misgiving that it might be fastened and she had no idea where the key would be. But Edward swung the lid open easily, releasing a pocket of musty, perfumed air that reminded her of her grandmother who had lovingly maintained the family heirlooms and would, on occasion, exhibit them to her grandchildren provided they swore to be *very* careful.

The trunk contained two trays on which were ranged small bags of silk and linen with corded drawstrings, and inside each was a pocket watch. On the bottom tray, most of the watches had their own cases in which they nestled on beds of maroon and navy blue velvet. Rosemary began to search for the item she wanted, pulling the gleaming treasures out into the light. Feeling their weight in her fingers once more was like handling pieces of her past.

She resisted the pull of nostalgia, however. She didn't have time to indulge herself at the moment. The other two were content to remain an audience and let her hunt without interference. After all, she knew what she was looking for.

It took her a good ten minutes to unwrap each little package – there were seventeen in all.

'It's not here,' she said finally.

'Are you sure?' Katherine asked. 'They all look rather similar to me.'

Rosemary proceeded to explain why this particular timepiece was different.

'It's got a secret catch which opens to show a rude picture – a young man and his girlfriend by a river.'

'What? Having it off?' Edward laughed. 'You're kidding.'

'Of course not.'

'I thought you told me your grandmother used to show them to you.' He was grinning broadly, evidently tickled pink. Katherine was looking at him with wry disapproval. Rosemary avoided his eye.

'I doubt my grandmother was aware she had an obscene watch in her possession. It was only years later I found out about the secret catch. Anyway, apparently it's valuable and as of this moment I'd rather have the money.'

They went back through the bags and little cases for a second time. This time Edward and Katherine helped. It took a while, for they examined each watch closely, looking for a hidden catch which would transform a respectable antique timepiece into an erotic rarity.

At last they conceded it was not there.

'Damn,' said Rosemary with emphasis. 'It must be in one of the other boxes, though I don't know how that could have happened.'

'I'm happy to help you hunt for it another time,' said Edward. 'But not now. I should have been in bed an hour ago.'

Rosemary got reluctantly to her feet.

'Are you sure about that watch?' Katherine asked. 'I don't remember it.'

'Well, you wouldn't,' Rosemary snapped. 'Even your mother wouldn't have known about it, any more than I did. And she and I grew up in this house.'

There was an awkward pause, as there invariably was at any mention of Grace, her late sister. The gloom that had descended on Rosemary in the failure of her treasure hunt gripped her tighter. The loss of her sister was the other great burden of her life. Unlike the accident which had robbed her son of half his wits, she bore no direct responsibility for Grace's death. But Rosemary still felt guilty, like anyone close to a suicide. All the same, her sister had to be acknowledged – she missed her fiercely at moments like this. Grace should be here to bear witness to the past, she thought.

She felt Katherine's hand on her shoulder in silent support and shot her a grateful glance. She shouldn't have snapped at the poor girl in that way. She knew how deeply Katherine was affected by the memory of her mother.

'So when did you find out about this watch and its naughty secret?' Edward asked.

'A couple of Christmases ago. When we had a valuation done, it, er, came to light.'

'You mean Glyn spotted it,' said Katherine.

Rosemary felt foolish. They all knew perfectly well who had carried out the valuation.

Edward surveyed them sourly. 'Trust him to notice something like that.'

'I was grateful to him at the time,' Rosemary said. 'He assured me it was a highly desirable item for certain kinds of collectors and would probably fetch four or five thousand at an auction.' She sighed heavily, suddenly exhausted. 'I'll come back and look for it tomorrow.'

As they made their way out of the room, Edward said, 'You know there's an easier way of tracking it down than searching through all this stuff.'

'What do you mean?'

'There's an up-to-date inventory, isn't there? That was the point of Cole doing the valuation surely, to prepare a decent list for us and the insurance company.'

That was true but Rosemary couldn't see Edward's point.

'I mean,' he continued, 'you could save yourself the chore of looking by checking the inventory. If it's not on the list – well, obviously it won't be here.'

Rosemary was at the top of the stairs and Edward was halfway down the flight. 'Are you suggesting I imagined this watch?'

'Of course not, but memory does play tricks. You were convinced Salisbury was a left-handed track and it's not.'

'That was different,' Rosemary protested, on the brink of launching into an attack of her own on her son-in-law's deficiencies, when her foot slipped on the worn carpet on the top step. Suddenly she was tumbling downwards, her hands grasping at empty air.

Luckily Edward had turned to oversee their progress and he caught her in his arms. He placed her gently on her feet at the bottom of the stairs next to the hall table set with a display of early-season roses.

'What happened?' he demanded.

Katherine came rushing down the flight, almost tripping herself. 'Are you all right?' she cried.

'Yes, I'm fine,' Rosemary said, gingerly testing her limbs for suspicious aches. 'I wasn't really paying attention, I'm afraid.' Champagne and fatigue had played their part too, she knew, but she wasn't going to say so. 'Thank you, Edward.'

He was hovering by her side, regarding her with anxiety. 'It's just as well I was there. It could have been nasty.'

Freddy and Anna were waiting downstairs. If it had been up to her, Rosemary wouldn't have mentioned her fall but Edward boomed it out and Freddy's face turned pale.

Anna turned to Edward. 'We've got to put new carpet down on that staircase.'

'It wasn't the carpet,' Rosemary protested. 'It was my own stupid fault. I wasn't looking where I was going.'

Freddy insisted on making her a cup of tea – his standard treatment for his mother's ills – and as Rosemary sat down to drink it, she put on a stiff-upper-lip smile and shut out the conversation around her. Never show your weakness, was one of her mottos, even to your own family.

Inside, she conceded to herself that she was genuinely shaken up. It wasn't just the fall which, as it turned out, had not caused her any physical damage. But suddenly she was feeling less certain of events than just half an hour earlier. The watch – had she remembered events correctly? The vision of Glyn Cole, with his rich Welsh voice, lecturing her on its distinguishing characteristics was vivid. But, considering what had then transpired between Glyn and Anna, was it possible she had somehow invented the existence of the obscene picture? Was she, after all, going doolally?

She had never discussed the watch with Anna, for obvious reasons. Now she wondered whether her daughter knew about it and could back up her own recollection.

But there was no time to talk about it now. Katherine had come bustling into the room with Freddy in tow. It was finally time to leave.

For once Rosemary was grateful to be spared the walk along the drive and, as she got out of Katherine's car, she was fulsome in her thanks.

Her niece thrust something towards her through the car window.

'Edward asked me to give you this. He ran it off his computer while you were drinking your tea.'

Rosemary took hold of the sheaf of A4 paper stapled together in the left-hand corner. 'What is it?'

'The inventory he was talking about.'

'Oh.' Rosemary had an innate distrust of documents generated by computer, though she knew that was simply generational superstition. She had her own machine in the gatehouse, after all. 'If I must.'

She was turning into a grouchy old bat, she reprimanded herself. Anna's baby can't come too soon, she thought. A grandchild is what I need to soften my edges.

'Don't look at it tonight,' Katherine said. 'You look like you belong in your bed.'

Rosemary bent to kiss her goodnight. How her scramble-brained sister had managed to produce such a sensible child, she had no idea. But thank God for it.

Chapter Eight

Carmel was on an afternoon shift which, as a rule, meant a lie-in, followed by a few leisurely household chores. If Robbie had been on a late start too then the lie-in would have been extended and the chores forgotten. But not this morning, worse luck.

However, she had a task on hand which was almost as good as cuddling up to her boyfriend – trying to get more information out of Amanda Yates. It wasn't a task that fell within her remit as a support officer but what she did in her own time was her business. Besides, she'd promised Greening, which surely justified some amateur sleuthing.

She prepared in her mind what she was going to say as she nibbled at a piece of toast.

Amanda Yates worked just out of Hungerford at a company called Universal Logistics which, Carmel assumed, was some kind of delivery business, though that was neither here nor there. She rang and was transferred to an extension which, after half a dozen rings, referred her to voicemail. Amanda, it seemed, was away from her desk but invited her to leave a message which would be dealt with immediately on her return. (But when would that be?) Carmel declined the request.

She rang again and asked to be put through to Ms Yates's closest colleague. There was some hesitation and list-shuffling on the other end and then a phone was ringing once more. This time it was answered. A female voice said Amanda wasn't in the office and offered to be of assistance. She didn't sound as if she wanted to do any such thing.

Carmel claimed she was a friend who couldn't get through to Amanda on the phone – at which the colleague interrupted to say that wasn't surprising as Amanda had the day off and had planned to go to the gym. Carmel rang off and considered her options.

There were a few gyms in the area. The notion of trawling their car parks on the lookout for a scarlet Fiat was not appealing. On the other hand, she had observed a swimming costume spread out to dry in the back window of Amanda's car yesterday. There weren't many local health clubs that also had swimming facilities.

She drew a blank at the first one she tried, which was maybe as well because she wasn't a member and she'd have to wait for her quarry in the car. But at the second, the public leisure centre, she spotted the little red car parked in a side street. She parked up as close as she could and backtracked on foot. It was the right vehicle, she was sure of it. The swimming costume was gone from the back window but she recognised the green Wildlife Aid sticker.

Carmel felt immensely pleased with herself for about ten seconds. Then she debated how to proceed.

Fetch her own swimming things from her car and hope to catch Amanda – where? In the water or the gym? And would either of those places be right for any kind of conversation? And suppose Amanda was on a sunbed or somewhere else entirely? She could easily miss her.

In retrospect, it might be better just to go and wait outside the woman's house.

'Excuse me, that's my car.'

The angry voice came from across the road. Amanda Yates was advancing towards Carmel, her pink face even pinker from recent exertions and, as it appeared, irritation at some stranger peering into her vehicle. Her overall redness was exacerbated by her fucshia-coloured tank top and matching Capri pants.

'Hello, Mrs Yates.' Carmel put on her warmest smile. 'I thought I recognised your car.'

Amanda squinted at her. 'Do I know you?' she began. Then she stopped. 'Good God, you're that policewoman.'

'Community support officer, actually. Carmel Gibbs.'

'I didn't recognise you out of uniform. You look completely different.'

Carmel had made a point of appearing so. She wore her Chanel jacket again over a green and black pencil skirt she'd found in an Oxfam shop. On her lapel was an art deco antelope pin and around her neck a string of blue glass beads.

The effort wasn't lost on Amanda. 'What a gorgeous brooch,' she exclaimed.

'Not as nice as the one you were wearing yesterday.'

'Well, thank you. I hardly ever wear it but it seemed appropriate.'

'Yes, it was. I didn't really have the opportunity to say so yesterday but I am very sorry about Mr Cole. The discovery of his body must be very upsetting for you.'

Amanda regarded her suspiciously. 'Did you know Glyn?'

'Not properly. But his shop was on my patch and we'd say hello. And I used to go in for a nose around sometimes but he never recognised me – like you.'

Amanda grinned. 'Sorry about that.'

'It's OK. Perhaps it's best people just see a uniform. It means I can have an ordinary life off duty.'

'I suppose so. I'll look out for you in future.' Amanda had unlocked the car and dumped her bag in the boot. It was plain she had decided the conversation was over.

'How about a coffee?' Carmel suggested.

Amanda looked mildly surprised as she opened the car door. 'I've got to get home actually. Bit of a busy day.'

'It could be to your advantage.'

That stopped her. She turned and faced Carmel. 'What do you mean?'

'Well, we're having a pleasant chat right now. We could continue it, just the two of us, and maybe we wouldn't have to bother you again.'

Amanda's smooth forehead furrowed as she interpreted Carmel's remark. 'Which "we" are you talking about?'

'DCI Greening. The policeman I was with yesterday.

He thinks you know more than you told us. He wasn't joking about getting you down to the station with your solicitor.'

'So I haven't got much choice, have I?'

'I suppose not, Mrs Yates, but believe me, I'm on your side. I think you're in a horrible position, considering the way your husband obviously feels about Mr Cole.'

'I thought you said you weren't on duty.'

Carmel shrugged. 'Sorry. If you'd rather talk to DCI Greening, I understand.'

Amanda glared at her. 'You can buy me a drink, you devious bitch. Only one, because I'm driving. Just promise me you'll keep Ian out of this.'

'I'll do my best,' Carmel replied. She wasn't going to make any promises she wasn't sure she could keep.

Greening rang Katherine Pym's doorbell. The bungalow had been hard to find, down a small side lane in a village five miles from Lambourn, its white walls obscured from the road by a screen of hedging. The front garden was mostly gravel with a small patch of lawn fringed by shrubs – easy to maintain, he figured. He assumed from the black BMW saloon parked outside that this time he would find the lady at home.

He was unsure what to expect. He knew Katherine Pym worked as a book-keeper for a variety of businesses in the area, including the yard at Pitchbury and, until his disappearance, Glyn Cole Antiques. Rosemary Drummond had referred to Katherine frequently in the conversations they had had following the discovery of Cole's body and it was clear she saw plenty of her unmarried niece. So the picture he had built in his mind was of a spinsterish businesswoman – which didn't square with the husky and humorous voice on the phone when he'd managed to track her down to arrange the appointment for this morning.

'Let's not make it too early,' she'd said. 'You don't want to know me first thing, I'm horrible.'

Now, as the door opened to reveal a personable woman with a copper-coloured bob and an amused smile, Greening doubted very much that horrible would ever be an apt description for her. As she led him into a sparkling kitchen of off-white cabinets and gleaming chrome, he admired his surroundings. From his acquaintance with Rosemary and his glimpse inside Pitchbury Hall, this was something of a contrast. As was his hostess, in a dark blue tailored blouse worn over black slacks. Whether it was the cut of her trousers or the pointed high-heeled leather boots, Greening was aware that she was a tall woman. As she handed him a cup of coffee, her gaze was almost level with his.

She ushered him into a minimally furnished living room and a seat on a large sofa the colour of oatmeal. His eye was attracted by an array of recessed bookshelves and the amount of art on the wall, none of it familiar to him. He put all distractions out of his mind and tried to establish some basic points.

'How long did you know Mr Cole?' he began.

'Since he cut me up at a roundabout in Swindon in July two thousand and two,' she replied and sipped her coffee. Obviously there was a story to be told. He prompted her to tell it.

'I had a cherry-red convertible back then and I drove with the top down whenever I could. Quite quick too, though I probably shouldn't admit it to you, Mr Policeman. Some men won't stand for being overtaken by a woman in a fast car.'

And Glyn Cole would be one of them, Greening could understand that.

'So Glyn and I had a bit of a dice and he ended up asking me out while we were sitting at the traffic lights. I was going to tell him to get lost until he conceded I was the superior driver and asked me to name my favourite restaurant.'

'All this at a traffic light?'

'No, we'd parked up by then. I could tell he was a diverting man, Inspector, and right at that time I was in need of diversion. So we went out for a while. Not seriously, but that's how I met him.'

Greening was pleased she'd volunteered her romantic connection with the dead man. Amanda Yates had already marked his card but he was happy to receive confirmation without having to dig for it.

'I started doing his books about a year later. We'd stayed in touch. We both liked ballet so he'd take me to Covent Garden sometimes, which was sweet of him. He swore me to silence about his secret, said it wouldn't go down well if his drinking pals discovered he liked watching men in tights.'

Greening didn't know what to say to that and was happy to let her talk for the moment.

She appeared to misinterpret his silence. 'We'd go

up for the evening and drive back. It was all perfectly innocent. We were just friends by that stage.' Her expression changed. 'Special friends, actually. I've never known anyone like Glyn. What on earth happened to him, Inspector?'

'We're still at the early stages of the investigation, Miss Pym.'

'But he vanished two years ago. And you only found him because of some freak weather. He was up a tree all the time! It's just too grotesque.' She put her cup down on the glass-topped table in front of them and stood up. 'I'm sorry, Inspector, I can't . . .' And she clapped a hand over her mouth and headed for the door. As she disappeared down the hall, Greening could hear her sobbing.

Carmel led a sulky-looking Amanda to the nearest pub, a spit-and-sawdust boozer of the old school where the tang of nicotine still lingered in the beams of the roof and the shabby soft furnishings. It was dingy and unwelcoming but what did that matter? She had her fish on the hook and she needed to land her as soon as possible.

Amanda asked for a glass of white wine, plainly a poor choice for she screwed up her nose at the first sip but did not relinquish the glass.

Carmel didn't see any reason to beat about the bush. She'd already had to twist the woman's arm to get her into the pub. There was no point in trying to pretend she was Amanda's best friend. That didn't mean to say she would treat her unfairly, however, provided she got at the truth.

'Were you in love with Glyn Cole, Mrs Yates?'

'Piss off.'

'Were you sleeping with him then?'

'I'm not answering that either. Maybe I will get a solicitor.'

'It's your prerogative. I'm only trying to get at the facts.'

'What on earth has this got to do with Glyn being murdered?'

It was a fair question. 'If you were close to him at the time of his disappearance, it's possible you may know something which could help the inquiry into his death. Maybe he told you something and you don't realise its significance.'

'Well, he didn't. He gave me no indication he was about to clear off. Believe me, I've thought about it hard enough.'

'Well, what about the shop? Were there any business matters that were causing a particular problem?'

Amanda looked exasperated. 'How would I know? I only worked there part-time. But the answer is no, not as far as I'm aware.'

'Why was your husband so scathing about Mr Cole yesterday?'

'Ian has a strange sense of humour. Sometimes it doesn't come off.'

'It was more than that. He gave the impression he was jealous of Mr Cole. Why would that be?'

Amanda got up from the table. 'I've had enough of this. I'm going.'

Carmel remained seated. 'OK, but we'll be round to talk to Mr Yates himself in that case.'

Amanda glared at her, anger clouding her milky blue eyes, but she didn't make good on her threat. 'You're sick. Why do you keep coming back to this? What business is it of yours what was going on with me and Glyn?'

'A blonde woman was seen in Mr Cole's car on a couple of occasions before he vanished. Was that you?'

Amanda slumped back into her seat, the aggression suddenly gone. 'It could have been, he sometimes gave me a lift. It depends exactly when you mean.'

'At the beginning of April two thousand and eight. He was reported missing on the sixteenth. They were seen once in Hungerford High Street and then again on the road to Lambourn.'

'That wasn't me.'

'Can you be sure?'

'Definitely. I wouldn't have got in his car then. We weren't exactly getting on by that point.'

'Really?' Carmel observed her companion closely. She thought – she hoped – that she had finally worn the woman down.

Amanda drank deeply from her glass and set it down empty. 'OK, I'll tell you all about me and Glyn. You're going to get it out of me one way or another, aren't you?'

'Yes.' She had no doubt that was true.

'Just remember you've got my marriage in your hands.'

Carmel had already guessed as much.

Katherine Pym seemed embarrassed by her outburst. She returned after five minutes, full of apologies.

'I'm really sorry, you must think I'm some ghastly over-emotional female.'

'I can assure you, Miss Pym, I would never think less of anyone who shed tears for someone they cared about.' Greening was aware he sounded rather pompous but he meant it all the same.

'I imagine,' she said, 'you see a lot of emotional outbursts in your line of work.'

And how, he thought but said simply, 'True enough. If you're feeling better, why don't you tell me a bit about Mr Cole's business?'

'What would you like to know?'

'For a start I'm curious if he made money.'

'I only did his day-to-day accounts, his VAT, that sort of thing. He had a firm of accountants doing his year-end returns with the Revenue.'

'Surely you had some idea how his business was faring?'

'I suppose so. But I no longer have the laptop I used when I was working for Glyn, so I can't access any files. All the paperwork was handed over to his sister.'

'I'm not asking for specific figures, Miss Pym. They probably wouldn't mean all that much to me anyway. Just the general picture, as you remember it.'

She sat back in her seat and reflected for a moment. She seemed calmer now. He noticed a smudge of mascara below her left eye, where she must have hastily dried her tears. He felt a pang of distaste at having to press on with the interview but hastily dismissed it.

'When I first started working for him,' she began, 'he'd been in business for three years. He was only just beginning to turn a profit. I think his turnover for the first year I was involved was around fifty thousand. His lease was twelve and then there were running costs – wages for an assistant, keeping a car on the road, computers, taking stands at fairs. And buying stock, of course. He was also paying off loans.'

'I imagine starting up an antiques business is pricey.'

'Yes, but he bought an existing business and then he acquired a collection of military memorabilia which helped get him going. Having the right stuff to sell is the heart of the business – any business. Fortunately, he seemed pretty good at it. His turnover increased steadily each year. I imagine it might have got up to a hundred thousand for his last year. His overheads had crept up too, of course. I don't think he was ever going to be really rich but he was doing OK. He had gut instinct, that's what he used to say.'

'Was he trained? How did he learn the business?'

'I think he picked it up by working for people who knew what they were doing. He told me that after he left school he went to London and got a job on Portobello Road. He gained a lot of his knowledge there. Then he lived in Holland for a few years, working in the antique trade in Amsterdam.'

That tied in with what Carmel had discovered from the woman in the pub.

'Did he maintain contact with people from these times in his life?' he asked.

'With his old girlfriends, you mean? There were a few of those, I imagine, but I never liked to ask. He was quite secretive about that.' She smiled suddenly. 'But aren't we all?'

'How about blokes, then? Everyone has a few old mates, don't they?' As he spoke the words, Greening realised they hardly applied in his own case. Apart from former colleagues he'd prefer to avoid, he couldn't think of anyone of his acquaintance who would qualify as an 'old mate'. However, that was not the point at issue.

'There was Jan,' Katherine said. 'A friend from Holland.'

Greening was irrationally pleased. It was always satisfying when information was confirmed.

'Did Mr Cole see this man often?'

Katherine shook her head, then brushed a thick lock of hair out of her eyes. She did that a lot, Greening noticed, following it up with a quick apologetic grin. It was a signature gesture.

'No,' she said. 'At least, I don't think so. I only visited the shop every two weeks. But, now I think about it, Jan was there the last time I went in.'

'When was that?'

'A fortnight before the day we found Glyn missing. The first Wednesday of the month.'

About ten days before Cole's last sighting, Greening thought. Which didn't mean much – a lot could happen in ten days.

'Do you know how I could get hold of this Jan?' he asked.

'I suppose I might have a number somewhere. If you don't mind waiting.'

Greening didn't mind at all.

*

'I got on with Glyn from the start.' Amanda had moved on to tonic water and she sipped nervously as she spoke. 'I'd only been working with him for a couple of days before I knew I was going to fall for him. I seriously considered quitting.'

'Why?'

She shot Carmel a contemptuous glance. 'Because I was engaged to Ian, wasn't I? Ian is great, don't get me wrong. But we'd been together for ages and the wedding was still a long way off. I knew it was dangerous putting myself in the way of a hot guy like Glyn.'

'But you didn't quit,' Carmel prompted.

'No, I didn't. The job was too convenient – part-time, flexible and I loved the shop. It was full of fascinating stuff. Glyn had an eye for beautiful things.'

As if to prove this, Amanda leaned back and removed the large wooden barrette from her head and her hair escaped. She shook out the thick mass which tumbled over her shoulders in a golden cascade. 'It's still damp,' she said. 'I was going to dry it properly when I got home.'

Carmel made no comment. She guessed it bolstered Amanda's self-esteem to display her best feature.

'I tried to keep a distance from him but, you know the shop – small front room, small back room and a basement brimming with stock. You're literally bumping into each other all day long. I was horribly aware of him every time we brushed shoulders. He'd make a joke of it. Mind my BO, he'd say, but to be honest he smelt fantastic. Old wood, a touch of lemony aftershave, a hint of raw male – am I embarrassing you, Officer Gibbs?'

She was, a bit. But Carmel didn't care. She could hardly complain now she'd got her talking.

'Please call me Carmel,' she said.

'Honestly then, Carmel, we tried hard not to start anything. I convinced myself it was OK if we did friends stuff out of hours sometimes. He took me riding a couple of times and I promised I'd teach him to swim, because he let on he couldn't. That was a fiasco – he just panicked in the shallow end. But I got to check him out in a swimming cossie.'

Carmel's disapproval must have shown on her face.

'Yeah, I know. Who was I kidding with the good friends stuff? Glyn knew all about Ian, who'd pick me up from the shop sometimes. We'd even been to the pub over the road once or twice, the three of us. Somehow that made it more possible, I don't know why. I think I relaxed my guard once I saw Ian and Glyn getting on together. Anyhow, we were all mates and I was a good girl right up to that Christmas. I couldn't wait to go in to work, however. The days I spent at the shop were the highlight of my week.' She finished her tonic water.

'Would you like another?'

'You're joking. They must have invented gin to make tonic drinkable. Have you got a boyfriend, Carmel?'

That caught her off guard. She wasn't here to discuss her own love life. But this was hardly an official interview and, in the circumstances, it was only fair to share a little personal information. Especially if it helped keep Amanda talking.

'Yes. He's called Robbie. We've been living together for two months.'

'Ooh, the first flush of romance. How exciting.'

'You were telling me about Glyn,' she prompted. Maybe she shouldn't have said anything about Robbie at all. But she was new to this and making it up as she went along.

'You want to know how he first got into my knickers?' Amanda was enjoying making Carmel squirm, it seemed. 'It was ten days before Christmas and I was in the basement looking for something, a set of Edwardian teaspoons, I think, when the lights went out. Glyn said it was a fuse and came down with a torch because the fuse box was in the basement too. I told him I hated the dark and he told me to hold on to him if I was scared. So I did and he kissed me. I know it's disloyal to Ian but I swear that was the best kiss I ever had.'

Amanda's eyes were gleaming with the excitement of the memory and, Carmel guessed, the sadness of it too.

'It was a long time before he got round to mending the fuse,' Amanda went on. 'After that there was no stopping us. We'd waited so long it was like taking a pin out of a hand grenade or something. He said I was his early Christmas present. He was mine all right.'

'Didn't you feel guilty?' It was a naive question but Carmel couldn't help herself.

'I feel guilty about it now but I didn't then, when I was in the middle of it. My boyfriend before Ian had two-timed me, so when things kicked off with Glyn I just thought, so this is what it's like, now it's my turn. Like I was entitled. Do you know what I mean?'

Of course she didn't. Carmel couldn't imagine ever betraying Robbie that way but they were discussing Amanda's love life, not her own. She said, 'But it didn't last with Glyn?'

Amanda shook her head. 'It went on through Christmas and into January. Ian had to go and visit his grandparents and other relatives up in Yorkshire for New Year and I said I couldn't go because I had to work, which was a straight-up lie. I just moved into Glyn's flat above the shop for the best part of a week. We cooled it a bit when Ian came back and I made sure I was very nice to him so he wouldn't suspect. But the whole thing had shaken me up. I wasn't so sure marriage to Ian was what I wanted and I started to wonder what it would be like living with Glyn all the time.'

'Did he ask you to move in properly?'

'Not in so many words. But when I'd gone he told me how much he missed me. He led me to believe that if things fell apart with Ian then he'd be there to pick up the pieces. What a bloody fool I was, eh?'

'What do you mean?'

'I thought I was the one in control. That I had the pair of them on a string and I could choose which one to have long-term. I agonised over my choice. Then just as I decided to break it off with Ian, Glyn made it clear he was no longer that interested in me. Bit of a kick in the teeth.'

'When was this?'

'Towards the end of January. It was like someone had flicked a switch inside him and I was no longer the golden girl he couldn't keep but some minor irritation who wouldn't go away. It didn't stop him screwing me, of course. Reflex male behaviour. Half the time I think he only did it to shut me up. I should have quit the shop then, but I couldn't. So the answer to your very first question, Carmel, is yes, I was in love with Glyn. I realised I was in love with him at just the point when he fell for someone else.'

Carmel wasn't surprised to hear it. She'd pictured Glyn Cole as a serial seducer, a man who got his kicks from a new conquest and then moved on. However, she supposed Amanda might feel better about herself if she imagined she'd lost her lover to a towering new passion, rather than simply accepting that her own novelty had faded.

'Who was it?' she asked.

Amanda shrugged. 'I never found out.'

'Really?' Carmel was amazed.

'I didn't want to know. I'd been through all that with my previous boyfriend, obsessing about his other girl, finding out all about her so I could understand what made her better than me – it drove me nuts. So this time, after Glyn finally told me there was someone else, I didn't try to compete. We just broke it off and went back to working together. Only there was suddenly a lot of painful baggage. But I still needed the job and he upped my salary, because he felt bad about it all, I think. I planned to hang on until the summer when I'd finish my OU course. And he made a point of staying out of the shop when I was there.

He'd have appointments or just keep to his flat upstairs. He wasn't inconsiderate.'

Carmel wasn't so sure about that.

'When was all this going on?'

'During February and March, I suppose. In the month or so before he vanished we'd got things pretty much together again as work mates. I'd put him back in his box, if you know what I mean.'

'And Glyn's affair with this other woman continued?'

'Oh yeah. It completely screwed him up. I'd never seen him in such a state.'

'Did he confide in you about it?'

Amanda shook her head. 'I wasn't interested. I thought it served him right. Heartbreaker gets a taste of his own medicine. It cheered me up, if you want to know the truth.'

'And you honestly didn't know who this other woman was?'

'No. But she must have been married or in some kind of heavy-duty relationship she couldn't get out of. And I imagine she had blond hair.'

'Because he preferred them?'

'Because you said so, right at the start. He was seen in his car with a blonde girl. And I told you, it wasn't me.'

Greening passed the time by studying the artwork on the wall while Katherine was out of the room, searching for Jan's number. The pictures were unusual to Greening's eye. They had a modernist look but were clearly recognisable as landscapes. Most of them were prints, though there was one watercolour that particularly appealed, of a patchwork of fields surrounding a hill with trees silhouetted against a pale grey sky. It was sad but substantial.

'I like this one,' he said as she returned.

'It's my Paul Nash,' she said. 'A First World War artist but he painted that before the war. Glyn put me on to it.'

'And these?' He indicated the prints nearby. Now he looked closer he could see barbed wire in one and zigzag furrows on the ground. 'Are these First World War too?'

'Yes. They're a bit bleak to have in the living room, I suppose. But if you own special things you want them where you can admire them.'

Greening could understand that.

'Did you have any luck?' he asked.

She shook her head. The thick copper hair fell over her face again and she pushed it away. 'Sorry, I thought I had it in an old desk diary but I can't find it.'

'Pity. You don't remember this man's surname, do you?'

She smiled ruefully. 'I saw it written down once. It was confusing, full of Es and Ns. I don't remember it at all.'

'Anything you can tell me about him?'

'Only that he's tall and likes football – he used to come over to watch games, I think. That's all I know. Sorry.'

So that was that. As he drove off, Greening tried to convince himself that, diverting though it had been, spending the morning with Katherine Pym had not been a waste of time. All he had to do now was locate a football-loving Dutchman called Jan connected to the Amsterdam antique trade. Should be a piece of cake.

One thing still puzzled Carmel, though she wasn't sure she had the nerve to put the question to Amanda. It might count as simple prurience. She asked it all the same.

'Did your husband ever find out about your affair with Mr Cole?'

'No. Not really.'

'But he suspected? You said that the pair of them were friendly.'

'They were at the start. Then there was an unfortunate incident with this guy Glyn knew and Ian got suspicious.'

Carmel kept silent, hoping Amanda would tell her without being prompted. The tactic worked.

'When I was living with Glyn over New Year, a friend of his turned up out of the blue. It was embarrassing. It was about eleven in the morning and we were still in bed. You can imagine. Suddenly there was a knock on the bedroom door and this man walked in with two cups of coffee. I think I screamed. Glyn just laughed and told me this was his friend Jan from Holland. It turned out he had a key because he stayed every so often. Apparently he'd been trying to call but Glyn had his phone switched off so Jan had just let himself in and drawn the obvious conclusions. Anyhow, it was all smoothed over. Jan turned out to be an OK guy. He slept that night on the sofa next door and disappeared back to Holland. I thought that would be the last I'd see of him.'

'Yes?' Carmel prompted this time, eager to hear more of the Dutchman. It was the same guy Pam had mentioned – it had to be.

'Unfortunately, it wasn't. A couple of months later Ian and I were in the pub after work – a different one, I'd stopped going to the one across from the shop – when Jan loomed up. He said he was in town, looking for Glyn in all the locals and, naturally, he expected me to know where he was. I said I didn't and hoped he'd piss off but he hung around and I had to introduce him to Ian. I made a big point of saying, "This is my fiancé," because it was obvious to me he thought I was Glyn's girl. The dozy twit picked up on it and started in with, "Congratulations – when did this happen?" like it was new news. And when Ian said we'd been engaged for eighteen months, Jan almost contradicted him before the penny finally dropped. If I could have reached him under the table I'd have kicked his leg off. Then they got talking about football and I thought I'd got away with it but Ian hadn't missed a thing. I swore blind I'd never had so much as a Christmas snog with Glyn and he said if I had, he'd fix it so no one would ever want to lay a finger on me again.'

'He threatened you with violence?'

'He didn't just threaten. It wasn't nice, though he did apologise the next day. He's never forgotten about Glyn, though. All this about Glyn's body being found just sets him off again. So you can see why I don't want you dragging him into this.'

Carmel could indeed.

'Was that the last you saw of Jan?' she asked.

'No, worse luck. He turned up again the day before Glyn disappeared. He had another man with him. Do you want to know about him too?'

Ask a silly question, Carmel thought. 'Please, Amanda. You're being very helpful.'

'I hope you appreciate how much I'm putting myself on the line.' The blonde woman stared at her without expression. 'I've never told anyone else what I've told you. In case you're wondering why, I want you to catch the people who killed Glyn. The bastard could have treated me better but I loved him all the same.'

Carmel thought that sounded like a good reason.

Chapter Nine

Rosemary had been out of sorts all day, her routine disrupted by a late night and broken sleep. She'd been woken early by the dogs, eager for their morning walk. As she'd grumpily dressed herself she wished she'd asked Freddy to take them out before he'd left for the yard. Plodding across the meadows and along the stream, she'd been dazzled by the sunlight which had pained her head. She'd forgotten she'd drunk so much. The champagne celebration of the previous evening seemed a long time ago.

However, the fundamental cause of her discomfort was her failure to find that watch. She'd barely given it a thought in the two years since Glyn Cole had unveiled its smutty little secret. But last night it had surfaced in her memory as an apt and satisfying means of getting her charity donation up to a new level. To then fail to find it was infuriating – and puzzling.

Last night before bed she'd gone through the inventory, paying particular attention to the watch collection. It wasn't always possible to identify each timepiece by its listing but, by the time she had finished, she was certain that the item she sought was not included. Whatever her personal opinion of Glyn Cole, as an expert on pocket watches he obviously knew his stuff and the wording of his inventory was precise. There would be no mistaking the description of the saucy scene by the riverbank and no watch on the list came close.

As she'd lain there in the dark, brooding on the mystery, she'd once more questioned her fallibility. Surely she couldn't have imagined the whole episode. She'd even turned on the light and gone through the listings again, just to be sure she hadn't missed it. But there'd been no mistake, the dratted thing wasn't there. It wasn't anywhere but in her head. No wonder she'd barely slept.

Although she was itching to get back to the Hall and resume her search, she had a WI committee meeting in Lambourn in mid-morning which she couldn't, in all conscience, avoid. Rosemary prided herself on her commitment and other people's excuses of convenience irked her no end. So a lost watch, valuable or not, could not be allowed to stand between her and her long-standing obligations.

As she'd driven home afterwards, Mrs Jenkinson's seedcake lying like a stone in the pit of her stomach, she remembered something significant. Among her late husband's papers was a copy of the previous household inventory, the one Cole's document had been commissioned to replace. Why hadn't she thought of it before? Last night's over-indulgence had certainly dulled her wits.

The moment she entered the house she made straight for Jack's old desk in the front room, ignoring

Lodger and Porky's excited welcome. She found what she was looking for straightaway, in a faded green folder in the bottom left-hand drawer. The half-dozen pages of yellowing paper were headed 'Pitchbury Hall Inventory 1968'. It was a familiar-looking document though she had never read it through. Her father would have been responsible for compiling it.

She flicked through the pages until she found the timepieces. They were listed in similar language to the recent document but halfway down the page was an entry not included in the current list: 'Mid-nineteenth-century gold quarter repeater with concealed erotic scene of lovers dallying by a river.'

That was it! She held up the sheaf of paper in triumph and spoke to the dogs. 'See, I'm not going potty after all.'

They panted happily, tongues lolling and velvety brown eyes gleaming. Potty or not, they weren't bothered.

Greening was happy to let Yvonne Harris do the driving for the moment. He enjoyed watching her handle the car; it brought to mind Katherine Pym catching Glyn Cole's eye in her convertible. Whatever anyone said about women drivers, he was sure these two were a sight more proficient than he was.

He'd hoped to avoid the hundred and thirty mile trek to North Wales but another phone conversation with Dee James had convinced him his best bet of getting anything useful out of her lay in a face-to-face meeting. He'd considered deputing the task to Yvonne and Les Davis but thought better of it. Les was busy with Dougie, managing the physical evidence of Cole's death. He'd also asked him to have a go at tracking down Cole's friend from Amsterdam.

'His name is Jan, he's tall and likes football,' Greening had said. 'One call to Interpol should do it.'

Les had not been impressed by this information. 'How about I comb the antique shops of Amsterdam in person? I could do with a weekend away.'

Instead Greening gave him Pam Bellamy's number, courtesy of Carmel, and asked him to check her out.

Yvonne broke the silence in the car. 'How are you getting on with your little protégée?'

He pretended not to know who she was talking about.

'Your tame PCSO,' she prompted, obviously determined to discuss her. 'Carmel, isn't it?'

'She's a bright girl. There's a sight more to her than I first thought.'

'You've been spending enough time with her.'

'Not jealous, are you?'

She gave him a quick roll of the eyes while smoothly slipping into the outside lane of the motorway to overtake two lorries passing in slow motion.

'You sad-sack middle-aged geezers. I guarantee every woman under forty ceased considering you as a sexual being about ten years ago.'

Greening regarded her curiously. 'Don't pull your punches, will you, Yvonne? As a matter of fact, I ceased regarding myself as a sexual being about that time too. I meant, jealous in the professional sense.'

'Because she was hanging around with you yesterday? Honestly, I couldn't give a monkey's, just as long as you know what you're doing.'

Ah, that explained it. Yvonne was worried he'd been softened up by a youthful face. He supposed he appreciated her concern but what was she thinking?

She guessed his thoughts. 'It's OK, Alan, I know you're not an old lech. But you don't see much of Amy these days, do you? I'm a little worried you might be susceptible to a daughter substitute. And not everyone knows you as well as I do. I wouldn't want your behaviour to be misinterpreted.'

His behaviour! Greening bit back an angry retort. He supposed Yvonne might have a point.

'As a matter of fact,' he said, 'PCSO Gibbs is back on patrol this afternoon, having given the benefit of her local knowledge to the investigation. I doubt if I shall have further need of her services. Happy now?'

Yvonne considered the remark and smiled. 'Yes, boss,' she said.

Anna felt as if she had emerged from a long dark tunnel. Today her body was not in rebellion. The queasiness in her stomach was absent and she could contemplate food without the urge to vomit. Better than that, she had been properly hungry for the first time in months.

Today was not a racing day and Edward had accompanied Freddy up to the Hall for lunch. They had sat in the kitchen, rehashing the events of yesterday at Salisbury for the umpteenth time, while she cooked. To their surprise, she served them a proper hot fry-up – eggs, sausages, bacon, fried bread and all the greasy transport-caff trimmings she could muster.

'Good Lord,' said Edward as she set the plates on the table – including one for herself.

'Brilliant!' cried Freddy, reaching for the brown sauce.

'I'm feeling a bit better,' she said.

'I can see that.' Edward squeezed her hand impulsively. She hung on to his grip for a second or two. This was more like it. She was eating for two and her husband loved her still. Hang on to the moment, she thought.

Freddy was chewing hard. 'I've got a complaint. There's no black pudding.'

It was well known Anna hated black pudding at the best of times though, as she stuffed bacon into her mouth, the thought no longer seemed so repulsive. She felt as if she hadn't eaten all year. 'Next time,' she said. 'I promise.'

From down the hall came the sound of the phone ringing. It cut off and they heard the murmur of Tammy's voice as she took the call.

Anna had picked Tammy up in the car that morning as promised. The girl had seemed restored to her customary good humour and Anna was convinced her scheming of the night before must have paid off in some way. She had resisted asking Tammy about Will directly but she was determined to get the story out of her later and had hatched another plan.

Tammy came into the kitchen. 'Mrs Drummond says she's coming up to the Hall now to carry on looking for something upstairs. She just wondered if anyone was going to be here and I said yes. Is that OK? I'll be in anyway.'

'Actually,' Anna said, 'I was going to ask you to come shopping with me for nursery furniture.'

'Me?' Tammy looked startled.

'If you don't mind. I thought it might be fun. Since I'm feeling good today, why not?'

'If that's what you'd like. But I don't know anything about baby things.'

Edward chuckled. 'I bet you know more than Freddy and I do.'

'But what about Mrs Drummond?'

'She can let herself in. I've got an appointment with the vet,' Edward said. 'You go with Anna. If she starts feeling funny, make her come back at once.'

But Anna didn't think there was much chance of that. She hadn't felt so good in ages.

To Greening's eye the rolling green countryside looked more and more appealing as they left the road to Wrexham and drove deeper into Wales. As a boy he'd been on a school trip to Llandudno and enjoyed the daily outings to slate mines and castles and the peaks of Snowdonia. It couldn't be all that far from here. He was about to embark on a speech of reminiscence when Yvonne spoke.

'Jesus, we're deep in sheep-shagger country.'

'I think it's rather lovely.'

'Oh yeah? The road's are bloody slow, half the traffic signs are in a foreign language and there aren't any decent clothes in the shops. I don't think they know what a nightclub is on this side of the border.'

'I only said the countryside was pretty,' he protested.

'We've got fields just as green back in Berkshire,' she retorted. 'No wonder Glyn Cole got out as soon as he could.'

After a lengthy cruise down side roads flanked by hedge and stone walls, with inviting-looking hills in the distant west, Yvonne found the entrance to Dee James's farm. A two-lane track led them into a gravelled car park surrounded by a collection of one-storey buildings, behind which could be seen the bulk of a substantial farmhouse. Beneath an awning, tables and chairs were set out and a blackboard advertised a selection of foodstuffs and drinks.

'I see the caramel macchiato has penetrated this barbarous land,' Greening said but failed to get a rise out of his colleague.

'It's busy enough,' she said as she manoeuvred into a tight spot between two Range Rovers. 'No wonder this Dee James hasn't been down to see us, she's making too much money here.'

Yvonne had a point, Greening thought, as they entered the farm shop. The freezer aisles were full and people crowded in front of the lengthy butcher's counter. A selection of plump pies caught his eye, prettily garnished with fruit. 'Try our homemade steak and stilton quiche' read a label flag-sticked into an attractively glazed tart. He felt a pang of hunger. They'd eaten nothing since wolfing a hasty sandwich in the Farley Road canteen before departure.

His companion was plainly not seduced by her surroundings. 'Let's get this over with and head back to civilisation.'

They pestered one of the girls on the checkout until

she vanished into the back and returned with a woman in a dark suit with a white butcher's coat over the top. She shook his hand with a grip worthy of a blacksmith and led them out of the shop into a small cluttered office where she arranged a pair of uncomfortable-looking wooden chairs in front of the desk. She did not offer them any refreshment.

'Mrs James?' Greening ventured. No formal introduction had been made and it was as well to be sure.

'Call me Dee,' she said. It was more of an instruction than a friendly invitation. In person, her Welsh accent was stronger than on the phone. 'You're Inspector Greening, I assume. And this is?'

Yvonne introduced herself and added, 'I'm very sorry for the loss of your brother.'

Dee waved the sentiment aside as if it were an irritation. 'To be honest, I'm just damned pleased the matter has been cleared up. Now his body has been found, we can sort his affairs out properly.'

'I thought you'd already done that,' Yvonne ventured.

'You don't know much about the law of the land then, dear. Without a body or powerful evidence that he's not alive, I can't get a death certificate for seven years. Glyn's bank accounts are frozen and his life insurance won't pay up. I can't even sell his car.'

'You've still got his car?' Greening was delighted.

'Don't get your hopes up, Inspector. I can't insure it so we've been using it here on the estate and it's in a right old mess. I doubt it holds any clues. Now we can have Glyn officially declared dead, I'm hoping the government are going to revive the scrappage scheme so I can trade it in.'

'You managed to wind up his business though, didn't you?' he said.

'Up to a point. The lease was up for renewal and I simply didn't renew it. Technically, I don't think I could. I took a cash offer for his stock. Maybe that wasn't strictly speaking above board but sue me, is what I say. I settled the outstanding bills and paid the remainder into his business account. The whole thing was a pain in the neck.'

It appeared that, from his loving sister's point of view, Glyn's disappearance had been a cause of inconvenience rather than emotional distress.

Yvonne leaned forward slightly, her mouth pulled tight in an expression Greening was familiar with. She'd just been addressed as 'dear' and that must have rankled. Yvonne was eager to stick the knife in. She spoke gently, however.

'You mentioned life insurance.'

'I did. He has a policy due to pay a hundred thousand pounds on his death.'

'And you are the beneficiary of his will?'

'He didn't leave one. Hardly a surprise. The next of kin is my mother but she's got early onset dementia. She barely knows me half the time, though if Glyn had ever taken the trouble to come up and see her I'm sure she would have recognised him all right.'

Yvonne continued to pursue her line of inquiry. 'Apart from Glyn, are there any other siblings?'

'Not alive, no. Our sister died when she was ten. Leukaemia. Glyn left home about six months later.

Just after my dad drove his Land Rover into a petrol tanker on the A5 – he was three times over the limit.'

The more Greening heard about Glyn Cole's family circumstances, the more he sympathised with the young man's desire to flee his unhappy nest.

Dee's matter-of-fact account had banished his hunger pangs though it had evidently not dispersed Yvonne's suspicions.

'So, in effect, you will be the beneficiary of your brother's estate?'

Dee eyed the policewoman coldly. 'Eventually, I suppose. But between the nursing home and the taxman I shan't see any of it. You're not suggesting I killed my brother to get my hands on his life insurance, I hope.'

'I didn't say that.'

'Because if I had, I would have made sure his body was somewhere ruddy obvious so I could make a claim. I'm not the most patient person, officer, and seven years is a long time to wait.'

Greening rather thought Yvonne had asked for that.

Rosemary was barely out of puff by the time she reached the top of the back stairs that led to the storage room at the top of the Hall. That's what an active lifestyle did for you, plenty of fresh air and dog-walking with a twice-weekly ride-out thrown in. There were women a generation younger who could barely waddle to the local shops to buy a Mars bar. She, on the other hand, was as fit as a fiddle. Physically, she had no fears for the future, provided her mental health held up. That was her worry. Except it was an irrational phobia, as the discovery of the old inventory had just proved. There was nothing wrong with her memory or her wits.

She unlocked the small room and surveyed the cluttered interior. There were more boxes and trunks than she'd thought. If she was going to undertake a thorough search, it would take a long time. But she'd never shirked from a large task and prided herself on being thorough. If it took days, then so what? It would be done.

Of course, the job would be made a lot easier if she had some help. Edward had volunteered yesterday but he'd left a note to say he'd gone to the vets to see if Liquid Assets was well enough to return to Pitchbury after the hip injury he'd sustained at York. It was rare for a trainer to have an afternoon off.

She extracted her mobile and called Katherine. She wanted to talk to her anyway.

'You know that inventory you gave me last night?' she began, launching herself into the conversation without preamble.

'Yes, Aunty.' Katherine recognised her voice straight off, as always. If there was a hint of exasperation in her tone, Rosemary ignored it.

'Well, it's wrong. That watch I was talking about is not on it, but it is on an earlier inventory.'

'Gosh, I didn't know there was an earlier inventory.'

'Certainly there is, dated nineteen sixty-eight. Your grandfather must have compiled it. I found it this morning.'

'Really? Clever old you. But that's over forty years ago. Couldn't Grandad have sold the watch and not mentioned it? It sounds like the kind of family heirloom he might want to get rid of.'

'Possibly, but how do you explain the fact that Glyn Cole showed the wretched thing to me just over two years ago? It was definitely in the collection then and must have been left off the list by mistake. So much for Mr Cole's efficiency.'

'I daresay he had other matters on his mind, Aunty.'

And Rosemary had no doubt what – or who – they would have been. It wasn't funny.

'Where are you now?' she demanded.

'I'm in the office in the yard, doing Edward's books.'

'Good. You can come up here and help me look for the watch then.'

'You're at the Hall?'

'Yes and I could do with some assistance. It's going to take me ages to go through all this stuff on my own. But I'm determined to find that watch or know the reason why it's not where it should be.'

There was a pause. 'I'm sorry, Aunty, I can't at the moment. I spent the morning with the police and now I've got Edward's VAT to do, apart from sorting out a mound of receipts. Things are always in such a mess here.'

That was a nuisance though it plainly couldn't be helped.

'I hope you didn't tell the police anything you shouldn't,' she said.

'Of course not.' Katherine laughed softly. 'I thought Inspector Greening was rather a teddy bear.'

'Teddy bear or not I don't want him upsetting Anna about Glyn Cole.'

'Surely he's going to find out about her soon.'

'He might not. If you ask me, I think the police are dim. In any case, it's got nothing to do with the man's death.'

'I shouldn't worry about it if I were you, Aunty. As a matter of fact, I sent him off in a completely different direction.'

Rosemary listened half-heartedly to Katherine's explanation and Greening's interest in some Dutchman. But they'd talked long enough and she ended the conversation. She had work to do.

To be fair to Dee James, and Greening was conscious of his antipathy towards her, she had tried her best to be helpful. She had sorted out those belongings of Glyn's which she thought would be of most interest to them – his laptop and office computer, his sales book and other business paperwork.

'You're welcome to look at his other things. I put them in a spare bedroom in the farmhouse. His old room actually. I don't think anything much has been touched.'

They'd had a cursory look in the little room which still bore the hallmarks of teenage occupation from another era, with posters of Freddie Mercury and Ruud Gullit still on the walls. The wardrobe was full of adult clothes – Glyn's, Dee assured them – and Yvonne ran through the pockets of jackets and trousers. Greening thought of the blackened and weather-beaten garments that had been cut off the skeleton at the post-mortem. Once they would have hung next to these very clothes. It was a weird thought.

Dee had shown them Glyn's car which, as she had implied, looked as if it had been used to transport the entire farm back and forth. The bodywork of the old Volvo estate was battered and scratched, with interesting rust patches spreading along the trims like fungus. The interior upholstery was rotted and stained, wood was stacked in the boot area where Glyn Cole once loaded Victorian chairs and Tiffany lamps, and the back seat was covered in empty feed sacks. Straw, mud and dog fur lined the passenger footwell and the stench of petrol and creosote poisoned the air.

'I suppose I ought to hand this over to Sean and his lads,' Greening said.

'I suppose,' Yvonne echoed him. They both knew it was probable that Cole's murderers had dumped the car in Swindon. On the other hand, what were the chances of finding any relevant forensic evidence in the vehicle now?

Greening came to an executive decision. 'I'm going to forget the forensics on this. It's too late. We could tie up a team for weeks and get nothing. It's a waste of resources.'

They checked the glove compartment and door pockets, finding only rubbish.

'Here's a bag of mints,' Yvonne said. 'Looks like some mouse has already had a go at them.'

'I cleared out Glyn's stuff and put it with his other things,' Dee said.

'What about his phone?' Greening asked. Carmel had told him it had been found in the driver's door.

'It's in the pocket of his laptop bag. His charger's in there too.'

'Thank you, Dee.' She might not be the warmest of women but her efficiency was admirable.

They carried their spoils to the car, two cardboard boxes and the laptop. The shop was closed now and the car park all but empty.

'You've got a thriving business here,' Greening said.

'It's been damned hard work,' Dee said. 'But it's a team effort. My aunt and I do the shop stuff but my husband and his brothers take care of the farm. I've been lucky, I married into a family of real grafters.'

'Did you never get on with your brother?' he asked, suddenly emboldened.

She looked at him as if he had slapped her in the face and, for a moment, he thought she was not going to respond.

'If you really want to know,' she said finally, 'I used to worship Glyn. I was his adoring younger sister and thought everything he did was the best – all the books and films and music he liked. Together we looked after Chloe, our sister who was ill. I thought he'd always be there, my wonderful big brother. Then suddenly, after my father managed to get himself killed, he wasn't. He let my mother know he was still alive but that was it. We scarcely ever saw him again, except when he was in trouble. Mum used to send him money sometimes. The truth is, I loved him but he did not love me.

'So,' she continued, 'when he disappeared two years ago, it didn't mean much to me. Not compared to how it was when he disappeared the first time.'

Greening absorbed the information – it was more than he had expected to get out of her.

'Do you know where he went when he left home?'

'London. Then he lived abroad.'

'In Holland?'

'Yes. He got into trouble there and had to leave suddenly.'

'What kind of trouble?'

'My mother wouldn't tell me but I think it was drugs. A friend of his went to prison and he had to get out suddenly. Mum sent him the money. Next thing we knew, he was an antique dealer swanning around Berkshire but I'd given up on him a long time ago. Here.' She thrust a carrier bag into his hand.

Greening was surprised – was this more of Glyn's belongings? But the bag bore the emblem of the farm shop. 'What's this?' he asked.

'Just a few chops. I told you, we produce the best organic lamb in Wales.'

But it wasn't just a few chops, as he discovered when he delved into the bag as they began their return journey. The parcel included some of the other food that had caught his eye earlier.

'Fantastic,' he said as he bit into a pork pie. 'I misjudged that woman.'

'She's trying to buy you off,' Yvonne said as she drove the car down the narrow country lane – far too fast, in his opinion.

'You fancy her for the murder, do you?' He wasn't

serious and, he was glad to see from her expression, she wasn't either.

'Not as much as I fancy one of those pies. I'm starving.'

Rosemary's intentions were good. She'd begun her hunt through the contents of the upstairs museum room full of purpose, which was simply to locate the missing watch. Some boxes and packages had not been opened for years and had been wrapped up with the intention of putting them into storage. She'd had to go downstairs to fetch a pair of scissors and a knife with a retractable blade so she could slice through the cardboard. All this took time.

Then it transpired that unpacking and unwrapping family treasures that she'd not looked at for some time – for many years in most cases – was a distraction it was hard to ignore. It was also disloyal, she felt, to yank a photograph album or a set of cutlery or an old snuffbox into the light of day and simply bundle it up again. With each undressing, the clothes of the past came into view, memories of her grandmother and her sister Grace and the wet afternoons they would spend looking through 'the old things'. The past was owed its due.

So, distractions were many and progress was slow. But she felt she was putting the time to good use even if, so far, she had not found that dratted timepiece. She'd brought both inventories, old and new, and as she unearthed an object, so she checked it off on the two lists. She had her notebook on hand too.

It was satisfying to be reassured that what was

once in the possession of the family was still where it belonged.

When she came to a lacquered rosewood box her heart leapt in anticipation. This contained some of her favourite pretty things from the past – a small collection of mid-nineteenth-century glass paperweights. She remembered the vivid colours and intricate designs very well. As a fourteen-year-old girl she had coveted one in particular, a round ball of glass filled with hundreds of tiny blue and white flowers, interspersed with little silhouettes of animals. She had 'borrowed' it for a fortnight to weigh down the letters she was getting from an older boy who was pursuing her ardently. When her mother discovered them, Rosemary had been surprised it was the stolen paperweight rather than the passionate letters that upset her most. Her grandmother had explained that the weight was worth rather a lot of money, which hadn't impressed Rosemary at the time. She'd thought it was typical that her family should care more about material things than an assault on her virtue.

So it was with a nostalgic air that she opened the box. 'Her' paperweight was not there.

She reached hastily for the new inventory. The paperweights were headed as a group: 'Eleven glass paperweights, flower and animal designs, mid-19th century', followed by a line on each one.

Her heart pumping – something was wrong here – she skipped through the 1968 inventory. Here they were, listed individually, each weight given its own line of description. There were twelve lines in all.

Her eyes ran down the list, seeking one particular

entry. Here it was: 'Baccarat millefiori paperweight dated 1848, with silhouettes of horses and deer.'

'Millefiori' meant a thousand flowers; she remembered her grandmother explaining the term to her, which described the floral effect produced by the tiny slices of coloured glass.

But there was no millefiori weight here, just as there was no scandalous pocket watch.

She stood up, clutching the two inventories. They were proof of criminal activity and she was going to get to the bottom of it.

She heard footsteps in the corridor outside and turned to face the door.

'Is that you, Edward?' she barked. 'I've just discovered something very suspicious.'

Tammy had obediently followed Anna around Swindon, popping into shops that sold baby equipment. She wasn't complaining, though she was puzzled by the trip. Anna didn't seem all that interested in the merchandise on view and so far she hadn't bought anything. Maybe she was just happy to be on an outing and feeling better.

'Well,' Anna said, 'what do you think?'

They were surveying an item of furniture called a Little Treasures Changing Unit.

'I'm not sure you should go by my opinion,' Tammy said. 'I don't know anything about babies.'

'Me neither. I've been doing some homework though. I know you've got to have somewhere you can change the baby. This seems about the right height – I don't want to do more bending than I can help.'

'Yes, but it's only a chest of drawers with a little rim around the top. Why don't you just get a proper chest of drawers you can use for ever?'

'That's true. I knew you were the right person to come with me.'

'My friend Alison's sister had a baby last year,' Tammy said. 'According to her, the most useful thing she bought was a big rubbish bin with a foot pedal you could chuck nappy sacks in when they were full.'

'Brilliant. I'll get one of those then.'

As they were buying it in the shop next door, Anna said, 'How did you get on with Will last night?'

So that was the point of Anna dragging her along – Tammy saw it at once. Anna had plotted to put her and Will together and now she wanted to pick her brains about it.

'Oh, fine.' It wasn't that Tammy didn't appreciate Anna's machinations. The gloom that had gripped her spirit since York had vanished and the part of her that she'd dedicated to Will was no longer forbidden territory. This was down to Anna and she was grateful. But she was still suspicious – there was some kind of weird connection between them and she was instinctively jealous.

Anna gave her a knowing look. 'Just fine?' Her interest was blatant.

Tammy was unsure how to respond. She was struggling for the right words to tell her employer politely to mind her own business when Anna's phone rang.

'Edward?' Anna said. 'What's wrong?'

Tammy only heard half the conversation but it was

plain something serious had happened. The progress of her romance with Will was suddenly irrelevant.

Anna turned to Tammy, her face emptied of everything but shock. 'Mum's fallen downstairs and hurt her head.' She had trouble getting the words out. 'We've got to get to the hospital. They're taking her to the Great Western.'

Tammy put both arms round Anna. 'Is it serious?'

'Edward says he can't tell if she's breathing.'

Tammy steered Anna outside. They left the bin for the nappy sacks behind.

Chapter Ten

Anna had never seen Edward in such a state. He was a man who kept his cool in moments of stress. Two years ago, when she'd told him she was in love with Glyn Cole and wanted him to release her from their marriage, he'd been calm like ice. Like a soldier under fire. But now he was shaking. It added to the unreality of the moment as she faced him in the reception area of the hospital. It was a big space, with a vault of empty air above and a bustle of people around them, but it seemed claustrophobic to her.

Words tumbled in incoherent syllables from his lips and she had difficulty piecing together what he was saying – beyond the fact that her mother was dead.

The floor moved beneath her feet and only Tammy's presence by her side kept Anna upright.

'How?' she said. 'What happened?' Her mother was indestructible.

'I found her when I got back. She'd fallen down the top stairs and hit the hall table.' Edward's words came out clearly this time. 'The vase was lying on top of her head.'

It was a heavy stone vase with a swirling sandy surface, supposedly made of fossils. She'd always hated the ugly yellow thing. That's why she'd stuck it away at the end of the corridor.

'She slipped on those stairs yesterday,' Edward said, to himself as much as anyone. 'I was going to get new carpet.'

Anna took his hand. He was still trembling. 'Don't. It's not your fault.' At least, it wasn't his alone. If only she'd had the courage to chuck out that vase.

'Where's Freddy?' she said. 'Does he know?'

'Katherine's bringing him. She was in the office in the yard. I came in the helicopter.'

'Helicopter?'

'They brought her by air ambulance,' Edward said. 'That's the least they could do.'

Even in her state of shock, the irony was not lost on Anna.

'I want to see her,' Anna said.

'No, darling.' Edward said. 'She's not . . .' He stopped himself.

'I have to.'

'They're coming,' Tammy said, pointing to the door.

Anna saw her brother running across the atrium floor towards her. Katherine was just behind.

Freddy threw his arms around her and held her tight. She felt him sob but he said nothing.

'Will you come and see Mum with me?' she murmured into his chest.

Unless she saw for herself, she would not believe it.

*

It was after ten by the time Greening got back from Wales. His flat wasn't much to boast about but at least it was home, with a kettle, a TV and a bed – which was all he needed at the moment. Even though Yvonne had done the driving, the journey back had been knackering. He was no longer hungry but made himself a cup of instant coffee, added a slug of Famous Grouse and settled on the sofa with the remote control. There had to be something on the television that wasn't to do with weathered skeletons, unlucky families or sarcastic females – Yvonne had not been the best of company on the drive back.

Funnily enough, he found a programme about Great War artists on a digital channel he never watched. He settled down to have a look, his mind less on the subject than on Katherine Pym's quick smile and figure-hugging trousers. He was off duty, he could think what he damned well pleased.

When his phone rang he was tempted to ignore it but when had he ever done that?

'Hi, Inspector, it's Carmel.'

Funnily, she was about the one person – maybe the second, with respect to Katherine Pym – he was happy to hear from right at this moment.

She sounded full of beans. 'I've just come off my shift, so I couldn't call earlier. Sorry.'

'Sorry about what?'

'I've got things to report. About Amanda. I could come over now and tell you.'

'What, come here?'

'It'll only take ten minutes at this time of night. You showed me where you lived, remember?'

They'd passed his place the day before as they drove to the Yates house. He should have kept his mouth shut. The conversation he'd had with Yvonne in the car flashed back to him. A woman young enough to be his daughter should not be visiting his flat at any time, let alone this late. Already he could hear the canteen sniggers – heard the one about the inspector and the PCSO? She knows how to give good community support . . .

On the other hand, he'd welcome her company and the chance to chew over the events of the day. It might even be better to see her away from the nick and out of working hours when their meeting wouldn't come to the attention of his colleagues.

'OK, if you're up to it,' he said. 'But only for half an hour and no snide comments about the tip I live in.'

Anna didn't know where the time had gone but they were still in the hospital, in a small plain room that she imagined they kept for people in their position. Bereaved relatives.

Her mother hadn't looked too bad. There were no marks on her face and the medical staff had obviously done their best to clean her up and make her presentable. But Anna had not seen the back of her head. Edward had told her he'd found Rosemary face down with the heavy vase lying on the back of her skull. Anna could imagine the damage that had done. She hoped oblivion had come quickly – that any pain had been brief. The doctor who had spoken to her assured her that would have been the case. But then, what else could he say?

Edward had said he thought she was dead when he found her but the air ambulance medics had discovered a pulse and shipped her out as fast as they could. But all their speed and skill had not been able to save her. She'd been dead on arrival at hospital.

The paramedics must have called the police. Two uniformed officers had turned up at the hospital to take a statement from Edward. It seemed they had already visited the yard and Tom had let them into the Hall so they could view the site of the accident. There would probably be an inquest, they said, the timing would be down to the coroner. They were solicitous and sympathetic and Anna thanked them as they left.

Tammy had remained at the hospital, ferrying coffee and tea, most of which had gone cold in the cup. Anna had regularly told her to go home and then realised it would be a laborious journey for her without a lift.

'We must go,' Edward said.

Anna was reluctant. It seemed disloyal. And final – leaving without her mother was an admission that they had to get on with their lives without her.

Katherine said, 'My car's here. Who can I take?'

But it was agreed she should go straight on home. The rest of them would fit into Anna's car and Tammy could be dropped off on the way back to the Hall.

They said goodbye in the gloom of the car park. Katherine hugged them all.

Anna hung on to her cousin. 'Are you going to be all right?' she asked.

'Are *you*?' Katherine replied.

'I've got Edward. You're going home alone.'

'You know, the timing of this is all wrong. I can't get over the fact she's never going to see her grandchild.'

Anna said nothing – she couldn't.

Katherine released her and fumbled for her car keys. 'I've got sleeping pills. I'll call tomorrow.'

Anna watched her get into her car and then led the others to her own vehicle. She pushed the keys into Edward's hand and took a seat in the back, next to Tammy.

Edward turned to Freddy as he started the engine. 'You'd better stay with us tonight.'

For a split second of stupidity Anna wondered why. Then she realised with a lurch that her brother was suddenly without the rock on which his entire life was based. The woman who organised and fed him, who slept in the room next door and kept a benign eye on his every movement – his principal carer – was no longer at her post.

Of course, she'd always known a day like this would come, that one day her handicapped brother would be her sole responsibility, but it was not something she'd ever planned for. How do you plan for the unthinkable?

'Yes,' she said. 'We can pick up some of your things as we go by.'

Freddy shook his head. 'No thanks, better not.'

She leaned forward and put her hand on his shoulder. 'You can't be on your own tonight, Freddy.'

'Why not?' He turned to her. 'I've got stuff to do and I'm sure you have too. The dogs are going to need feeding and everything before I turn in.'

'Just bring them up to the Hall. They're used to it.'

He shook his head and stared mulishly at the road ahead. 'No. Mum wouldn't want that. Things are fine as they are.'

'Come on, mate,' Edward chipped in. 'We'll just worry about you down the drive on your own.'

'I don't want you to worry about me. I'll be all right. Mum and I talked about this, you know. She said there was no reason why I couldn't look after myself in the house. I've just got to stick to my routines, like she said.'

Anna didn't know what to say to that. She knew better than to try to bully her brother into doing something he didn't want to do. But after they'd dropped Tammy off at her home, with a hug and profuse thanks for her help, Anna had another try.

Freddy remained adamant. 'Look, Mum's still keeping an eye on me down here, me and the dogs. The house is mine now, anyway. She told me it was fixed that way in her will. But you can come and stay with me, if you like.'

They left him there fussing around Lodger and Porky. What else could they do?

In the event it was twenty minutes before Greening opened his door to Carmel.

'Doesn't your boyfriend mind you heading out this late?'

She laughed. 'It's only eleven. Late is four in the morning – when we go clubbing.'

'I see.' Not that he did particularly. He'd done his

share of partying in his youth, though nothing that could fall under the heading of clubbing.

'Anyway,' she added, 'he's spending the night with his mum in Reading. He often does that when I'm working in the evening.'

Greening made no comment. He was pleased Carmel had lost her shyness in his company and seemed happy to share the domestic trivia of her life. He couldn't deny it reminded him of conversations he'd have with Amy. Now Yvonne had put the idea of a daughter substitute in his head, he could see he would not be able to get rid of it.

She accepted a mug of coffee, minus the whisky, and curled up in the opposite corner of the sofa. Without prompting, she launched into a description of her encounter with Amanda.

Greening wasn't surprised to hear that Glyn and his assistant had been having an affair. So some of Mrs Shaw's gossip had some substance after all. What was more surprising was that Carmel had got it out of her.

'She's worried we're going to talk to her husband. He was very jealous of Glyn.'

Greening had worked that out long ago.

'Talking to Mr Yates sounds like a good idea. He's the closest we've come so far to a likely suspect.'

Carmel blinked at him in surprise.

'Come on, Carmel, you must see that. He's a possessive young fellow, angry that his fiancée's fallen for her boss, so he takes him out of the picture. He'd probably have to get a mate to help him but it's a possibility.'

'But I sort of promised her we wouldn't go bothering him if she told me the truth about her relationship with Glyn. She thinks her marriage is on the line.'

'That's not our concern. I don't think your sort of promises count for much in these circumstances.'

'So I've lied to her?'

'Welcome to the real world of policing, Carmel. Look at it this way, if you've pointed the finger at the culprit by telling a few porkies then you'll have done us all a favour. Including Mrs Yates, I may add. Would she want to spend the rest of her life with a killer?'

Carmel sipped her coffee, plainly thinking things over. 'She as good as told me he'd beaten her up when he first suspected her.'

Greening smiled. 'I think I shall enjoy talking to Mr Yates.'

Carmel nodded. She appeared to have accepted that there was no cushioning Amanda from the blunt end of the investigation.

'She told me it was all over with Glyn by the time he disappeared and that it couldn't have been her in his car in April two thousand and eight.'

'And you believe her?'

She thought for a moment, weighing the matter in her mind. 'I do, actually. The way she tells it, she was seriously considering dumping Ian for Glyn when he fell for someone else. He confessed as much and they ended the affair. She says the blonde in the car must have been the new woman.'

'Who is?'

'She doesn't know. She says she didn't want to find out because she'd had a bad experience obsessing over another woman in a previous relationship. Does that sound likely?'

She looked at him seriously. Obviously she had never been in such a situation. Long may that last, he thought.

'Personally,' he said, 'I think there's no limit to a woman's curiosity about a rival. But maybe she's telling the truth. Once bitten, twice shy and all that.'

'I believed her. If she does know, why didn't she say? She told me other things. She brought up the man Pam told me about in the pub. I didn't even have to ask. The Dutchman – you remember.'

Greening remembered very well. He eagerly cross-referenced Carmel's information with what he'd learned from Katherine about the tall, football-loving Jan, the one friend they had identified so far from Cole's past.

'Amanda says Jan showed up just before Glyn disappeared. He had another man with him, a big guy in a fancy leather coat called Errol.'

Oh? That was interesting.

'It was Saturday afternoon and she was on her own in the shop because Glyn was at an auction. She says he was late back and the men hung around because Errol wanted to talk to him about a deal.'

'What kind of deal?'

'She didn't know. She got Glyn on the phone and he said he was on his way and it was OK for her to go because it was after closing time. So she left them in the shop and went home. That was the last time she spoke to Glyn.'

'Did she say anything else about this Errol?'

'Just that she didn't take to him. They'd fixed a time to meet Glyn and Errol had a bit of a tantrum at being kept waiting. He took it out on her, apparently.'

'Took it out how?'

'Shouted at her. Was rude and aggressive. She said she was happy to get on her way.'

Greening considered what she'd told him. 'Well done, Carmel. Before you walked in I had no suspects and now you've just handed me two.'

'Two suspects?'

'Ian, the jealous boyfriend who knocks his fiancée about – we already mentioned him. And now there's Errol, the aggressive visitor who wants to do some kind of deal. Maybe Glyn won't play ball and things go wrong. Errol and Jan could easily get a body up a tree. Of course, Jan makes three. Thanks to you, Carmel, it's raining suspects.' He chuckled. 'Are you considering a career as a regular police officer?'

She didn't join in his merriment. Her mouth set in a small hard line. 'Are you making fun of me?'

His laughter died abruptly. He was tired and the whisky hadn't helped.

'Certainly not, Carmel. I think you are a very impressive young woman. And as a consequence of what you have just told me, my team will shortly be taking proper statements from Mr and Mrs Yates.'

She nodded, somewhat mollified, and stood up.

'It's time I went home.'

At the door he said, 'I wasn't joking about you becoming a regular officer. You ought to think about it. I'd back you.'

She gave him a solemn look. 'Thank you, sir.'

'Alan,' he corrected but she was already walking down the steps to her car.

It had been raining, not hard but enough to muddy up the footpaths and soak the grass, so the dogs were wet by the time Freddy got them back to the gatehouse. After he towelled them dry he gave them some biscuits as a treat. His mum did that sometimes when they'd been left waiting or gone for an extra long walk – whenever their routine had been particularly disturbed. And it had been disturbed today. They never normally had to wait until nearly midnight for their evening walk.

'Good doggy, Lodger,' Freddy said. 'Good doggy, Porky.'

These words were not part of his usual vocabulary, they were his mother's. Rosemary spoke to the dogs like that whenever she was pleased with them. Now she was no longer here, he would have to replace her as best he could. They were his responsibility now.

Lodger the lurcher suddenly dashed from the kitchen and the little terrier bustled after him down the hall. The pair began to bark in chorus. Someone was at the front door.

Freddy approached warily. Whoever it was did not ring the bell, they must know the dogs' clamour made that unnecessary. He anticipated Anna or Edward. Why wouldn't they understand he didn't need a babysitter? Even tonight.

But it was Will. He stood awkwardly on the doorstep. 'I just heard.'

Freddy held the door open for him to come in.

'I'm not intruding, am I? Tell me to go away if you want.'

'It's OK.' Freddy did not want him to go. Will was his friend. It felt right that he had come.

The dogs were quiet now, though still frisky. They trotted happily beside the two men as they returned to the kitchen. Freddy shooed them away with a stern command.

'I've got to look after them like Mum did,' he explained. 'This is my place now.'

Will nodded. He was going to say stuff about Rosemary, Freddy could tell. He wished he wouldn't but people always felt they had to say stuff when someone died.

'I'm so sorry. Your mother was a great woman.'

That was true. He was glad Will thought that. He just hoped his friend wouldn't go on about it, though, or he would get upset. Mum had taught him he should try not to get emotional. If he cried he would find it hard to stop. Then he wouldn't be able to sleep and if he didn't sleep he'd find it hard getting up and getting on with things. And he had two lots of jobs in the morning now before he went to the yard.

'Are you all right, Freddy?'

Will was looking at him as if he was about to give him a hug, which would be terrible. He'd cry then for sure.

'I'm good,' he said firmly. 'Would you like a cup of tea? We have Jammie Dodgers.'

'Er, thanks.' Will was still looking uncertain but he backed away as Freddy filled the kettle and hunted out the biscuit tin.

'I suppose Anna sent you to check up on me.' It had just occurred to him. 'She's worried I won't be able to look after myself but I'm fine. As you can see.'

'No. I've not spoken to Anna.'

'So who sent you?'

'No one sent me. Tammy rang me when she got home from the hospital and I thought of you.'

Tammy. Freddy had not considered her. She'd been very nice to him at the hospital even though she'd been upset too. And she'd been in the car when they were driving back so she knew that he'd be on his own.

He decided he didn't mind whoever had sent Will. He was glad he had come by. It helped that he wasn't on his own.

He had an idea.

'Do you want to watch a DVD?'

Will hesitated. 'Sure.'

'We can watch *Star Trek*.'

Freddy picked up his mug and the biscuit tin and led the way into the front room. Will followed.

As he loaded the player he had a thought, about Tammy and Will. At dinner the other night they'd not even spoken to each other.

'I didn't know you were friends with Tammy,' he said.

'Sure we are.' Will was being casual but Freddy could see through it.

'Are you in love with her?'

'Leave it out, Freddy.'

'Don't sound shocked. Yes or no will do.'

Will's mouth flapped. He didn't know what to say, obviously.

Freddy laughed. It felt good to laugh even on a night like this. 'Caught you. You love her, don't you?'

'I like her a lot.'

His friend had coloured up, gone all embarrassed. Freddy didn't blame Will if he loved Tammy, she seemed the kind of girl a man could easily love. He himself had never been in love and didn't want to be. He'd seen what it did to people, even nice, good people like his sister.

Who would have thought little Anna could kill someone? Yet she had, because she'd been in love. And he and Will had had to protect her from the consequences.

'Just you be careful,' he said.

Will stared at him. 'What do you mean?'

'What I say, mate. Tammy's a lovely girl but you take care.'

Will considered the advice. 'OK. Thanks.'

'No problem.'

Freddy leaned back on the sofa and pressed Play on the remote. As the screen sprang to life, he couldn't help smiling.

If his mum had been here he would never have been allowed to do this.

Greening had run out of milk so he made his breakfast porridge with water. He'd read somewhere that porridge was ideal for people with a chaotic working life. Even if you only ate rubbish food all day, the article said, a nutritious and sustaining breakfast of oats was the secret to healthy living. He made it standing over the stove, stirring slowly and that, he reckoned, was its chief benefit. Stirring time was thinking time. It gave him a moment of calm to plan the day ahead.

His mobile rang mid-stir, which was a nuisance as he needed one hand to anchor the little saucepan and the other to wield the wooden spoon.

'Morning, boss.' It was Yvonne. 'Have you heard? Rosemary Drummond died last night.'

Rosemary Drummond? For a second he was at a loss. Mrs Drummond with the smartly cut grey hair and lively eyes and a bark like a sergeant major when she called her dogs? The energetic walker who had found a man's corpse in a tree and held a press conference spellbound as she described picking up his disembodied foot. A woman like that was built to last forever.

He turned off the gas and sat down at the kitchen table. 'Tell me.'

'She fell down some stairs up at Pitchbury Hall, crashed into a table at the bottom and a vase fell on her head.'

'A vase?'

'An ugly great stone thing, according to the officer who attended. Air ambulance got her to the Great Western in half an hour but she was dead on arrival.'

'A freak accident then.'

'Looks like it.'

Jesus. He took a moment to absorb the information. He'd talked to Rosemary on a couple of occasions, the first time shortly after she'd discovered Cole's body. She'd been unflustered and precise as she'd described what had happened. He'd thought to himself at the time that his job would be a sight easier if all witnesses were like her. And when, a few days later, he'd given her a lift home after the press conference, she'd told him a bit about life at Pitchbury Hall.

Her family would be devastated. Her daughter was pregnant and Edward, the son-in-law, was a hotshot horse trainer – he'd seen him on the television. And Rosemary had introduced him to her son when he'd dropped her off – big, sandy-haired Freddy. Who'd nearly died as a boy and still suffered from the effects of his near-drowning. Rosemary could certainly talk – it hadn't been that long a car journey.

'I'm very sorry to hear it,' he said. 'She was an admirable woman.'

'I suppose so.' Yvonne was hard to impress. 'At least it's not going to screw up the investigation. Everything's in her statement, isn't it?'

'That's true.' He couldn't imagine a reason why he would have needed to talk to Rosemary further – apart from the pleasure of doing so, of course.

Time to return to business.

'I'm glad you called. I want Glyn Cole's assistant, Amanda Yates, and her husband Ian brought in to Farley Road pronto. Keep them apart.'

'What's going on?'

'It turns out Amanda was having it off with her boss, and her husband, who was her fiancé at the time, was suspicious.'

'Just suspicious?'

'Suspicious enough to thump his girlfriend. He's the jealous type. Jealousy and aggression add up to a possible murder motive in my book. I've also been puzzling over Cole's broken fingers. Maybe he was tortured before he was killed. A jealous lover might be nasty enough to go in for that kind of thing.'

'You bet.' Yvonne sounded almost enthusiastic.

'So we bring Ian Yates in and make him feel uncomfortable, see what we get out of him. OK?'

'Some proper action at last then. Excellent. I'm curious, though.'

He feared she would be. 'Yes?'

'You saw this Amanda and her husband the other day. What's changed?'

'A little bird tells me that Mrs Yates is now prepared to admit to her liaison with Cole.'

There was a pause. Greening could imagine Yvonne's sniffy expression on the other end of the line. 'A little bird spelt PCSO, I suppose. Are you having late-night chats, Alan?'

'This is work, Yvonne. Spare me the lecture.'

There was a heavy sigh before the connection was cut without even a barbed sign-off.

Greening returned to his porridge, adding more water and stirring vigorously to try to get it back to life.

How old was Rosemary Drummond? They'd printed her age in the paper – sixty-four. Jesus, that was only ten years older than he was. Ten years, that was close. It would be gone in a blink and then maybe some stupid collision with a vase of flowers would claim him too.

The phone rang again. 'Yes?' he snapped.

'Ooh, Dad, you sound grumpy. Is this too early for you?'

Amy, his daughter. His mood flicked from black to sunshine yellow in an instant.

'Too early for *me*? I didn't think you students saw the world in daylight.'

She laughed, a breathy hiccup she had inherited from her mother. Somehow it didn't irritate when Amy did it.

'Actually, it is early for me but it's a big day and I've got to muster the troops for tonight. That's why I'm calling.'

'Yes?' He was none the wiser.

'Dad, you are coming, aren't you?'

'Coming to what?'

'Hal's show in Oxford. It's the opening – don't say you didn't get the invitation.'

Invitation? Nobody invited him to anything, unless you counted crime scenes and post-mortems.

'I asked the gallery to put you on the VIP list,' she said, sounding anxious now.

'Gallery' rang a bell. There had been a card in the post the week before, glossy on one side with writing in a funny texture on the other, like the feel of an emery board. A bit weird. The writing had spelt: Harold's House of Haptics. Hal – Amy's artist boyfriend.

Suddenly Greening felt stupid. Somebody must have told him the lad's proper name but he only knew him as Hal, a lanky tongue-tied individual with no dress sense. He seemed attentive to Amy though, so he was OK in Greening's book.

'Yes, of course,' he said heartily. 'Hal's show tonight – wouldn't miss it for the world. But, er, just remind me of the time and place, would you? I've put the invitation somewhere safe but I can't remember where.'

She gave him the details in a tone that suggested she knew very well he'd chucked it out.

'Will your mother be there?' he asked casually.

'No. She's got some dinner in the City with Archie.'

Archie was Sir Archibald Stanhope, a big-deal investment banker and Justine's boyfriend. The only good thing about the recent financial crisis, in Greening's opinion, was that it was open season on bankers.

'Is that why I've been invited, because your mother's somewhere else?'

'No, Dad. Of course not.'

'One more question. Am I going to understand this art?'

'That's not the right question to ask. You've just got to be open to new things – check your prejudices at the door. You can do that, can't you?'

'I'll try my best, sweetheart.'

He rang off, the excitement of hearing from her dissipated by the thought of the evening ahead. Only ten years of his life left and one whole night of them spent staring at things he didn't understand surrounded by people less than half his age.

He suspected that the porridge wasn't the only thing beyond salvation.

Chapter Eleven

Greening was gratified to discover that Les Davis had got his teeth into the materials that he and Yvonne had brought back from Wales. Les had turned the computers over to a lad who specialised in IT, and Cole's account books and bank statements to another with a head for figures. He himself had hung on to the phone and general correspondence.

'I suppose it's a bit early to ask if you've come up with anything,' Greening said as he started on the muffin he'd brought to his desk in lieu of the failed porridge.

'You suppose right,' Les said. 'I've only had a quick flick through the papers and I haven't even turned the phone on. It's still charging.'

'Your flick through didn't unearth any threatening letters? Or perfumed billets-doux?' Greening took a sip of his Americano with hot skinny milk: if you asked for a white coffee these days the girls in the fancy café down the road looked at him blankly – he'd had to learn a whole new vocabulary.

Les eyed the drink enviously. 'If I'd known you were going out I'd have put in an order. I've been here since half seven.'

'Find me the motive for Cole's murder in that stuff you're looking at and I'll buy you one of these every morning.' Greening raised the coffee carton in a toast. Actually, it wasn't that marvellous. And how long did it take, exactly, before you stopped missing sugar?

He dismissed the thought and ran through his mental list of outstanding matters. 'Any news on Cole's wristwatch?'

'I've just heard back from Mr Venables,' Les said. Venables was the expert who'd agreed to take a look at it.

'And?'

'He didn't come up with any great insights. The glass face is missing but that could have been caused by any kind of knock.'

Greening nodded. They both had a pretty good idea of the knock in question. Whoever had been so keen to smash Cole's hands had probably clouted his wristwatch at the same time.

'The hands were stopped at three thirty-eight, quite possibly because of the blow that removed the face. That could be morning or afternoon, of course. But he says be careful not to read too much into the exact time because it's possible the watch could have gone on working after it was damaged.'

'So it could have carried on ticking away on a dead man's wrist?'

'Indeed. And packed up any time over the past two years.'

'Good God.' It was a macabre thought. And not a very helpful one.

Greening moved on to the next item on his list.

'How's Dougie getting on with Cole's clothes?'

'I haven't heard anything. I don't think he's got the lab report yet.'

'Can't he sniff anything out for us? Hasn't he got a mate over there who can give us a steer?' Waiting for the official report could drive a man crazy.

'I'll give him a call.'

'You do that. I'd put a rocket up his arse myself but I've got Cole's assistant twiddling her thumbs in an interview room.' He got to his feet.

'We still don't have a clue, do we?' Les said, following suit. 'About why poor old Cole got bumped off. Or even how.'

'You're not going defeatist on me, I hope. I think we're starting to make some progress.'

Les raised his eyebrows but said nothing. He continued to look glum – which was par for the course.

Greening said, 'You haven't had any luck with the Dutchman, have you?'

Les shook his head. 'I spoke to the internet clothes lady, Pam Bellamy. She told me she'd only met him a couple of times and knew very little about him. She promised to ask her husband, see if he had any idea how to get hold of him.'

'OK. And there's a good chance he'll turn up in your trawl through Cole's stuff, I suppose.'

'If he's there, we'll find him.' Les turned for the door, then stopped. There was something else on his mind. 'Pam Bellamy said she told some off-duty PCSO about the Dutchman, in a pub. That would be this Carmel, would it?'

'Correct.' Les must have been talking to Yvonne.

'She handled Cole's missing person report in the first place and has been assisting the inquiry.'

'So I gather. The pair of you have been out drinking together.'

'The pub was Cole's local. It's on her patch. Don't look at me like that, Les. Yvonne has already given me a lecture about Carmel but it's all legit.'

'OK.'

'She's been useful. Carmel is a smart girl.'

'And looks barely out of school, so I'm told.' Les shot him another lugubrious stare. 'Be careful, boss, won't you?'

Amanda Yates had brought a solicitor with her for her interview, a woman not much older than herself, dressed in a severe dark suit and rimless spectacles. Miss Bracken was on her feet before Greening had a chance to close the door behind him.

'I want it on the record, Inspector, that you are harassing my client.'

'That's not my intention, I can assure you. I see you've had some tea.'

He'd left them kicking their heels for twenty minutes but had made sure their creature comforts had been attended to.

'You have already visited my client at home and your colleague accosted her in the street the other day.'

'You mean PCSO Gibbs? She's just been aiding us in an informal capacity.'

Amanda was on her feet as well. 'She promised me if I told her about Glyn you'd leave Ian alone and now you've arrested him!'

That was true. Yates had been booked into the custody suite in the bowels of the building. Greening would get to him later.

'I'm sure you appreciate, Mrs Yates, that the investigation of a murder is a serious business. The information you gave PCSO Gibbs has important implications and, I'm afraid, she was in no position to make promises to you.'

'That's outrageous.' Her face was thunderous. Greening hoped that she would not be running into Carmel any time soon.

'You are not currently under arrest and are free to leave,' he said pleasantly. 'However, may I suggest that if you want to clear this matter up – and be of most help to your husband – we take a statement from you now.'

Amanda and Miss Bracken held a whispered conversation. By his side Yvonne shot him a quizzical glance. If the two women walked out, it was plain she would not be impressed.

But they didn't. Miss Bracken made a speech about the lengths to which her client had already gone to assist the police and how keen she was to dispel any misunderstandings which might have led to her husband's arrest.

Greening summoned more tea and, to show good will, biscuits, which they all ignored. He then prompted Amanda to supply a summary of her affair with Glyn Cole, which she did in rather less rapturous terms than Carmel had reported.

'And what was your fiancé's reaction when he found out?' Greening asked.

'He doesn't know about it. Please don't say anything to him, Inspector.'

'If he doesn't know about it, why did he beat you up then?'

Amanda almost dropped her teacup. 'He never did.'

'That's what you implied when you spoke to PCSO Gibbs.'

'Look, Ian became jealous of Glyn but it was finished by the time he suspected anything. We had the odd row but it all blew over. We're very happily married.'

'So he never hit you?'

'He might have done but I think I hit him first. We made it up later – you know, like couples do.'

Greening ruminated for a moment. He didn't know whether to believe her or not.

'So,' he continued, 'it's not true that he discovered proof of your affair with Glyn Cole after it was over and flew into a rage, which he took out on you physically—'

'No, it's not true!'

'And then he subsequently took it out on Mr Cole, with fatal results.'

'No!' shouted Amanda.

The solicitor jumped in. 'Are you suggesting my client is an accessory to murder?'

Greening was considering the possibility. After all, it would have taken two people to get Cole's body up the tree. But Amanda, with her memorial brooch and impassioned confidences to Carmel, didn't fit his idea of an accomplice, before, during or after the fact.

'I wasn't suggesting that. Should I be?'

'Don't be ridiculous,' said Amanda. 'Neither Ian nor I had anything to do with Glyn's death. I made a bit of a fool of myself and Ian was upset about it but it was over by the time Glyn went away.'

Greening decided he'd prodded that particular wound for long enough. He had sympathy for Amanda's predicament, though that was an irrelevance.

He turned to asking her what had gone on at the shop just before Cole's disappearance. She gave him an account that matched the one she had described for Carmel. That she'd had two visitors, Jan the Dutchman and Errol in the leather coat.

'What nationality was Errol?'

'English, a southerner but not local. They'd come down from London specially to see Glyn. Errol was fed up because Glyn was late. He gave the impression that his time was precious and if Glyn was serious about doing business he'd have shown up as agreed. I didn't like him.'

'What kind of business was he talking about?'

Amanda shrugged. 'He didn't tell me – I wasn't important enough. He mostly just spoke to Jan and poked around the shop like it was his place. I had to stop him going upstairs.'

'Why did he want to do that?'

'He knew – from Jan, I suppose – that Glyn lived above the shop. It was like he thought he might be up there. "Is he hiding from me?" he said. "Does he want to do the deal or not?" In the end I got Glyn on his mobile and he told me something had come up to delay him but he was on his way. I was running late myself, so he said I could go and it was all right to leave them in the shop.'

'And you have no idea what kind of deal he was talking about?'

'Absolutely not. It could have been anything. Glyn's whole business was doing deals.'

It had been a long and terrible night for Anna. She and Edward had sat in the kitchen. He'd fixed himself a sandwich but she'd refused to eat anything. And now, the morning after, her sickness had returned with a vengeance.

The hours had gone by in a haze of nausea but she'd welcomed the discomfort. Her mother was dead, stolen from her without warning, and physical pain seemed appropriate.

Edward had hovered around her at first until she'd ordered him away.

'Aren't you needed in the yard?' she'd said. 'I thought you were going to Windsor today.'

'Yes, but in the circumstances . . .'

'The circumstances are horrible but you're doing no good here. Mum wouldn't want you moping around – she'd tell you to buck up and do your job. You know she would.'

It had taken a while to persuade him to go. She'd had to promise she'd get Tammy to look after her before Edward agreed. Then she'd just lain in bed, punctuated with trips to the bathroom to throw up. She had no intention of calling Tammy. She was suddenly conscious of how much she was leaning on her. Last night at the hospital had been an emergency, of course, but there had been the dinner the night before. She was being very selfish with Tammy. The poor girl had her own sick mother to worry about.

But during a phone conversation with Katherine – Anna had urged her to stick to her plans too – Tammy had appeared. She'd caught a taxi, she said – her bike was still at the Hall.

Anna had to admit it was a relief to see her and they hugged like sisters – or as she imagined sisters would – then she made herself get up and eat the toast Tammy prepared for her in the kitchen.

'Will spent last night at the gatehouse with Freddy,' Tammy said.

This was news to Anna. She knew Freddy was OK this morning because Tom had called from the yard to say he was going about as usual.

'I called him when I got home,' Tammy continued, 'and he said he was going straight there. Then he texted to say he was staying over.'

Anna wasn't surprised, Will had an interest in keeping an eye on Freddy, as she did too. She thought back to this time the day before, when all she'd had to worry about was whether her plan to push Tammy into Will's arms had succeeded. It seemed a distant concern now.

'You can rely on Will,' she said. 'He won't let you down.'

She noted that Tammy did not disagree.

Greening ate a sandwich in the canteen, as much to clear his head as to fill his stomach. It had the added advantage of keeping Ian Yates waiting a little longer.

Let the steam build up inside that choleric young man, he thought, and see if he blows his top. It was invariably revealing to hear what a suspect said when he was too angry to watch his tongue.

As he chewed without tasting, his phone rang. At first he couldn't tell who was on the other end. Then the penny dropped.

'Hi, Dougie, what have you got?'

It was hard to make out the Scotsman's words against the canteen clatter so he took the call in the corridor.

'Les says you're getting het up about the clothes report. Don't you fret, sir, you'll get it soon. They're snowed under.'

'So, what's new? I don't want them thinking that because our man's been dead for two years they can take just as long doing my report.'

Dougie laughed. 'No chance of that. I've been on the phone to one of the guys I know. I've got something for you.'

Thank the Lord for that. Greening listened eagerly.

'They found hairs on his clothes. At least four different kinds. They're analysing them now.'

'Four different kinds? You mean colour? Texture?'

'I think it's more a question of species. Apparently two types are human but they're not certain about the others.'

Greening reflected. An image of Buster, Cole's walking hearthrug of a cat, sprang instantly into his head. Removing the animal's long white hairs from his trousers had taken an age after their encounter at Mrs Shaw's house.

'Cole had a black-and-white cat. Very hairy. That will account for one set, I bet.'

'OK, good. Another is going to be the deceased's own hair.'

'And the other two sorts? Got any info on them?'

'Yes. Blond hair, apparently, just a couple of strands. Long.'

That made sense. A woman's hair, Greening would put money on it. The new lover – Cole's mystery blonde.

'And?'

'The last lot is short and coarse, brown in colour. It hasn't yet been officially confirmed but my pal tells me he's sure it comes from a horse.'

Greening didn't know what to think about that.

'Thanks, Dougie. Tell your mate he's a genius and keep sitting on him. We need that lab report.'

As expected, Ian Yates was not a happy bunny. He was more like a hopping mad bunny, to Greening's eye. The eruption on his cheek was still there, no longer a fresh pink spot but an ugly maroon blotch, firmly established. He'd been arrested and cautioned at his office – a recruitment consultancy in Reading – and taken to Farley Road police station where he'd been booked into a cell and left to fret. Now he faced Greening across an interview room, his solicitor – provided from the duty pool – by his side.

Yvonne was in charge of recording the proceedings, which promised to be lively as Yates immediately began to shout.

'What the bloody hell do you think you're playing

at? I've been dragged out of my office like I was some psycho terrorist. I knew you were a bastard when you barged into my house and upset my wife. I had meetings scheduled all morning and instead I've been sitting in a prison cell. You're costing me money! Is that the idea? I'm going to sue you for wrongful arrest.'

The solicitor, Anthony Buckley, a cadaverous fellow of Greening's generation, laid a restraining hand on Ian's sleeve.

'Let's listen to what the inspector has to say. Perhaps he can explain why you have been subjected to an entirely unnecessary ordeal.'

'Hardly an ordeal,' Greening said calmly. 'I'm sure the custody sergeant has been solicitous of Mr Yates's well-being and informed him of his rights.'

'I've been fingerprinted and photographed. They took my bloody DNA! It's outrageous.'

'We have only treated you in the manner which is prescribed by law.'

'But was this arrest necessary?' Buckley said. 'I'm sure my client would have been more than happy to answer your questions in less threatening circumstances.'

'We are investigating a murder. It's a very serious matter.'

'You're off your rocker if you think I've got anything to with Glyn Cole getting killed,' Yates shouted. 'It's ridiculous.'

'How did you get on with Glyn, Mr Yates?' It was time to ignore the bluster and proceed with the interview.

'He was a smarmy ponce,' Yates snapped, then added, 'but I got on with him OK.'

'You seem a little confused.'

'No. I got on with him all right at the beginning – he was Mandy's boss so I had to. We used to go to the pub. The three of us.'

'When was that?'

'When Mandy first started in the shop.'

'The autumn of two thousand and seven?'

'If you say so. Yeah. He was all right then, bought plenty of rounds. He didn't act like Mandy's boss.'

'So, what changed?'

'Nothing really. I got a bit sick of him, that's all.'

'Sick of him because . . . ?'

'Because he got too pally. I just went off him.'

'Did you go off him because he was too pally with Amanda?'

Yates glared at Greening, no doubt calculating how much he knew.

'Glyn Cole had women drooling over him all day long. Some of us work hard at getting a girl and keeping her. He didn't have to try.'

'So you were jealous of him?'

'Not exactly. But I was concerned that my fiancée was working so closely with a guy like that. Wouldn't you be?'

'I certainly would. And were your suspicions justified?'

Yates blinked. 'What do you mean?'

'Did Cole and Amanda have an affair?'

He thought about that. 'Not to my knowledge.'

'So you were just jealous on principle?'

'No. We were going through a bit of a bad patch in the New Year. I thought she'd gone off me. Was getting cold feet about us getting married, anyway.'

Yates had calmed down now and was talking slowly. Greening wondered if this was the first time he'd seriously reflected on how their relationship had developed at that time.

'There was a misunderstanding. Mandy and me ran into a mate of Glyn's who thought she was Glyn's girlfriend. He tried to cover it up, but it was bloody obvious. That freaked me out a bit. Afterwards me and Mandy had words.'

'And that's when you hit her, I suppose.'

Yates was out of his seat in a flash. 'That's a lie, I never.'

Buckley reached out a restraining hand once again and gripped his client's elbow. Yates remained standing, quivering with emotion as he demanded, 'Who told you that?'

'She did. About an hour ago.'

'What? You've banged her up too?' His face was anguished.

'No. Mrs Yates attended of her own free will and has now left the premises.'

Yates slumped back into his seat, deflated by the information and calculating, no doubt, how damaging his wife's testimony might be.

'Yeah,' he said quietly. 'We had a flaming great row about Glyn, it went on all night. In the end, I slapped her, I admit it. You know what women are like—' He stopped, staring guiltily at Yvonne. 'I mean, they can really wind you up. She twisted my words so I was the paranoid bastard who wanted to flush our relationship down the pan when she was the one who was two-timing me. That's what I thought anyway. Of course, the moment I touched her, I suppose I lost the argument.'

Silence fell, broken by the solicitor who said, 'Surely, Inspector, you're not thinking of charging my client over an ancient domestic dispute?' He looked at Yates. 'How long have you been married?'

'Nearly two years. Things have been great since then. I admit I went a little crazy when I thought I was going to lose Mandy to Glyn but she stuck by me. We got over it.'

'Good for you.' Greening smiled. 'It must have helped when your wife was no longer working for Glyn Cole.'

'That's true.'

'So you were pleased when the job came to an end?'

'Sure.'

'Of course, the reason it ended is because Mr Cole disappeared. Did you have anything to do with his disappearance?'

'You're joking! Of course not.'

'But we have established that you believed Amanda was having an affair with him. That your jealousy made you a little crazy. That it made you violent. Can you honestly say you didn't turn that violence on Glyn Cole.'

'No, I bloody didn't.'

'But you must have wanted to. Considering what he was getting up to with your fiancée. And when he disappeared, all your troubles with Amanda were over. I'm looking for the person who killed Glyn Cole and it seems to me that you had a very good motive.'

'This is ridiculous.' Yates turned to his solicitor. 'He can't say these things about me, can he?'

'Just remain calm. The inspector needs to present evidence to a court to substantiate his lurid allegations.'

'But I had nothing to do with him getting killed. And by the time he vanished I wasn't that bothered about him and Mandy anyway. Maybe they had had a fling and maybe they hadn't but I knew it was all over, like she told me.'

'How did you know?' Greening asked.

'Because I saw him with another woman.'

That was interesting. 'Would you like to expand on that?'

'Before he disappeared Mandy told me she was sure Glyn had fallen for someone. Fallen like a ton of bricks, she said. I couldn't make out why she'd told me, except to put me off the scent. It made me more suspicious, I admit. So I used to keep an eye on Glyn sometimes. Evenings when Mandy said she was going to the gym or meeting a friend, I'd pass by Glyn's place and see what he was up to. A lot of it was a waste of time but once I saw him with a girl.'

'Can you describe her?'

'She had long blond hair – that was the first thing I noticed and it gave me a turn. I was looking up at the window of his flat from the street and I saw this flash of hair. I thought it was Mandy.'

He stopped.

'Would you like a glass of water?' Greening offered.

Yates shook his head. 'I waited on the pavement, just staring at that window, my guts all tied up in my stomach. Part of me wanted to break down the door and go charging in. Another part said it was my own fault. I'd come looking to catch them out and I'd done it and only made myself feel worse. Then the woman came back to the window and looked directly down into the street. It wasn't Mandy.'

'Do you know who it was?'

'Not a clue. Pretty, I suppose. Young. And she wasn't wearing much that I could see. Just a bra. What you'd expect of a woman in Cole's bedroom. When she saw me looking up, she backed out of sight.'

'Did you tell anyone else about this?'

'Who am I going to tell? I'm hardly going to say to Mandy that I've been snooping on her. And it's not something you tell a mate, either. They all thought me and Mandy were solid. And we were. Why does it matter?'

Greening didn't answer that. It had the ring of truth but he would have liked to verify it. He was pretty sure by now that Yates, for all his belligerence, was not Glyn Cole's killer. But he would prefer to eliminate any doubts.

'I'd like you to test your memory, Mr Yates,' he said. 'Can you remember any of your movements in mid-April two thousand and eight? Specifically the week beginning Sunday the thirteenth.'

Yates snorted. 'Don't ask much, do you?'

'I realise it might be difficult to come up with an

answer right away. You may need to consult old diaries and talk to friends. And your wife, of course.'

Buckley reacted to the implication. 'So you won't be charging my client then?'

'Not on this occasion.' It wasn't an offence in Greening's book for a young man to behave like a prat when his girlfriend put him through the wringer. Yvonne would doubtless disagree.

'You'll be able to go home shortly,' the solicitor said but, surprisingly, Yates did not react.

'I know where I was that weekend in April,' he said. 'Cricket tour in Cyprus.'

Greening wondered whether he'd ever heard a more unlikely alibi. Whether he'd even heard the words 'Cyprus' and 'cricket' in the same sentence.

Yates was smiling for the first time. It had to be said, it improved his sullen appearance no end.

'Yardley Green Old Boys go off for a pre-season cricket tour every year. It's a bit of a jolly really, we go where there's cheap booze and a bit of sun. Cyprus is brilliant.' He saw the disbelief in Greening's eyes. 'There's a fair bit of cricket there, you know. Because of the army bases. And there's leagues and some youth cricket in the schools. We usually get walloped but who cares? I can show you the pictures, Inspector.'

Greening got to his feet and held out his hand. 'I'll look forward to it, Mr Yates,' he said.

'Am I free to go then?'

Greening nodded. The interview was over.

Tammy fetched a bucket of warm soapy water and a black plastic bin bag from the kitchen and climbed the stairs to the first-floor landing. Anna was in the bedroom. She'd been persuaded to lie down after a lunch of soup and crackers. Tammy hoped she was asleep. Fortunately the bedroom was at the opposite end of the corridor from where Tammy intended to work.

Edward had called earlier, after Anna had gone upstairs, and Tammy had answered the phone.

'Don't disturb her,' he'd said. 'I'm just checking to see she's all right.'

Tammy had asked if there was anything in particular she could do.

Edward had paused, then said, 'I don't like to ask but would you mind taking a look where Rosemary fell? There was a mess, flowers and water everywhere. And, well, blood. If you don't feel up to it, say so.'

'It's OK.'

'All you've got to do is straighten things up and get rid of the flowers, just so Anna doesn't see it like that. I meant to do it but I forgot.'

She hesitated. 'Is it allowed? I mean, the police don't need to take photographs or anything, do they?'

'They've taken them. They told me they've done all they have to do and won't be coming back.'

Now Tammy got down on her knees beside the hall table and gathered up the roses and broken greenery which had formed the flower display. Heavy feet had trodden the stems into the grey of the hall carpet. She placed the pieces in the bag.

Lying on its side in a dark circle of moisture was the vase that had toppled from the table on to Rosemary's head. Tammy didn't want to touch it but dismissed all superstition and gripped the yellowish patterned marble. She'd been told – by Rosemary, ironically – that it was called fossil stone and contained plants, shells and other ancient tiny organisms, which accounted for its swirling patterned surface. The thought had given her pleasure in the past as she'd dusted around it. Now the thing filled her with disgust.

She righted the vessel and examined it for damage. There was none, which seemed unjust. She wiped its outside surfaces and lifted it back on to the table. It was certainly weighty enough. The thought of it smashing into the back of Rosemary's skull made her sick.

She surveyed the floor and the ominous wet patch. There was a darker staining close to the table. That would be the blood. There was less of it than she had imagined.

She used the soapy water, letting it dilute the stain and then wringing out her cloth in the bucket. She wouldn't be able to clean it all away but it was the attempt that mattered. Edward had said he would be replacing the carpet. For the moment she just needed to expunge the worst.

She did her best and stood back. Something about the arrangement didn't look right but what more could she do? When the carpet had dried she'd find a rug to hide the stain.

Along the corridor, the bedroom door opened.

'What are you doing?' Anna called. 'Oh,' she added as she took in the bucket and the bag.

'Edward asked me to—'

'I see. Thanks very much.' Anna had changed into jeans and a dark blue top and brushed her hair. She looked pale but stronger than before. 'Will you come with me upstairs?' she said.

'Of course. Why?'

But Anna didn't answer. Tammy put the bucket down and followed.

The gallery seemed more of a nightclub to Greening than a venue for displaying art. He entered through a heavy door and followed a line of people heading downstairs. A voiceless soundtrack of electronic music played, drowning out the possibility of casual conversation.

So far he had not seen Amy or Hal and he knew no one. He trailed behind the woman ahead into a dimly lit cubicle where a gust of warm air enveloped him, followed by a blast of cold. Then into another small space where invisible threads caught at his face. This enclosure was succeeded by another – unseen hands plucked at his clothes.

He was beginning to get the idea. This was about isolating the senses and stimulating them individually. 'Harold's House of Haptics'. Didn't 'haptics' mean something to do with the sense of touch?

He hadn't anticipated a conventional display of artwork but this was beneath his minimal expectations. He had given up an evening in front of the TV for this?

No, he admonished himself, he had come to please his daughter. If only he could find her.

He raced through the succession of little rooms,

trying to note the trick encapsulated in each so that he could pretend enthusiasm when he came face to face with Hal.

The space below was dark and cavernous, and much larger than he could have anticipated from ground level; it seemed to take an age before he was through. He'd been a good sport, he reckoned – taking off his shoes to walk in warm green sand, thrusting his bared arm through a curtain where it was caressed by something cool and slimy.

If this was art, then so was the average five-year-old's birthday party.

At last he was at the foot of stairs which led him up into a brightly lit room, full of people. Animated chatter and bursts of laughter filled the air. Girls with too much lipstick proffered glasses of wine. And on the walls hung brightly coloured abstract paintings – conventional and derivative no doubt, but no less welcome to his eyes.

He stepped closer to look at one. There was no sign of his daughter and genius boyfriend, so he might as well.

'What do you think of it?'

He turned to find a woman in a stylish cream suit by his side. She was well groomed, glamorous and, unlike most of the company, not young enough to be his child.

'Hello, Miss Pym. What are you doing here?'

Katherine treated him to a wide smile. 'I'm a friend of the gallery owner. I once bought one of his paintings. Nothing like any of this dross though.'

They turned away from the wall to face the crowd.

Still no Amy, though that seemed to matter less right at this minute.

'Before you're rude about the exhibition downstairs,' Greening said, 'I must tell you the artist might one day become a member of my family. My daughter is very keen on him.'

'I'd like to meet him. Young artists are always entertaining.'

Greening had finally spotted Amy in the far corner where the laughter was loudest and the girls the most ostentatious. He imagined that Hal was embedded somewhere in the throng.

'You're in luck,' he said. 'Follow me.'

Anna sat on the sofa while, across the room, Edward consulted the computer, making notes as he did so. There were many things to be done in the wake of her mother's death and she was glad he was prepared to take charge. In a few moments they would drive down to the gatehouse so he could root through Rosemary's desk and trace some necessary information – her National Insurance number, marriage dates, tax references and so on. Edward had been told he had five days in which to register the death, unless the coroner decided an inquest was required. They were waiting to hear.

She felt both guilty and grateful that Edward was taking the lead. She would do her part – she'd already spent over an hour on the phone notifying cousins and friends. But she'd not made half as many calls as she'd intended, for each had taken time. People were shocked, they wanted chapter and verse, some wanted to reminisce, others had cried. On reflection, maybe notifying another human being of a death was more demanding than dealing with the bureaucracy.

She knew her thoughts were confused at the moment and she was in no state to get to grips with the sudden loss of her mother. But it seemed important to hold on to what she could so she would be able to think about it later. That's why she'd gone with Tammy to the little room where Rosemary had been rummaging through the family heirlooms. She'd peered accusingly at the carpet at the top of the stairs where her mother must have tripped, though there were no obvious holes or rips in the material, just the same wear and tear as before.

The door to the room had been closed, the key in the lock but not turned – she guessed her mother had been intending to return. As she stepped inside, she thought to herself, 'Mum was here yesterday.' It seemed unreal – she must have accepted the fact of death already.

The room looked much as it had the evening before last, when Rosemary had begun hunting for that damned watch. Anna hated the thought of the thing, real or imagined. If an inanimate object could be held responsible for a death then that horrible watch was guilty.

She noted more boxes had been opened and articles lined up on the floor. She recognised the paperweights her mother had been fond of.

'Mum would have been the last person to stand in this spot,' she said aloud, as if it would somehow bring her back. That was silly. Her mother remained no less dead.

'What was she doing up here?' Tammy asked.

'She was looking for an old watch. She thought it had gone missing.'

Tammy absorbed the information as she looked around. She picked something up off the top of a chest of drawers.

'Didn't this belong to Mrs Drummond?'

It was a little book with a floral fabric cover and Anna recognised it at once. Her mother carried it in her handbag and regularly produced it.

'Yes. Mum was always making lists.'

The book was now on Anna's lap as she sat in sombre silence, her brain a whirr of activity.

Her mother had been making a list in the upstairs room just before she fell. Written in red ballpoint, which she habitually used, the entry was the last in the book and headed 'Missing', underlined twice. There were three items:

1 Curio watch
2 Millefiori paperweight
3 Great Exhibition snuffbox

Why had she made this little list? Anna knew her mother was convinced the watch was missing but did it mean the other items were missing as well?

She knew that this was significant but now was not the moment to bother Edward with it. Somehow she'd fathom it out.

Greening stood on the steps of the gallery, his duty done. All the same, he was vaguely dissatisfied. He'd have liked to be able to prise Amy away from her crowd.

He'd tried. 'Fancy a bite to eat?'

'We're all going out together later, Dad. You're welcome to come with us.'

But he'd ducked that and he could see that Amy had been relieved. He'd have cramped her style no end and he could see that the competition for Hal's attention on his big night was fierce.

She'd felt guilty about it though. 'I'll come and see you next week and we can spend some proper time together,' she'd said.

'Is that a promise?'

'Of course!'

And they'd left it at that. Now he was hanging around in the street outside, telling himself he should go home.

The door opened behind him and Katherine Pym appeared.

'Had enough of the teenage fun?' she said.

'Yes. And you?'

'They're all very sweet but they will insist on reinventing the wheel.'

They stood there for a moment, contemplating the empty street. The sky still held light, it was not late.

'I was sorry to hear about your aunt,' he said.

She looked him full in the face. She had almond-shaped eyes. Almond in colour, too – at least in this soft light.

'You must think badly of me, coming to a frolic like this the day after her death.'

He'd made a note of it but he wasn't going to judge her.

'To be honest,' she added, 'I couldn't stay at home

and I couldn't face going up to the Hall. This seemed like a way of trying to get it all out of my mind.'

'And I've just reminded you. Sorry.'

'Don't be. These things don't go away.'

He jingled the keys in his pocket. Time to say goodbye.

Instead, he said for the second time that night, 'Fancy a bite to eat?'

Chapter Twelve

'Are you sure you're comfortable with this? It's not against the rules or anything, is it?'

Katherine put these questions to Greening as he led her into the dining room of the Crested Grebe near Lechlade. They had driven there in convoy. The place had been recommended to Greening by Yvonne as 'an OK gastro pub, nothing special'. He'd had it in mind to take Amy, if he'd been able to lure her away from her friends, but here he was with a different dining companion altogether. It was a bit late to be questioning this spontaneous dinner arrangement. Besides, Greening was hungry.

'Having a meal with a friend is not against any rule I'm aware of,' he replied as he took his seat. 'In any case, I'm off duty.'

'That's a relief. I was worried you were going to subject me to another grilling about poor Glyn's death.'

'I promise I'll spare you this evening.'

'In that case, I can relax.' She smiled at him – a conspirator's smile. 'Thanks for stealing me away. This is nice.'

Through the window by their table, the lawn sloped down to a river where swallows flitted in the dusk. On either side of them, diners were toying with glasses of wine and a waiter was hovering with a set of menus.

They quickly ordered food and, after a moment's hesitation, a bottle of Prosecco. Greening justified it on the grounds they didn't have to drink it all.

'Women don't make toasts, do they?' Katherine said but she raised her fizzing glass all the same. 'Here's to Aunt Rosemary.'

Greening drank to that – how could he not?

'She was almost a mother to me,' Katherine added.

'Really? What about your own mother?'

Katherine shook her head. 'Let's not go there, Inspector.'

He pulled a face – what did he have to do to get people to see him as a person, not a police functionary?

She fielded his displeasure.

'That is – Alan,' she placed a cool hand over his briefly, 'I mean I'm having too good a time to get into my family history. Maybe later, if you're still interested.'

Their food arrived.

'So,' she said, spearing a piece of broccoli, 'have you found out how Glyn died yet?'

'I thought you didn't want to talk about it.'

'It's better than talking about my mother. Anyway, it's a bit of a mystery, isn't it? The whole up-a-tree thing. I'm intrigued to know how you go about solving it.'

He shrugged, swallowed a mouthful of steak and considered how much it was prudent to tell her. When he thought about it, there was little to do with Cole's remains that he had to hold back. The broken fingers. For reasons of taste, if nothing else.

'The fact is, there wasn't much left of the body by the time it was found. Once the natural process of decomposition is over, no soft tissue remains – no flesh, no organs, no skin. Just bone and hair. The pathologist could find no skeletal damage which would have accounted for his death.'

'No sign of anyone bashing him on the head, you mean?'

'Exactly. No broken neck, no bullet holes, though it's possible he was shot in some vital area which did for him. No damage to the bone though. Bit of a pity.'

Her almond eyes pinned him with reproach. He recalled that the dead man had not only been her friend but, once, her lover.

'I'm sorry. I didn't mean to suggest it was a pity he hadn't been shot.'

'Don't worry about it.' She drank deeply. 'I suppose doing what you do makes you . . .' She searched for the right term.

'Professionally insensitive. That's true, I'm afraid.' Except he'd always prided himself on being able to see the human being in the victim – the father or daughter in the ravaged corpse. Sitting opposite this elegant and vulnerable woman, he suddenly felt as if he were just a cold-blooded flatfoot.

She treated him to one of her inclusive smiles. 'You're not insensitive, I can tell. People like me can afford to be sensitive, we just swan along enjoying our comfortable lives, but you confront the horrible things that people do every day of the week. We should be grateful a man of your taste and intelligence is doing such a cruel job on our behalf.'

He was aware he'd just been shamelessly flattered but the remarks had been timely. It had been too long since an attractive woman had issued a compliment to his face.

While he was still basking in its glow, she said, 'It must have been difficult getting Glyn up that tree. Do you know how it was done?'

Relieved to be on home ground, he explained his theory of how the body had been disposed of.

'I think a couple of men rigged up a block and tackle and hauled him up there. Probably soon after he was killed. You're right, it wouldn't have been easy. But you can get a car off the road by those trees where he was hidden and there's a few hours in the middle of the night when you're not likely to be disturbed.'

'You think it was two people?'

'Mr Cole was a decent-seized fellow, so I think that rules out one man. Two seems the most likely but there could have been more – another to keep a lookout, for example.'

'It sounds very organised. Do you think it was a criminal gang?'

It had occurred to Greening. If Cole had been mixed up in a dodgy deal that had gone sour, or withheld money from some nasty people, that might account for the damage to his hands. Professionals would not be squeamish about torturing a man for information or, simply, revenge.

'To your knowledge,' he asked, 'did Mr Cole have any business relationships with people who were at all suspicious?'

Katherine laughed, a low mischievous sound. 'If he did then I wasn't suspicious of them. The antique business is full of funny characters. None of them are likely to kill you and put you up a tree, though. I'm sorry, but aspects of this are so bizarre.'

'That's OK. I just thought, as you did his books, you might know of anyone he'd fallen out with in some business matter. Or maybe a deal that was a bit iffy.'

All laughter had gone from her face now. 'As far as I'm aware, Glyn's business affairs were completely above board. I can't answer for anything he didn't put through the books but Glyn was not a criminal. I can assure you of that.'

There was a sticky silence, covered by the removal of their plates. She waved away the dessert menu but said, 'You go ahead,' which, of course, he didn't feel able to do. But, for once, the lure of a pudding was dimmed by his new companion. If he could eat with a woman like her every night he'd have a double incentive to turn down sweet things.

'Was Mr Cole a horse lover?' he asked, thinking of his conversation with Dougie and the hairs that had been discovered on Cole's clothing.

'Of course,' she said. 'We're all horse lovers around here, aren't we?'

He nodded in agreement, though his own

enthusiasm for the gee-gees was limited to the office sweepstake at Grand National time. He suspected this level of ignorance was not likely to impress a woman closely connected to the Pitchbury yard.

'I mean,' he continued, 'did he go riding?'

'Sometimes.'

'Where?'

She thought for a moment. 'He hunted occasionally and he knew plenty of people who had horses.'

'Attractive young blond people, by any chance?'

She sipped her drink and stared at him over her glass. 'What makes you say that?'

'I thought it was well known Cole had an eye for blonde women.'

'He had an eye for women, Alan.'

He considered her own colouring, a rich dark brown in the candlelight. Cole had found Katherine Pym attractive, he knew that, and he doubted that such an acknowledged ladies' man would have restricted himself to just one type. The evidence was doubtless coincidental. Nevertheless, Dougie's information was not restricted to horses.

'We're pretty sure he was involved with a blonde girl at the time of his death. And we've found blond hair on his clothes.'

'Amanda,' she said. 'The girl who helped him in the shop. You are aware that he was thick with her, aren't you?'

She didn't look as if she approved of Amanda.

'We've spoken to Mrs Yates. She says that their romance was over by the time of his disappearance and that he was in love with someone else. Someone fair-haired like her. Have you any idea who that might be?'

In the kitchen at the gatehouse, Tammy took out her purse. Supper plates were in the sink and Freddy was out walking the dogs. Will sat opposite her. It was the first time they'd been alone since he'd taken her home from the dinner party at the Hall.

'Anna gave me some money,' she said and fanned some notes out on the table. 'She just took this out of Mrs Drummond's handbag and said I should have it.'

The handbag had been in the living room at the Hall and Tammy had found it. Anna had looked through the contents and said, 'Mum didn't pay you for the other night, did she? Take this.'

It amounted to just under £200.

'I feel uncomfortable,' Tammy said. 'But she wouldn't take it back.'

'This isn't instead of your wages, is it?'

'No. That's paid into my bank, it's all set up properly.'

'I should take it, if I were you. And if Rosemary was going to pay you for the dinner party, you've earned it.'

'Not this much. I was expecting twenty quid.'

He shrugged and flashed a big all-encompassing grin. He didn't see her problem, that was plain, and she wasn't sure she could articulate it. Her relationship with Anna was proving a puzzle. She felt that, with the events of the past few days, she'd crossed the boundary from employee to friend. She'd been the happy victim of Anna's scheming which had put her back in Will's arms, stood by Anna's side at the hospital throughout the nightmare of her mother's death, and discovered the notebook in the upstairs room which Anna had seized on gratefully. But being given these banknotes was like a slap in the face, a reminder that she was just paid help. Not that she couldn't do with the money but how exactly did Anna look on her?

Then there was the continuing puzzle of Anna's hold over Will.

She didn't know what to think. She only knew she was involved with affairs at the Hall and couldn't extricate herself even if she wanted to.

Will caught her hand and lifted it to his lips. 'We could go upstairs,' he said.

Freddy had asked Will to stay at the gatehouse and the three of them had been discussing the arrangements over supper. Fortunately there were three rooms upstairs, two bedrooms used by Freddy and, until yesterday, Rosemary, and a tiny box room which had been equipped as a spare bedroom. It was cramped and awkward, having accumulated a variety of belongings that Rosemary intended to house elsewhere. Freddy and Will had shifted these things into Rosemary's room, leaving just a narrow bed, a wardrobe and a chair. But that, of course, was enough.

Will ran a long finger up the inside of her wrist, a gentle touch that made a large impact. She knew he wanted to take her upstairs to bed and that, in another minute or so, she wouldn't be able to resist. But it didn't feel right. Not yet, not here.

'Will,' she began, then she heard the crunch of wheels on the drive outside. The vehicle stopped.

Will rolled his eyes in exasperation and released her hand.

The wine was having an effect, Greening realised – on Katherine, not on him. She had polished off most of the bottle in her quiet way.

Somehow the matter of her mother had returned to the agenda. Sufficiently mellowed, she now seemed prepared to talk about her.

'Grace was four years younger than Aunt Rosemary,' she began. 'I always called her Grace, she never wanted to be called Mummy. I used to think that was very sophisticated when I was ten or so, it made us sort of equal – I was her best friend, she said, a shoulder to cry on. She used to tell me everything, more than she should, about her boyfriends, her politics, her hang-overs, all the stuff a kid needs protecting from. I thought it was great until I realised that she was my responsibility. It should have been the other way round.'

'What about your father?'

She pulled a face. 'I had a dozen fathers or none at all, depends how you look at it. Grace was twenty when she had me. That was nineteen seventy, so you can work out just how old I am.'

Greening did so, of course. He wished he was still forty but he'd never looked as youthful at that age as she did. These days, it seemed to him, women looked fantastic at any age – some of them, that is.

She emptied the last of the bottle into her glass.

'Grace was supposed to be studying in Exeter. Teacher-training. But she'd gone off to live in a derelict farmhouse with a group of other drop-outs to live the hippy dream. They kept pigs and geese – and just about any animal they could get hold of – baked their own bread, lived off benefits and what they could flog. To be fair to them, they stuck it out. I was the eldest child but other women had babies too. Childcare was "collectivised" – that's how Grace described it to me when I was older. All the adults there were meant to be my parents. But I knew Grace was my mother. My father, on the other hand . . . I never found out.'

'Surely your mother knew.'

She shrugged. 'She said she wasn't sure. It could have been one of three or four. You remember the age of free love surely?'

He nodded, though in his opinion love had never been free in any age. But he didn't want to debate the matter. Katherine's personal history was more interesting.

'So what did your grandparents make of this? Your mother was brought up in pretty conventional circumstances, I imagine.'

'Not entirely. Grandad had turned the Hall into a hotel after the war and I think it was hard graft for the whole family. I remember Grace saying that she was forced to work as a maid in her school holidays and only got an extra half-crown in her pocket money. But it's true she had all the conventional creature comforts. And more – private school, her own pony, the Pitchbury acres as her own secret garden. She was privileged but she rebelled, of course. After she dropped out, she scarcely ever saw her parents. They freaked, especially after Grace had me, couldn't understand what she was doing. Bitter family breakdown. The usual drama. You can imagine.'

'Where was Rosemary in this?'

'Aunty was the good daughter, naturally. She was virtually running the hotel in her twenties, keeping the family business afloat. A dashing horse trainer came to stay one weekend and she targeted him. That was my Uncle Jack. He was fifteen years older than her, obsessed with winning Classic horse races and with a string of old girlfriends who'd all failed to tie him down. A bit of a sexist pig, if you want to know, but I adored him, he was always sticking up for me. He met his match in Aunty. Within a year she'd married him and they turned Pitchbury into a training yard. Jack had the Two Thousand Guineas winner in his first season there and they were never short of owners after that. Are you sure you aren't finding this a little boring?'

He shook his head.

A waiter appeared and offered them coffee. They agreed.

'And a large cognac,' she added. 'Don't worry, Alan, I'm catching a cab home. I'll pick the car up tomorrow.'

He wondered if she was saying that just because he was a policeman.

'Anyway,' she continued, 'Aunty kept in touch with Grace. I think she used to give her money. She regularly brought me back to Pitchbury for visits when I was little. I was a bridesmaid at her wedding even though, at first, Grace refused to go because her parents would be there. But Aunty talked her round. Then, later, I went to live at the Hall so I could go to a decent secondary school, which was a relief. The hippy commune had broken up by then and Grace went off to Greenham Common. To the women's peace camp.'

Greening remembered the protest of the early eighties. He'd been a uniformed constable when it attracted a media frenzy. At the time he'd wondered how he would feel if he was asked to police the camp. His colleagues had been scathing about the 'wimmin' but he'd kept his mouth shut. He'd thought they'd showed a lot of balls. He said as much to Katherine.

She grinned. 'It was also quite convenient. Greenham's not that far. Aunty used to take me over there and Grace would come back with us for a bath. On one of these visits she was upstairs for ages and we were waiting so we could have lunch. Aunty sent me to see what was taking her so long.'

She stopped and sipped her cognac, swirling the pale liquid in her glass for what seemed like an age. Greening wondered whether to prompt her but held his tongue. He knew that she was playing up the drama but he was a willing audience.

'She was in the bathroom on the top floor, she always used that one because she was used to it from when she was a kid. I knocked on the door but there was no answer. I knew she was in there because the door was locked, which I thought was odd. Grace was a great one for railing against locked doors – they'd even taken the doors off the toilet back in the early days of the commune. Symbols of the barriers between people and all that. And she was always walking around naked, embarrassing the hell out of me. So I was suspicious.'

This time he did prompt her. 'What did you do?'

'I looked through the keyhole. There wasn't a key because the door was locked with a little bolt higher up. I couldn't see much, just the sink and the side of the toilet pedestal. The bath was out of sight but the clothes she'd been wearing were on the floor. Some grotty old dungarees and her Indian scarf. I banged hard but she didn't answer. I thought maybe she'd fallen asleep and I wondered if you could fall asleep in the bath and drown. And God knows what she had taken. She'd seemed sober enough that day and she claimed she'd given up drugs now she'd become political but I knew she was taking pills for her depression so I panicked. I called her over and over. "Mummy," I said. I didn't call her Grace like normal, I just screamed, "Mummy!" There were a pair of horse statues in one of the bedrooms, horrible old metal things – iron or bronze, I'm not sure. Anyway, they were heavy. I fetched one of those and stood in front of the door. She still didn't respond to me shouting. I knew I should go to fetch Aunt Rosemary but that would lose time. And, anyway, I thought if she had done something stupid and I could get to her first, then maybe Aunty and everybody wouldn't need to know. I felt protective of her. I was twelve and she was thirty-two but sometimes I felt like the grown-up. So I broke down the door.'

She finished her brandy and looked Greening in the eye.

'I suppose you've seen plenty of dead people. I'd never seen one before. She'd fallen asleep in the bath, all right, only the water had turned raspberry red, like a jelly before it sets. It looked very pretty. And so did Grace. She didn't look careworn or disconnected or angry like she usually did. She was smiling. She looked happy. That's always been a comfort.'

'She'd cut her wrists?'

'Just one. The left. They found a Stanley knife in the bath water. I found out later – Uncle Jack told me because it impressed him – Grace only made two cuts. Deep, right through to the artery. No tentative slashes or anything. She knew what she wanted to do and she did it.'

'That must have taken courage.'

'That's what Uncle Jack said. "Your mother didn't live in the real world," he told me. "But she had real guts." ' Katherine smiled to herself. 'You could say she wasn't a woman for half measures.'

'So where did that leave you?'

'Feeling guilty, of course. I should have saved her. I could have got up there quicker, I could have kept an eye on her – I should have been less happy living with Aunt Rosemary and Uncle Jack. I'd got a new life I loved. I'd abandoned her.'

'Come on, you were a child. None of this could possibly be your fault.'

'I know that. I knew it at the time really but you can't help what you feel, can you? Anyway, my lovely new life wasn't so great after that. Not long after Grace died, Freddy fell in the horse swimming pool at the yard and poor Aunty had a terrible time. We all did, just waiting to see if he'd recover. How well he'd recover.'

'He seems to do all right to me. But I only met him once.'

'He was a brilliant kid before the accident. Very bright. After, it was as if someone had replaced a hundred watt bulb with a forty.'

Greening didn't know what to say to that.

She covered his hand with hers. 'Sorry to be such a downer. I'm not always a depressing date.'

'You'll have to prove that to me then,' he said as he called for the bill.

Tammy, in the garden behind the gatehouse, heard the back door open and footsteps on the path. She hoped it wasn't Anna or she'd feel obliged to kill the cigarette she'd just lit. But it was Will. He didn't say anything, just pulled her into his arms and kissed her.

'I taste of smoke,' she said when they finally broke away. 'I'm sorry.'

'You taste of you. You should never be sorry about that.'

'I'm going to give up, honestly. But it's hard at the moment.'

'Ssh.' He kissed her again, hungrily. She knew what he wanted. One of the advantages of him moving into the gate-house was that they could spend time together. He hadn't been able to take her back to his old digs and every move they made at her parents' house was under scrutiny.

She pulled back, it wasn't easy. 'I'm sorry, Will, but would you take me home?'

There wasn't much light at the end of the garden but she could make out the disappointment on his face. But he didn't complain or whine, like some boys would when they were itching to get a girl to stay.

'OK. Do you want to go now?'

'Please.' Now was a good time. Anna and Edward were still in the house with Freddy, going through Rosemary's things. And if she got home now she could sit with her mum and talk to her before she got too tired.

She didn't say any of this though. She threw away her cigarette and hugged Will tightly. 'I'm sorry.'

'Don't be.' She could hear the smile in his voice though she couldn't see it. If he'd asked her to stay then she would have given in. But he didn't.

For a woman who appeared a bit squiffy, Katherine dealt efficiently with the three locks on her door and her burglar alarm. Greening could understand why a woman living on her own in a secluded spot would need that kind of reassurance. He had driven her home and, at her request, was accompanying her inside her house. Though she had tripped on the doormat in the dark porch and leant on him for support, she tapped a code into her security system by reflex.

'There wouldn't be much point in calling the police out tonight,' she said. 'Not with you here.'

He'd laughed but, as she'd walked ahead of him into the kitchen, flicking on lights as she went, he began to feel awkward. Though he was sorely tempted, making a pass at a witness in a current murder case when she'd had a few too many drinks would not be a bright move. Besides, he really liked her. He didn't want to spoil anything.

'Coffee?' she offered, as he'd known she would.

'Not tonight,' he said.

'Who says there will be another night?' She leaned back against the kitchen counter, kettle in hand. She had fine legs, as she was doubtless well aware.

In the restaurant, she had insisted on splitting the bill, producing a credit card for the waiter and asking him to divide it up. Greening's protests had been dismissed on the understanding he could treat her 'next time'.

'I mean,' he said, 'why don't I call you tomorrow? Maybe we could fix another occasion then – if you still want to.'

She put the kettle down and brushed the hair out of her eyes. 'Sure,' she said and pushed past him to walk ahead of him down the hall. She held open the front door and smiled without artifice. She didn't seem at all drunk now.

'Thank you for a lovely evening,' she said.

'Thank *you*.' There was an awkward moment while he wondered if a kiss was expected. But, a friendly peck or something more?

She solved his dilemma by kissing his cheek and leaning the length of her body into his.

'Next time,' she said softly, 'let's talk about you.'

She pulled back, then plucked a hair from his jacket. It was long and brown, one of hers. She considered it.

'You say you found hair on Glyn's clothes?'

'I haven't had the lab report yet but that's what I've been told. Blond hair.'

'How are you going to find who it belongs to?'

He shrugged. 'That's why I was asking.'

She giggled. 'You could take samples from all the blonde girls in the county. I bet you'd get volunteers for a job like that.'

'They'd be queuing up, I'm sure.'

'It would take you ages,' she said. 'The place is full of blondes.' She held up the brown strand. 'Grace was dishwater blonde. Aunty had hair like ripe wheat before she went grey. I'm about the only brunette in our family.'

He'd got it wrong – she was still pissed. And entertaining though he found it, he knew he should go.

With a final 'Goodnight' he turned for his car. It was too dangerous to stay.

Greening's phone had been turned off all evening. He'd obeyed a request at the gallery to shut it down while going through Hal's display and had forgotten it. Now, as he stepped inside his front door, he remembered and turned it on.

There were three missed calls and one message. The message was from Amy saying how great it was to see him and sorry she couldn't get away and she'd visit him next week – all the things she'd already told him. He hoped she wasn't feeling too guilty about leaving her old man to fend for himself. After all, he'd not done too badly.

The missed calls were all from the same number. He didn't recognise it. While he was trying to figure it out, the number called again. It was Carmel.

'I'm sorry to disturb you,' she said breathlessly, 'but I thought you'd want to know.'

'To know what?'

'I had a call from Pam Bellamy. She's the woman—'

'Your friend from the pub. I remember.'

'Yes. She's found the Dutchman's name.'

Excellent. He said so.

'Her husband had an old business card and she read me out the details. It's a bit of a funny name – you'll need a pencil.'

But Greening had already worked that out. He sat at the kitchen table with a pad from the drawer. 'Fire away,' he said.

When she'd finished spelling it out, he found he'd written 'Johannes Vandeneijnde' and the name of a company, Cornelius Bakker Fine Arts, with an Amsterdam address.

'It's in the Spiegelkwartier,' Carmel told him. 'You know.'

He didn't but he knew she'd tell him.

'It's a historic neighbourhood near the Rijksmuseum. The heart of the antiques trade.'

'Have you been reading a guide book?'

'It's true. Google it and you'll see. You do have a computer at home, don't you?'

There was a note of exasperation in her tone – very Amy, he had to admit. Where was the girl's deference towards him now?

'Yes, Carmel, I have a computer and am quite able to use it. What's more, I have a team of IT nerds at my beck and call. Why, incidentally, did your Mrs Bellamy bother you with this? DS Davis spoke to her on this specific point earlier, she should have called him.'

It was a bit unfair to put Carmel on the spot for that but it didn't hurt to reassert the chain of command. And she was right at the bottom of it.

'Oh,' she said. 'I think she just likes me. And she sort of knows me from being out on patrol.'

That was fair enough. He could see why someone might prefer to talk to sympathetic and unthreatening Carmel than lugubrious Les. And there was no denying the girl did seem to come up with the right answers.

He'd thought of something else to test her with.

'Your boyfriend plays a bit of cricket locally, doesn't he?'

'Yes?' She sounded puzzled, which was not a surprise, it had been a sudden change of tack.

'He doesn't play for Yardley Green Old Boys, does he?'

'Of course not. He didn't go to Yardley Green.'

That would have been a bit of a coincidence.

'But he does play against their seconds,' she said. 'I don't think they take it too seriously.'

'Would you happen to know whether their first team head off to Cyprus in the pre-season?'

'I can find out. Why?'

He told her about Ian Yates. It was the nuttiest alibi he'd heard for ages, so nutty he had little doubt Yates could stand it up. Still, it made sense to check it out independently.

He ran through the details with Carmel and she promised she'd get Robbie to ring one of his Yardley Green mates.

Chapter Thirteen

Carmel had given Greening two numbers for Jan. He tried the mobile first but it only connected him to telephone limbo. The second was a landline, to the antique business, he assumed. At least it rang.

'Met Geerd Bakker.'

'Alan Greening.' Carmel had given him a lecture on Dutch manners – he was supposed to say his name first. He had no idea how she knew this stuff but he was beginning to trust her. 'Do you speak English?'

'Of course, Mr Greening.'

Of course. Greening guessed he was a Dutch antique dealer – he probably spoke ancient Sumerian as well.

'Is it possible for me to speak to Johannes Vandeneijnde?' He had a valiant stab at the pronunciation. 'Shall I spell that for you?'

'There is no need. I know exactly who you mean but Jan is no longer associated with this company. May I be of assistance?'

'I'm sorry, Mr Bakker, but I'm not a customer. I am an English police officer and I would like a word with Mr – with Jan – about an inquiry.'

'Oh, I see.' The man sounded more English than most of the people Greening spoke to in the course of a day. 'May I ask what kind of inquiry?'

Greening wondered how much to divulge. The advantage of telling the truth was that requests for information were liable to be taken seriously. He'd found people more likely to be generous with their time and endeavour once he'd mentioned the word murder. Which he did now.

Geerd Bakker was impressed. Greening could clearly hear the inrush of breath as he gasped.

'Surely you don't mean Jan has killed someone?'

'That's not what I said. But if he had, would that surprise you?'

'Very much. Jan may have had his troubles with our own police, as I'm sure you know, but I never thought of him as violent. Oh dear. Do you mean to say we might have been in danger? This has come as a bit of a shock.'

Plainly the Dutchman was a man of a sensitive disposition. Greening quickly backtracked.

'I didn't mean to alarm you, Mr Bakker. There's no suggestion that Jan has harmed anyone but he may possess information which would be useful to me. Do you know how I can find him?'

'Oh no. I haven't seen him for years – not for two years at least. And we were just work colleagues, nothing more.'

'You don't know where he went to work after he left your firm?'

'No. Absolutely not. I know nothing about him.'

Mr Bakker was beginning to sound flustered.

'You say he was in trouble with the police – can you tell me when that was?'

'A long time ago, ten years at least. My father only took him on because he said every man deserves the benefit of the doubt. It was an act of generosity.'

'Is it possible for me to speak to your father?'

'He died in two thousand and seven, Mr Greening. I run this business now and I have a very busy day ahead of me.'

That was a hint, in anyone's language.

'I'm most grateful for your assistance, Mr Bakker. Just one more question. Do you know why Jan had a problem with your police?'

'Oh yes.' His voiced dropped to a horrified whisper. 'Drugs.'

'Was he dealing?'

'I couldn't possibly say. I know nothing about it – absolutely nothing.'

Greening smiled to himself. He'd thought all the sophisticates of Amsterdam were blasé about illicit substances. Obviously not.

Thanking Bakker for his time, he left his contact numbers and rang off.

Anna ran off two copies of the Pitchbury Hall inventory from Edward's computer. Fortunately, it wasn't hard to locate. As in everything he did, Edward was methodical and the files on his side of the computer were organised with military precision. Good luck to anyone who went hunting for stuff in the chaos on hers.

So, under a folder titled Hall, she located a document

named 'Inventory 208' – February 2008. As the printer chuntered away, she tried to suppress her memories of that time and, as ever, failed to do so. Those were days when joy and despair had greeted her waking self each morning, when she'd longed to slip back into sleep to escape. And this document she was printing had been the cause of the turmoil. If her mother had not insisted on its compilation then she'd never have met Glyn Cole. But how could she wish she'd never met the man who had given her the most vivid and thrilling moments of her life?

She pulled the sheets of paper out of the machine and organised them. The guilt was still strong. Even to be handling the list that Glyn had painstakingly created made her feel she was being disloyal to Edward. It was unfair the way negative feelings endured for longer than positive ones. It was easy to feel again the dead weight of betrayal on her shoulders yet so hard to recapture the wind of ecstasy that had once promised to carry her away.

Maybe she was fooling herself, trying to keep alive the memory of her passion. What was that passion anyway, when it came down to it? Just the urge to possess someone exclusively and use them for your selfish needs. And her selfishness had resulted in her lover's death. Glyn had remained exclusively hers, all right. Maybe she had got what she wanted all along.

'Shall I make up your bed?' Tammy was in the doorway. She could have been there for some time.

'No. I want you to help me with something.' Anna stapled the loose leaves into two sets and held one out. 'Forget about the cleaning. This is more important.'

Tammy looked curious. 'What is it?'

'When Mum moved down to the gatehouse with Freddy she had an inventory done. She was checking the items on it the other afternoon, just before she fell down the stairs. I want us to go over it and finish the job she started.'

Tammy took the sheaf of paper. She looked uncertain. 'Is this to do with insurance?'

'Not really. Mum thought some things were missing.'

'The things on the list in her notebook?'

Anna nodded. 'I'd like to know what she was thinking before she fell. I'm probably just being neurotic.'

Tammy shook her head. 'In your place, I'd want to know too.'

'Then let's get started.'

Greening flicked through the half-dozen pieces of paper Les had placed in front of him – a list of phone calls generated from Glyn Cole's mobile phone. The bottom three sheets were an actual phone bill from Orange which Les said he had discovered in the papers supplied by Dee.

For the past five minutes, Les had been giving him a breakdown of the callers he had identified. A separate sheet listed the names in the address book stored on the phone itself.

'As far as we can tell, and it's early days, most of these people are customers or drinking mates plus a couple of family members.'

'I didn't think he was in touch.'

'Well, his sister is there. Dee – that's her, isn't it? And there's an Aunt Claire.'

Greening remembered Dee mentioning the aunt who ran the farm shop with her. Maybe Glyn had kept an eye on his family after all, though at one remove. The sibling relationship had obviously been tricky.

'What about Jan?'

'Oh, he's here.'

Les had been busy with his magic markers. He'd blocked in Glyn's conversations with the Dutchman in blue, of which there was a little sea on the page. There was just one snag.

'It's the same number I've already tried,' Greening said. 'I didn't get anything.'

'That's a Dutch mobile, isn't it?' Les said. 'Starts zero six. Let me see if I can trace it with the phone company.'

The office door opened. 'Found anything?' Yvonne said.

'Too early to say. We're still hunting this bloody Dutchman.'

'Just as well you've got me to help out then, isn't it?' She plonked a sheet of paper on Greening's desk with an air of satisfaction.

It was a fax page, with a blurry photo of a man captioned in a language he could not follow.

'What's this?' he said.

'The bloody Dutchman, I believe.'

'Good Lord, really?' He looked more closely. The man was shaven headed and thick necked with a solid mono brow and a sullen expression.

'How did you get hold of this?'

Yvonne favoured him with one of her superior smiles. 'Through a friend of a friend. He knows some of the guys in Customs at Dover. They've been working with the Dutch on stopping shipments of ecstasy. Apparently Holland is full of labs pumping the stuff out. And Glyn Cole's mate Jan is something of a big wheel in the business – or was. He's now doing serious time in a high security jail in Maastricht.'

The moment Bakker had mentioned drugs, Greening's mind had flashed to Cole's sister Dee saying that he'd got mixed up in drugs in Holland and had to leave in a hurry after a friend was arrested. He wouldn't mind betting that he was looking at a photo, albeit a badly reproduced one, of that same friend right now.

'According to Amanda Yates,' he said, 'Jan was at Cole's shop just before he disappeared. And he had a flashy character with him throwing his weight around.'

'Cole only had a piddly little business, didn't he?' Yvonne said. 'Maybe it was just a front for flogging more lucrative stuff.'

There was a thought.

Les, sitting opposite, shook his head. 'If he was a serious player he'd have serious money. And we haven't found any indication of that. He drove a car that was eight years old.'

'Suppose he was just getting into the ecstasy business,' Yvonne said. 'And he screwed it up and that's why he got killed.'

Greening mulled it over. Maybe the 'deal' that had been agitating Errol, the flashy guy, was a drug deal. Being involved in that kind of business was hazardous.

'Well done, Yvonne,' he said. 'Good work.'

She acknowledged the compliment with a lift of her head. 'We can't have you running to your new little friend for everything.'

Greening understood that she was referring to Carmel. 'Leave off, Yvonne,' he said.

Ignoring this interchange, Les tapped the fax page, which he had been studying.

'Are we sure this is the right guy? I can't read Dutch but I can make out his name. Look.'

They both turned their attention to the line of type above his blunt forefinger. It read: Jan-Arnoldus Vandeneijnde.

'The name you gave me this morning,' Les continued, 'was Johannes and this fellow is Jan-Arnoldus. Obviously both of those are a bit of a mouthful so he's called Jan, but is it the same man?'

It was a good question.

'We can get this translated,' Yvonne said. 'And I'll go back to my source and see if we can talk to a Dutch copper.'

'I don't think you've got to be a great linguist to read some of it,' Les said, squinting at the page. 'It says "09 januari 1974" – got to be a date of birth and here's his height "1.81 metres".'

Greening worked it out. 'That makes him thirty-six, born the year before Glyn Cole. Sounds right. Dunno about the height though.' His school had gone metric just after he'd done maths O level – precise conversion always gave him trouble.

'Five eleven,' Yvonne said promptly. 'That's short for a Dutchman.'

'Short for our man, too,' Greening said. 'I keep being

told how tall he is.' He held up the fax page. 'Let's make some copies of this. Yvonne, you go ahead and talk to the Dutch. Les, get someone to show this to Amanda Yates, see if she recognises the fellow. And I'll try and get an ID elsewhere.'

'Who from?' Yvonne asked.

'Cole's book-keeper. Katherine Pym.'

He avoided looking at her directly. It was difficult to hide things from Yvonne.

Tammy was concerned about Anna. 'Are you feeling all right?' she asked.

It was stuffy in the little museum room on the top floor and they hadn't been able to unstick the window to get it open.

'I could fetch us a cold drink,' Tammy continued.

Anna shook her head. 'Let's have a proper break in half an hour.' She shot Tammy a quick grin. 'Don't worry, I'm not feeling sick today.'

They were squatting on the floor amongst the boxes and trunks, surrounded by items big and small that they had pulled into the daylight and released from their packaging. Dust swam in the air, and the floor, despite the thin carpet, was hard. It seemed to Tammy that a pregnant woman should not be sprawling in such discomfort. But Anna's real discomfort, for once, was clearly not physical.

They had started with the watches.

'Mum was looking through these after you left the night we all had dinner,' Anna said. 'Edward told me she insisted on dragging him and Katherine up here to look for a particular watch but she couldn't find it.

She said she'd come back the next day to continue the search and that's what she was doing just before she died.'

'Why was she looking for it?'

'She wanted to sell it and give the money to the air ambulance. Edward said she had a bee in her bonnet about writing them a cheque for twenty thousand and even after all her fund-raising, she was still short.'

Tammy couldn't imagine ever being in the position of giving away such an enormous sum of money. Suddenly she didn't feel so bad about accepting the two hundred pounds Anna had given her. These people were rich.

She looked in awe at the collection of pocket watches. 'How much are these worth then?'

'A few hundred each, some a bit more, I think. Look at the back of the inventory. Glyn listed the valuations separately.'

'Glyn?'

Anna stared at her defiantly.

'Glyn Cole, the antique dealer?' Tammy persisted. 'I didn't know he'd been here. Did your mother know him?'

'Katherine used to do his books. She recommended him to Mum and she got him to redo the inventory.'

Then Mrs Drummond had discovered his body two years later. And now here they were trying to find out what she'd been up to just before she herself had died.

Tammy wasn't superstitious but it was pretty spooky. She would have asked a few more questions but Anna had turned her face away and said, 'We'd better get on with it,' so she took the hint.

An hour later, they had checked and rechecked the old watches, marking them off on their pieces of paper once each individual timepiece had been identified. When they'd finished, they packed them away carefully.

There were seventeen antique pocket watches in total, exactly the same number as described in the inventory.

'I suppose it's no surprise that the watch Mum was looking for is not here. She hunted for it twice and couldn't find it. And she marked it missing in her book.'

Tammy had looked at the entry. 'She called it a curio watch – what does that mean?'

To her amazement, Anna began to giggle. 'Apparently it shows a couple having a shag on the riverbank.'

'No!'

'That's what Edward told me. He said Mum called it rude. That's one of the reasons she wanted to sell it and, of course, it's probably why it's valuable.'

Tammy smiled at the thought of it. The notion of respectable Mrs Drummond looking for a dirty watch was incongruous, as was the thought of sex in these circumstances.

Maybe it would be all right to stay with Will tonight. She blushed.

Anna misinterpreted her confusion. 'Don't worry, I don't think there's much chance we're going to find it.'

'Do you remember it?'

'No, but I thought all these musty things were boring when I was a girl. Apparently you could only see the naughty picture if you pressed a secret catch. I suppose I might have taken more interest if I'd known it was here.'

'Do you think it's mixed up with some other stuff then? There's lots to go through.'

Anna considered the question. 'I'm sure it won't be here. Glyn would have found it and listed it.'

'So what do you think happened?'

'Either Mum got confused and imagined it. Or else she remembered it from years back and someone, Granny or Grandad maybe, got rid of it long ago.'

'I can't imagine Mrs Drummond getting confused.'

Anna gave her a wan smile and shifted uncomfortably. 'No, neither can I.'

Greening was dithering about putting in a call to Katherine Pym. He could have got someone else to show her the fax and try and get an ID on Jan but he'd grabbed the task for himself. And now he was hesitating over giving her a call to set something up. He was acting like a nervous suitor. It was pathetic.

More to the point, he was a detective with a job to do. He reached for the phone on his desk. Before he could lift the receiver, it rang.

'Greening,' he snapped, irritated at being sidetracked.

'It's Dee James, Inspector. I'm sorry to disturb you.'

She sounded less frosty than usual. The image of her presenting him with a bag of goodies from her shop instantly sprang to mind.

'You're not disturbing me, Mrs James. I meant to call and thank you for your generosity the other day. Those pies were a life-saver.'

'And the chops?'

'Delicious, the best I've ever tasted.' He'd given them all to Yvonne since he knew he'd never get round to cooking them. 'How can I help you?'

'I've been talking to the coroner's office.'

'There isn't a problem, is there?'

'Not really. They said they were going to open an inquest just so they could issue the documents I need to arrange Glyn's funeral. Then they said it would be adjourned and might be opened again depending on the result of any criminal proceedings.'

'That's correct. If the full facts of your brother's death are established at a trial then there may be no need to resume the inquest.'

'Well, what *are* the full facts? Are you any closer to finding out?'

'We're making some progress, I promise you.'

'Such as?'

Such as your brother might have been murdered by an international drug cartel. But he couldn't say that.

'It's too early for me to say anything at this stage. I'm sure you understand.'

He heard an exasperated grunt on the other end of the line and added quickly, 'I'm grateful for the material you provided the other day. It's been very useful.'

'You think the answer to him being murdered is on his computer?'

'It might be. We're still analysing the hard drive.' He had a fresh thought. 'Did your brother enjoy horse-riding?'

'Not particularly, not as I remember.' She sounded surprised. 'But he did ride. He grew up on a farm, after all. Why do you want to know?'

He wondered whether to tell her and couldn't see any harm in it. He'd already told Katherine about the preliminary results of the examination of Glyn's clothes.

'They've found horse hair on the clothes he was wearing.'

'Which means what? He's up a tree with horse hair on his trousers. So?'

He wished he knew. 'It might not have any significance, I admit.'

'To be frank, Inspector, I'm sure you're trying very hard but it doesn't make a lot of sense to me. What killed him, that's what I'd like to know. Have you found that out yet?'

'No.'

'Oh dear.' She sounded upset, far more than he'd come to expect from her. Then he remembered her admission that she'd once worshipped her absent brother. She was softer than he'd first thought.

'We discovered one thing from your brother's phone. I think he was more concerned about the welfare of your family than he let on. You should have a word with your Aunt Claire.'

'Who?' She sounded suspicious.

Greening instantly regretted this conversational foray. He'd begun it with the best of intentions but family politics were tricky.

'Your Aunt Claire. According to his records, Glyn talked to her regularly.'

'Really.' Her voice was flat. 'That's very interesting, Inspector, but I don't have an Aunt Claire.'

Tammy was getting tired. The novelty of trawling through the Pym family treasures had worn off sometime between her left leg going to sleep and the onset of the headache that was gripping her temples.

'Can we break for lunch now?' she said, putting down an amber glass ashtray, one of several outsize monstrosities – it seemed Mrs Drummond's father had enjoyed a cigar.

Anna was sitting with her back to her, immersed in reading her copy of the inventory. She didn't respond.

'Anna?' she prompted.

'You go. I'm all right.' Her voice was thick and dull.

Tammy looked at her closely. Barely perceptibly, the paper in Anna's hand was shaking.

Tammy put her hand on Anna's shoulder. Beneath the thin cotton of her top, Tammy could feel her trembling.

'You're not all right – I thought you said you were feeling better.'

Anna's face was hidden by the fall of her hair. All the same, Tammy could see the tear as it fell with an audible plop on to the paper.

This wasn't anything to do with pregnancy sickness,

she realised. How stupid she was. Poor Anna had just lost her mother and she was suffering.

Tammy leaned forward and put both arms around Anna who gulped in air, seeming to fight the turmoil inside her. Then the paper dropped from her grip and she began to weep without restraint.

They crouched there awkwardly, Tammy ignoring her dead leg and listening to the sobs echoing in the small room, as she hugged Anna to her. She had a horrible premonition of her own grief. Would this be her in a few years – maybe just months – when her mother finally lost her fight with cancer? If so, would there be someone by her side just to hold her? And would she want that? Who knew what a person wanted in moments as terrible as this.

They seemed to sit there for an age, locked in a clumsy embrace, Tammy holding Anna up, taking her weight. At last, Anna pulled away and rubbed her eyes with her bare fingers.

Tammy shifted position – what a relief – and searched in the back pocket of her jeans for paper tissues. 'Here,' she said.

Anna dried her face and pushed the hair off her forehead. The unforgiving sunlight streaming into the room showed the red-rimmed eyes and features swollen from her tears. All the same, she looked tragically beautiful.

When my turn comes, Tammy thought, I'll just look a mess.

'Come and eat something,' she said. 'Your mum wouldn't want you making yourself ill.'

Anna studied her carefully. 'You should go home.'

'Why? I don't think it's a good idea for you to be on your own.'

'This afternoon then. Go and spend it with Will.'

Tammy was puzzled. 'Will's riding this afternoon.'

There was a meeting at Warwick and Will had four rides. Life had to go on.

'Yes, of course.' Anna sat up straight and gathered together the scraps of tissue that surrounded her, collecting them into a ball. 'All the same, you shouldn't be around me. I'm just a horrible person.'

What? Tammy stared at Anna in confusion.

'I might look harmless but I'm not. Bad things happen to people near me. People I love.'

Her voice was wobbling and the tears were coming back. Her fingers were still plucking at the tissues on the carpet. They brushed the fallen paper of the inventory and she seized it.

'Look!' She held it out. 'The person who did this died because of me. I'm evil – I'm a liar! I'm not even crying because of Mum.'

'Why are you crying?'

Anna pitched forward and buried her face in Tammy's shoulder. What she said was muffled but still distinct.

'Because of Glyn.'

'So there is no Aunt Claire?' Yvonne seemed amused.

'Apparently not.' Greening relayed the information Dee had supplied. 'The aunt who works there is called Bethan and was never, to Dee's knowledge, in touch with Cole. Apparently she was not his greatest fan even before he left home. Dee said she'd ask Bethan but reckoned there was no chance she'd have been taking phone calls from him.'

'It's a code then, isn't it?' Les looked excited by the idea. 'From the records, he was talking to this person regularly as far back as January. Just the occasional call at first, then at least once a day. Some of them go on a bit too. Looks like this drugs deal to me.'

Greening began a doodle on his pad. Little circles. 'Could be. And he calls his business partner – Errol, say – "Aunt Claire" for security reasons.' The little circles looked like pills.

Yvonne barked a contemptuous laugh. 'What kind of security is it to use his regular contract phone? You're both way off base.'

Les looked miffed. 'Cole was an amateur, wasn't he? Using his own phone was a mistake. Probably one of those that got him killed.'

Yvonne shook her head, a straw-blond loop of hair over her ear catching Greening's attention. 'The place is full of blondes,' Katherine had said and it was true.

'I'm not dismissing the dope deal,' Yvonne said. 'But this won't be it. I guarantee Aunt Claire is another little secret altogether. And she's probably got him on her phone as Uncle Bill, or something.'

Greening kicked himself. Of course, she was right. 'So this is the latest girlfriend? The blonde he was in love with.'

'I bet you any money. Well, a gin and tonic will do.' Yvonne got up. 'That looks like a T Mobile prefix. Whatever, I'll get the subscriber's details.'

That sounded good to Greening. It might solve one

of the mysteries surrounding Glyn Cole's death. He fervently hoped so. Dee James's questions were still ringing in his ears.

He looked down at his pad. The pills had turned into eyes in a woman's face. Maybe they were about to put a name to that face. It was about time.

Tammy put together a simple lunch while Anna was upstairs in the bedroom, recovering from her earlier outburst. A lot more had come spilling out of her than tears and Tammy wasn't sure she'd wanted to hear half of it. If she were honest, she felt a little out of her depth.

Anna had confessed to an affair with Glyn Cole. Not a quick thrill kind of thing, she'd said, or a meaningless thrash in a spare bedroom at a party, but a full-blown love affair that had turned her inside out.

Mrs Drummond had commissioned an antiques expert to prepare the inventory in mid-January 2008 and had met him at the Hall to show him round. That was the occasion Anna had first met Glyn Cole. She'd told Tammy about it in a low, matter-of-fact voice, without hesitating or seeming to choose her words. As if she'd told herself the story many times and she was simply repeating it.

'I didn't take much notice of him when I first met him. He looked a bit scruffy, with his hair uncombed and a shirt that hadn't been ironed. I thought Mum would be sniffy about him but not a bit of it, she sang his praises after he'd gone. About how he was so amusing and perceptive and how it was extraordinary a man of his age could know so much. And wasn't he good looking? I presumed he'd given her the soft-soap treatment when they were upstairs together and so I pegged him for an oily shit.

'The next time he came back, Mum had some other engagement and she expected me to look after him. I tried to leave him alone upstairs with the stuff but he said he'd be happier if I stayed, so I could keep an eye on him. Otherwise, he said, if anything was missing and he'd been unsupervised then he'd get the blame. Later, he told me that was complete bollocks – that's how he put it – and he'd only said it to get me to stay with him. "So you were intending to seduce me from the start?" I said and he said, "It was because I'd never met a woman before who looked like a Renaissance angel." You can tell he never stopped talking bollocks to me.'

Tammy had laughed, as intended, but she knew why Glyn had said that. Pale and ethereal Anna did look as if she had stepped out of an Old Master painting.

'So I stayed with him,' Anna said. 'I thought he was going to suck up to me like he'd done with Mum and show off with his knowledge, but he didn't. At least not so I was aware of it. He seemed genuinely interested in all the old objects that the family had accumulated. Some things were weird – a lot of stuffed birds and display cases of dead butterflies. He said he didn't know much about them but knew where to get rid of them. The sooner the better, I said, because they give me the creeps. I explained that my mother was moving out and I wanted a few changes. Not many, I hope, he said. This is a very beautiful place, you are lucky to live here. I knew that was true but I didn't feel lucky, I felt trapped. I felt as if I'd never had any choices in life. That I'd only been conceived as a replacement for my brother, after his accident, and that I was meant to have been a boy. As it was, I'd ended up getting married too young to a man ten years older than me who had been foisted on me by my mother. It was like she'd had a son-in-law made to measure – a brilliant trainer able to take over the yard, a hard worker who'd come from nothing and proved himself in the army, good old steady Eddie who'd fit right into the family because he needed us as much as we needed him. And I'd gone along with her choice like I always did.'

'Oh.' Tammy had been shocked. It made her uncomfortable hearing Edward referred to in this way.

Anna had noticed her unease. 'I mean, that's how I felt at the time. And I didn't immediately dump it on Glyn. I think I said something like, the grass is always greener, I suppose. And he said, you're not kidding, and we left it at that. But when I rang him to arrange his next visit, we ended up talking. We did a lot of talking on the phone – there was always some excuse for him to call or the other way round. He'd started to have an effect on me by then – a physical effect, I mean. So when he was there, I couldn't always concentrate on what we were saying. It was easier on the phone, just to listen to his voice without distraction. I told him how I felt, that I was in a gilded prison, living my life the way other people wanted me to. And

I told him about the big disagreement between Edward and me, the thing that was between us at the time. I should never have told him about that.'

'About what?'

'Edward wanted kids. Mum wanted me to have kids. What else was I supposed to do with my life but raise Pitchbury children? It was expected. And I felt that once I'd had a child that would be it, there'd be no chance of me doing anything with my life. Anything just for me, that is. I'd studied history of art but I'd not done anything with it afterwards because Dad got ill and I was needed here. Anyway, college was only in Reading so I never felt I'd really left home and made my own life. I told Glyn all this and we made fantasy plans for me. Like, I could do an English teaching course and teach in Florence while I studied art, just for me. He said, that sounds great, can I come too? I said, what about your business? He said, I'd give it up tomorrow if I could live in Italy with a Botticelli Venus like you. He missed his next appointment to come to the Hall and I was so upset I shoved Edward's supper in the oven and drove to Glyn's shop. When I walked in, he just put the Closed sign on the door and took me upstairs. By the time I got home, Edward's supper was carbonised and I was in love.'

Tammy laid two places at the kitchen table. She'd made a salad with tuna, green beans and cold potatoes diced small – one of the few dishes she was confident about making. As she put out plates, Anna's words whirled around her head. There were parallels in their lives. Her mother, like Anna's father, being ill. Anna's days as a student hadn't given her the independent life she craved and no more had her own. That feeling of being trapped was all too familiar.

But, things were different for her. She would make sure she had her own choices.

For a start, she would choose Will.

Will left the changing room at Warwick with an extra pulse of nervous energy pumping through his veins. Despite the dramatic events of life at Pitchbury, his concentration was entirely focused on the first race of the afternoon – a five-furlong maiden for horses of modest ability. And Flashback, his mount, was the most modest of them all, an animal who had come a distant last in his only race and on two other occasions had failed to even reach the starting stalls. Flashback was not a horse of much value, trained by a local farmer and owned by a woman whom Will barely remembered. Yet, compared to the other animals he was due to ride that afternoon, this was the horse on which he most wanted to do well.

As he headed through the crowd to the parade ring, his stomach knotted in anticipation. He looked out for Alf, the trainer, and tried to locate him in the melee of connections in the middle of the ring. Will had met him the week before when he had driven up to a farm near Banbury to ride Flashback in a piece of work. It had been an unseasonably wet morning but Alf had been bubbling over with excitement even then. Will wondered how he would handle the big occasion.

As for the horse – a scruffy-looking character – despite doing nothing on the racecourse he definitely had an engine. Will knew that no matter what horses looked like or how inexperienced they were, they had to show you something.

A hand suddenly seized his and Alf's grinning face was looking up at him as he pumped with enthusiasm. By his side was a middle-aged woman in a faded Barbour jacket. The owner.

'Jenny Burgess,' she said as she gripped the hand that Alf had reluctantly released. 'It's been a long time. I used to watch you ride out on my father's horses.'

Fred Burgess had owned the stables next door to old man Pilling's farm in Shropshire, where Will had grown up. Pilling had leased a paddock to Mr Burgess, who had taken a shine to Will.

'It's thanks to your father I'm riding for a living,' he said to Jenny. 'I was very sorry to hear he's no longer with us.'

Will had taken a call from Alf two weeks earlier, telling him Fred Burgess was dead but his daughter Jenny had inherited the horses and was in need of his services. Will had received the news with mixed emotions. Burgess and his horses were part of a past he wanted nothing more to do with. But he was in Fred's debt.

'Dad said you were the best young rider he'd ever seen so I've been following your career. You've got something to live up to this afternoon.'

Will spotted Flashback being led into the ring by his groom, a burly young man whose face was pink with the effort of trying to keep Flashback under control. The horse did not like the occasion and he was making his feelings plain.

Jenny groaned at the sight. 'We took him to Windsor

first time out and thought it was a bit of a disaster when he was tailed off, but at least he took part. Since then he's behaved so badly we can't even get him to start. This is his last chance.' She looked round at Will with a grin. 'Dad said you were a bit of a miracle worker.'

For a fleeting moment, Will regretted that the late Fred Burgess had been so generous with his opinion. Then he strode towards the plunging horse.

Time to repay that debt.

Chapter Fourteen

Anna finally appeared for lunch. She had changed, brushed her hair and added a touch of make-up to her eyes.

'Katherine's coming over,' she said as she sat down at the table. 'She just called.'

Tammy couldn't imagine it was necessary for Anna to smarten herself up for her cousin's sake and presumed the change was as much for her own self-esteem. Though Anna was no longer the trembling reed who had clung to her upstairs, Tammy could see that Anna's façade was brittle.

All the same, she thought she was entitled to ask a few questions before they were interrupted.

'This looks nice,' Anna said, putting some food – mostly lettuce, Tammy observed – on her plate.

'You said Glyn died because of you.'

Anna didn't look at her. 'Did I?'

'Upstairs. Just before. You held out the inventory and said, "The person who did this died because of me."'

Anna shot her a look of reproach. But Tammy stared right back.

'I was upset.'

'Of course you were. You have every reason. But you can't just tell me that and not explain. I don't know what to think.'

'I'm sorry. I shouldn't have said anything at all.'

'But you did.' It was Tammy's turn to look reproachful. She hadn't asked to listen to Anna's confession but now she had heard some of it, she had to hear the rest. 'You said that bad things happened to people around you and that you were evil. What did you mean by that?'

Anna put down her knife and fork.

'I didn't mean . . . evil is too strong. I never meant anyone any harm. But back then I was weak and selfish. I shouldn't have married Edward in the first place but I did and I should have tried to make it work. But I wanted something for myself and when Glyn came along, I thought that was it. Then I lied to everyone, to Edward and my mother and to Glyn. I said I'd leave Edward and run away with him and at the last moment I didn't have the courage to go through with it. I broke Glyn's heart, I know it. Oh God, I'm getting upset again.'

Tammy got up from the table and fetched Anna a glass of water. She felt like a shit but she couldn't leave things like this, she had to press on and get to the truth. She sat across from Anna and looked her in the eye.

'But Glyn didn't die of a broken heart, did he? And he didn't kill himself – the police say it was murder.'

Anna sipped from the glass but said nothing.

'So, you have no idea how he died?'

'Of course not.'

'But you said—'

'I was a bit hysterical before, Tammy. I know he was in a terrible emotional state just before he vanished and that was because of me. I feel responsible for whatever horrible thing it was that happened to him. Do you see?'

Tammy wasn't sure, this was so much out of her own experience. But she could imagine the guilty load that was weighing Anna down.

'I keep thinking,' Anna said, 'if only I'd had the courage to keep my word, he and I would be living in Italy right now and this,' she put her hand on her stomach, 'would be his baby.'

Tammy's questions had dried up. She was out of her depth. Poor Anna. But poor Edward, saddled with a wife who didn't love him, and poor Glyn who had no life at all.

She thought of Will with a fierce possessiveness and swore to herself that whatever happened between them, nothing would be hidden. Better to be honest and lonely than live with lies and deceit.

Anna took her hand. 'I've never told anyone these things before.'

Footsteps sounded on the garden path. Katherine burst in and hugged Anna and then Tammy, who was surprised to be included. But the three of them had shared the awful night at the hospital when Rosemary had died. She guessed she was honorary family now. She wasn't sure how she felt about that.

'I'm sorry,' Katherine said, 'but I've just had a call from Inspector Greening. He's coming here now.'

'Why?' Anna asked. To Tammy, her voice sounded shrill with fear.

'He's got a photograph he wants to show me. I tried to put him off but he says it's urgent.'

'What photograph?'

'He wouldn't say but I think it might be a man Glyn knew. A Dutchman. I met him at Glyn's shop.'

'Why are they interested in him?'

Katherine hesitated. 'He was around at the time Glyn disappeared so they want to talk to him. I suppose.'

'Is that the only reason this inspector is coming here?'

To Tammy's surprise, Katherine's mouth curved into a smile. 'Possibly not. He's actually quite a sweet man.'

While they were absorbing this information, a bell rang from the front of the house.

'I'll let him in, shall I?' Katherine said and exited the room.

Anna stared at Tammy in panic.

'Don't worry,' she said in answer to the unspoken question, 'I'll keep your secrets.'

At least Will had got Flashback into the starting stalls at Warwick. It had not been easy. The horse had been most unhappy when Will had jumped into the saddle and the longer they'd spent among the crowds and noise in the parade ring, the more wound up he had become. Will had steered him out on to the course as soon as he could and Flashback had repaid him by trying as hard as he could to dump him on to the turf.

'You really don't like it here, do you?' Will had muttered to him. It seemed to Will that something about his early racing experiences had so spooked the animal that he'd decided racecourses were not for him – an unfortunate conclusion for a racehorse to draw.

But Will had not been as easy to dislodge as his previous riders. Apart from any superior skill he might possess, Will guessed it was because he rode longer than other jockeys on the circuit and consequently had more of his leg in contact with his mount. The other lads liked to perch high up, legs bent under them, which was fine when the horse underneath knew his business. With an animal who misbehaved you needed to be firmly seated to keep your balance and exert control. And so far Will had defeated all Flashback's efforts to unseat him.

But getting Flashback to the start was only half the challenge. Now he had to persuade him to participate in the race itself. The horse was a big-priced outsider – all things considered, a fair price – and to win on him would be a miracle. Will wasn't foolish enough to think he could bring that about but if he could just get Flashback to show some of the basic speed he'd demonstrated on that rainy morning in Banbury he would be well satisfied. And Jenny Burgess would not have put her faith in him for nothing.

Greening got Davis's call just as he turned off the road into the drive leading up to Pitchbury Hall.

'We've found something on Glyn's computer. Thought you'd like to know about it straight off.'

Of course he would. 'Fire away, Les.'

'We've been going through his emails and it appears he'd been doing some work for Rosemary Drummond a few months before he died.'

'What kind of work?'

'There's a mail here dated the twenty-fifth of February saying he's attaching the finished inventory as agreed and hopes she finds it satisfactory. On a personal note, he says, it has been a great pleasure to have worked on such a fascinating task and the opportunity to spend time in the beautiful setting of Pitchbury Hall has been positively inspiring.'

'That's what he says? Smooth bugger. What else?'

'Just thanks very much for the job, he'll drop her a back-up CD and, if all is in order, he'll send her an invoice.'

'I bet that would have been a pretty decent size. You pay through the nose for flannel like that.'

'I wouldn't know, boss.'

Neither did Greening if the truth were told, but it seemed likely. But, apart from casting some light on the late antique dealer's effusive style, the tone of Glyn's mail was beside the point. The substance, however, was more intriguing.

'So Rosemary knew Cole? Had him up to the Hall to prepare this inventory, where he spent time – he must have made a few visits. And then she finds his body but doesn't recognise it.'

'She wouldn't, would she? Not the state it was in.'

That was true. Why would she connect the fleshless corpse with the antique dealer she'd employed two years earlier? Of course, she must have known Cole had disappeared. Aside from local gossip and a snippet or two in the paper, Katherine would certainly have told her aunt about it. Come to think of it, it was possible Katherine had provided the link between the two in the first place.

'It's a pity Mrs Drummond isn't alive so I could ask her about Cole.'

'It would give the old dear the heeby-jeebies, I should think.'

Greening doubted whether anything would have done that.

'Thanks, Les. I'm just arriving at the Hall now. I'll give you a call when I know what Katherine Pym thinks of this photo.'

He was about to end the call when Davis said, 'Hang on, boss, Yvonne wants a word.'

A couple of minutes later he was standing in the porch of Pitchbury Hall, waiting impatiently for the door to be answered. Suddenly things had become a lot more interesting.

A five-furlong sprint – which is over in little more than a minute – is not the best race to start slowly but, as the runners bolted out of the gates, Flashback followed as if he was wearing lead boots. The ground had plenty of give in it and the animal didn't seem willing to exert himself. Will desperately wanted to lift his whip and give him a couple of cracks behind the saddle, but instinct told him that if he did that, Flashback was likely to down tools completely. Instead he took a tighter hold of the reins to give the horse some confidence.

Alf had told him that when Flashback had his first

run, the jockey had pushed him from the moment they'd left the stalls and he'd hated every moment of it. Will knew it was his job to turn the horse's feelings round and get him to enjoy the race. But it took another furlong for the animal to begin travelling with some sort of enthusiasm.

For all Flashback's greenness, they were not quite last. A grey horse was struggling alongside them and that seemed to give Flashback extra encouragement. Gradually Will could feel his mount come to life and begin moving forward with belief. Will's hopes rose as he realised that they were making ground on the pack of runners ahead.

They came to the elbow in the straight, a kink to the left where the five-furlong start joined the main course. Ahead lay the stands and the crowds and all the activity of the busy racecourse – the aspects of racing to which Flashback had developed an aversion and which so far had been hidden from sight. But the horse appeared unaffected as he galloped into the crowd of horses ahead.

Will quickly scanned the other runners in an effort to spot the one travelling easiest and moved Flashback into his slipstream. They were past the furlong marker now and it was time for Flashback to put in some serious effort. Will began to push with his hands and heels. He wondered how the horse would respond but he need not have worried. Flashback was now up for the task and he moved alongside the horse they'd been tracking. His head lowered, his ears back, this was a different animal to the one who had left the stalls; now he was in a battle with the horse beside him and he was fighting to reach the finishing line first.

Will had decided that, whatever happened, he wasn't going to use the whip. In the end, he didn't have to and they won by half a length.

This was the most unlikely winner of Will's short career but undoubtedly the one that gave him the most satisfaction. It was just a shame that Mr Burgess wasn't there to see it.

'Next time,' he said to Jenny and Alf in the unsaddling enclosure, 'he'll be even better.'

Jenny grabbed him in a crushing embrace. 'That was brilliant,' she said. 'Dad was right about you. You'll ride him again, won't you?'

How could he refuse?

Tammy observed Inspector Greening as closely as she could without making it obvious. He wore a navy suit which looked as if it could do with a good pressing to get rid of the wrinkles and so could the man himself. He had a baggy, lived-in look common among the fathers of her friends, most of whom she found much easier company than her own. Having been taken into Anna's confidence, she felt she must be wary of the policeman. Suppose he started asking her questions and she let something slip? She would feel awful.

But the detective, beyond a genial nod when she was introduced, appeared to have no interest in her at all. She was quite overshadowed, she could tell, by Anna and Katherine.

'I'm sorry to intrude at this time, Mrs Pemberton,'

he said. 'I didn't know your mother well but on our short acquaintance I could tell she was an outstanding woman. Her accident is a tragedy for us all.'

What did he mean by that? Tammy wondered. One person fewer to interrogate, she supposed.

Anna didn't say much to this; in fact, to Tammy's eye she seemed terrified, and she offered to leave Katherine and the inspector to get on with their business.

'Oh no, the more the merrier,' he said. 'I'm only looking for an ID.'

So tea was offered and accepted and Tammy happily got on with making it. The three others sat round the kitchen table as Greening reached into his jacket and produced a folded sheet of paper which he opened out and laid flat.

Katherine, sitting next to him, shifted closer to have a look. Tammy was a little surprised to see that she was leaning companionably against his shoulder. She remembered Katherine's remark about him earlier, when she'd called him 'sweet', and felt a frisson of distaste. He must be well over fifty. Surely Katherine could do better?

'It's not a great picture, I'm afraid,' he was saying. 'But you should be able to see a likeness. If there is one.'

'That's not Jan,' said Katherine. 'Jan is a slim man, smiling face, open features – quite good looking. This guy looks like a thug.'

'He *is* a thug,' Greening said. 'He's a convicted drug smuggler. Are you sure there's no resemblance?'

Katherine picked up the page and studied it closely.

'If you took some of the flesh out of his neck and cheeks, there could be. He has Jan's long nose and there's something familiar about the eyes. I guess if he was smiling they might look more alike.'

'So, could it be the same man?'

She shook her head. 'I don't think so. No.'

Greening pointed to the text beneath the photo. 'Is that the name – the one you were trying to remember?'

She said, after some consideration, 'It might be.'

'What about you?' He turned the page round so Anna, on the other side of the table, could get a good look.

'Me?' she said in surprise. 'I've never seen him before.'

'Are you sure? He may be a friend of Glyn Cole's.'

Anna shrugged. 'Why would I know Glyn Cole's friends?'

Uh-oh, Tammy thought. She shouldn't have said that.

'But you did know Mr Cole, didn't you?'

'Briefly. My mother asked him to prepare an inventory of some family heirlooms before she moved out to live in the gatehouse.'

That sounded OK to Tammy. As if, maybe, Anna had avoided a trap.

'Really?' Greening smiled encouragingly. 'When was that exactly? We're still trying to piece together Mr Cole's life before he, er, disappeared.'

'Mum moved out in the New Year of two thousand and eight. She said it was time for a new start. I think she brought Glyn up here in about mid-January.'

'Was that it? He did the inventory in one visit?'

'Oh no, he came up a few times over the next few weeks, until he'd finished.'

'And when was that?'

'He'd done it by the end of February. I know that because we've just been checking the inventory he made and it's got a date on it.' She looked at Tammy. 'Can you remember?'

Tammy was surprised to be included but she could understand why Anna wanted to move herself out of the spotlight. 'I think it was the twenty-fifth. Would you like me to go and check, Inspector?'

He turned to face her. He had warm brown eyes, like a friendly spaniel. 'No, my dear, don't trouble yourself at the moment. Maybe later one of you could give me a call just to confirm it.'

He shifted his attention back to Anna. Before he could resume his gentle but sly questions, Tammy said, 'Would you like some more tea, Inspector? We've got some banana bread too.'

'My mother made it,' Anna said. 'I don't think any of us are up to eating it now.'

'No thank you,' he said.

'Perhaps you'd like to take it back for your colleagues?' Tammy said. 'I could wrap it up.'

This was interesting, Greening thought. The girl Tammy – how did she fit into the household exactly? – was trying to protect Anna Pemberton. But that wasn't going to happen.

'Would it be possible, Mrs Pemberton, for you to show me some of these heirlooms that Mr Cole was listing for your mother?'

Panic flashed across the blonde woman's face. She really was very fair. And lovely in a fine-boned, porcelain-complexioned fashion. A classical beauty.

'Shall I show you, Inspector?' Tammy again. 'It's not good for Anna to keep climbing those stairs in her condition.'

Greening was amused. This Tammy was a feisty one, obviously. But he was becoming irritated, he didn't have time to pussyfoot around.

'In that case,' he said, looking first at Tammy and then at Katherine sitting silently by his side, 'would you ladies mind if Mrs Pemberton and I had a private word?'

Tammy might have argued the point further but Anna said, 'It's OK, Tammy. I'm feeling OK.'

Katherine got to her feet. 'You won't be long, will you?'

I'll be as long as it takes, he thought, but said, 'Of course not. Just a couple of questions.'

When they'd left, he said, 'What condition was your friend referring to?'

'I'm pregnant.'

'Many congratulations.'

'Thank you.'

She didn't look happy about it but, in the circumstances, that was not a surprise.

'I've got a daughter,' he said. 'She was born within a year of my mother's death and I've always thought of her as a kind of replacement.' He didn't know why he'd started this. It was clumsy. On the other hand, he felt it was true. 'You know, one life ends and another begins.'

She shot him a small smile which lit up her pale face. 'That's a nice thought.'

'So, Mrs Pemberton, I'd be interested to hear –' enough niceness – 'how well you knew Glyn Cole.'

The smile had vanished. 'Not particularly well. As I said, Mum brought him in to do the inventory. On Katherine's recommendation, because she worked for him. I used to see him when he came up here to do the job.'

'How often did he come?'

'I don't remember. About once a week maybe, for a month.'

'And after he had finished on the twenty-fifth of February?'

'I never saw him again.'

He looked directly into her pale amber eyes. She met his gaze with, for the first time, a hint of defiance.

'How would you describe your relationship?'

'We were friendly. He was an interesting man and seemed very knowledgeable. But we weren't particular friends.'

'I see.' He paused, giving her time to say more but she did not take up the offer. 'Did you ever talk to him on the phone?'

'I might have done. To arrange when it would be convenient for him to visit.'

'Not often then?'

'Not that I can remember.'

'Do you have a middle name, Mrs Pemberton?'

'Claire, why?'

He'd have put money on it.

'Because we have been examining Mr Cole's phone records. And there are frequent calls to someone listed in his address book as Aunt Claire.'

She glared at him defiantly again, though this time it was less convincing. 'Are you suggesting that this person is me?'

He took his notebook out of his pocket and opened it so she could see the mobile phone number he had written there.

'Do you recognise this number?'

She said nothing, just sat there dumbly.

He continued. 'The phone company have told us the subscriber is Mrs A. Pemberton of Pitchbury Hall, near Lambourn. It is the same number listed on Glyn Cole's phone. According to our calculations –' Yvonne had been thorough – 'he spent two hundred and twenty-three minutes in March and one hundred and forty-seven minutes until the middle of April, when he was murdered, talking to Aunt Claire. I'd like to know what you were talking about. And please don't tell me you were discussing antiques.'

Greening should have been elated. He had found the mystery blonde in Glyn Cole's life. Anna Pemberton was entirely the kind of ethereal beauty he could imagine a man of taste and culture falling for – certainly in preference to the earthier charms of Amanda Yates. Anna had not denied she had been having an affair with Cole – it would have taken a tougher character altogether to have brazened it out in the face of the telephone evidence. In fact, she had crumpled without further resistance, admitting that she had been besotted with Cole, to the point of agreeing to leave her husband and run off with him to Italy.

This information had come streaming out of her unprompted. Once the dam had been breached, the flood had been inevitable. Maybe it was the tears that had accompanied the outpouring that brought the image to mind.

But though the information was valuable – at last he felt he was closer to the issues that had preoccupied Cole before his murder – the getting of it had not lifted Greening's spirits. He plodded back to his car better informed but heavier in heart. He had subjected a grieving pregnant woman to the ordeal of reliving an unhappy love affair and reduced her to tears.

He sat in the car for a few minutes, ordering his thoughts.

Just how useful would this information prove to be? It might be entirely irrelevant to Cole's murder – it beggared belief that Anna was involved in smuggling drugs – in which case he had put the poor woman through an unpleasant experience for nothing. For the bottom line, if she was telling the truth, was that she had ended the affair with Cole two days before he disappeared from sight. She said she had visited his flat on the evening of Friday, 11 April, to tell him it was over. And that was the last she had seen of him.

His passenger door was flung open and Katherine threw herself into the passenger seat. 'You bastard,' she said.

'I'm just doing my job.'

'Sod your bloody job. Have you no compassion?

That poor girl was suffering enough already. Her mother died two days ago! You should be ashamed of yourself.'

He considered Katherine's blazing eyes and the pulse that beat in her slender neck and felt a tug of want in his guts that he thought had disappeared for ever. Well, he'd probably just screwed up any chance of extending their acquaintance into any other sphere.

He let her curse him some more. It was enjoyable in its way. She was angry at him on a personal level which had its, admittedly minor, satisfaction.

He waited till she'd run out of steam and then said, 'Why didn't you tell me your cousin was having an affair with Glyn Cole?'

'Because it was none of your business,' she hissed.

'Everything going on in Cole's life before he was killed is my business. I'm investigating his murder. I have no cause of death and I have no motive for the killing. There's only a skeleton hidden up a tree with hair on his clothes – some of it blond human hair, you knew that. You also knew I was looking for a fair-haired woman who was involved with him in the weeks before his death. You should have told me it was Anna. You must have known.'

'Of course I knew. So did Aunt Rosemary, and the last thing she wanted was for it to become public knowledge. Our family has been through hell over Glyn's behaviour with Anna. Did you know he almost wrecked her marriage?'

'She told me she was on the brink of leaving her husband and changed her mind.'

'Exactly. She finally saw sense. It's taken two years and a lot of effort by everyone for those wounds to heal. It would be unforgivable if you trampled all over our lives in your hobnail boots just because of the coincidence of Glyn's death.'

'Coincidence?'

'Yes, of course. What else could it be?'

He didn't answer the question but that's exactly what he was wondering.

Greening briefed Yvonne and Davis on his return to the incident room.

'I'd like you to visit Anna Pemberton and take a proper statement. She thinks I'm a complete ogre so I'll leave it to you,' Greening instructed. 'Kid-glove treatment, though, please.'

'We'll handle her like precious china,' Yvonne said.

Greening sincerely hoped so; Yvonne had previous experience in the china-smashing department.

'So we'll be after the husband now, will we?' said Davis.

Greening had been considering the matter as he drove back. Jealousy was a powerful motive – it had put Ian Yates in the frame. Just because Yates had proved a blind alley didn't mean that Edward Pemberton might not be the road to the truth of Cole's murder.

'I like him for it much better than Yates,' Yvonne said. 'After all, Cole was found on his land. Murderers stick bodies under their patios all the time. It's the same thing.'

'Yes, but those trees are near a public right of way,

just by the main road. Anyone could get at them.' Davis made the counter-argument. 'And because they're by the road, anyone who went by regularly would know about them. So any local could have used them to hide a body.'

All these things were true and didn't sway matters either way. Something else nagged at Greening.

'It would be helpful to know if Pemberton was aware his wife was carrying on with Cole. If he was blissfully ignorant then he has no motive.'

'Surely he would know,' Davis said with some force. 'I'd know if Eileen was doing the dirty on me.'

'Oh yeah?' Yvonne was sceptical. 'Go through her phone calls, do you?'

'Of course not. We respect each other's privacy.'

Yvonne looked at Greening and rolled her eyes. 'That makes your point. Pemberton might well have been the last to know.'

'We don't know if Pemberton even met Cole,' Greening said. 'How many horses has he got in that yard? Almost a hundred, isn't it? And he's off at the races half the time.'

'Hang on, boss,' Davis said. 'He's a Flat trainer and I don't think the season starts till the end of March.'

'So?' Yvonne was typically belligerent. 'Getting horses in shape for the season is time-consuming. And there's Flat racing on the all-weather throughout the year. Pemberton would have his hands full, probably wouldn't have much time to keep an eye on his wife. Anyway, he might not care.'

'What do you mean?' Greening couldn't imagine a man married to the lovely Anna not caring.

'Those horsey types are in each other's pants all the time. It's well known.'

Davis grinned. 'You seem to be well acquainted with the racing fraternity, Yvonne.'

She flashed him a rapier look and the grin disappeared.

Greening ignored them. 'Ring the yard and get Pemberton's mobile number. Then see if you can find any evidence of communication between Pemberton and Cole in those records you've got.'

'Why don't we just get Pemberton in?' Yvonne suggested. 'If his wife's affair with Cole is a sore point I bet he won't be able to hide it. We could interview Cousin Katherine at the same time, see if their stories match up and what falls between the cracks. We're bound to turn up something damaging.'

Greening pretended to consider her request. Sometimes he thought Yvonne had been born out of time – she'd have done a great job for the Spanish Inquisition.

'No,' he said. 'The heavy-handed stuff can wait. You have another look at those phone records.'

'Of course.' Yvonne somehow kept the disappointment out of her voice.

'I'd like to get an idea of the lie of the land before approaching Pemberton. Especially since we have no evidence he and Cole were even in the same room.'

His best bet was to go back to Katherine. He hoped she might have calmed down by the time he did so.

Greening got a cool but civilised response when he called Katherine. He'd offered to drive to her house or to return to Pitchbury but she'd vetoed those. He picked an old-fashioned tearoom in Swindon which, he could tell, did not impress her. He wondered whether that was because it didn't serve alcohol.

She'd driven directly from the Hall, she'd said. He noticed that she'd taken time to freshen her eye make-up.

'How's Mrs Pemberton?'

'How do you think? Miserable. She thinks you tricked her.'

'I could have questioned her under much less congenial circumstances. Some of my team would have taken her into the nick for interview.'

'I suppose so. I'm sorry I got a bit emotional.'

'It's an emotional time for you all.'

'I guess it was bound to come out about Anna and Glyn.' She sipped her tea. 'So, what do you want from me now? I assume this isn't the lavish date you promised me.'

'You could tell me who that young lady is who was looking after your cousin.'

'Tammy? She's just a girl who helps out in the Hall. Student drop-out, aiming to go back to college next year, I think. Anna hasn't been well during her pregnancy and Tammy has been keeping an eye on her.'

'She's certainly protective.'

'We're all very grateful to her.'

'All of you being?'

'The family – Aunty liked her and Freddy thinks she walks on water.'

'What about Mr Pemberton?'

'Edward, too, of course. Edward more than anybody, in fact.'

'Why would that be?'

'That's a bit of a daft question, Inspector. You *are* playing policeman at the moment, aren't you, Alan?'

He sighed. 'I'm afraid so. Just tell me why Edward Pemberton is so grateful to Tammy.'

'There's nothing sinister in it. Because she's looking after his pregnant wife. He's desperate to have children and it's taken a while to get to this point.'

'How long have they been married?'

'Four years.'

'That's not long to wait for kids.'

'He's ten years older than her. And he's the incomer into the family. He didn't bring much money with him – his family haven't got any. His contribution is his skill with horses. And his sperm. God, I sound like Aunty talking.'

'Mrs Drummond spoke very highly of him to me.'

'She adored Edward – she practically chucked Anna into bed with him. But one of the reasons she liked him is that he always delivered. The yard has been going great guns under him and Anna is expecting. Aunty was very happy.'

'So Edward had a lot riding on his relationship with Anna.'

'Doesn't every man with his wife? You should know, shouldn't you?'

He'd told her he'd been married twice – 'shop-soiled' was how he'd put it. Too late to take it back now.

'I mean, his position at Pitchbury Hall, his stewardship of the yard, they would have been affected if his marriage had broken up.'

'I see where you are going with this, Alan, and I think I've said too much already.'

'You're only giving me some background. I'm not taking an official statement.'

'Is it going to come to that?'

He couldn't see how. She was too valuable off the record – leaving any personal considerations aside, of course.

'Just tell me one thing. Did Edward know Anna was having an affair?'

'Do I have to answer that?'

'I'm only trying to find out how your friend and employer Glyn Cole was murdered. You've told me that's what you want too.'

'Of course, I do.'

'So then, did he know?'

Greening's phone rang. Brilliant timing. He ignored it.

'Aren't you going to answer?'

He looked at the little screen, intending to shut it off. It was Davis.

'Where are you, boss? Dougie rang in just now and said he's got the lab report. He said he'd be ten minutes. Can you get back here?'

'Did he tell you what was in it?'

'He said he couldn't wait to show you. He sounded excited.'

'OK, I'm coming now. If he shows before me, just wait.'

Katherine had listened to this with interest. 'Am I saved by the bell?'

'Just tell me about Edward. Does he know about the affair?'

She nodded. 'He knows. But you'd better ask him when he found out.'

'Thanks. I intend to do just that.'

In the event, Greening and Dougie arrived in the Farley Road car park at the same time. Greening could see the young Scot was bursting with anticipation. His usual relaxed demeanour had been replaced by a twitchiness of movement and a nervousness of step. Greening wondered what could have got him so agitated but he refrained from asking for a preview as the two of them entered the building.

He summoned Yvonne and Davis and the three of them provided an expectant audience in the cubbyhole that passed for an office.

'You've heard some of this already,' Dougie began. 'We found a variety of hairs on the deceased's clothes. Cat hair, horse hair and some fair human hair.'

'We think we can identify two of those,' Davis chipped in. 'Cole owned a cat and we believe the blond hair belongs to Anna Pemberton. She's being interviewed tomorrow so we can ask her for a DNA sample to confirm it. We have no idea about the horse, however.'

'As a matter of fact,' Dougie was grinning, 'it's horses plural.'

'More than one horse?'

'I believe that's what plural means.'

Dougie was looking positively cocky, Greening thought. He must have something good.

Davis was put out. 'Go on then. How many horses?'

'The lab have identified at least four distinct animals, maybe as many as six or seven. I don't think they're used to dealing with animal suspects.'

Greening didn't know what to make of this information. Nobody had suggested Cole was that keen on riding. It seemed bizarre.

'Maybe he was wearing riding clothes he never cleaned,' Yvonne suggested. 'Over the years he might have ridden a string of different horses and the hairs just . . . accumulated.'

Dougie appeared to be enjoying this floundering conjecture. 'You might be interested in a couple of other substances found in the material. Some surviving particles of horse manure.'

'Horse poo.' Yvonne wrinkled her nose. 'See, he never cleaned his clothes. I used to know guys like that.'

'No,' said Dougie. 'The particles were tiny and they had penetrated right into the fabric, that's why they hadn't decomposed.'

That brought a halt to the conversation. It wasn't easy to account for the phenomenon.

'What was the second thing?' Greening asked. 'The other substance found in his clothes.'

Dougie looked almost disappointed to reveal his final card.

'Chlorine,' he said.

For a moment Greening's mind fogged over. That made no sense.

'Like in a swimming pool?' Yvonne said. 'You're not telling us he drowned, are you?'

'A drowned man hidden up a tree,' Davis said. 'I'm going to enjoy telling my grandchildren about this.'

The fog cleared in Greening's head.

'I think I've got it,' he said. 'And I know exactly what we do next.'

Chapter Fifteen

Greening was not familiar with horse swimming pools. In fact, the notion of taking horses swimming struck him as a bit bizarre, though he conceded his ignorance was profound. However, he'd been aware that top training yards had pools and that one existed at Pitchbury – Freddy Drummond had nearly drowned in it, so he'd been told. The presence of chlorine and horse evidence on Glyn Cole's clothes, together with the proximity of the skeleton's place of concealment, had pointed him to where he stood the next morning, by the side of the Pitchbury yard pool, overseeing Green Watch from the local fire service as they cheerfully pumped it empty of water.

The pool was circular, with an island in the middle reached by a footbridge which could be swung across as required. It had been explained to Greening by Tom, who'd introduced himself as the Pitchbury head lad though he looked a strapping thirty years old, that a groom would stand in the middle and another on the outside of the pool and together they would swim a horse round with leads attached to its head collar.

'They love it,' he said. 'Most of them anyway. It's good exercise, especially for those carrying an injury. Often we can't get an animal up on the gallops but we can pop him in the pool and keep up his condition.'

Tom was proving a mine of information and Greening picked his brains while he waited for the draining process to be completed. He was keen to get up to speed before Edward Pemberton returned from some business in Newbury. He gathered that the boss had been alerted to the police presence in his yard and was not best pleased. He was doubtless hotfooting it back to make his feelings felt. Greening, however, would be ready for him.

'You just carry on as usual,' he'd said to Tom. 'Unfortunately you can't use the pool until we're done. I'm sorry about that.'

Tom hadn't seemed too bothered, though Greening doubted Pemberton would be that sanguine. It would be interesting to gauge his reaction.

'What are you hoping to find down there?' Tom had asked, but Greening had simply said it was necessary for his ongoing investigation. The groom had chewed on that silently. Since the discovery of the corpse up the hill, everyone was well aware what that investigation was about.

At Greening's request the fire brigade had supplied a tanker big enough to hold the water, so it could simply be returned after they'd had a chance to examine the empty pool. Les Davis had put in a call for forensic assistance and a SOCO team was expected. As to what Greening was hoping to find, he had no idea. Anything that would link this pool to the dead man would do, even if it was just a couple of matching horse hairs.

He'd asked straight off if the water was treated with chlorine.

'Sure, like any swimming pool – got to zap the bacteria.'

That was one box ticked.

'How often do you drain the pool completely?'

'Every three or four years,' Tom had said. 'Then we can redecorate and do any serious maintenance. We're due for a refurbish at the end of this season.'

So the pool had not been emptied since before Cole's death – that was another box ticked. Greening had given the green light to the operation at that point.

Now he said, peering at the pale blue surface twinkling in the morning sunlight, 'How do you keep the water clean?'

'It gets backwashed every day.'

Greening looked at him expectantly. 'Backwashed?'

'We suck the water out through a grille at the bottom of the pool and filter it under pressure through a big drum of cleaning sand. The sand gets rid of all the crap that's accumulated and the clean water is returned to the pool. Simple.'

He made it sound simple anyway.

'And then we've got our special pool minder,' Tom added.

'What's that?'

Tom pointed to the broad figure of a man standing on the other side of the pool. Greening recognised him.

'You mean Freddy Drummond?'

'Freddy, yeah. He likes the pool. Hosing the horses down before they get in, keeping the area clean, helping swim them. He keeps an eye on everything. It's his responsibility.'

Greening raised a hand to Freddy, who was staring in his direction. 'I'll go and have a word,' he said. Tom had babysat him long enough.

Freddy kept a steady watch on him as he rounded the pool's edge.

'Alan Greening,' he said, offering his hand.

'I met you already,' said Freddy, accepting the handshake with unnecessary firmness. 'You brought Mum back from that press conference.'

'I'm very sorry about your mother. She was splendid.'

'Not half. She wouldn't have let you lot muck around in here like this. We got three horses to swim this morning and now we can't.'

'I do apologise. We can't put it off, I'm afraid.'

'What are you looking for?'

'I shan't know until I find it. Maybe nothing – it's just a precaution.'

'We're not the only ones round here with a horse pool. Are you going to look at them too?'

'If we have to.'

'You're going to be pretty busy then, Mr Greening. There's loads around Lambourn.'

It flashed through Greening's mind that if he came up blank here then he might indeed have to search other pools. The thought was grim.

Freddy was staring at the water. The level had dropped noticeably.

'The horses walk in down the ramp and then they have to swim,' he volunteered. 'It's deep – goes down twelve foot. I fell in once.'

'What happened?' This would be the lad's accident, Greening assumed.

'I was only a kid. But I was all right, they got me out. I never learned to swim though.'

'That's understandable. I've never much liked swimming myself.'

'You can't swim either?' Freddy's eyes were wide with interest.

'No, I can swim. I just don't enjoy it much.'

'Oh.' Freddy appeared to think about it. 'Everybody can swim except me. Although—' He stopped himself. 'Perhaps I shouldn't say.'

'Shouldn't say what?'

'Glyn Cole – he couldn't swim. He told me.'

Really?

'Were you friendly with Glyn Cole?'

The younger man turned his attention from the lapping water and looked Greening full in the face. 'I was once. But he turned out to be a bastard.'

'What makes you say that?'

But Freddy had no time to reply for, suddenly, a square-shouldered man in a dun-coloured waxed jacket was standing between them. His grey eyes were stormy and his jaw jutted with menace.

Greening had not met Edward Pemberton before but he had no doubt who the newcomer was. He hoisted his most affable smile as he introduced himself.

Pemberton cut him off. 'I know who you bloody

well are but I don't know why you are disrupting my yard. Or why your detectives are up at the Hall upsetting my wife.'

Carmel waited an age on Mrs Shaw's doorstep. She might have given up and gone had she not heard the shuffle and drag of a large and infirm presence making its way down the hall on the other side of the front door.

'Who is it?'

'PCSO Gibbs, Mrs Shaw. Carmel.'

The door opened slowly to reveal the old lady leaning heavily on her walking stick. Her hair was wild and she wore a dressing gown. She looked in some disarray though she smiled as she took in her visitor.

'Hello, dear. I thought you were my home help – she's late.'

'Is that why you're not dressed yet? Why don't I give you a hand?'

Carmel's intention was to have a quick chat, just to see how the old lady was doing. There were a number of infirm people on her regular beat, living on their own, and she checked on them when she could. Which was the point of community support, in her book.

Mrs Shaw led the way back down the hall to the kitchen, grumbling about her hips as she went. Her second replacement operation had been postponed again, she said. She declined the offer of help in getting dressed in favour of a cup of tea and a chat.

'Joan'll be along in the end to sort me out, though

frankly I can't see the point in getting dressed just to watch the telly.'

Carmel made herself useful as the kettle boiled, drying the dishes on the draining board and putting away some shopping that had been left in a Tesco bag on the kitchen table. A bundle of newspapers and cardboard recycling material had spilled over on the counter and she sorted those out too. She wondered exactly what this Joan did when she pitched up. Probably made tea and had a chat, she thought.

'Why don't you sit down,' Mrs Shaw urged. 'You're wearing me out just watching.'

'What's this?' Carmel pointed to a pile of letters and junk mail hidden behind a row of empty milk bottles.

'Don't touch those, dear. They're letters I've got to deal with.'

'Some of them go back a while.' Carmel was looking at the postmarks.

'I know. After I came out of hospital I couldn't be doing with the post. I just shoved all the letters on one side. But I'm catching up now, that's why they're there. Hand me that white one on top, will you?'

Carmel did so.

'I came across this the other day and I thought it might interest that nice inspector. I couldn't find his number though. Perhaps you'd like to give it to him.'

'What is it?'

'It's from one of Mr Cole's friends. He said he'd lost touch with him and asked if I had an address.

Someone ought to write back and tell him poor Mr Cole's dead – I thought that might be a job for the police. I'm never going to manage it.'

Carmel withdrew a single sheet of paper from the envelope. The message, written in a neat round hand, blue ink on graph paper, was short:

> Dear Mrs Shaw,
>
> Maybe you remember a Dutch fellow who used to stay with Glyn Cole who had the antiques shop next door to you. That fellow is me and I am writing to ask if you know what has happened to Glyn as I have lost touch with him. I myself have now moved to the UK and I give you my address in case you can pass it on to Glyn. Or maybe you have a number you can tell me about. I would very much like to see him again as he was my good friend.
>
> I hope you are in good health and ask forgiveness for this request, which means a lot to me.
>
> With very best wishes,
>
> Jan Vandeneijnde

Beneath that was written, in block capitals, a London address and a mobile phone number.

'Don't you worry about this, Mrs Shaw,' Carmel said. 'I'll look after it for you.'

Greening and Pemberton were sitting in the yard office. The trainer's anger had been replaced by a coolness that was barely polite. Pemberton sat behind a cluttered desktop while Greening perched on a wobbly chair opposite. It was an inadequate seat for a man of fourteen stone but he presumed not many of his stature ever used it, the yard staff he had encountered being almost half his weight. He also imagined that few of them spent any time sitting around on their bottoms.

Though Pemberton seemed in icy control, Greening wouldn't mind betting that the anger he had seen earlier was not far from the surface – which could be useful. An angry man did not usually keep a watch on his tongue.

Greening had held firm on the necessity of draining the pool.

'What on earth do you hope to find in there?' Pemberton demanded. 'I thought this antique dealer died up a tree.'

'How do you know that?'

'I don't *know* anything about his death at all, but that's where he was found, isn't it?'

'Correct. But the evidence suggests he was killed before his body was concealed.'

'Killed in my pool? How on earth do you work that out? It's mad.'

'We have good reasons—'

'Let's hear them then.'

'Which I cannot divulge at present.'

'Look, officer, I have a pretty good idea what you're up to and it's nothing to do with gathering evidence.'

Greening nodded encouragingly. 'Go on, sir.'

'Basically, you haven't a clue. You've got a two-year-old skeleton and no idea how he died. You've managed to dig up some old gossip about this man and my wife and, since that's all you've got, you're trying to put pressure on my family. That's why you're harassing my wife and turning my yard upside down. You've got half the county fire service here and men in little white suits strutting around as if they're on the television. If you think I'm impressed, you must be barking. I'm appalled at the waste of public money, quite apart from the sheer insensitivity of subjecting us to this within two days of the death of my mother-in-law. Without whom, may I remind you, you wouldn't even have a body to investigate.'

This speech was delivered with mounting intensity which Greening thought promising. If Pemberton kept it up he'd blow his top for sure. He decided to stoke the fire in the most obvious fashion.

'Tell me, Mr Pemberton, when exactly did you discover that your wife was sleeping with Glyn Cole?'

He could see in the trainer's steely grey eyes a considerable desire to inflict pain. He guessed that right now Pemberton was suppressing the impulse to leap over the desk and punch him in the face. He felt a frisson of apprehension, as any sensible – and out of condition – man would in these circumstances. However, he was practised in concealing such feelings.

Pemberton said, 'You've got a flaming nerve even asking that question.'

'You raised the matter, sir. And it is relevant to my inquiry.'

'I said gossip and that's all it is. Glyn Cole did not have an improper friendship with my wife.'

'That's not what she told me yesterday. And I don't suppose that's what she's telling my colleagues who are taking a statement from her at this moment.'

'What? She told you she had an affair with Cole?'

'She couldn't deny it. We have Cole's phone records. The pair of them spent hours talking until two days before his disappearance.'

'Oh.' The man appeared to sag like a punctured balloon.

'I'm sorry if this is news to you but I thought you were already aware of the situation.'

'Of course I was aware, you fool, but a man doesn't go broadcasting his wife's infidelity.' He took a deep breath. 'Let me explain. We had a difficult start to our marriage. I thought everything was cut and dried, that we both wanted the same things – a successful yard and a house full of kids. This place was a dream come true for me. Growing up, I thought I'd be spending my life fixing people's central heating like my father and I ended up in this fantastic place with the kind of woman I'd always thought was out of my league. But instead of enjoying our lives here, Anna wanted – well I couldn't work out what she wanted. She went on about freedom and space and hating the thought of being tied down with children. I loved her but I thought she was spoilt rotten. Didn't know how lucky she was. Then I found that all the airy talk boiled down to her shacking up with some greasy antique dealer. If thinking about murder is a crime, Inspector, you can arrest me now. I don't mind admitting that I would have relished putting a bullet between that man's eyes.'

Greening had done a little homework on former Squadron Corporal Major Edward Pemberton and discovered that his service in the Household Cavalry had not been entirely ceremonial; he had served in war zones in Eastern Europe. Greening had no doubt he was capable of killing. But had he killed his wife's lover?

Maybe he'd just heard the answer.

'I see.' Greening filled the silence, willing Pemberton to go on.

'I only found out about the affair after she put an end to it. She confessed to me out of the blue and asked me to forgive her. It's taken me a bloody long time to do that, I can tell you. But now we have a child on the way and a new understanding. She's grown up and now I realise there are more important things than getting my own way. I can tell you I felt responsible for her infatuation with Cole. I left a space for him to ooze into her affections.'

'So she told you she'd broken up with him just before he disappeared?'

'Correct.'

'That would be the weekend of the twelfth of April two thousand and eight?'

'If you say so.'

'Can you tell me what your movements were that weekend?'

Pemberton rummaged in a drawer of his desk, produced an old desk diary and flipped through the pages.

'I had some runners on the all-weather at Kempton on the Saturday and I went to a jumps meeting at Newton Abbot on the Sunday.'

'You didn't stay with your wife following her admission of the affair?'

'Are you implying I should have done?'

Greening thought that if he'd been in Pemberton's shoes he would not have let Anna out of his sight. He kept the thought to himself and the trainer continued.

'As I remember, Anna, Rosemary and I were due to go down to Devon. But Anna said she was too exhausted – we'd been up half the night rehashing the whole business. She swore to me it was over with Cole, that she was committed to life at Pitchbury and that we should try to start a family. So, I left her behind to recover and took Rosemary. Actually, it gave me a chance to talk to her about it. She knew Anna and I had been going through a rough patch but she didn't know why. I put her straight. Rosemary was a woman I could talk to.'

Greening reflected that it was a pity she wasn't on hand to verify Pemberton's story.

Carmel had a small tussle with her conscience before she dialled the number on the letter Mrs Shaw had given her. She should really just hand it over to Greening and get a pat on the head for her trouble – that's if she even got a chance to talk to him.

At his request, she'd rooted out a load of information about Ian Yates's cricketing exploits. According to one of Robbie's mates in the Yardley Green Old Boys first eleven, Yates was the spearhead of the attack. She could imagine that lanky frame delivering a mean bouncer and his snarling spotty face spitting abuse at the batsman. Thanks to Robbie's pal, she'd verified the Yardley Green trip to Cyprus in April 2008 and even copied a couple of photos which showed Yates in action. She'd dutifully delivered this package to the Farley Road incident room. And heard nothing. When she'd followed it up with a call to Greening's mobile she'd been diverted to a number manned by DS Harris.

'Yeah, thanks, Carmel, but we already got a load of cricketing snaps from Yates himself,' was all the acknowledgement she got.

So she wasn't inclined to hand over the prime lead that had miraculously fallen into her lap. She'd always maintained that she didn't want to be a detective but this taste of life in the fast lane had whetted an appetite she didn't know she had. Surely she could at least be as good an officer as that surly, patronising, offhand DS Harris.

The phone was answered immediately.

'Hello, this is Jan speaking, how may I help you?' The voice was warm and cheerful with a slight inflection – much as she would have expected.

She declared herself to be a police officer from Hungerford calling about Glyn Cole who used to run a local antique business. She name-checked Mrs Shaw.

'So she gave you my letter and you called – this is great. I am very pleased to hear from you.'

Carmel moved quickly to dampen his enthusiasm. 'I'm sorry to inform you, Mr Van—'

'Just call me Jan. Everybody does.'

'Jan, this is not good news. I'm afraid Glyn Cole is dead.'

He said nothing. The silence dragged on and Carmel wondered whether she'd screwed up royally. This kind of information should be delivered personally.

'Are you still there?'

'Yes. I'm just – this is a shock. I had feared as much for him, of course, but to have it finally . . . What happened? Was it a car accident? He didn't have a heart attack, did he? He seemed always so healthy.'

Carmel let him run on a little. The news of Glyn's death had plainly knocked him for six.

'Jan, I can't answer all your questions. However, we believe that Mr Cole died two years ago, shortly after you last saw him. It would be very helpful if we could talk to you face to face.'

'Of course. I'll come at once. I just need to arrange who will take over in the shop and I will catch a train. Thank God I am here in London now.'

'I can pick you up from Swindon station any time after half past two. Take down my mobile number and give me a call when you know what time you'll be arriving.'

After she'd rung off, Carmel wondered if she'd done the right thing. Maybe Greening would have wanted Jan picked up in London or otherwise dealt with. She knew he was suspicious of the Dutchman. But surely it was better this way, to have a fully cooperative suspect walk right into their arms. Her arms, in fact, which was even better.

*

'Weird kind of swimming pool, if you ask me.' Sean the SOCO was contemplating the circular ditch in the Pitchbury yard, now empty of water. 'A bit like a doughnut. One with a hole in the middle.'

'It's not meant for humans,' Greening said. 'Apparently horses don't mind going round and round in circles.'

Sean laughed. 'Like your investigation, you mean.'

Greening chuckled along with him, though he felt the barb in the joke. 'I'm confident we're getting somewhere at last. And with your excellent forensic skills to hand we'll soon have a result.'

'You think we're going to find you something down there two years after the event? To help in the murder of a man found up a tree?'

'A tree not far away. And the man's clothes contained chlorine. What's more, this pool hasn't been emptied completely in the intervening time. So, yes, if this is where he died then I think there's a chance you'll find something to link it to the body.'

'One of your hunches, is it?'

'If you like.'

'If you ask me it's about time we put you old guesswork merchants out to grass. We need proper scientific analysis in this day and age.'

'That's why I've got you, Sean.'

The SOCO grunted, unconvinced. 'What sort of thing have you got in mind?'

'The lab report said there were horse hairs on Cole's clothes, probably from half a dozen different animals.

You find just one that matches and I'd say we're in business.'

'Well, we'll do our best.'

Sean might be a pessimistic sod but that went without saying. Greening was banking on it.

'I don't understand why they're draining the pool.' Tammy had just returned to the Hall from the yard, where she had hoped to catch sight of Will. Tonight, she'd decided, she would spend the night with him as he'd been entreating her to do. Her brother had come up from Exeter for a couple of days so she didn't feel she'd be letting her mother down by staying out. But she'd failed to find Will, he was up on the gallops apparently, and she'd returned to the Hall, puzzled by the goings-on.

At least the short walk had given her the opportunity to sneak a cigarette. She was still determined to give up, but now was not the time.

She had joined Katherine in the upstairs room where they had resumed the task of checking the inventory. After her interview with the two police officers, Anna had been persuaded to lie down in her bedroom and recover. Without her presence, the inventory business seemed less urgent. Tammy had come to the conclusion that they were doing it to kill time as much as anything else.

'I mean,' Tammy said, 'what do you think they hope to find in the pool?'

Katherine was peering into a trunk that contained a collection of antique racing tack – saddles and leads and whips. Tammy supposed they must be mementos of famous horses. It was funny what some people considered valuable.

'I haven't a clue,' Katherine said. 'I daresay they have their reasons.'

'You like Inspector Greening, don't you?'

Katherine let the lid fall on the equine relics. 'Up to a point. He's quite an interesting man. For a policeman anyway.'

Tammy wasn't so sure about that but she recognised her own personal antagonism. She'd spent a long time the previous afternoon, after Greening had gone, trying to stem Anna's tears.

'Can't you ask him what they're up to?'

'Edward says he thinks they're just trying to harass him.'

'Why would they do that?'

Katherine laughed. 'You might have an old head on your shoulders, Tammy, but you're still a bit naive.'

Tammy was puzzled. 'Sorry, but I don't get it.'

'OK, look. Poor old Alan Greening has got very little information to work with. Just the skeleton of a man who was killed, by some method or other, over two years ago. But now he's discovered that Anna had an affair with Glyn just before he died. So that automatically casts suspicion on Edward – he had a motive to do away with Glyn. And Glyn's body was found nearby.'

'That doesn't prove anything though, does it?'

'No. But Edward thinks that going to the lengths of draining the pool is meant to send a signal that the police will turn over the yard and the Hall and the grounds in search of any tiny thing that can link it to Glyn's death. Maybe more important, it will put enough pressure on Edward and Anna and the rest of us so that one of us will do something daft.'

'Such as?'

'I suspect they think the only way they're going to crack this is if someone confesses. Alan is just piling on the pressure to make that happen.'

Tammy considered this. It still didn't add up.

'Surely no one is going to confess to something they didn't do?' she said. 'Or is that just me being naive again?'

'No. I think you're absolutely right. Even if he did it, Edward is the last man who's ever going to confess.'

Greening curbed his impatience as the forensic examination of the empty pool took place. Sean only had one other SOCO to assist him and the search was bound to take time. But the longer it went on, the darker the cloud of gloom that seized his mood. This was turning out to be a complete waste of time.

Freddy Drummond came to join him as he stood by the side.

'Found anything yet?'

'It's too early to say. They're still searching.'

'They're forensic scientists, aren't they? I've seen them on the TV in those funny clothes. You know – *CSI*.'

Greening knew the programme he was talking about but he'd always steered clear of shows to do with dead bodies.

'I don't watch it often, though,' Freddy went on. 'I prefer *Star Trek*. And *Doctor Who*.'

Greening remembered the conversation they'd been having which had been interrupted by Edward's arrival.

'You were telling me about Glyn Cole earlier. About how you were friends but he turned out to be a bastard.'

Freddy looked at him. 'I'm sorry, I shouldn't have said that. It's rude.'

'No, that's OK. I'm just interested to know why you thought that.'

'Because of all the girlfriends he had. He was OK to me but he was very bad with women.'

'How do you know this?'

'Mum told me. After he'd disappeared she said to me it was good riddance to bad rubbish.'

Greening could understand how she might have thought that.

'Oy, Alan.'

Sean was calling to him from the pool. He was standing halfway up the ramp where the horses walked down into the water.

Greening strode over and squatted down. 'How's it going?'

Sean was giving him a look that implied both irritation and admiration. 'You jammy bugger.'

Greening's spirits lifted instantly, the gloom banished.

'What have you got?'

'You'll be happy to know we've got a load of horse hair. That's what you wanted, wasn't it?'

'What else, Sean? Don't muck me about.'

'There's only one thing. We found it wedged in the filter.'

The SOCO lifted his hand into sight above the parapet. It held a small, see-through evidence bag. For a moment, as he squinted at it, Greening thought that it was empty. Then he spotted the transparent disc, thinner than a coin but about the size of an old half-crown. He remembered them from when he was a boy.

The glass face of a wristwatch.

Sean was grinning now, happy for once. 'Isn't Mr Tree Man missing the face of his watch? You'll have to check that this is the one but it looks like your hunch might have paid off after all.'

Greening stood up, disregarding his creaking knees. Sometimes there was no better feeling than being right. He reached for his phone.

'Les, got a bit of news. We found something in the pool – what looks like the face of a wristwatch. We're going to need your expert to confirm that it's the missing piece from Cole's watch.'

Davis promised instant action and added a 'Well played, boss', which was praise indeed from him.

Greening slid the phone back into his pocket with a smile on his face and turned back to the pool.

A solid figure blocked his way. Freddy.

'I heard what you just said –'

Damn, he should have been more careful.

'– and I want to give myself up.'

'Sorry, Freddy, I don't follow.'

'I want to give myself up for the murder of Glyn Cole. I pushed him in the pool and he drowned because he couldn't swim. I did it because he was a bastard to my sister and I'm not sorry.'

Greening gaped, speechless, searching for a smile or wink, something that would betray that the man in front of him was winding him up. But he doubted that poor damaged Freddy was capable of that.

'Well, Inspector, aren't you going to arrest me?'

Chapter Sixteen

Freddy had refused to have a lawyer present at his interview. Greening offered to send for the duty solicitor several times and was rebuffed on each occasion. He made sure the refusal was recorded on the tape.

As he sat across the table and began to gently probe his self-proclaimed prime suspect, Greening attempted to clear his mind of all misgivings. He could almost feel the excitement emanating from Yvonne, by his side. Confessions were meat and drink to her and the first route to a conviction. Greening wished he could share her certainty. It would make his life a heck of a lot easier.

Freddy began, unprompted, to repeat the admission he'd made by the pool in the Pitchbury yard, that he'd killed Cole by pushing him into the water.

'Back up a bit, would you, Freddy?' Greening said. 'Can you start by telling us how well you knew Glyn Cole.'

Freddy obliged. Saying he'd first met Cole when he came to do the valuation at the Hall for his mother and that Glyn had made a point of seeking him out when he came through the yard.

'He was always nice to me. He asked about the horses and asked me to show him my favourites. He asked me for tips too but I told him he'd be better off asking Mum which one was going to win. He thought that was funny but he did ask her and he told me she was good at tipping. And he used to bring me DVDs and, once, some computer games. He said he'd got them as part of a job lot at an auction and I could have them. I thought he was a good bloke. I didn't realise at the time he was only being nice so he could suck up to my sister.'

'So when did you change your mind about him?'

'Not for ages. Though I didn't see him much after he stopped going to the Hall. But I saw what he was really like when Anna made me drive her over to his shop. I saw him in his real colours then.'

'When was that?'

'Friday the eleventh of April two thousand and eight.'

Greening was taken aback.

'That's very precise. Are you sure of that date?'

'I remember lots of dates. I remember that one because of what happened. Anna came to the gatehouse just as I was going out. I always go to the White Hart on Fridays, unless there's an emergency. She said she needed me to do her a favour and would I mind taking her to Hungerford instead. I said was it an emergency and she said yes, so I agreed. She wanted me to drive her in Mum's car but Mum was out so I went up to the yard and got the Land Rover. I asked why we didn't go in her car and she said it was out of petrol but I don't think it was. When we got to Hungerford she asked me to park in front of Glyn's shop. I realised afterwards that she didn't want anyone to see her car outside Glyn's and that's why she said about being out of petrol.'

'Who do you mean by anyone?' Greening wanted to be clear what was running through Freddy's mind.

'Edward, of course. Or Mum, or anyone who knew her and might tell. I worked that out later. I'm not as stupid as some people think.'

Greening was tempted to say he didn't think Freddy was stupid at all, but he didn't want to interrupt the flow of information. In any case, Freddy didn't look as though he needed reassurance. He looked like a man eager to shift a heavy weight from off his shoulders.

'Anna told me to wait for her. She was going into the shop to talk to Glyn and she wouldn't be long. If she wasn't out within twenty minutes she said I was to come and get her. She made me promise that I would not go home without her, which I thought was strange because how else would she get back? I said I would wait as long as she wanted and she said twenty minutes would be enough. She was very determined.

'So she went in. She had to ring on the bell because the shop was closed and Glyn let her in. I just sat there and listened to the radio. After twenty minutes I went and rang on the bell. There was no answer, so I rang again. I thought maybe the bell wasn't working properly upstairs – that's where Glyn's flat was – so I just kept pressing. Eventually I heard noises, footsteps rushing down the stairs and voices, like they were arguing.'

'Could you make out the words?'

Freddy nodded. 'Glyn was shouting. He said, "For God's sake, you promised. I'm giving up everything for you." And my sister just said, "I'm sorry. I told you I can't." That's what I heard. Then the door opened and Anna came out. She was very upset. She pushed past me and ran to the car. She had her head down but I knew she was crying. Glyn was right behind her. He came out of the door and yelled after her. He said, "Go then and have a nice life. You've just wrecked mine." Then he looked at me. His face was red and angry and I thought he might hit me. He said, "Get her out of my sight and screw the lot of you." But he said a worse word than screw.'

Freddy had recited the exchange in an unemotional tone but it brought a vivid picture to Greening's mind nonetheless.

Yvonne said, 'Are you sure that's exactly what was said?'

'Oh yes. That's correct.'

'You're good at remembering conversations, are you? As well as dates?'

'Yes,' Freddy said. It was a fact.

'Then what happened?' Greening prompted.

'I got into the car and Anna said, "Go quickly. Just drive." So I did. Glyn was still on the pavement, watching us go. She was in a terrible state, shaking and making funny noises in her throat, and she didn't even have her seat belt on but she wouldn't let me stop for ages. Then she said, "I can't go home like this," and I drove off the road into a pub car park, up the back where it was dark. Then she just sat and cried. I put my arms around her and she was shaking like she had flu. I felt like crying too and I didn't know what to do. "Shall I call Mum?" I said. "Or Edward?" She shouted, "No!" and started crying even worse. We must have sat there for ages before she stopped. She'd used up all my packet of paper tissues and was drying her eyes on the sleeve of her blouse. I was scared to ask her anything in case I set her off again but I wanted to know what had happened. So eventually I did ask and she said, "I fell in love with him. I couldn't help it." I knew Glyn had a reputation with girls. One of the lads in the White Hart knew him and said he had a lot of lady friends. And sometimes Glyn used to talk to me about women, man to man, you know.'

'Not really,' said Yvonne. 'Could you be more specific?'

'One of those DVDs he gave me was a bit rude and he asked if I minded and I said no but I'd have to hide it from Mum. Then he asked if I had a girlfriend and I said not at the moment, and he said he'd have to fix me up, but he never did. I knew that there were women he went to bed with but I never thought one of them would be my sister. I was shocked when she told me. Then she said something even worse, that she'd been planning to go away with Glyn to live in Italy. "What – run off from your husband?" I said. "Like a shot," she said. "You'd leave Mum and me? And Pitchbury?" I couldn't believe she would ever think of such a thing. "I can't," she said. "That's why I'm not going through with it."

'Then she told me the reason she'd asked me to come with her was that she couldn't trust herself. She had decided to break it off with Glyn and if I was outside waiting for her she would have the strength to do it. Otherwise there was a risk she might not be able to.

'Eventually, I took her home. She said she'd be all right because Edward was at an evening meeting and Mum thought I'd been at the pub. I wished I had been. I was very unhappy at what had happened and scared what might still happen. Anna said to me never to mention Glyn's name to her because she must not allow herself to think about him. She had to cut him out of her life forever and I had to help her. "I don't have much willpower," she said to me. "You've got to help me be strong." I promised I would but I didn't know how.'

Freddy drank from his glass of water.

'At first I thought Glyn Cole was my friend. But he was only pretending so he could get close to my sister and get her to run away with him. Now do you understand why I'm not sorry he's dead?'

Greening looked at Yvonne. 'Stop the recording,' he said. 'I think we could all do with a cup of tea.'

Carmel spotted Jan immediately as the passengers streamed off the London train. He was a head taller than anyone else, a thin floppy-haired fellow with a scarf knotted fashionably round his neck and a leather shoulder bag. From a distance, he looked like a fresh-faced student but as he approached the barrier where Carmel was waiting, she realised he would be in his mid-thirties - Glyn Cole's age, had he still been alive.

Spotting the uniform, he made straight for her and

they shook hands awkwardly. 'I came as soon as I could,' he said, 'but I'm working in a shop in Westbourne Grove and I couldn't just leave.'

'An antique shop?'

'That's right. It's very nice but the things are expensive. Fortunately, it seems there are always some people who have enough money.'

They drove to Farley Road, with Jan asking questions about Glyn that Carmel was reluctant to answer in any detail. She planned to deliver the Dutchman to Greening and it would be up to him how much to give away. But it seemed only fair – if Jan was as ignorant of Glyn's death as he appeared to be – to give him the information that was available to any other member of the public. She'd brought with her a copy of the local paper which carried the original story of Rosemary Drummond's discovery.

He read it in silence, then said, 'It doesn't mention Glyn.'

'The body had to be identified from dental records.'

'That's unbelievable. What happened to him?'

'We are trying to find out.'

'I mean, was it an accident? Or suicide? He'd be capable of climbing a tree and, well, I don't know – something could have gone wrong, I suppose.'

'We have reason to believe it wasn't an accident or suicide.'

'You mean he was murdered?'

'Yes.'

Jan said nothing more for the rest of the journey.

*

Once again, Freddy refused to have a solicitor present while he was questioned which, as Yvonne had muttered to Greening in their break, was his funeral. As before, Greening made sure that the offer of representation was recorded.

'When did you next see Glyn Cole?' he asked as they resumed.

'Sunday the thirteenth of April. I had lunch at the Hall with my sister. She was on her own because Edward had gone to the races with Mum. Anna said she could have gone too but she couldn't face it. She said she had told Edward about Glyn and they had been arguing about it. She wished now she'd never said anything but she'd wanted to be honest and make a new start. I said that she had done the right thing because if you are married you are meant to be honest. Though I've never been married myself, so I'm not the best person to ask. But I reminded her she'd forbidden the mention of a certain person and she was already talking about him. She had to be strong and I had to help her – she'd said so. She laughed but I could see she didn't find it funny. She said, "Oh God, Freddy, I wish I could just run away from it all," and I said she mustn't think like that. Then we watched a movie on the television. It wasn't the kind of film I like but I just watched to keep her company. It was in black and white, about a woman who was married and in love with someone else. Anna starting crying but she wouldn't let me turn it off, she said it was good for her. So I left her to it and went down to the stables to see Miletus, Mum's horse. He was kept in one of the stables in the old barn on the other side of the yard. I spent some time with him and the horses over there. Then I thought I'd go and sweep up round the pool because that's one of my jobs, and that's where I saw Glyn Cole.'

'What exactly was he doing?' Greening asked.

'Just standing by the pool.'

'Why was he standing there?'

'I don't know. He was watching the water. People do – I often do.'

'What did you do?'

'I went over to him and told him to leave. I said he wasn't welcome any more. But he refused and I hit him. He fell backwards into the pool.'

'You hit him?'

'I thought he was going to go to try and persuade Anna to go away with him. The way she was feeling, I thought she might say yes. I was trying to protect her from herself. Like she'd asked me to.'

'But,' Greening said, 'before, at the yard and on the way here, you said you pushed him. You didn't say you hit him.'

'Does it matter? He went in the water and he couldn't swim.'

'Where on his body did you hit or push him?'

Freddy thought. 'I punched him in the face. He deserved it.'

'And what happened when he hit the water?'

'He shouted. He wanted me to help him out because he couldn't swim. But I wouldn't. I just watched him drown.'

'Didn't he try and climb out?'

'He tried but I pushed him back in again.'

'Yes, but the pool has an island in the middle. Why didn't he try and climb out on the other side, away from where you were?'

'Well, he didn't. He splashed and shouted and then he went under. He just drowned.'

'How long did it take?'

Freddy thought. 'Not long. Two or three minutes.'

Greening paused for a moment, studying Freddy. He looked more flustered than before, though considering that he was confessing to murder, that was probably not a surprise.

'Then what did you do after he was dead?'

'I got him out of the water.'

'How?'

'I used one of the poles we use for the horses. I sort of pushed him round with it on to the ramp. Then I was able to get hold of him and pull him out.'

'Would you describe this pole for me please?'

'It's just a pole – made of wood, about six foot long.'

'What is its purpose?'

'If there's just one of you swimming a horse you need it to keep the horse straight.'

'So what did you do when you got the body out of the pool?'

'I put it in a wheelbarrow and covered it with a muck sack.'

'What's that? Some kind of garden sack?'

'It's just a big bit of plastic. You use it to clear out horse muck.'

'I see.' Greening changed tack slightly. 'Were you alone all this time?'

'It was Sunday afternoon. There was nobody there.'

'But don't people come back to feed the horses?'

'Oh yes. At four o'clock. This was about half past three. Anyway, the pool is hidden from the stables, it's round the corner in front of the office.'

Greening nodded. He'd noted the arrangement of the buildings.

'Then what happened?'

'I waited until it was night and then I put him in the Land Rover. I drove up to the top end and tied Glyn to the tree.'

'What made you think of hiding him like that?'

Freddy grinned. 'Well, nobody ever looks up, do they?'

Greening thought that he had a point.

'How did you manage to get him up?'

'With a pulley. There was a block and tackle in the shed and I used that. I've used it lots before. It was easy.'

Greening let that pass. He could hardly imagine a more difficult task, manoeuvring the stiffening corpse of a man the same size as yourself twenty-five feet up a tree in the dark.

'How long did it take you?'

'I don't know exactly – not more than an hour. I finished about two o'clock.'

'Then what did you do?'

'Glyn's car was in the car park in the yard. I'd taken his keys from his jacket and I drove it into Swindon.'

'How did you get back?'

'Oh. I caught the night bus to Lambourn.'

Greening leaned back in his chair. He had only one more question.

'Who helped you, Freddy?'

The man across the table from him blinked. Then said firmly, 'Nobody.'

'I can't believe you let him go.'

Greening could see that Yvonne was seething as they returned to the incident room. A car had been summoned to drive Freddy home. He'd seemed perplexed by the dismissal, though not as much as Yvonne.

'He's not going to run away,' Greening said. 'We can get him back any time we like.'

'But he just coughed to murder, Alan. What on earth are you playing at?'

'Did you believe him?' He turned to face her on the stairs. 'Is that what you think happened to Glyn Cole?'

'I don't see why not. It answers all the questions, doesn't it?'

'Hardly. When it comes to the murder, his story's got more holes than a Swiss cheese.'

'Such as?'

'Such as he can't decide whether he pushed Cole into the water or hit him. And what was Cole doing there anyway? If he was on his way to talk Anna into changing her mind, why go and stand by the pool? I also don't believe that a strong and healthy man like Cole just drowned in a couple of minutes even if he couldn't swim.'

'But we've been wondering what killed him and

drowning makes sense, doesn't it? How would he know about that?'

'Beyond us draining the pool, you mean? But I take your point.'

Yvonne flashed him a grin. 'Getting through to you at last, eh?'

'Look, I'm not saying he's not in this up to his neck. All that stuff about taking Anna to see Cole in Hungerford sounds spot on to me. But I don't believe he killed him, though there's a good chance he fished the body out of the water and hid it.'

'Yeah?'

'So, the question is, who did put Cole in the water? And smashed his hands – probably with that pole – when he tried to get out? I bet he beat Cole over the head with it too, while he was in the water, shoved him underneath the surface. It would have been bloody and horrible and taken a while. Nothing like Freddy's account.'

'And you think whoever killed him got Freddy to help hide the body?'

'Don't you? Putting Cole up the tree is a two-man job at least. And then you need another car to go into Swindon alongside Cole's Volvo to bring the driver back. I bet there isn't a night bus to Lambourn.'

'I'll check.'

'Good. And I want the Pitchbury yard searched, especially round the pool and in the shed he referred to. You know what to look for – poles, block-and-tackle kit, rope, wheelbarrow.'

'Leave it to me, boss.'

*

Greening barely had his foot inside the incident room when Davis waylaid him.

'Your PCSO girlfriend is here to see you.'

'I don't have time for her at the moment.'

'Actually, Alan, I think you do.' Davis was grinning. 'I've made her comfortable in a room upstairs. She's been waiting a while.'

'What's going on, Les?'

'Just go and see her. She's brought someone to talk to you.'

Greening tramped up the stairs in mild irritation, thinking as he went that young Carmel had managed to charm old Les more successfully than she had Yvonne. But why should that surprise him?

Two figures leapt to their feet as he pushed open the door to the meeting room. One was so tall his mop of brown floppy hair threatened to brush the ceiling. By his side Carmel looked like a little doll.

'I'd like to introduce Jan Vandeneijnde,' she said proudly.

The visitor rushed forward with an outstretched hand. 'Delighted to meet you, Inspector. I hope you don't mind me coming to see you about this terrible business of my friend Glyn. Carmel has shown me the press reports of his death.'

Greening had been feeling a bit bushed after the session with Freddy but as the visitor's warm fingers clasped his, he felt new wind in his sails.

'I'm sorry to keep you waiting,' he said.

'That's OK, you weren't expecting me. I've had time to teach Carmel how to say my name.' Jan grinned. He seemed a cheery sort of fellow and not an obvious candidate for involvement in the international drugs trade.

Carmel was explaining about a letter to old Mrs Shaw. She was still on her feet, unsure whether she was allowed to remain. Well, why not? She'd performed a service in pulling the Dutch rabbit out of the hat.

He waved her back into her seat and pulled out the faxed photograph he'd been carrying around. It bore only the most general resemblance to the man in front of him.

Jan's face fell as Greening handed it to him.

'Why do you have a photograph of my brother?'

Greening explained.

'I see. It is a terrible thing for my family about my brother. I don't make excuses for him, however.'

'Do you have any criminal convictions yourself?' Greening asked.

'Excuse me, Inspector, but I came here voluntarily to find out what happened to my friend. Why are you asking me a question like that? And bringing my brother into it? Am I under suspicion?'

The answer to that was yes – at least, it would have been before Freddy Drummond had stuck his head above the parapet. Greening could detain Jan if he wanted to but he didn't see the advantage in antagonising him. Better by far to have the Dutchman's cooperation.

'To be honest, Jan, it has been difficult discovering exactly what happened to Mr Cole two years ago, beyond the fact of his murder and concealment. We have been pursuing every lead with suspicion. Your name came up as a frequent visitor to Mr Cole's shop in Hungerford, in particular we believe you were present on the day before Mr Cole disappeared. When we made inquiries with our Dutch colleagues, your brother's name – and conviction for drug-smuggling – came to our attention.'

'You thought that I was responsible for Glyn's death because my brother was in jail?'

'We've been under the impression that both you and Mr Cole were known to the Dutch authorities because of your involvement in the drugs trade.'

Jan shook his head wearily. 'That is completely untrue.'

Greening waited for him to continue.

'I met Glyn in Amsterdam about fifteen years ago. I was a student and he was working on a market stall. He was sleeping on people's floors and I offered him a room in a flat I shared with my brother. And that is the only connection either of us ever had with the drugs trade, as you call it. I confess we went to the brown cafés sometimes and smoked a little but that's not a crime in my country. But my brother is – well, he is my brother and I love him but he lives by different standards to me. He should have been a proper businessman. He would have made a lot of money and people would have been impressed that I was his brother. As it is, people think worse of me because I am related to a criminal and accuse me of behaving in ways I would never do. I believe the phrase is guilt by association. Neither Glyn nor I ever had anything to do with the drugs business and I will happily refute any specific allegations you put to me.'

'Thank you for clearing that up,' Greening said. The

fact was, he didn't have any specific allegations, just rumour and innuendo. But you made bricks out of whatever straw came to hand. He dismissed the drug suspicions for the moment. 'Would you like to tell us about the last time you saw Mr Cole?'

'Oh, OK.' The Dutchman looked slightly mollified. 'Glyn had told me some weeks before that he was thinking of selling his business. At first he wouldn't tell me why, then he admitted he had finally found a woman he was serious about but it was complicated. I got the impression she was married or in a really serious relationship but he was confident he could persuade her to go away with him. I'd seen him recently and he'd been buzzing about getting five thousand pounds for a Regency table which he'd had for ages because he couldn't bear to part with it. Now I realised why he'd sold it.'

'Why was that?'

'Because he was planning to take this woman out of the country. He said he needed the money from the business and asked me if I knew anyone who would be interested. Though I was still living in Amsterdam at that time, I had contacts in the antique trade in London and I asked around. I was introduced to a possible buyer and we set up a meeting in Hungerford for the Saturday you are talking about.'

'The twelfth of April two thousand and eight.'

'If you say so – it sounds right. The buyer and I arrived at the shop in good time but Glyn wasn't there and we had to wait. Unfortunately, Errol – that was the buyer's name – took this badly. I think he thought it was some kind of negotiating tactic but I knew Glyn wasn't that kind of guy. Anyway, when Glyn finally showed up, things didn't go so good. Errol made some ridiculously low offer for the stock and Glyn told him to get lost, or words to that effect, and Errol walked out. He'd given me a lift down from London in his car and he said he'd wait five minutes for me, otherwise I'd have to make my own way back. I apologised to Glyn for Errol's behaviour and he said sorry to me, because he'd been rude but he was out of sorts. The woman he loved had changed her mind about going away with him. I asked if he still wanted to sell now he'd lost the girl and he said the way he was feeling he wanted to pack the business in anyway. By now, Errol was pooping his horn outside and I suggested I stay the night and we talk things over. But Glyn said he would be bad company. He promised he'd call me the next day and so I went back to London.'

'Can you tell us how to get in touch with Errol?'

'So you can check my story? For sure.' Jan pulled a notebook from his bag and wrote down the contact details, verifying them with the address book on his iPhone.

Greening tucked the slip of paper into his shirt pocket. Jan's account was interesting. It certainly seemed more likely that 'the deal' Amanda Yates had overheard Errol discussing was a straight business negotiation.

'I rang Glyn the next morning,' Jan continued, 'and asked if he still wanted to sell his business. There were other people apart from Errol I could approach on his behalf. He said that he couldn't talk about it right at the moment because something urgent had come up.

I asked if it was to do with his failed romance and he said there was a connection but he couldn't talk because he was waiting for a call. He would ring me later in the week to explain. But he never did and he didn't answer my messages. I was back in Amsterdam and time went by and I still didn't hear. But the next time I was in London I went down to Hungerford and his shop was closed. I tried to talk to Mrs Shaw, the lady next door, but I was told she was in hospital. So, I just thought that he'd sold up and moved on after his unhappy love affair. I hoped he'd be in touch with me but he never was. I was a little hurt but, you know, you lose friends in life. I never expected to lose a friend like this though.'

Greening thought that if this was an act, it was worthy of an Oscar. But why would Jan bother to act? He'd initiated his appearance at this interview himself, by writing to Mrs Shaw and responding to Carmel's phone call. If he had murdered his old friend, it was a strange way to behave.

'Mr Cole said he was waiting for a call – did he say who from?'

'Yes, but it sounded funny to me – Scratch. Is that a name in English?'

'Scratch could be a nickname. Are you sure about it?'

'Not really, Inspector. I wished I'd asked him about it at the time but I could tell he just wanted me off the phone. I'm sorry.'

There was nothing for Jan to be sorry about, Greening thought. Quite the contrary.

*

Doing the dishes and tidying up the gatehouse was not Tammy's idea of a romantic evening. Realistically, she'd not expected to have Will to herself given the dramas that had been going on, but she was disappointed not to have his company at all.

Freddy had spent all afternoon with the police in Swindon and the shock at the Hall and in the yard had been almost palpable. Edward and Katherine had held a whispered conversation, after which they had enlisted her support: Anna was not to be told – for the moment anyway. After that, Edward disappeared to his study to phone a lawyer in London.

Then, remarkably, Freddy reappeared, driven back to the Hall by an affable policeman. He had refused to say much about what had happened and had even calmed Edward down when he'd started talking about suing the police for wrongful arrest. In the event, he had returned to the gatehouse to walk the dogs as usual and Will had collected a takeaway for the three of them.

But now, it being Friday night, Freddy had insisted on going to the White Hart and Will had accompanied him. Tammy would have gone too, except that Will had taken her aside and asked her not to come. He had been apologetic but firm – he needed to talk to Freddy on his own and find out what had happened at the police station. Tammy could see the importance of that and had agreed, on the understanding that Will made it up to her soon. However, the promise of a future night out did not erase the mundane nature of the evening ahead.

When she'd finished in the kitchen, she sorted out

the front room which was plainly missing Mrs Drummond's touch. Mugs and plates had accumulated, cushions were flattened into unrecognisable shapes and sections of a racing paper were scattered like leaves across the floor. Lodger and Porky followed her as she tidied, chasing the newspaper into the corners of the room and prodding her with their noses, eager for play. She didn't mind – any attention was better than none, after all.

'When I've finished in here, I'll take you out,' she told them. Why not? She had nothing better to do.

She hurried. There was only the desk in the bay of the window and that wouldn't take long to sort out. The top surface, around the computer and on top of the keyboard, was covered with faded olive-green folders which were kept in slings in the drawers beneath. Edward had been rooting through Mrs Drummond's papers the other night and hadn't put half of them back.

The slings were labelled but Tammy didn't bother with trying to match things up. She just shoved the folders into the available slots. As she manoeuvred the last folder into place, something solid fell out on to the floor. Porky, the terrier, dashed for it but couldn't get it in his mouth.

Tammy pushed the dog away and picked it up. It was a CD in a plain jewel case with a piece of paper attached by a rubber band. As Tammy was about to pop it back into the folder, a handwritten word on the paper caught her attention: 'Glyn'. She smoothed out the paper – a complimentary slip from Glyn Cole Antiques – and read: 'Dear Mrs Drummond, here's the back-up of the inventory I promised you, together with my invoice. Once again, may I say what a pleasure it has been to work on this fascinating task. Sincerely yours, Glyn.' On the note, in a different hand, was pencilled, 'Paid by cheque, 6 March 08.'

How spooky it was. This inventory seemed to lie in wait for her at every turn.

She turned on the computer and inserted the CD. Lodger the lurcher nuzzled her thigh.

'You'll have to wait,' she told him and fondled his ears as the document opened on the screen.

She was familiar with its layout by now and quickly scrolled down to the listing of the old watches. But though she might be familiar with the format, the detail was different. Eighteen watches were described and not seventeen. Tammy was certain the last one on the list was not on the inventory Anna had been using at the Hall. It described a mid-nineteenth-century gold timepiece with a hidden erotic scene of 'amorous couple making love on a riverbank'. It was the watch Mrs Drummond had been hunting for.

Tammy didn't dwell on the implications. She moved on quickly, ignoring the nagging of the dogs. She found the two other items that were listed as missing in Mrs Drummond's notebook, a paperweight and a snuffbox.

It was tempting to pick up the phone to Anna but she didn't. It would be better to talk to her face to face.

'OK, doggies,' she said, 'it's your lucky night. Two walks. But I want you to know that I would rather be walking with someone else.'

That didn't bother them in the slightest.

Chapter Seventeen

Greening took the call from Davis when he was already on the road to Oxford the next morning.

'I think I've solved it, boss. On Sunday the thirteenth Cole made three calls to a guy listed in his address book as Martin S. I've been on to the phone company and the subscriber is Martin—'

'Scratchwood of the Scratchwood Art Gallery in Summertown. Yes, I know.'

'Bloody hell! *How* do you know?'

'I worked it out, Les. I have connections in the artistic community, don't forget. But, as ever, you are a most reliable back-up.' Greening could imagine the expression of pique on Davis's face and it tickled him. He had no intention of revealing that he had been on the receiving end of another of Carmel's late-night phone calls.

'I've been talking to Pam Bellamy, sir,' she'd said. 'There's a gallery owner in Oxford called Martin Scratchwood and everyone calls him Scratch. Do you think it could be him?'

Of course there'd been a price to pay for this latest

titbit from his young informant. She'd somehow talked herself into this morning's trip to Oxford. Or maybe he'd invited her along. Whatever, she was a handy second pair of eyes and the rest of the team had their hands full.

'We've found a lot of likely stuff at the training yard,' Davis said. 'The forensic guys are crawling all over the pool area. And Dougie's over there too, collecting rope samples.'

'Excellent. Any word from your watch man?'

'Mr Venables. He's ninety-eight per cent certain the face is a match.'

'Big of him to be so sure.'

'He says he's wrong about these things two out of a hundred times. He's a precision workman.'

'Fair enough. There's one more thing you can do for me, Les. Pick up Edward Pemberton and stick him in Farley Road till I get back.'

'Yes, boss.' Davis sounded enthusiastic for the first time. 'Do you think he's the guy?'

'I'm keeping an open mind but he had a good reason to bump Cole off – he as good as said to me he'd have enjoyed it. And I reckon that if he ordered Freddy to help him, the lad would have hopped to it without question. The pair of them could easily have hoisted the body up a tree.'

'But wasn't he off at the races in Newton Abbot?'

'He says he went with Rosemary Drummond but he'll have to come up with something better than that. It's not usual for the dead to alibi the living.'

'Well, not unless she left a diary or—'

'You know what I mean, Les. Anyway, I looked at

the back pages of the paper this morning for a change. Pemberton has four runners at Newbury this afternoon so you'd better nip over there smartish and nab him before he clears off.'

Tammy arrived at the Hall to find a note for her on the kitchen table from Edward. It said that Anna had been unable to sleep and had taken a sleeping tablet at four in the morning. Would Tammy check to see she was OK but try not to wake her. And he would appreciate it if she would tidy his study, which was a bit of a mess.

First she looked in on Anna, who appeared dead to the world. This was frustrating as Tammy wanted to tell her what she'd found out about the inventory. She'd brought the disc with her from the gatehouse but any discussion would have to wait. Maybe that wasn't so bad.

Edward's study had the fug of stale alcohol and late-night occupation. A blanket was crumpled on the sofa next to a pillow which belonged in the main bed. Tammy assumed that Edward had left Anna in the night so she could sleep undisturbed, maybe around the time she took her pill. It wasn't the first time Edward had slept in the study during Anna's difficult pregnancy.

She plumped cushions, collected up the bedding and opened the windows to freshen the air.

Then, feeling like a criminal, she turned the computer on. If Anna had been awake she would have asked permission which, she knew, would not have been refused. All the same, it felt sneaky checking out a man's computer files behind his back.

The Windows XP screen opened and she clicked on Edward's name. If he really cared, she told herself, he should have installed a password.

Greening was not surprised to find Carmel had beaten him to the Scratchwood Gallery, a double-fronted window on a side street off the Banbury Road. She was in her stylish civilian gear today, studying a window that featured outsize photographic sunsets, cunningly shot so that they might not in fact be sunsets at all. The red tones of the largest frame could be a sandstorm in the desert or clouds on a mountain or even, Greening thought uncomfortably, blood swirling through the filter of a swimming pool.

'These have got something,' Carmel said, 'but I prefer that over there.' She pointed to the other window, which showcased one colourful canvas, of a woman with a pink and gold head-dress and a glittery necklace. Greening admired it for a second then turned away. He wasn't here to look at art.

'Is he in there then?' he asked.

'Pam says he's a tall bloke with a big nose and a bald head,' she said. 'So I guess that must be him.'

Through the glass door a man answering that description was sitting behind a desk watching them with faint curiosity, probably calculating whether they were prospective punters or – Greening was getting used to the idea – father and daughter who had used the gallery doorway as a meeting point.

He strode in and the owner got languidly to his feet. 'So you finally plucked up your courage to come in. That's your first good decision of the day.'

'What's my second going to be?' Greening asked.

'When you buy one of my wonderful paintings, of course.' The man was beaming, plainly enjoying himself.

'Then I'm going to be a disappointment to you, Mr Scratchwood.' Greening took out his identity card and introduced himself.

Scratchwood smiled ruefully. 'I've sold art to police officers before, Inspector. And I have high hopes for this young lady who, I see, has sufficient taste to wear a rather fine art deco brooch.'

Greening was amused to see Carmel blush.

'Do you have the time to answer a few questions?'

Scratchwood gestured to the empty gallery. 'Ask away.'

'Are you acquainted with Glyn Cole, of Glyn Cole Antiques in Hungerford?'

'Of course. Has he turned up? Last I heard he'd packed it all in.'

It transpired that Scratchwood had no idea Glyn's body had been found, or the circumstances of the discovery. He sat down heavily and gestured to the chairs by the desk. 'Please take a seat. This is a shock. I don't read the papers much – they're too depressing. Poor Glyn. What on earth happened?'

'It's a mystery we are currently trying to unravel. We believe you are one of the last people to talk to him.'

'Me?'

'He disappeared on or shortly after the thirteenth of April two thousand and eight. That was a Sunday. According to his phone records he rang you that morning and you called him back. Do you recall those conversations?'

'Yes. It was a bit odd. Glyn was very stewed up and he wasn't a guy to get hot under the collar about anything. Unless it was a pretty girl.' He nodded to Carmel, evidently beginning to cheer up. 'He'd have loved you and your brooch.'

'What was he stewed up about?' Greening asked, keeping his impatience in check.

'Actually, it was a watch. A beautifully made Victorian timepiece which I had taken in part payment for a painting. I have a background in antiques, you see. I've done a fair amount of business with Glyn in the past.'

'And you offered to sell this watch to Mr Cole?'

'Indirectly, yes.'

Tammy found the inventory file without difficulty. She opened it and compared it with the printout Anna had given her, the one they had been using to check items upstairs. It was identical. She closed the file, then opened its Properties box which gave the details of its origination.

The Word file had been created on 22 February 2008 at 20:57:51 – which made sense. That's when Glyn Cole would have sat down at his computer and begun work on the list. It had been accessed on 15 May 2010 at 10:46:46 – which was just a few minutes ago when she had opened it up. The line between was the one that grabbed her attention.

It read, 'Modified: 22 November 2009, 14:57:51.'

So someone had altered the text last November.

Someone who, surely, had removed an item from the collection upstairs and then changed the record to cover their tracks. Of course, the inventory could have been altered many times between its origination and the November date. Maybe the computer held that information but Tammy didn't know how to access it. But that was beside the point. The question was, who had done it?

Tammy didn't waste time racking her brain. She was sitting at Edward's computer, in the house where he lived and where he had twenty-four-hour access to the objects upstairs. Why he should be stealing from the family treasures she had no idea. Only that Mrs Drummond had been very unhappy when she'd stumbled upon it, so the things must have been taken without discussion or permission.

Her first impulse was to tell Anna that she had solved the mystery of the missing items. Let her deal with the consequences. Tammy wasn't happy being in sole possession of such a secret.

She went upstairs to the bedroom to find Anna still lost in a deep sleep. She debated waking her. But it seemed cruel and, anyway, if Anna was still doped up, what would be the point? Much better to curb her impatience and wait till Anna was in full possession of her wits.

Tammy returned to the study and set the printer to churn out a copy of Glyn's original inventory, from the CD she'd brought with her. Then she went to the kitchen to fetch her dusters and other cleaning equipment. Whatever happened, she still had a job to do.

She unfolded a black plastic rubbish sack and emptied into it the contents of the wastepaper basket, first retrieving a dead Biro and an empty paracetamol blister pack. This was her usual routine, to separate out the recyclable rubbish as she went round the house. She knelt down beside the paper shredder and removed its lid. Unless it was emptied carefully you ended up with ribbons of paper all over the carpet, as she knew from experience.

It wasn't the best shredder in the world. It simply sliced each sheet of paper into long strips, half a centimetre wide. Tammy had thought more than once that it wouldn't pass muster in the offices of MI5. Personally, she wouldn't trust it to chew up her bank statement.

So it was no surprise to find herself holding strips of thick yellowing paper on which words and parts thereof were not only visible but easy to sequence. The letters 'Exhi' caught her eye. She matched the strip next to it – it was partially attached – and made out 'Great Exhi'. Her fingers snatched at the next piece. It didn't marry up but the next one did, to spell out 'Great Exhibition'.

She knew just where she had last heard mention of the Great Exhibition – the third entry in Mrs Drummond's notebook: 'Great Exhibition snuffbox', under the heading 'Missing'.

She looked at the curling mass of paper pieces in the bin of the shredder. The yellow paper stood out. She had no doubt that she'd found another list of the family valuables, one that pre-dated either of the other documents. This paper came from an age before computer files. Suppose Mrs Drummond had dug it up from somewhere and used it to check against? She could see flecks of red ink against the yellow – it could be the dead woman's writing.

Tammy's heart was racing in her chest but she forced herself to take a deep breath. She'd read somewhere that, after the collapse of the Berlin Wall, women had been employed to piece together the millions of documents that been shredded in the last days of the GDR. They were still at it years later, reconstructing whole files and unearthing secrets of the past.

Compared to that, this was a simple task.

'Indirectly?' Greening's tone was gentle but his gaze was piercing as he considered Martin Scratchwood's words. 'How do you sell something indirectly?'

'I was selling it through a third party. I don't have time to go hanging around too many auctions these days. I've got a tie-up with a Cork Street gallery in London now. Around here's lovely but it's a bit provincial. Certainly as far as making money goes.'

'A third party, Mr Scratchwood?' Carmel said, steering him back to the point.

'Yes. I know a guy called Bubble who handles specialist stuff for me. Did I mention this watch had a false cover and a naughty picture underneath? All very genteel compared to what you get these days but there's nothing new under the sun. Anyway, Bubble took the watch to an auction on the Saturday to see if he could get any interest.'

'Why didn't you sell it in the auction?' Greening asked.

'Can't be doing with catalogues and viewings and all that. I wanted a quick sale and Bubble would be doing the rounds. He knew the kind of guys who'd be interested anyway.'

'Like Glyn Cole, you mean?'

'That's what Bubble hoped. He took Glyn to one side, showed him the watch and asked if he was interested. He was interested all right.'

'He wanted to buy it?'

'No. He wanted to find out how I'd got hold of it. He thought it was stolen.'

Tammy heard footsteps in the hall a second before the study door opened. Anna must be awake at last. But it wasn't Anna.

'What on earth are you doing?' Katherine looked astonished as she took in Tammy's form, bent over the desk, reassembling bits of the old inventory with Sellotape.

'Look at this,' Tammy said and explained her discovery in the shredder. 'It's an inventory from nineteen sixty-eight. See?' She pointed at the heading on the first page, which was clearly visible. 'I think Mrs Drummond must have found it – that's her writing in red, isn't it?'

'Good Lord. She told me she'd unearthed it from Uncle Jack's papers but I forgot all about it.' Katherine pored over the bits.

'And look at this.' Tammy opened Cole's inventory on the computer screen. 'Glyn sent in a copy on disc. This one here. But it's been altered on the file on this computer.' She demonstrated how. 'Those items that

Mrs Drummond listed as missing in her notebook are precisely those missing from the most recent document. But they are present on Glyn's original and,' she tapped the reconstituted pages on the desk, 'on the nineteen sixty-eight original.'

The surprise and mild amusement which had been present on Katherine's face slowly hardened. 'I don't know what to make of this.'

'It's obvious. Edward has been taking things and amending the file to cover it up. Taking things without Mrs Drummond's agreement.'

'Well,' Katherine reflected, 'I'm not sure it's any of our business.'

'I suppose you're right. It's not *my* business anyway. Except – come with me, I want to show you something.'

She made for the door, Katherine following reluctantly behind.

'The watch was stolen?' Greening queried.

'Glyn said he thought it was. He said he recognised it as part of a collection he had valued a couple of months earlier. I said it was perfectly legitimate. I knew where the watch had come from. It had been in the hands of the same family for over a hundred years. They live in some fancy pile near Lambourn. This particular watch didn't really fit in with the rest of the collection – not very PC. So they'd decided to raise some cash on it.'

'I thought you said it was given in part exchange for a picture?' Carmel was in quickly, before Greening.

'It was. One of his.' Scratchwood pointed to the

canvas of the woman in the window. 'An exceedingly good deal on their part, I must say. That's a Rory Picard. Do you know how much he goes for up in London?'

Greening shook his head. Might as well ask him the chemical composition of rocket fuel – he wouldn't know where to start.

'A hundred thousand,' Carmel said.

Scratchwood's eyes goggled as he pantomimed being impressed. 'Not only well dressed but well informed. Last month a Picard that size went for one hundred and ten thousand pounds. I spotted him when he was at art school in Manchester. All the southern dealers were snotty about him but I bought up his leaving show and he's loved me ever since. Long may it last. That's not for sale incidentally, so you can keep your chequebook in your pocket, Inspector. It's already spoken for.'

Greening was getting lost in this fog of verbiage. He was going off Scratchwood fast.

'When Glyn Cole rang you that Sunday morning he wanted to find out who sold you the watch. That's what it boils down to, am I right?'

'Yes, that's correct. He wanted to have a word with them about it.'

'You keep saying "them", Mr Scratchwood. Who precisely was it?'

The gallery owner sighed and got to his feet. 'I'll have to fetch my old sales book. If you'll excuse me.' And he headed towards a flight of stairs that appeared to lead down to the basement.

When he'd gone, Carmel met Greening's stare.

'Got any idea what name he's going to come up with?' he asked.

'Edward Pemberton,' she said with confidence.

Tammy led Katherine to the top landing, just along from the museum room. She pointed back down the narrow flight of stairs they had just ascended.

'What do you see?' she asked.

Katherine regarded her unhappily. 'I see the staircase where poor Aunty died. Is that your point?'

'Not quite. What do you see at the bottom of the stairs?'

'A rug that hides a bloodstain. What's up with you, Tammy? You're being ghoulish.'

'Sorry, it's just that when I cleared up the day after Mrs Drummond's accident, I knew something didn't look right but now it's back to normal. You can't see the table from here but on the day of the accident you could. It had been moved a foot or so along the corridor.'

'Why does that matter?'

'Because if you fell down the stairs now you wouldn't crash into the table and you wouldn't be able to knock the vase over.'

'Oh.' Katherine weighed the matter. 'You're saying that someone deliberately moved the table so Aunty would fall into it?'

'I'm saying that Edward knew Mrs Drummond was on to his thieving and he pushed her down the stairs. Then he dropped the vase on her head to kill her and moved the table across to make it look like an accident. And now he's moved the table back to its proper place.

I know exactly where it should be – I've been hoovering round it for months.'

Katherine's jaw dropped. 'That's mad, Tammy. You can't go around accusing people of murder.'

'I know it's hard to swallow but what about the old inventory? I bet Mrs Drummond was up here that afternoon checking stuff against it and that's why Edward killed her. Then he put the inventory through the shredder, thinking he'd destroyed it.'

'I can't believe Edward is a murderer.'

'Why not? He was in the army, wasn't he? That's what soldiers do. Anyway, you were the one who put the idea in my head.'

'What do you mean?'

'Yesterday when we were talking about the police putting pressure on Edward, you said that even if he killed Glyn he wouldn't confess. It admitted the possibility. I've been turning it over ever since and it fits. He killed Glyn because of the affair and he killed Mrs Drummond to hide his stealing. Besides, with her out of the way, doesn't his wife inherit everything?'

Katherine looked at her with exasperation. 'How old are you, Tammy? Twenty? This is just wild speculation and potentially very damaging. I know you're not a member of this family but you're a trusted friend. How do you think my aunt would feel to hear you talking like this? You've really got to be very careful what you say.'

'I intend to be. I'm only going to tell Anna what I believe. What happens after that is up to her.'

'You can't tell Anna her husband has murdered her mother. It's like some ridiculous Greek tragedy.'

'But what if it's true?'

'It's not and I'll prove it to you.'

'How?'

'For a start, at least one of those things on Aunty's list has not gone missing at all. I've seen that snuffbox, I'm sure. Come on, I'll show you.'

Tammy followed her into the room with the disputed family treasures. Even if Katherine produced the snuffbox, she wasn't convinced that would make a difference to what she now believed.

'What about your friend Inspector Greening?' she said, as Katherine rooted in a pile of boxes. 'Why don't you tell him about the table and the old inventory? You could do it off the record, couldn't you?'

Katherine lifted her head from her task. 'You're joking. I'm not going to waste Alan's time with any of this stupidity.'

Tammy could understand that maybe Katherine would be reluctant to make herself look a fool in front of a man she had designs on. She, on the other hand, had no such constraints. And, on second thoughts, talking to the police would be more responsible than dumping the decision on Anna, who wasn't in the best of shape.

'I'll talk to him myself then. If I'm spouting rubbish, he can tell me so. At the very least, I want them to investigate Mrs Drummond's death properly. I bet they don't know about the table. But they took photographs of the scene – they should prove my point.'

'Here.' Katherine was handing her a small leather hold-all. 'The snuffboxes are in there.'

Tammy laid it on the top of the card table and opened the lid. She was about to say that there was nothing inside but old photograph frames when something hammered into the side of her head and robbed her of the power of speech. Robbed her of the capacity to do anything at all.

Scratchwood returned, a blue notebook in his hand. He resumed his seat and fiddled around in a desk drawer. 'I'm always losing my reading glasses. They must be in here somewhere.'

'Do you only sell contemporary art?' Greening asked.

'Not necessarily. I'd sell anything if it was good enough. If you had a Turner tucked away in the attic, Inspector, I think I could find it wall space.'

'I was thinking of something a bit more recent. Paul Nash, for example.'

'Oh yes.' Scratchwood's face lit up and he stopped his hunt – he was now on the third drawer. 'Slade artist of the Great War. Lovely landscapes. He and his brother John are highly prized.'

'So his paintings wouldn't be cheap then?'

'Good Lord, no. Oh dear, I don't seem to be able to find . . .'

Carmel reached over the desk and pulled a pair of spectacles from Scratchwood's shirt pocket. She looked a trifle smug, Greening thought, and he anticipated that self-satisfaction being replaced by surprise in just a matter of seconds. It would be good for her to understand that she wasn't always right.

'Here we are,' Scratchwood said, finding the entry at

last. 'Rory Picard's Simone II, oil on canvas, was sold to Katherine Pym on 5 April 2008 for £7,500. I've a note here that she paid £4,000 in cash and I took the nineteenth-century lovers pocket watch in lieu of the balance.' He shut his book with a smile. 'The Pyms of Pitchbury Hall in Lambourn, that's the family.'

Tammy woke in pain. She couldn't move. She lay on the floor among the boxes and trunks, her hands and feet bound together by the reins of the old horse tack.

'If you shout or scream, I'll hit you again.'

Katherine stood over her. She held one of the pair of bronze horses in her hand.

Tammy understood that she had been knocked down and tied up but she couldn't fathom why.

'What are you doing?' she said, the words thick, the sound of them distant in her buzzing head.

'I tried to tell you that you couldn't be allowed to go mouthing off, not to Anna or the police. You didn't give me a choice.'

'I don't understand. Why are you protecting Edward?'

Katherine squatted down next to her. 'You're a smart girl, Tammy, but only up to a point. Edward is an arrogant little corporal who has been promoted way above his true rank. He doesn't need to kill anybody to get his share. He's been handed it on a plate.'

Tammy's wits were clearing. 'Unlike you, you mean.'

'Precisely.' Katherine was gripping a knife; the blade caught the sunlight streaming in from the window. 'My mother was born into the good life and she rejected it. She made it very hard for me to get back in. I've had to fight for my place and I still don't have my feet properly under the table. Who could blame me if I pinched a few crumbs? Yet the way my aunt went on about that stupid watch, you'd think I'd stolen the crown jewels. She asked for it in the end.'

'*You* killed her?'

'I knew I'd never stop her otherwise. People can be remarkably blind sometimes. They don't seem to realise that it's dangerous to take a person for granted. My aunt assumed that the booty our family have accumulated was hers to give away to one of her good causes. But if I asked for anything she just turned me down flat.'

'So you pushed her down the stairs?'

'Smart of you to spot that I moved the table and shredded her bloody inventory. Not so smart to tell me, of course. Now I have to decide what to do with you.' She held up the knife. 'How am I going to get rid of your body? That's the question.'

Tammy began to shake. She couldn't believe the situation she found herself in. Katherine was joking, surely? She listened in mounting terror, her eyes on the shining blade in the other woman's unwavering hand.

'When I killed Glyn I panicked and ran away. He was in the pool in the yard and there was a bit of a mess. I'd had to hit him a lot with one of those big poles and there was blood all over the side – he took forever to die. I knew I couldn't cover it up so I just drove home and waited for the news to break. I steeled myself to brave the storm. But it never happened. Glyn just disappeared into thin air. It was a kind of miracle. Edward must have got rid of the corpse to avoid scandal. But I don't suppose he'll be so helpful with you.'

Bewildered, Tammy stared into the other woman's brown and beautiful eyes and read absolute conviction. Anna had told her Katherine had once had psychiatric problems but had recovered. She must have relapsed.

'You're not well, Katherine. You need help.'

'Shut up. I'm just the product of my experience, like everyone else. Did you know my mother killed herself in the bathroom just down this corridor? With a knife like this one here. Perhaps you'd like to cut your wrists in the bath too.'

'I'd never kill myself. No one would believe it.'

'Oh, I don't know. You're an emotional young woman whose mother has terminal cancer and your new boyfriend has been sleeping with Anna Pemberton for years.'

'That's a lie!'

Katherine chuckled. 'Are you absolutely sure?'

Outside the Scratchwood Gallery, Carmel looked at Greening accusingly. 'Why aren't you surprised?'

'It just came to me. Katherine's the one who collects art. She's got a fancy security system at her home to keep it safe. From what I now understand, she needs it – her paintings appear to be worth a lot of money.'

'Well, so what? Even if she was pinching stuff from the Hall to fund her art habit, what's it got to do with Glyn?'

But Greening didn't reply, he was answering a call from Davis.

'Boss, I've got Cole's accounts back.'

'And?'

'He was bumping along OK, nothing dramatic in either his personal or business accounts. No sign of that fund he was building up to make a move, though.'

'So you haven't found the five grand he got for the table?'

'No. But it could have been in cash, couldn't it? In which case, it might not show in the books.'

'It ought to show up somewhere.'

'Unless someone pinched it, boss.'

'Indeed.'

'That's not why I rang,' Davis continued. 'I've found a letter from his accountant dated the eleventh of April, the Friday before he disappeared. He must have got it on the Saturday.'

'So?'

'Let me read it to you: "Dear Mr Cole, We have just received a letter from HMRC relating to a discrepancy between your VAT return and your business turnover. According to our records, the sums paid to them do not tally with the sums they should have received. You will shortly be hearing from them and I suggest you contact us as a matter of urgency." It's signed by a Mr Saul who has written across the bottom: "Glyn – call me at home if you need to."'

Greening reflected – something Dee James had said, that when Cole's life insurance paid up, it would be swallowed by nursing home fees and the taxman.

Not precisely the taxman, it turned out, but the VAT. Which Katherine was responsible for preparing.

'I've been to see Saul, he's got an office in Swindon. He says Glyn called him in a panic on the Sunday morning – he'd only opened the letter the night before, after he'd got back from an auction. Saul told him that the VAT had just twigged they'd been underpaid going back five years and were going to hit him with a bill.'

'How much?'

'Just over forty thousand pounds.'

'Good Lord. That's enough to spoil anyone's Sunday. How did Cole take it?'

'He was incredulous, said he would speak to the woman who did his VAT return. He said he had a bone to pick with her anyway. Then he made an appointment for the Monday which, of course, he didn't keep.'

'Thank you, Les. That's very interesting. Now, have you got Pemberton in custody?'

'He's downstairs now, waiting for some expensive brief from London.'

'How is he?'

'How do you think? He's pissed off big time. Frosty cold on the surface but steaming inside. If we leave him long enough I think he might explode.'

'Go and get him. I'll call you back shortly and have a word with him. Tell him that if he plays ball I guarantee he'll be at Newbury for the first race.'

'Aren't you coming back to interview him properly?'

'Not today, Les. I've got a more attractive fish to fry.

And a damned sight more slippery one,' he added for Carmel's benefit as he ended the call. 'Come on. Follow me in your car.'

'Where are we going?'

'To find Katherine Pym.'

Anna woke slowly, summoned from the bottom of a well of sleep by an unfamiliar sound. She would have ignored an alarm, a vacuum cleaner, even a revved-up car engine and plunged back into the depths. But this noise could not be dismissed. It was a high keening sound, like an animal in pain.

She dragged herself into a sitting position. The bedroom was in half light, sunlight spilling through a gap in the curtains and spearing a golden shaft across the floor on to the foot of the bed. She gulped from the glass of water by the bed. The noise had stopped, thank God. A familiar nausea was in her stomach but she ignored it as she stood up gingerly. She knew this particular queasiness. She wasn't going to be sick, it just felt as if she was. As she pulled on her dressing gown, the noise began again.

In the corridor the sound was more distinct. The cry of a person, not in physical pain but in mental anguish. And there were words in it.

She walked towards it, down the corridor towards the far staircase. The cry was coming from above. It was a woman's voice.

And it was calling her name.

Greening was not surprised to find an empty driveway in front of the white bungalow. Finding Katherine at home would have been too easy. Carmel parked her car alongside his and got out.

Greening rang the doorbell without expectation. There was no reply.

'Why don't you have a snoop around,' he suggested. 'I've been inside but I'd like you to have a squint through the windows. Take a note of what she's got on the walls.'

He phoned Davis. 'Les, have you got Pemberton there? Put him on, will you?'

'Inspector.' Cold did not adequately describe Edward's tone. Arctic was more accurate.

'Mr Pemberton, many apologies for today's inconvenience. I'm sure DS Davis has told you we intend to get you to Newbury shortly. If you'll be so good as to indulge me first.'

'Get on with it, man. I've been indulging you all blasted morning.'

Greening wasn't going to argue with that. 'Can you confirm that Katherine Pym does the books for your yard?'

'Yes, she does. And a few others too.'

'It's not a full-time post, is it?'

'No. It's an afternoon a week and she puts in some extra time when required.'

'What's her usual afternoon?'

'When the yard is at its quietest. Sunday, as a rule.'

'And where does she do her work?'

'In the yard office, of course.'

'Which is in the row of buildings facing the swimming pool.'

'Correct. Why do you want to know, Inspector?'

'I'm curious to find out if Katherine was working in your yard on the afternoon of Sunday the thirteenth of April two thousand and eight. Was she?'

'I couldn't say for certain off the top of my head but it's very likely. She's there most Sundays. There's nobody around then. My God, I've just realised what you're suggesting.'

'I'm not suggesting anything. Though, if I were you, I would have an independent adviser look at the day-to-day finances of your yard. Pay particular attention to your VAT returns.'

'What?'

'Have a successful day at the races, Mr Pemberton.'

Carmel appeared from around the side of the house. 'I see what you mean about security. She's got gates on all the back windows. I could see through though.'

'And what did you see?'

'Everything's very swish. All that fancy designer furniture and the kitchen must have cost a mint. And hanging on the wardrobe door is a Lee McQueen – or else a good copy.'

'What's a Lee McQueen?'

She rolled her eyes. 'A designer dress.'

'Worth?'

'A thousand? I don't know. I couldn't possibly afford one.'

'And the art?'

'It's like a gallery, isn't it? There's a big painting by the artist we just saw, Rory Picard, hanging in the hall.'

Greening smiled, though his heart was heavy. 'Handy for us she lives in a bungalow.'

'What are you thinking? What's Katherine Pym got to do with Glyn Cole's murder?'

It looked to Greening as if she had everything to do with it.

'She's been stealing,' he said. 'Katherine's got expensive tastes, as we know. She took a watch from Pitchbury Hall and traded it to Scratch whose man, Bubble, approached Cole with it at the auction on Saturday afternoon. Cole recognised it and traced it back to Scratch, who he'd done business with before. He might have been keen to track it down to get back into Anna's good books but once he found Katherine was involved, he smelt a rat. Then he opened a letter from his accountant and got a nasty surprise. So he started looking closely at his finances and found some of this cash he'd been raising was missing. By then it was Sunday afternoon, when he knew Katherine was doing her regular stint at the Pitchbury yard. So he went to have it out with her. The office is right there, by the pool. I don't know how she got him into the water but you can imagine them arguing outside. All she's got to do is catch him off balance. He can't swim and there are poles by the side the handlers use to control the horses in the water. She's a tall, strong woman. I can see her smashing his hands as he tries to get out.'

He could too. Though he'd found Katherine powerfully attractive he could easily imagine her giving vent to her anger and passion and vindictiveness. Maybe he was programmed to gravitate to women like that.

'But,' Carmel immediately fingered the weak spot

in his theory, 'how did she get Cole's body up a tree?'

'I don't think she did. I think she just left him there.'

'And?'

'Other people disposed of him. Freddy was certainly involved – he probably fished the body out and hid it as he described. And he knew how to go about hiding it in the tree. I just think someone else told him what to do.'

'Why did they do that? Why not call the police?'

'Would you, knowing that you were bound to be blamed for Cole's death, even if only in the press? A scandal would be certain. Wife's lover found dead in top horse trainer's pool – suicide or murder? Plenty of owners might take their horses away in those circumstances. And if it hadn't been for the tornado, Glyn Cole would still be just a missing person.'

Just before she opened the door on the top landing, Anna had a premonition that she would find something horrible. Given the howling from within, that was inevitable.

She stepped into an other-worldly space, bathed in sunlight, humid and muggy, smelling of rust and salt, and filled with the sound of pain.

First she saw Tammy lying on the floor, her hands and feet bound, the lead lashed to the radiator underneath the window. Around her pooled a puddle of blood.

'Anna.' The sound came from Tammy's lips.

Anna dropped to her knees and scrabbled at the girl's bonds. The wetness soaked instantly into her nightdress.

'Are you all right?' she heard herself say, over and over. 'Where are you bleeding?'

The girl stared at her, shivering and traumatised, on the verge of death. She had to be – there was so much blood.

'I'll get you an ambulance.' Damn it, her phone was downstairs.

'It's OK.' Tammy's voice was hoarse but suddenly strong. 'It's not me.'

Then Anna saw Katherine in an old button-backed velvet chair by the side of the window. Her head was tipped back against the headrest. Her eyes were closed and her left hand hung down. From the tip of her index finger Anna saw a drop of red liquid fall to join the lake on the floor.

Greening got the call from Yvonne as he was already on the way to Lambourn.

'Are you driving, boss?'

'I'm approaching Pitchbury Hall. I want a word with Katherine Pym.'

'Can you pull over for a moment.' It wasn't a question.

For once Greening did as she told him. There was something in her voice.

'Katherine Pym's dead, we've just had a call from Anna Pemberton.'

'What?' His heart skipped in his chest.

'She confessed to Glyn Cole's murder to Tammy Turner, the girl who helps out at the Hall. She had her tied up. Tammy thought she was going to get knifed but Katherine suddenly sliced through her own wrist.

Chop, chop – straight to the artery. Then she sat down and bled out right in front of this poor kid.'

His hands were shaking. He turned off the engine and sat breathing hard.

'Alan? Are you all right?'

'Yes, I'm OK.'

'You liked her, didn't you? I bet you never thought she was the killer.'

Though he was tempted to contradict her, he didn't.

Epilogue

Tammy marvelled at the way Anna put away her hot dog. She was still only halfway through hers when Anna was licking her fingers.

'I could eat another of those,' Anna said. 'It must be the air up here.'

They were standing on the roof of the members' stand, surveying Bath racecourse, supposedly the highest above sea level in the country. Certainly the wind whipping across Lansdown Hill kept the air fresh on this hot August day – and sharpened the appetite.

'Here, finish mine.' Tammy offered her half-eaten bun.

'I shouldn't. If I carry on like this I'll never get my figure back after.' After the baby was born, that is, but there was no need to say that. The days of sickness were gone, replaced by a steady growth that was transforming the svelte and skinny Anna into a sturdy, glowing picture of health, prone to ravenous enthusiasm for fat and carbohydrate. 'OK, then, hand it over.' And she polished off Tammy's food too.

Anna had insisted on the trip to Bath to follow the fortunes of Liquid Assets, now fully recovered from an operation three months back. It was a trip to the vet to see the recuperating Liquid Assets that had taken Edward out of the house on the afternoon Katherine had killed Mrs Drummond. Somehow that added a poignancy to the occasion.

'Mum would have loved this,' Anna had already said more than once as they'd prowled the racetrack before the meeting began. 'She'd be down on the rails with the bookies, planning her bets with Freddy.'

It was only Tammy's second trip to the races. There'd been that time at York and after that, despite Will's regular entreaties, she'd stayed away. She knew jockeys fell off sometimes and she couldn't bear the thought of seeing Will get hurt. Everyone had insisted she come today, though. Win or lose, they were going to have a party.

'I've still got that two hundred pounds you gave me,' she said to Anna. 'I've given it to Freddy to put on Liquid Assets for me – I don't know how to bet.'

If she lost it, she wouldn't care. And if she won, she'd give half of it to the air ambulance in Mrs Drummond's memory and put the other half into her student fund for when she went back to college. If indeed she did go back to college. She'd deferred it for another year because her mother still needed her at home – that's what she told people, anyway. But she couldn't bear to be away from Will at the moment and she certainly wasn't going to miss the arrival of Anna's baby.

She and Anna were closer than before – it was inevitable after what had happened. And after Anna had found her lying in a pool of blood the day Katherine killed herself, their roles had been reversed for a while. Anna had become the carer, turning up at Tammy's house to sit with her and do chores for her mother.

Tammy had told her all that Katherine had said while she'd held her captive in the room at the top of the house. And what she'd told her when she'd sat in the chair by the window and cut her wrist.

'She said that she was with Freddy when he had his accident. They were playing by the pool – which was forbidden – and his ball went in the water. He fell in trying to rescue it and she couldn't get him out. So she ran for help and his life was saved though he was never the same. She said it was terrible for everyone, especially your mother. She blamed Katherine and wanted to send her away but your father said that would be wrong and put his foot down. She said Uncle Jack was always on her side but it had taken years for your mother to treat her in a civilised fashion.'

'And that's why she pushed her downstairs?' Anna said in disbelief.

'She said it helped. And when she killed Glyn it helped that she still loved him. "Why didn't he ask me to go to Italy?" she said. I think that's why she didn't kill me – she had no reason to love or hate me. It might seem like she was a cold-blooded killer but I don't think that's the whole truth.'

Anna had squeezed her hand and said, 'Going to Italy – all that sounds so stupid now.'

'She also said you'd been sleeping with Will.'

'What?' Anna had seemed reassuringly surprised.

'I thought you might have been. You have secret

phone calls and talks with him. You call him a lovely boy. What goes on between you and him?'

'It's because he did me a favour. The kind of selfless favour I couldn't believe anyone would do for another.'

Then Anna had told her what it was.

'On the afternoon Glyn died, I was up at the Hall watching television. *Brief Encounter* – great choice, eh? Freddy had been with me but it wasn't his kind of film and he left before the end to go see the horses in the old barn. He knew all about me and Glyn and he didn't judge me. Then the phone went. It was Will. He asked if he could come and see me but he wouldn't say why. I said I'd meet him in the barn. I thought Freddy was going to be there but he wasn't. Will arrived with a bunch of flowers and said he wanted to thank me. Edward didn't like him because of the way he looked and said he wanted him out of the yard but I'd persuaded Mum to let him ride one of her horses and he'd won brilliantly. So Edward had changed his mind about Will and he was going to stay. I was happy for him and he was very grateful.

'We walked back into the yard together, looking for Freddy. We got as far as the swimming pool and saw a dark shape on the ramp, half in and half out of the water. There were bloody puddles around the pool and a pole on the side near the thing in the water. It was Glyn. Just then Freddy came out of the shed. He looked at us and said, "He's dead. Don't worry, I'm taking care of it." I was speechless with shock. I thought Freddy had killed Glyn for me. That Glyn must have come to the yard to find me and Freddy had stopped him. All I could think then was how to protect my brother. He wasn't equipped to cope with the situation I'd put him in. Then Will said he'd help us hide the body. He knew Freddy would never survive in jail.'

'What did you do?'

'Will and Freddy got the body out of the water into a wheelbarrow and hid it in the shed. Will said they'd drive it to a quarry or lake in Glyn's car and submerge it. He and I were debating where to go when Freddy suddenly said, "Let's put him in a tree. No one will ever look there." I told him not to be silly but Will said that was a fantastic idea. So that's what they did, that night. Then Will drove Glyn's car into Swindon and Freddy followed in the Land Rover and brought him back when he'd abandoned it. It was our secret, the three of us. Only it turned out there were four of us involved. If I'd known about Katherine I'd have called the police. And my mother would still be alive.'

Tammy had reached for Anna's hand, anticipating tears, but they had not come. The returning squeeze of the fingers had been firm. She'd known then that Anna's crying days were over.

Will had been amused to be greeted by Sir Sid Tobin liked a long-lost son. He'd not ridden for him since York when he'd pulled off the startling victory on Paper Sun.

'My boy!' Sid had exclaimed as they encountered each other in the parade ring. Hearty handshakes were exchanged and joshing comments passed about jockeys who wore earrings.

Will wondered whether to invest in a nose stud for

the next time Sid put him up on one of his horses. If he ever did, of course. In any case, he thought as he took Liquid Assets down to the seven-furlong start, he couldn't go ahead and get himself some facial jewellery without consulting Tammy. In the past he might have resented this loss of autonomy. Now he rather enjoyed it. It was a bit like being married.

When he'd told her about his part in hiding Glyn's body he'd been surprised to find she knew already. She was very thick with Anna these days and said it was due to her that she'd allowed Will back into her heart. Again, he might once have resented this manipulating sisterhood, now he was just grateful.

He'd told Tammy about the night he'd taken Freddy out to discover what he'd said to the police. It seemed Freddy had confessed to killing Glyn but the police had not been convinced and they'd sent him home. In the pub, Freddy had told Will that he'd found Glyn's body in the pool and a bloody pole on the side. He'd tried to drag the body out, thinking Anna was responsible. She was the only person in the yard and he'd witnessed a row between her and Glyn just two nights before. He'd told Will he'd been amazed his little sister had the guts to kill the man who was ruining her life but he was glad she had and he was prepared to take the blame for it himself.

Only, it turned out, it was someone else altogether who'd committed the murder.

Will shook these thoughts from his head as he approached the starting stalls. Time to concentrate – loading into the starting gate was how Liquid Assets had injured himself at York. But the horse appeared to have no memory of the event. He was about to happily pop into the stall when there was a commotion to their left. One of the other horses reared away, around the gate, and bolted off down the course.

A delay was now inevitable and Liquid Assets wheeled fretfully, his tail whisking from side to side in agitation.

Damn. They could lose the race right here.

Edward swore under his breath as Hang Up Your Boots, the outsider in the race, ran off with his rider, delaying the start and spooking Liquid Assets into the bargain.

By his side, Sid Tobin registered his unhappiness and patted him companionably on the back. 'Cheer up, Ted. That's one of the competition done his chances.'

Edward wasn't so sure about that, given the touch on Miletus just before Rosemary died. Hang Up Your Boots, however, was the least fancied horse in the race and would likely be withdrawn – the usual fate of horses who bolted before the start. He was more worried about the effect on Liquid Assets who could do without the delay and the additional test of his nerves.

Sid had his binoculars fixed on the far corner of the course. 'Crikey me, Ted, he's gone miles. He'll be cream-crackered.'

Edward couldn't help smiling. He no longer resented being called Ted. For all his fancy title, Sir Sidney Tobin was a down-to-earth companion and one who stood by his friends in time of trouble. In the wake of Katherine's suicide, there had been a string of lurid stories in the press about goings-on at Pitchbury Hall. One or two of Edward's more straight-laced owners – friends of Rosemary's – had taken their animals elsewhere. Sir Sid had stepped in to fill the empty stalls.

As far as Edward was concerned, Sid could call him what he liked.

It seemed to Will an age before the runaway horse was brought under control and returned to the start. Then the process of loading began all over again. This time, Liquid Assets was far less amenable. He hung back nervously and, with a heave from the handlers, was the last to load. Will was vaguely aware that Hang Up Your Boots was among the field as the eleven runners set off.

As they raced slightly downhill towards the tight bend which would bring them round into the home straight, Will was relieved to feel his mount slipping into an easy rhythm. He remembered the strange feeling on his back all those months ago at York, when he'd known the animal wasn't right. And though he'd been working him on the gallops for a couple of weeks and knew the horse was sound, riding in a race was different. This was the real test of ability and fitness.

He judged the bend nicely, shooting out of it in third place with Liquid Assets cruising. The two most fancied horses were already battling it out three lengths ahead, a trifle prematurely in Will's opinion. He tracked them up the half-mile long straight and, as the stands came closer, he could see their private contest had taken its toll.

Inside the last furlong, he gave his mount a couple of smacks and the horse responded at once, moving up on the leaders within a dozen strides. Then they were past at speed, leaving the other two toiling in their wake. The winning post was approaching rapidly and Will could already taste the victory.

Afterwards, he had no cause for regret. He had not let up. He had ridden Liquid Assets to the line as hard as he was able. There had been nothing he could do to prevent Hang Up Your Boots, the runaway outsider, from sweeping past to beat him into second place.

The worst of it was, as the other riders congratulated their triumphant colleague and expressed surprise at his feat, Will knew exactly why the other horse had won.

Tammy tried not to be downhearted at her loss. She'd never really considered that £200 as hers anyway. All the same, Liquid Assets had been so close to winning. Beaten by half a length in the last few strides.

'That's why I'll never be a gambler,' she said to Anna as they pushed their way through the crowd to the unsaddling enclosure. Will was going to be hopping mad at the last-minute defeat and she wanted to put him on an even keel.

But Will turned out to be philosophical. 'There was nothing I could do about it once the other fellow ran off. He warmed up properly and my horse didn't.'

Tammy hadn't time to ask what he was talking about before Freddy turned up, looking sombre.

'I'm sorry, Tammy. I only backed Liquid Assets to win so you lost your money on him.'

'That's OK, Freddy, that's what I asked you to do.'

He nodded gravely. In fact, he looked unusually serious, considering he reacted to most events in the same way.

'Actually,' he said, 'I only put a hundred on Liquid Assets. I remembered what Mum told me to do at Salisbury with Miletus and I put the rest on the horse that ran off.'

'What?' Anna grasped immediately what he was saying.

Freddy grinned suddenly, like the sun bursting from behind the clouds. 'He went out from twenty to thirty-three to one.' He pulled a roll of banknotes from his pocket and held them out to Tammy. 'You made three thousand three hundred pounds. I hope you don't mind.'

Whoever said Freddy was mentally deficient needed their head examined.

Greening didn't understand horse racing but he liked a day out as much as anyone, especially in present company. Amy and Carmel made a fuss of him, Robbie and Hal bought him drinks and asked his advice, as if he knew one end of a horse from another.

He'd had a funny feeling when he'd spotted Edward Pemberton's name on the race card. After Katherine Pym's death there had been formal interviews with Pemberton with his fancy solicitor present. Greening had been convinced the trainer had masterminded the disposal of Cole's body but he'd had no way of proving it. In the end, Greening hadn't been able to lay a glove on him and his heart wasn't in harrying

Freddy Drummond, his likely accomplice, either. There had been interviews with Freddy, too, this time with Pemberton's lawyer in attendance, and Freddy's mental competence had become a serious issue. Greening doubted that the matter would be taken further. He didn't think the CPS had the stomach to put a man who was clearly a victim on the stand.

In his own mind, it hadn't been an investigation that covered him in glory. He'd asked himself over and over whether his attraction to Katherine had blinded him to the truth. And, crazy though it was, he couldn't decide whether she represented a lucky escape or a missed opportunity. The truth was, he'd never been much of a judge of women.

The name of one of the runners in the third race caught his eye. Edward Pemberton had been visiting Liquid Assets at the vet at the time Rosemary Drummond had died. It was hardly a bona fide racing tip but he'd recommended the animal to his young companions anyway. He hadn't mentioned his other bet because it was purely sentimental. But for a man approaching retirement, how could he not wager on a horse called Hang Up Your Boots?

And, when it turned out he had bet on both first and second, he was happy to be hailed as an expert tipster.

'It could be a new career, Dad,' said Amy.

There was no chance of that.

Deadly Finish

John Francome

Shot through with twists and skulduggery, John Francome's new thriller will leave you breathless . . .

With a blossoming career as a trainer and a beautiful Brazilian fiancée by his side, everything is going Simon Waterford's way. To cap it all, his two-year-old colt has just won a top race at Royal Ascot.

But as the victorious party board a train for London not everyone is in the mood for celebration. Unknown to Simon, the lovely Mariana is not the innocent he takes her for and Simon's uncle, Geoff, is on the brink of revealing her secret. Then a brawl erupts in the carriage, leaving Geoff lying dead on the floor.

Is his death a lucky twist of fate for Mariana, or something more sinister? Either way, her secret is safe. For now . . .

Acclaim for John Francome's thrillers:

'Genuinely exhilarating descriptions of races that capture the tension and excitement . . . could be written only with a jockey's insight' *Daily Mail*

'Francome provides a vivid panorama of the racing world . . . and handles the story's twists deftly' *The Times*

'Mr Francome adeptly teases to the very end' *Country Life*

978 0 7553 4992 0

headline